PACK UP YOUR TROUBLES

Adopted from birth, Pam Weaver trained as a Nursery Nurse working mainly in children's homes. She was also a Hyde Park nanny. In the 1980s she and her husband made a deliberate decision that she should be a full-time mum to their two children. Pam wrote for small magazines and specialist publications, finally branching out into the women's magazine market. Pam has written numerous articles and short stories, many of which have been featured in anthologies. Her story *The Fantastic Bubble* was broadcast on BBC Radio 4 and the World Service. This is her fourth book.

PAM WEAVER

Pack Up Your Troubles

AVON

A division of HarperCollins*Publishers*
77–85 Fulham Palace Road,
London W6 8JB

www.harpercollins.co.uk

2

A Paperback Original 2013

First published in Great Britain by
HarperCollins*Publishers* 2013

Copyright © Pam Weaver 2013

Pam Weaver asserts the moral right to
be identified as the author of this work

A catalogue record for this book is
available from the British Library

ISBN-13: 978-1-84756-362-0

Set in Minion by Palimpsest Book Production Limited,
Falkirk, Stirlingshire

Printed and bound in Great Britain by
Clays Ltd, St Ives plc

MIX
Paper from
responsible sources
FSC
www.fsc.org
FSC™ C007454

I should like to thank my agent Juliet Burton, my editors Caroline Hogg and Helen Bolton, and the wonderful team at HarperCollins Avon for their encouragement and above all their friendship.

This book is dedicated to my brother, Barrie Stainer. After a whole life-time apart, it was wonderful to discover your existence. Thank you for your warmth and generosity even though I was such a surprise!

VE Day 1945

One

By the time they reached Trafalgar Square, the sheer weight of the crowd forced the bus to a standstill. As the passengers turned around, the conductor gave them an exaggerated shrug and rang the bell three times. 'Sorry folks, but this bus ain't going no fuver.'

Irene Thompson and Connie Dixon had planned to go on to Buckingham Palace but they had to get off with the rest of the passengers. The bus couldn't even get anywhere near the pavement but nobody minded. Today, everybody was happy; everyone that is except Connie who couldn't hide her disappointment.

She had planned to be here with Emmett but he had written a hurried note, which she had stuffed into her shoulder bag as she left the billet. It was terse. *Can't make the celebrations. Mother unwell and she needs me.* She knew she shouldn't be annoyed. Emmett was always keen to help others, and he was devoted to his aged mother but it was very galling that he should pick this moment to be noble, just when the celebrations were about to begin. He had said he would telephone her that evening but even if she got back to the barracks in time, she had made up her mind to be 'out' when he called. She frowned crossly. Why couldn't he be like the others? Betty Tanner's boyfriend brought her flowers all the time and Gloria's man friend had given her a brand new lipstick. Emmett never did anything like that. It really was too bad.

'Cheer up, Connie,' Rene chided as she took her arm. 'We're making history. Don't let Emmett spoil it for you. Be happy.'

3

As they stepped onto the road, Connie had never seen so many people all in one place. Soldiers, sailors and airmen, from what seemed like every country in the world, had been drawn here to join the people of London to welcome this much longed for day. After five years of war and hardship, peace had come at last. It was rumoured that Churchill and the King had wanted Monday, 7 May to be called VE Day, but the Yanks had insisted that it should be today, Tuesday, 8 May. Connie supposed it was because they were cautious enough to make sure that everything was signed and sealed before enjoying the victory. The German troops had capitulated and signed an unconditional surrender at Eisenhower's headquarters at 2.41 a.m. Whatever the reason, the grey war-wearied faces had gone and Connie was met with smiles and handshakes from complete strangers. Ever since the news had broken that Adolf Hitler and his mistress had committed suicide, the whole nation finally believed what they had not dared to, that the war in Europe was over at last. The war in the Far East was still raging but the smell of victory was in the air.

The bus had come to a halt because an Aussie soldier, waving the Australian flag, his arm linked with a merchant seaman, was leading a group of revellers down the middle of the street. They were being watched by a couple of eagle-eyed Red Caps but there would be no trouble today. No one was in a fighting mood. The military police were in for a lean time. Even the US MPs – 'Snowdrops', as they were known because of their white caps, white Sam Browne belts and white gloves – were redundant. The joyful crowd following in the Aussie soldier's wake was made up of American GIs, WAAFs, ATS girls and civilians all singing at the tops of their voices.

'Bless 'em all, the long and the short . . .'

'Come on,' cried Rene as Connie held back, 'let's join in.'

An American GI caught Rene's arm and pulled her into the body of moving people. '. . . this side of the ocean, so cheer up my lads bless 'em all.'

4

'Oh Rene,' cried Connie, 'it's really, really over.'

Picking up the lyrics, they lurched with the crowd towards Nelson's column, the base of which was still covered in hoarding to protect it from bomb blasts even though the last air raid warning had been sounded on 19 March. Someone had stuck a poster on it with 'Victory over Germany 1945' on one side and 'Give thanks by saving.'

Connie nudged Rene in the ribs and jerking her head, shouted over the noise, 'Give thanks by saving? I should cocoa!' and they both laughed.

After so much hardship and sacrifice, did the government really think everyone was going to keep on being frugal and sensible with their money? Some might, but not her. She was twenty-one and she'd already spent the best years of her life scrimping and making do, first in the munitions factory and then, after a spell of sick leave, in the WAAFs. Now that the war was over, Connie had no idea what she wanted to do but she was sure of one thing. She was in no mood to save for the future. Hadn't she just blown all her coupons on her new outfit, a lovely pale lemon sweater and some grey pinstriped slacks? And then there was Emmett. She had hoped he would have asked her to marry him by now, but he hadn't, presumably because he was anxious about his mother's health. He'd asked her a few times to go further but Connie had told him she wasn't that sort of a girl. Still, Rene was right. This was no time to nurse her disappointments. Today was the day to enjoy herself.

In the press of the crowd, Rene was standing on tiptoe to see if anything was happening. 'We should have got away earlier,' she grumbled good-naturedly. 'There's too many people here.' Despite the noise all around her, Connie heard a distinct tapping sound just behind her and froze. Someone was tapping his cigarette on a cigarette case. Her blood ran cold and her heartbeat quickened. A surge in the crowd made the woman beside push her and she apologised. 'Sorry, luv.'

'Has Churchill given his speech yet?' Rene asked.

Connie listened hard. The person behind her clicked a cigarette case closed. It couldn't be . . . could it? No, it was impossible. It would be far too much of a coincidence.

'It was supposed to be at nine o'clock this morning,' the woman went on, 'but we're still waiting.' She rolled her eyes towards the lions. 'They've been putting up speakers so that we can hear him but as for when that happens, your guess is as good as mine.'

'You all right, Connie?' said Rene. 'You look a bit peaky.'

'Three o'clock,' said a man's voice behind them. Connie turned sharply to look at him. Sure enough, he was putting his cigarette case into his inside jacket pocket and was reaching for a lighter. He lit the fag between his lips and took a long drag. 'That's what the copper on the steps told me,' he went on. 'Three o'clock.'

A wave of relief flooded over her. The man was old, forty or maybe fifty with greying hair and a tobacco-stained moustache. It was all right. It wasn't him. Connie relaxed and looked at her watch. It was quarter past ten. A group of Girl Guides gathered together at the base of Nelson's column and were turning around to face the crowd. If the authorities were planning to entertain them, the man must be right. Churchill wouldn't be giving his speech for ages yet.

'Rene! A girl's voice rang out above the noise. 'Rene Thompson, it's me, Barbara.'

Rene searched the sea of faces and eventually spotted her friend waving as she came towards her. 'Barbara Hopkins. Well, as I live and breathe. Fancy seeing you here!'

Laughing, the two girls hugged each other. Barbara, dressed in her WAAF uniform, was thickset with very dark curly hair. The girl with her was dressed in civvies and hung back shyly.

'I haven't set eyes on you since our training,' Rene cried happily and Barbara hugged her again. 'Oooh, it's so good to see you.'

They stepped apart and introduced everybody.

'This is Eva O'Hara,' said Barbara. Eva was tall but with an almost elfin-like face, and a lot of laughter lines around her eyes. She wore dark slacks and a pale blue hand-knitted jumper.

'And this is Connie,' said Rene. 'We share the same billet.' The hand shaking was soon over and somehow or other the girls had reached one of the fountains in the middle of the square. The day was warm and the water inviting and while Rene and Barbara caught up with old times, Connie, unable to resist, began to roll up the legs of her slacks. 'Come on,' she laughed. 'Which one of you is game for a paddle?'

After a feeble protest from the others, Eva rolled up the legs of her slacks as well. As she climbed in, a sailor gave her a hand and then he rolled up his trouser legs and stepped in. The water was cold, but not unbearable, and it came just above their knees. The sailor and his mate, who joined them, were taller than Connie and Eva so there was less chance of them getting their clothes wet. The sailors were nice looking lads. One had brown Brylcreemed hair and a ready smile and the other one had fairer hair and slightly bucked teeth. He plonked his cap on Connie's head as they stood together. The blond one carried a knobbly walking stick and Connie wondered if he had some sort of injury, but she didn't like to ask. They all had to hold on to each other because the bottom of the fountain was covered in algae and a bit slippery. If they weren't careful, they'd all be under the water and soaked. The singing grew louder.

'*There'll be blue birds over the white cliffs of Dover . . .*'. The two girls swayed with the sailors as they sang and after a few minutes, the sailor's cap began to push Connie's rich chestnut-coloured hair out of place. She wore her hair with curls on the top of her head and pulled away from her face. When her comb landed in the water, her hair fell in attractive loose tendrils around her face. The sailor bent to pick the comb up and at the same time spotted a newspaper photographer taking pictures.

'Here you are, mate' he called. 'Two pretty girls and two good looking sailors. What more could you want for the front page?'

The photographer came over and the sailor planted a kiss on Connie's cheek as the shutter came down. Connie wasn't offended but she gave him a playful shove before he was tempted to take any more liberties. She didn't want Emmett or her own mother to see a picture of her kissing someone else on the front page of the paper and despite the improbabilities, she found herself scouring the faces in the crowd.

'Which paper are you from?' laughed Eva as the four of them posed again.

'*Daily Sketch*,' said the photographer before moving on.

Connie heaved a sigh of relief. None of her family read the *Daily Sketch* and with a bit of luck, her great aunt (they called her Ga) had never even heard of it.

Their legs were getting cold so the four of them climbed out of the water and Connie gave the sailor his cap back. She and Eva only had handkerchiefs to dry their legs but they didn't care. They held on to each other because in the surging crowd it was difficult to keep a balance on one leg while drying the other. Someone shouted a name, and waving, the two sailors merged back into the crowd.

'You in the WAAFs as well?' Connie asked Eva. It seemed very likely considering that her friend Barbara was in uniform.

Eva nodded. 'And you?'

Connie nodded too.

'Did you and Rene come on your own?'

'Actually my boyfriend was meant to be here but he couldn't come.'

'Nothing wrong, I hope?'

Connie shook her head. 'He's got a sick mother.'

'I hope it's not too serious,' Eva remarked.

Connie shook her head. It was funny that Mrs Gosling always seemed to be ill whenever she and Emmett had something planned but as soon as the thought went through her head, she scolded herself for being so churlish. Nobody could help being ill, could they?

'No doubt my lot will all be back home and listening to the radio,' Eva said. 'My parents are at home and my brother is in the Royal Engineers. He's still being kept quite busy, and will be for a long time, I'm afraid. He's in the bomb squad.'

Connie frowned sympathetically. 'That must be tough on you.'

'I try not to think about it,' Eva smiled. 'What about you? Do you have brothers and sisters?'

'A brother two years older than me,' said Connie with a sigh, 'and a little sister called Mandy. She's just coming up for six.'

'What about your brother? Is he in the army?'

Connie shook her head and willed her voice not to crack as she said matter-of-factly, 'We lost touch.'

Eva stopped what she was doing and looked up. 'I'm sorry,'

Connie looked away, embarrassed. It wasn't bloody fair. Families should be together, especially at times like this. Her emotions were all over the place. After her scare of a few minutes ago, now she was fighting the urge to cry. She looked around. 'Have you seen my other shoe?'

Eva shoved it towards her with the end of her foot.

'Thanks,' Connie smiled, glad that Eva hadn't asked any more questions. She looked at her watch. It was still only 11.30 a.m. If they stayed here, they were in for a long wait and it wasn't as if Churchill would be coming in person. He was only going to speak over the loudspeakers. Connie blew out her cheeks. She was bored. She wanted something more memorable to happen. Something she could tell her children and grandchildren about when she was old and grey.

'Let's go to Buckingham Palace,' she said suddenly.

Barbara looked around helplessly. 'Where will we get a bus?'

'We can walk from here,' said Eva. 'It's not that far.'

They pushed their way back through the crowd and when they finally reached the fringes, all four of them struck out for Buckingham Palace. Rene and Barbara linked arms and walked on ahead so Connie walked with Eva. With a lack of anything else to say, they shared their war experiences.

'So, where do you come from?' asked Eva dodging a drunk man staggering along the pavement in the opposite direction.

'Worthing. It's on the south coast, near Brighton.'

'Really?' Eva laughed. 'How weird. My folks live near there.'

They could hear the sound of a mouth organ playing, 'When the lights go on again, all over the world . . .' and all at once, an American airman grabbed Eva around the waist and waltzed her into the middle of the road. His companion held out a bottle and leaned into Connie's face. 'Hey babe, want some beer?'

Laughing, she pushed him away and another serviceman, this time a jolly Jack Tar, danced Connie into the street next to Eva and the two of them spent a hilarious few minutes with their newfound dance partners. As suddenly as they'd grabbed them, the two men hurried off to join their companions, blowing kisses as they went.

'Where's Rene?' said Eva as they came back together, laughing. Connie shrugged. 'No idea,' she said. 'I can't see Barbara either.'

They stayed where they were for a few minutes but as there was no sign of either of their friends, Connie and Eva struck out on their own. All the way to the palace, they were craning their necks and calling out occasionally but it was hopeless. The crowd was every bit as big as it had been in Trafalgar Square but thankfully, because the area in The Mall was much bigger, they didn't feel quite so much like sardines. After a while Connie said, 'This is stupid. We haven't a hope of finding them.'

'I think you're right,' said Eva, linking her arm through Connie's. 'It's time to give up and enjoy ourselves.'

'I second that,' Connie laughed. She suddenly liked this girl.

'It's a pity we never got stationed together. I've been in Hendon for a while, after I was re-mustered from Blackpool. Were you ever there?'

'I was stationed along the south coast mostly,' said Eva shaking her head. 'Poling, Ford and Rye. That's where I met Barbara.'

'I was hoping to be posted to those places,' said Connie wistfully.

Eva looked sympathetic. 'Why? Did you have it bad where you were?'

Connie shrugged. 'Not really.' It wasn't that. 'It was closer to home, that's all.'

'We didn't have too many bombs,' said Eva, 'but we were on the front line for the invasion. They were bombed in Poling just before I got there.'

'I suppose,' Connie said with a broad grin, 'as soon as ol' Hitler heard you were coming, he pushed off elsewhere.'

Eva chuckled.

'What do you do in the WAAFs?' Connie continued.

'Telephone operator,' said Eva. 'Mum seems to think it'll hold me in good stead when I get demobbed. She says I could join the GPO as a telephonist but I'd much rather join the police or something.'

'Oh no,' cried Connie. 'I can't wait to get out of uniform. I hate it. All those damned buttons to polish, no thank you!'

Eva chuckled.

'I mean it,' Connie said defensively. 'When I went for training in Blackpool, our billet was so damp that every single one of my buttons was green by the morning and that was even after I'd used the button stick and a duster. I had to polish the darned things up again with my uniform cuffs before parade.'

By now, Eva was laughing heartily.

'You may well laugh,' Connie continued, 'but I was forever getting into trouble. There was a constant film over them.'

'I trained in Blackpool as well,' said Eva wiping her eyes. '1942. I had the choice of factory work or the WAAFs.'

'I was there in September 1943,' Connie said. 'Blowing half a gale on the seafront, it was.'

11

'And if your hat blew off while you were marching, you weren't allowed to stop and pick it up,' laughed Eva.

'Yes, and how daft was that?' Connie remarked.

'Did you have old Wingate?'

'You, that gel over there,' Connie said mimicking Sgt Wingate, the WAAF officer who presided over new recruits, perfectly. 'Head up, chhh . . . est out.' And they both roared.

'So, what will you do when you get demobbed?'

'I want to be a nurse,' said Connie.

'And they don't have a uniform?' Eva teased.

'Yesss,' Connie conceded, 'but it's much sexier,' and they both laughed again.

Even after the long walk down The Mall, the crowd outside Buckingham Palace was every bit as good-natured as the crowd had been in Trafalgar Square. People milled about, meeting old friends and new faces with equal enthusiasm. The area around the Victoria Memorial was so overwhelmed with people, you could hardly see the mermaids, mermen or the hippogriff. People sat on the plinths beneath the great angels of Justice and Truth either side of Victoria herself. The statue depicting Motherhood was just as beautiful but it was facing the wrong way. Nobody was interested in what was happening down The Mall. Today all eyes were on the palace.

'At least he's home,' said Eva, rolling her eyes upwards.

Connie turned her head and glanced at the royal standard on the roof, fluttering in the breeze. 'Oh good-o,' she grinned as she put on a posh voice. 'Shall we knock on the door and ask for tea?' and Eva laughed.

According to one woman in the crowd, the King and Queen had already come out onto the balcony four times so Connie and Eva didn't hold out much hope that they would be lucky enough to see them. An impromptu conga snaked its way through the crowds and Connie and Eva joined in until they were breathless with laughter.

'What do you reckon?' said Eva eventually. 'Do you want to wait a while?'

'May as well,' said Connie with a shrug, 'now that we've walked all this way.'

'What if we don't see them?'

'It doesn't matter,' said Connie. 'At least we were here.' In her heart of hearts she was hoping they'd be lucky. Two disappointments in one day was too much to bear.

All at once, the cry went up, 'We want the King, we want the King.'

As it gathered momentum, Connie and Eva joined in. The volume of noise reverberated all around and it felt as if the whole world was stilled by the cry of the crowd. 'We want the King.'

Dodging one of the few cars still travelling in the area, they crossed the road and joined the people nearer the railings. Connie stared at the imposing building beyond the iron gates and especially at the red- and gold-covered balcony.

'They say Buckingham Palace has 775 rooms,' said Eva.

Connie wrinkled her nose. 'Just think of all that dusting. You'd hardly be bloomin' finished before you had to start all over again!'

'Look!' Eva nudged her arm and Connie's heart nearly stopped with excitement when a small door within the great centre door opened and a tiny figure in naval uniform came out onto the balcony. The King! King George VI, King of the United Kingdom and the Dominions of the British Empire, and here she was, looking right at him! He raised his arm and with a circular motion of his hand began to wave to the crowd. The Queen in a pale green hat and matching coat and dress had followed him out onto the balcony and when she began to wave as well, the crowd opened its throat and roared. A sea of waving hands and cheering people in front of them, Connie and Eva were carried along with the thrill of it all. In a moment of sudden frustration, Connie stamped her foot. Damn it, Emmett! You should have been here with me, she thought.

13

Two more figures had joined the King and Queen. Princess Elizabeth in her ATS uniform and Princess Margaret Rose, not yet fifteen and too young to join up, was in a pretty aqua-coloured dress. From where Connie and Eva stood, they were no more than tiny dolls behind the long red- and gold-covered balcony but it was enough. Connie and Eva cheered themselves hoarse.

When eventually the royal family went back inside, the two girls looked at each other with satisfied smiles.

'I'm starving,' said Eva. 'Fancy something to eat?'

'I've got a couple of fish paste sandwiches in my bag,' said Connie taking it from her shoulder. 'They'll be a bit squashed but you're welcome to share them with me.'

'Thanks for the offer,' laughed Eva, 'but if you don't mind, I think I can do a bit better than that.'

'But where are we going to get anything around here?' Connie cried.

Eva tapped her nose and pulled Connie towards Green Park. When they reached the road, they turned into a side street. Connie hadn't a clue where she was, but she didn't feel the least bit nervous. Presently they came across a small crowd laughing and dancing outside a café.

'Is this where we're going?'

Eva nodded.

'How on earth did you know this was here?'

'My husband's family has been here for quite a while,' she said matter-of-factly.

Connie was taken by surprise. Eva had never mentioned a husband. She wasn't wearing a wedding ring either. She was about to mention it when she was swept up with hugs and kisses and handshakes as the family welcomed Eva's new friend. Someone called out, 'Queenie, Queenie luv, look who's 'ere.'

Queenie, a small woman, middle-aged, with a lined face, hair the colour of salt and pepper and wearing a wrap-around floral apron, came out of the kitchen. The two women looked at each

14

other, unsmiling, then Queenie opened her arms and Eva went to her. Such was the difference in their height, Queenie had to stand on tip-toe and Eva had to lean over, but there was a moment of real tenderness and, Connie supposed, if Queenie was Eva's mother-in-law, a sense of shared grief. For a moment, Connie felt like an intruder so she looked away. Eva and Queenie went into the kitchen and shut the door.

Another woman sitting at one of the tables touched her arm. Connie looked down and smiled thinly.

'Why don't yer sit down, ducks,' said the woman indicating a vacant chair opposite. 'They'll be back in a jiffy.'

Connie nodded her thanks and sat down.

'Been to the celebrations?' asked the woman fingering a pearl necklace she had around her neck.

'To the palace.'

The woman lifted what looked like a glass of milk stout. 'Here's to His Majesty, Gowd bless 'im. Did you see him?'

As they talked, Connie discovered that Eva's mother-in-law, Queenie O'Hara, had lived in London all her life. She and her late husband, an Irishman, had taken over the small café in 1941 after their dockland home had been bombed out of existence.

'Queenie used to clean 'ouses for the nobs round 'ere,' said the woman, 'but when she saw this place was up for sale, it were an hoppertunity too good to miss. He died in '44 just before her son got married.' She pointed to a photograph over the counter of an Irish guardsman in his Home Service dress of scarlet tunic and bearskin. 'That's her Dermid. The light of her life.'

So this was Eva's husband. He was certainly a striking man.

'How long have they been married?' Connie asked.

The woman shrugged. 'No more than a couple of weeks.'

Connie frowned. Only a couple of weeks and already Eva had taken off her wedding ring?

'This damned war,' muttered the woman. 'The day he died the light went out of Queenie's face.'

Connie was appalled. Dead? She looked at the picture of the handsome young man in uniform again. How could it happen? Now she realised that she'd been so concerned to avoid talking about her own troubles that she hadn't even asked Eva about herself. Losing touch with Kenneth was bad enough but to lose a husband so soon after marriage seemed grossly unfair. And yet coming down The Mall, Eva didn't seem to be that upset. She was more like the life and soul of the party. Was she callous or was it bravado? But when she emerged from the kitchen and came over to join them at the table, Connie could see that Eva's eyes were red and she'd obviously been crying. 'Queenie's going to rustle something up for us,' she said matter-of-factly to Connie and then turning to the woman with the pearl beads and the stout, she said, 'And how are you, Mrs Arkwright?'

Connie's table companion leaned over and squeezed Eva's hand. 'Mustn't grumble, ducks. Mustn't grumble.'

Someone in the café had a piano accordion. He squeezed the box and one by one, the songs, especially the one penned during the war to end all wars, the same one which had meant so much to the country for the past five years, filled the air.

'*Pack up your troubles* . . .'

Yes, that's what the whole world wanted but for the first time that day, Connie felt uncomfortable. The war might be over but people like Eva had to live with the consequences for the rest of their lives. Her mind was full of unanswered questions. How did Eva's husband die? Was it really only a couple of weeks after they'd been married?

'*What's the use of worrying?*
It never was worthwhile . . .'

Of course, she couldn't ask. She hardly knew the girl and it seemed far too intrusive.

'*Pack up your troubles in an old kit bag and*
Smile, smile, smile . . .' they sang.
Connie could hardly bear it.

All at once, Queenie bustled in from the kitchen and put two plates of meat and veg pie, mash and gravy in front of them. Despite the fact that Connie had to search for a piece of meat in her pie, it was hot, delicious and very welcome.

'I'm sorry about your husband,' said Connie as Queenie went off to get them both a cup of tea. Her remark felt lame but she felt she had to say *something*.

'You weren't to know,' said Eva.

Connie smiled awkwardly and Eva looked away. 'Not much to say really,' Eva said, addressing the brick wall. 'We met in Hyde Park, got married by special licence and he was killed six weeks later.'

Connie stopped eating. 'But I thought . . .' She glanced sideways at Mrs Arkwright who was stubbing out a cigarette. Two weeks or six, it was still terrible. 'God, Eva, that's awful.'

Eva ran her fingers through her shoulder-length blonde hair and shrugged her shoulders. 'It happens.'

She'd only known the girl for a few hours but Connie wasn't fooled. She might be trying to sound tough but Connie could see that Eva's eyes had misted over. Connie had obviously reopened an old wound and now she didn't know what to say. Rescue came once more in the form of Eva's mother-in-law who reappeared with the tea. Planting a kiss on the top of Eva's head she said to Connie, 'Isn't she lovely? My Dermid picked a real gem. Like a daughter to me she is.'

Connie nodded vigorously and embarrassed, Eva shooed her away with, 'Get away with you, Queenie.'

'Now that it's all over, my gal,' said Queenie earnestly, 'you mind you keep in touch.'

'Of course I will,' said Eva, looking up and squeezing her hand.

As they finished their meal the man with the accordion struck up 'A Nightingale Sang in Berkeley Square' and they all sang along. Or at least, Connie mouthed the words. Her throat was too tight with emotion to sing but the jolly songs had the others dancing and clapping and the more poignant ones brought a sentimental tear to the eye.

'I presume you've got a SOP,' said Eva. 'If you need a place to sleep, I'm sure Queenie will put us up, won't you Queenie?'

''Course I can,' smiled Queenie.

Mrs Arkwright frowned. 'What's a SOP?'

'Sleeping Out Pass,' laughed Eva.

Connie's jaw dropped and she gasped in horror. 'Oh Lord, no! Since we started double summer time, these long light evenings make such a difference. Whatever's the time?'

'Eight forty-five.'

'Oh hell,' cried Connie grabbing her handbag from the floor. 'I never gave it a thought. I haven't even got a late pass and I've got to be in by ten.'

'Where are you billeted?' asked Eva.

'Hendon. Can you tell me how to get to the nearest tube station? I shall be all right once I get there.'

'Doug is going near there,' said Queenie balancing the empty plates up her arm. 'He'll be here in a minute. He can take you in the pig van if you like.'

Connie raised an eyebrow. 'Pig van?'

'He collects pig food from all the restaurants around here,' said Queenie. 'If you don't mind the smell, I'm sure he'd give you a lift.'

Connie looked at Eva and they laughed. It was hardly ideal but at least she had the chance to be back to the camp on time.

Connie stood to go. 'Thanks Eva,' she said giving her an affectionate hug. 'I've had a wonderful day.'

'Me too,' said Eva. 'We must keep in touch.'

'I'd like that,' said Connie.

Her new friend purloined two pieces of paper and gave one to Connie. 'I've no idea where I'll be when I get demobbed,' she said, 'so I'll give you my mother's address. She'll always know where I am.'

'That'll be good,' said Connie writing her own name and address down. 'I guess it won't be too hard to meet up. You started to tell me that we lived near each other.'

'I come from Durrington,' said Eva handing her details over to Connie. 'It's near Worthing.'

'I know where that is,' Connie smiled.

Queenie leaned over the counter and interrupted them. 'Doug's here, darlin'.'

'Thanks Queenie,' said Eva.

'I'll tell him you'll be out in a minute, shall I?'

'Thanks Queenie,' said Eva once more. Her mother-in-law went out through the kitchen door.

'My folks live in Goring,' Connie smiled. 'That's a small village the other side of Worthing.' She handed Eva her slip of paper and glanced down at the name and address Eva had written down.

Beside her, her new friend gasped. 'Connie Dixon? You're not one of the Dixons from Belvedere Nurseries, are you?'

'Yes,' said Connie. She stared disbelievingly at the address Eva had just given her. Mrs Vi Maxwell, Durrington Hill. She couldn't believe what had just happened. She'd spent the day with a girl her family heartily disapproved of. 'When we met,' she accused, 'you said your name was O'Hara.'

'Of course,' said Eva, tossing her head defiantly. 'That's my married name. I was born a Maxwell, and I'm proud of it.'

'I had no idea,' said Connie quietly.

'I can't quite believe it either,' said Eva. 'And we've had such a lovely day.'

Connie nodded. 'What are we going to do?'

'Tell you one thing,' said Eva. 'I don't think my mother would be too happy if you turned up on the doorstep.'

Connie's heart began to bump but she wasn't sure if she was angry or deeply offended. How could this girl be a Maxwell? She had been so nice. 'After what your family did to mine . . .' she began.

'After what *my* family did?' Eva retorted. 'I think you'll find the boot is on the other foot.'

'Now hang on a minute,' said Connie, her hand on her hip. 'I don't want to get into a fight but get your facts straight first.'

They glared at each other, their jaws jutting.

'What's up with you two?' said Queenie, reappearing in the café. 'You both look as if you lost half a crown and found a tanner.'

'She's been buttering up to me all day and it turns out that she's a bloody Dixon,' spat Eva. She turned away and Connie thought she heard her mutter, 'Cow.'

Connie was livid. 'It's hardly surprising,' she said to Eva's receding back, 'that the Dixons and the Maxwells have nothing to do with each other, especially when one of them is so bloomin' rude.'

Queenie O'Hara looked helplessly from one girl to the other. She seemed confused. 'I don't understand. A minute ago you two were best friends. How come things have changed so quickly?'

Connie recovered herself. 'Buttering up to you all day? What's that supposed to mean?'

'You know perfectly well what it means,' Eva countered huffily. 'My folks would have leathered me with a strap, if I'd have had anything to do with the Dixons.'

'Would they really?' said Connie putting her nose in the air. 'Well, mine would do no such thing. I'm lucky enough to come from a *loving* family.'

'If I had known you were a Dixon, I never would have invited you here,' cried Eva.

'Don't worry,' said Connie. 'If I had known you were a Maxwell, I would never have come!'

'Girls, girls,' cried Queenie, 'don't let this spoil a lovely day. For Gowd's sake, you're like a couple of bickering schoolkids. Doug has to get going and you have to say your goodbyes.'

'Goodbye,' Eva snapped, carefully avoiding Connie's eye.

Connie put her nose in the air. 'Goodbye.'

'I don't understand', said Queenie, shaking her head. 'Here we are with the first day of peace and you two are at war. Whatever it is, can't you bury the hatchet?'

'After what her family did to mine? No, I can't', said Eva. 'Don't keep Doug and the *pig* van waiting, Connie.' And with that she swept out of the room.

Furious, Connie followed Queenie through the kitchen and out of the back door. Her stomach was in knots. She had really liked Eva and she'd had more fun today than she'd had in a month of Sundays but Eva was a Maxwell. Her emphasis on the word *pig* hadn't gone unnoticed either. For a time back there, she had seemed really nice. She could have fooled anyone with that dear friend act she'd put on. Ah well, at least Eva had shown her true colours before it was too late and besides, Connie knew only too well that if she stayed friends with a Maxwell, there would be hell to pay. Hadn't she been brought up with her great aunt's stories about the Maxwells? Cheats, liars and vagabonds, the lot of them, according to Ga.

When Queenie hugged her before she climbed into the passenger side of the lorry, Connie hugged her back. It wasn't Queenie's fault and her full stomach reminded her that she had been more than generous. Doug turned and gave her a toothless smile as she sat down. He turned out to be a fifty-something in a greasy looking flat cap and leather jerkin.

'Straight over to Hendon now, Doug,' said Queenie, closing the passenger door. 'The girl has to be back by ten.'

'Right you are, missus,' said Doug, starting the engine.

As the lorry moved off, Connie caught a glimpse of Eva's pale face at an upstairs window before she let the curtain drop. At the same moment, Connie screwed up the piece of paper with Eva's name and address on it and deliberately dropped it out of the van. Queenie's eyes met hers and Connie felt her cheeks flame. Thankfully, that second, Doug put his foot on the throttle and the van lurched forward.

Doug wasn't very talkative and Connie was too upset to make much conversation. What a perfectly rotten end to a lovely day. It had started out disappointingly because Emmett couldn't be with her, but from the moment they had paddled in the fountain, she had had a wonderful time. When Eva had said her family came from Worthing, Connie had no idea of the bombshell that was to come. Her mind drifted back over the years. Now that she came to think about it, her great aunt had never been that specific about the rift between the two families. In fact, Connie hardly knew anything about the Maxwell family, but whenever Ga spoke of them, the contempt in which she held them was written all over her face. She never had a good word to say and when Ga voiced an opinion, no one dared argue. Connie had grown up believing that the Maxwells were dishonest, conniving, deceitful wretches who were to be avoided altogether. Eva was the first Maxwell Connie had ever spoken to and look how nasty she had been when she'd found out who Connie was. She'd certainly shown her true colours, hadn't she? Ah well, good riddance to bad rubbish.

The cab smelled musty and a bit like a compost heap on a sunny day. After a while it made her feel queasy so Connie was more than relieved to see the gates of her camp looming out of the darkness. She thanked Doug profusely and walked the few hundred yards to the sentry post. She fancied that the guard wrinkled his nose as she walked by and her only thought was to have a good strip-down wash or if she was lucky, a small bath before lights out.

'Connie! There you are,' Rene sounded really pleased to see her as she walked in their Nissen hut. 'Where did you and Eva get to? We looked everywhere for you both but you'd completely disappeared. I'm so sorry. Did you have a terrible time? I mean, you don't know London at all, do you? Oh, I feel perfectly dreadful about it. How on earth did you get home?'

'If you'll let me get a word in edgeways,' Connie laughed as she threw her bag over her iron bedstead, 'I'll tell you.'

As Rene sat on the bed beside her, Connie told her some of what had happened. Listening to her friend's abject apologies, Connie felt a twinge of guilt. She'd been having such a good time, she hadn't given Rene and Barbara a moment's thought since they'd lost sight of each other on The Mall. 'Please don't worry,' she smiled as Rene apologised yet again. 'It wasn't your fault. I had a great time anyway.'

'If you don't mind me saying so,' said Rene, pulling a face, 'you don't smell too good.'

'Neither would you if you'd sat in that awful van,' Connie laughed. 'Let me go to the bathroom.'

Sitting in the regulation five inches of water, Connie sponged away the smell of the pig food, but somehow she didn't feel clean. She'd already gone over some of the things Eva had said to her, and now she was remembering the unkind things she had said in return. She shouldn't have been so sharp with her. After all, Eva was a war widow and being with her mother-in-law again had obviously brought back some painful memories. Hadn't she suffered enough?

She climbed out of the bath and towelled herself dry. What could she do about it? The Dixons and the Maxwells had been at loggerheads for donkey's years. She pulled the plug and watched the dirty water swirl around the plughole before disappearing. Wrapping herself in her dressing gown, Connie sighed. There were some stinks that needed a lot more than soap and water to wash them away. Ah well, it was done and dusted as far as she and Eva were concerned. She'd never see her again anyway.

The dream came in the early hours. It was one of those strange moments when you are asleep and you know it's only a dream and yet you are powerless to wake yourself up. She struggled to make sense of it but as the moving forms in front of her grew darker, the overwhelming fear reached panic proportions. The tap-tapping of the cigarette on that case grew louder. *Wake up, Connie. Wake up.* Oh God, he was coming for her. Her eyes locked onto his and she couldn't get the door shut. The door . . . the door . . . Now he was inside the room . . . coming closer and closer. She could smell his breath, feel his hand pinning her shoulders down. *Connie, wake up.* She was screaming but no sound came from her lips. His rasping voice filled her ears. *You'll like it . . .* He opened his mouth and beyond his yellow teeth she saw his fat, pulsating tongue. She felt that if he came any closer, he would devour her whole. The weight of his body suffocated her. She thrashed her arms to push him away and the rushing sound in her ears grew louder.

'Connie, it's all right. It's just a dream.' The moment Rene's voice penetrated the terrifying sounds, they vanished as quickly as someone turning the radio off. Her eyes sprang open and she saw a torch on the pillow beside her. Rene was leaning over her, her hands as light as a feather on her shoulders but she had obviously been shaking her to wake her up. Connie sat up suddenly and blinking in the half light, saw a dozen anxious faces gathered around her bed. At the same time, she became aware that her nightdress was drenched in perspiration and her hair stuck to her forehead.

'You had a bad dream,' said Rene. 'You were shouting out.'

'I'm sorry,' she said. 'Sorry I woke you all up.'

The girls began to move away and get back into their own beds.

'Do you want to talk about it?' said a disembodied voice in the darkness.

Connie lay back on the pillow and shook her head. 'No, thanks. It was only a dream.'

Two

As Connie staggered through the front gate of Belvedere Nurseries with her suitcase two months later, the dog opened one eye. He was lying across the path, snoozing in the early July sunshine. A mongrel, he had a black and white coat, a feathered tail and more than a touch of the sheepdog about him. When her father had bought him as a pup for her thirteenth birthday, they were told that he was a Border collie, cross retriever but his legs were too short and his mouth lopsided. Connie didn't care what he looked like; she had loved Pip at first sight. 'You always did go for the underdog,' Ga had mumbled in disgust when they brought him home. As soon as the puppy was placed on the mat, he peed a never-ending stream, never once taking his coal black eyes from the old lady's face. Hiding her smile, Connie knew that like her, Pip had a rebellious streak and they became inseparable. Later on, it was Pip who helped her get over the loss of her father and her brother Kenneth going away like that. She took him for long walks and unloaded her brokenness onto him. When she sat on the grass to cry, he would lick her tears away and wag his tail in sympathy. Although she was careful to obey Ga and never mention 'that business,' Pip seemed to understand exactly how she was feeling. Pip was her adored companion until she was nineteen years old and joined the WAAFs and he had never quite forgiven her for leaving home. As the gate clicked shut behind her, Connie called out, 'Here, boy. Here, Pip.'

He rose to his feet, yawned, stretched lazily and she noticed that he was getting quite a few grey hairs around his muzzle. He was nine years old, much more than that in doggie years. She watched him turn around and walk ahead of her to the front door where he waited. When she got to him, Connie reached down and patted his side before ringing the doorbell. 'Silly old dog,' she said softly.

As the door opened and her mother stood on the step, Pip came to life, panting and jumping in the small porchway like a thing demented. 'Connie!' Gwen laughed as Pip's joyful barks obviously delighted her. 'What a wonderful homecoming Pip is giving you.'

'Warm welcome my eye,' Connie laughed. 'He hasn't even come to my call. He's doing all that jumping about for your benefit.'

Her mother smiled uncertainly. 'Well, come on in, darling, let me look at you. I like your new hair.'

'They're called Victory curls,' said Connie patting the back of her head. 'I have to curl them up with Kirby grips every night and wear a scarf in bed but I think it looks quite nice.'

'It certainly does,' her mother enthused.

Gwen Craig was small with high cheekbones and an oval face. Her hair was still dark but Connie could see a few grey hairs and she had tired eyes. It alarmed her to see that her mother had lost weight. Her clothes positively hung on her. Gwen had married Connie's father Jim Dixon in 1919 when she was only eighteen and bore him two children, Kenneth, now twenty-three, and Connie aged twenty-one. 1936 was an eventful year. First she'd had Pip, then soon after their father had died after a long illness, and Kenneth had left home abruptly. Her father's illness had sapped them of all their money and because they were living in a tithed cottage, Gwen and Connie would have been homeless if Ga hadn't come to the rescue. In exchange for housework, Gwen and Connie moved in with her in her small cottage in the

26

same village. A couple of years later, and much to Connie's surprise, Gwen had married Clifford Craig, a man she had thought was only a nodding acquaintance. Their union had produced Mandy now aged six and the exact image of her mother. Gwen held out her arms and, dropping her case on the mat, Connie went to her.

Behind her, a commanding voice boomed out of the sitting room. 'Gwen? Is that Constance?'

Connie grinned and ignoring her great aunt's calls, she deliberately stayed in her mother's warm embrace for several more minutes. 'It's sooo good to see you, Mum.'

'And you too,' said Gwen. 'Where's Emmett? I half expected him to be with you.'

Connie shook her head. 'I'm not with him anymore, Mum.'

Her mother looked concerned.

'It's all right,' Connie said quickly. 'It wasn't very serious and we lost touch soon after VE Day.'

'I'm sorry,' said Gwen shaking her head sadly. 'I thought he seemed like a good man.'

Connie couldn't argue with that. She had wanted Emmett to get in touch again but it never happened. She had eventually written to his last known address only to have her letter returned to her unopened. Someone had written in the top left-hand corner, 'Unknown at this address'. Connie had been upset, of course, but what could she do? She had cried. She had gone over and over their last date in her mind, Saturday night at the pictures followed by a fish and chip supper on a park bench, but there was nothing to say why he hadn't contacted her again. Maybe his mother had taken a turn for the worse, or, perish the thought, maybe she had died. Connie had no idea where she lived so there was little point in fretting about it. 'Well, it's all over now,' she said again.

'If that's you, Constance,' Ga called imperiously, 'come in here where I can see you.'

Gwen kissed her daughter and let her go, the two of them rolling their eyes in sympathetic unison.

'Come on,' her mother smiled, 'or we'll never hear the last of it.'

Connie advanced but her mother caught her arm. 'Shoes.'

Connie bent to unlace her shoes. Pip watched her and Connie patted his side again.

'You certainly fooled Mum,' she whispered, 'but you don't fool me. We'll go for a walk later, okay?' Ignoring her, the dog yawned in a bored way and sauntered towards the kitchen where he flopped into his basket.

'Hello Ga,' Connie said cheerfully as she walked into the sitting room.

'What took you so long?' said Ga, feigning her disapproval. 'And what were you whispering about out there?'

'Mum was asking me about Emmett, that's all,' said Connie, 'and I was explaining that it's all off.'

Connie kissed her proffered cheek. 'I can't say I'm sorry,' she said into Connie's neck. 'I didn't really take to him.'

Olive Dixon was a formidable woman. She was solidly built with spade-like hands from working the small market garden, which brought in the lion's share of the family income. Unlike most women of her age, her sunburnt face was relatively free of wrinkles and she wore her steel grey hair piled on the top of her head in a flat squashed bun.

'What the devil have you done to your hair?' she frowned.

'Don't you like it?' said Connie.

'Indeed I do not,' said Ga. 'With all those silly curls you look like something out of a Greek tragedy.'

Connie chose to ignore her. Usually when Olive said jump, everybody said, how high. Ever since Gwen and Connie had come to live with her after Jim Dixon died, she had quickly established herself as the undoubted head of the family. When Clifford and Gwen married in 1938, he had tried to exert his authority, but at a mere five feet, Olive towered over everybody by the sheer force of her personality. They had moved from Patching to Goring to make a completely new start but because Ga had bought the Belvedere Nurseries and the house they all lived in, Gwen and Clifford were expected to run everything, while she remained firmly in charge.

'I'll get the tea,' said Gwen, leaving the room.

Ga was sitting at her beloved writing bureau and Connie noticed for the first time that her right leg was raised up on a pouf. Her knee was very swollen.

'Ouch, that looks painful,' said Connie reaching out.

'Don't touch it!' Olive cried. 'I'm waiting for Peninnah Cooper.'

Connie took in her breath. 'The gypsies are here?'

'They turned up about a week ago,' said Olive. 'Reuben parked the caravan down by the lay-by near the field.'

'And Kez?'

Ga pursed her lips. 'I never did understand why you wanted to hang around with that ignorant girl. Yes, she's here too. She's married now, with children.'

Connie was thrilled. She couldn't wait to see her old childhood friend. Kez a wife and mother . . . Imagine that . . .

The gypsies had been a part of her life as far back as she could remember. When the family lived at Patching, they had turned up at different times of year to work in the fields.

The Roma like Kez and Peninnah had no time for other travellers like the fairground showman, the circus performer or the Irish tinkers, because they felt they had given them a bad name. The Roma were in a class of their own. Normally they didn't even mix socially with Gorgias, a name they gave all house dwellers, which is what made Kez and Connie's friend-ship all the more unusual. They had met as children during the short periods of time that Kez went to Connie's school. Because Kezia's parents always kept to the familiar patterns, Connie would wait in the lane in early May when the bluebells came out in profusion in the local woods. Kezia and her family would pick them by the basketful, tie them into bunches held together by the thick leaves and hawk them around Worthing. Connie was allowed to help with the picking and tying but her father drew the line at selling what God had given to the world for free. It was always a bad time when the season was over, but Kez would be back in the autumn to harvest in the local apple orchards.

Everything changed in 1938. Kezia's mother had died, old before her time. Then there was that business with Kenneth, after which Connie's mother married Clifford and they had moved to Goring.

'Why is Pen coming?' Connie asked.

'She's bringing a couple of bees.'

Connie raised an eyebrow. 'A couple of bees?'

'For my knee,' said Olive impatiently. Ga feigned disapproval of the gypsies until it suited her to call upon them.

Peninnah Cooper, Kez's grandmother, was well known for her country cures and many people swore by them. They may have been part of a bygone era but funnily enough, Pen's 'cures' often worked. All the same, Connie couldn't imagine how bringing some bees could help Olive's bad leg.

She heard the sound of tinkling cups and her mother came in with the tea trolley. Connie took off her coat and sat down. Teatime in the Dixon household was always a cosy affair and today her mother had tried to make it a bit special. She had got out the willow pattern tea service and the silver spoons Ga had kept in the top drawer. Connie appreciated her mother's effort. 'Thanks Mum,' she smiled.

Whenever she was homesick, Connie used to picture this little ritual. Gwen put the tea strainer over the cup and poured the tea. When the first cup was full, Connie handed it to Ga.

'So,' said Olive, 'now that you're finally out of it, we'll be glad of your help in the nursery.'

Connie winced. She had stayed on in the WAAFs for an extra couple of weeks because there had been a lot to do in the aftermath of the war. As well as doing her usual general office duties, her work had mainly been making sure that war-damaged RAF personnel were being followed up and getting help from the right channels. Not that there was a lot she could do. Most men were simply discharged and left to get on with it, something which left her with a yearning to do something constructive with her life.

'Actually,' said Connie taking a deep breath, 'I've made some plans of my own. I've decided that I want to be a nurse.'

She knew they'd be surprised but Gwen almost dropped her teacup and Ga's mouth fell open. 'A nurse?' she said in a measured tone. 'Do you think you have the stomach for it?'

'I've toughened up a lot because of the war', said Connie.

'We really need another pair of hands on the smallholding,' said Ga, glancing at Connie's mother.

'We'll manage', Gwen smiled.

'Manage?' Ga challenged. 'It's hard enough to cope now. Your mother and I are not getting any younger and we'll need every pair of hands we can get.'

The nurseries weren't large by the standards of other nurseries in the area. They grew seedlings and vegetables and her mother kept hens for the eggs. There were a couple of stretches of waste ground which had never been developed but there was plenty of work to be done. Connie knew that if she stayed at home she would be expected to work in the small lean-to shop attached to the side of the house or in the greenhouse. She didn't mind helping out, but she certainly didn't want to do it for the rest of her life and besides, she wasn't sure the nursery could support so many people.

Connie sipped her tea. She'd always known it would be a bit of a job persuading Ga and her mother that she wanted a career of her own. She wasn't afraid to go ahead with or without

31

their blessing, although she would much prefer them to be happy to let her go. She was determined to stand her ground, come what may. She was nearly twenty-two for heaven's sake. The war had changed everything. Girls had more opportunities than they'd ever had before, and besides, now that Emmett was out of the picture what else was there? She didn't want to leave it any longer. The training took four years. By the time she'd finished, she would be twenty-six . . . quite old really. Ga's reaction was predictable but it took Connie by surprise that her mother didn't put up more of a fight.

Pip barked.

'That'll be Mandy, home from school,' said Gwen as the dog hurried outside. Connie's younger sister Mandy had been at infants' school for about a year. 'Mrs Bawden, next door, and I take it in turns to take Mandy and Joan to school. It's her turn this week.'

Connie stood up as Mandy burst through the door and threw herself into her arms. 'Connie, Connie!' Laughing, Connie twirled Mandy around in a circle.

'How many times do I have to tell you, Mandy?' Olive grumbled petulantly. 'No outdoor shoes in the house.'

Connie let her go and Mandy slid to the floor. Obediently the little girl retraced her steps to the back door and took off her shoes, placing them next to the umbrella stand. Connie caught her breath. With her hair in plaits and wearing a grey pinafore and white blouse her little sister looked so grown up.

A couple of minutes later, Pen Cooper knocked on the door and stepped into the house. She had a jam jar in her hand. Inside the jar, an angry bee knocked itself against the glass. Pen was not only a gypsy but she was also a bit of an eccentric. She wore a long flowing dress and plenty of beads. She had make-up too, which was unusual for a traveller. Thickly layered powder and some kohl around her pale mischievous eyes. When she saw Connie she stopped and held out her arms. ''Tis good to see ye.'

'It's good to see you too, Pen,' Connie smiled. 'I'll come up later and see Kez if that's all right.'

'You knows it is,' Pen beamed, 'and welcome.' She turned her attention to Olive. 'Now, are you ready, dear?'

'As ready as I'll ever be,' said Olive. 'It's killing me and some-one's got to get the ground ready for the calabrese and winter cabbages.'

Connie saw her mother's back stiffen.

'Yoohoo.' They heard another voice call from the front door and Aunt Aggie came into the room. Aunt Aggie wasn't really a relation but she was Ga's oldest friend. A rather prim woman, Aggie never had a hair out of place. She always seemed to be dressed in her Sunday best and today was no exception. She wore a yellow floral dress, white peep-toe shoes, newly whitened, and she carried a white handbag. She and Olive had been friends since they were at school together. Peeling off her white crochet gloves, Aggie offered Connie a cold cheek to kiss. 'How nice to have you home again.'

'I'd better make a start,' said Pen and Gwen took a protesting Mandy away from Connie's arms and upstairs to get changed out of her uniform. 'But I want to see, Mummy. Why can't I watch?' They could hear her complaining all the way to her room.

Connie watched fascinated as Pen took some tweezers from her pocket. 'Ready?' she said again and slid the lid from the jar.

'Are you sure about this Olive, dear?' Aggie asked.

'Pen knows what she's doing,' Olive snapped.

Aggie poured herself a cup of tea and sat down with one leg swinging as she crossed it over the other. The bee continued to bang itself against the jar until eventually Pen caught its wings with her fingers and put it onto Olive's swollen knee, holding it there until thoroughly enraged, it stung her. Olive winced. Pen removed the dying bee and eventually the sting it had left behind.

Gwen reappeared at the door. 'While Mandy is getting changed, I'm going outside for a bit.'

Connie left the three women to watch Ga's swelling knee and followed her mother outside to where she found her picking runner beans.

'There's so much to do this time of year,' she said matter-of-factly as Connie made a start on the broad beans in the next row. Their smallholding was very popular and the shop was always busy. Their customers knew everything was very fresh, perhaps only just picked. Olive kept the prices down while Gwen did her best to keep the supplies from running out, in between the housework and looking after Mandy. Connie knew how hard her mother's life was and the unease slipped in.

'You don't mind me not working in the nursery, do you Mum?'

'I'm pleased you're going to make a career for yourself, dear,' said Gwen. 'You'll make a good nurse.'

'Ga was a bit cross,' said Connie. 'I don't want to leave you in the lurch.'

'We'll be fine,' said Gwen.

The nursery was hardly making its way when Olive bought it but Clifford was such an excellent nurseryman that he had pulled it back from the brink and made it a going concern. When he was called up in 1943, the two women took over. Gwen used to serve in the shop, but these days she preferred to work on the land, leaving Ga to look after the business side of things. It was never voiced, but the arrangement was so much better since Olive's knee started playing up. On bad days, Olive could sit in the shop, which was little more than a glorified lean-to, and let the customers serve themselves.

Although the family managed to lift the early potatoes them-selves, they generally hired casual labourers to help with the main crop in September. They mostly used the locals because the gypsies didn't often come this way. When Connie was a child and the gypsies came to Patching, she and Kenneth were invited

34

to share in their communal meal. Connie loved it, especially when Peninnah, Kez's grandmother, would take her pipe out of her mouth and tell them about the old days. She had an encyclopedic knowledge when it came to family and some of them sounded such wonderful people. 'They called 'e Red shirt Matthew on account as he always wore a red shirt . . .' 'So they stuffed the two rabbits under 'is big ol' hat and legged it all the way 'ome . . .' 'She'd stolen 'is trousers, so when 'e got out of the lake, 'e was as naked as the day he were born. He had to walk 'ome without a stitch on 'is back.' Pen would stop to chuckle. 'That learned him not to mess about with a gypsy girl . . .' Connie and Kenneth would roar their heads off even though they hadn't a clue who she was talking about. They were hard workers, the women and children selling handmade pegs and bunches of flowers around the centre of Worthing and the men doing any kind of manual labour on offer.

The war had changed everything. The government had created the Land Army pushing the gypsies further to the fringes of society perhaps, but the hope was that if the powers-that-be disbanded it, farmers would use gypsy labour once again. However, the fate of Kezia and her family was not Connie's main concern right now. As they worked side by side, she noticed how tired her mother looked.

'I'm fine,' said Gwen when Connie remarked on it. 'I've had a bit extra to do with Ga being laid up but things are easing up a bit now. We've taken on a local girl to work in the shop, and Clifford will be demobbed soon.'

'Have you been to the doctor?'

'Connie, I'm fine,' Gwen insisted.

Connie knew better than to argue. 'When's Clifford coming home?'

'At the end of the month.'

Connie breathed a silent sigh of relief. With Clifford back, he could take some of the workload off Mum and she could begin her training at the hospital in September as she had planned. She relaxed as she carried on picking. 'What's she like?' Connie asked.

'Who?'

'The girl in the shop.'

'Sally? She's a bit scatty at times but a good worker,' said Gwen, her bowl now full. 'The runner beans have been really good this year.'

Mandy had come out of the house and begun skipping. Connie watched her half-sister and was impressed.

'She's only just learned how to do it,' said Gwen proudly. 'I think she's quite good for someone not quite seven, don't you?'

There was a movement by the back door and Peninnah appeared with Ga. Olive was limping and she had to hold on to the doorposts to keep herself steady but at least she was mobile again. Her leg was heavily bandaged. The two women said their goodbyes and Pen blew a kiss to Mandy.

As she watched her great aunt turn around in the doorway and walk painfully back indoors, Connie turned back to the job in hand. The two boxes were full, one with runner beans and the other with broad beans in the jackets as they headed towards the shop. As they took the supplies inside, Connie met the girl working there.

Sally Burndell was a pretty girl with dark hair and full lips who made no secret of the fact that she was going to go to secretarial college later in the year and was only in the shop for a short while. Connie liked her directness. They arranged the fresh beans underneath the beans already in the boxes to make sure the older beans picked the day before were sold first. Gwen went round picking out failing fruit and vegetables and making sure the supplies were topped up. Connie fetched some fresh newspaper from the storeroom and showed Sally how to make it into bags by folding them a certain way. She also got her to fan out the paper wrapped around the fruit in the orange boxes.

'Press them flat and put them in a pile,' said Connie.

'Whatever for?' said a voice behind them.

Connie turned to see Aunt Aggie watching them from the doorway.

'They could be used as toilet paper,' she said. 'It's a lot softer than newspaper. It's a tip I picked up from the WAAF.'

'Huh!' Aunt Aggie scoffed. 'What's wrong with newspaper?'

'I must go in and get the tea,' said Gwen, wiping her hands on a towel.

'And I'm off for the bus,' said Aggie turning to leave. 'Olive said I could have some beans. Not too many. There's only me.'

Sally wrapped a few runner beans in newspaper and handed them to her. Aunt Aggie took them without a thank you.

'See you soon, Aggie,' Gwen called.

They watched her go.

'When you've got a bum as big as hers,' Sally said, 'I guess you'd need a newspaper as big as *The Times*.'

'Shh,' Connie cautioned. 'She'll hear you.' But she and her mother couldn't help giggling.

Thankfully, Aggie hadn't heard the remark because she walked on.

'Play with me, Connie,' Mandy pleaded as Connie followed her mother outside.

Gwen turned around. 'No need for you to come into the house,' she smiled. 'I've made a sausage in cider casserole. All I have to do is take it out of the oven. Stay here and play with Mandy.'

The two sisters grinned. Mandy flicked her plaits over her shoulder and before long, Connie was holding the rope and they were skipping together. Connie hadn't done this for years. She was a bit out of breath but she hadn't lost her touch. Pip wandered outside.

'When I was little', she told Mandy, 'I used to tie the rope on the down-pipe like this and when I turned it, Pip would join in.'

As soon as she said it, and much to Connie's delight, he joined in. Mandy clapped her hands in delight. By the time their mother called them for tea, she, Pip and Mandy had become great friends.

Three

Teatime over, Connie tucked Mandy up in bed and after a bedtime story they sang her favourite song, 'You Are My Sunshine'. It was a precious time for both of them and one that Connie had started when her little sister was very young. Every time she'd come home on leave, Mandy had begged her to sing it as she said goodnight. Connie crept out of Mandy's room and had what her mother would call *a cat's lick in the bathroom* and changed her clothes. She put on the pale lemon sweater and same grey pinstriped slacks she had worn in Trafalgar Square and after calling out her goodbyes, headed in the direction of Goring-by-Sea railway station. Pip invited himself along with her, sometimes running on ahead, occasionally stopping to sniff something. She watched him scenting a blade of grass, a telegraph pole and the postbox and marvelled at his carefree love of life.

They reached the Goring crossroad and walked up Titnore Lane. All at once the dog stopped and motionless, sniffed the air, then he took off at breakneck speed. A few minutes later she could hear him in the distance barking joyously. Connie quickened her step and as she rounded a small bend in the lane, she saw them – the gypsies. By now Pip was hysterical with delight, jumping from one to the other, his tail wagging as he let out little yelps of pleasure. Connie was surprised. The dog had only been a puppy when he'd last seen the gypsies but he clearly remembered them.

Connie could pick some of them out even from here. Peninnah Cooper, Kez's maternal grandmother was stirring something in the black pot hung over an open fire, and was that Kez's cousin sitting on the caravan steps? Reuben Light, Kez's father, his frail old body bent low with arthritis and it seemed that he had developed an unhealthy cough. Reuben spotted her and stood up to wave but where was Kez?

Connie recalled how devastated she had been when her mother and Ga moved to Goring in 1938. How would Kez know where she was? Writing a letter was hopeless. For a start, what would she put on the envelope? 'To the gypsy caravan somewhere near Patching pond in May' hardly seemed appropriate and besides, Kez couldn't read. Connie had wept buckets at the injustice of it all, which was why the fact that Kez was just down the road from where she now lived after all this time was so amazing.

There was a movement by the caravan and there she was. She had a baby in her arms but as soon as she saw Connie, Kez called out her name and pushed the child into Pen's arms. Connie broke into a run. The two women met in the lane and flinging their arms around each other they danced in circles, laughing as they went. Kezia smelled of rosemary and lavender, her flaming red hair tied untidily with a green ribbon flapped behind her as they spun together. She was wearing a long floral dress with a tight bodice and loose unlaced boots. They broke away and held each other at arm's length to look at each other and the questions flew. *How are you? You look great. Is that your baby? How long has it been since we met? It must be eight, nine years . . . Where have you been all this time?* A little boy had joined them and was tugging at Kezia's skirt. She bent to pick him up, settling him comfortably on her hip. As they wandered towards the caravan a delicious smell of rabbit stew wafted towards her.

'Stay and eat with us,' said Kez.

Connie linked her arm in Kezia's. Oh, it was good to see her again. 'I've just eaten but I'd love to share a cuppa.' She smiled at the child on Kez's hip. 'And who is this?'

'This is my son, Samuel,' Kez beamed. 'He's nearly three. Say hello Sam.' But the child turned his head shyly into his mother's neck.

'Pen told me you had kids,' said Connie. 'But two?'

'I had three,' said Kezia, her voice becoming flat. 'Pen is holding the babby but my little Joseph went to be with the angels.'

'Oh Kez, I'm so sorry,' said Connie suddenly stricken for her.

When they reached the caravan, there were more greetings and now that she was up close to him, Connie could see that Reuben was but a shadow of his former self. All the same, he was delighted to see her. 'It must be ten year since I laid eyes on ye,' he smiled, his gold tooth flashing in the failing evening sun.

'Nine,' Kezia corrected.

'It does seem a long time ago, doesn't it?' said Connie shaking the old man's hand.

Behind Reuben's traditional gypsy caravan, she caught a glimpse of a long motor trailer, an ex-army vehicle. Kezia explained that using his army pay, her husband, Simeon, had just bought it for the family and now he was converting it into their home.

'He says it's the way of the future,' said Kez proudly.

Other members of the family, including Kezia's husband, Simeon (how they all loved their Old Testament names) tumbled out to greet Connie respectfully. If they seemed a little surprised that a Gorgia would be joining them as they ate, they said nothing. Reuben offered Connie an upturned box and as she sat down a sullen-faced lad came out of the trailer.

'Isaac!' Connie cried. There was about six years between them so Kezia's baby brother was about fifteen or sixteen now. She remembered how when he was a year or so old, the two girls had taken it in turns to hoick him on their hip as they played together. He looked a lot like Kez. He had the same flaming red hair which was tousled and untidy but he was fresh-faced. He wore a kerchief at his neck and his shirt was open to reveal his hairless chest. Isaac's greeting was polite but nowhere near as enthusiastic as his sister's. As always, the men ate first.

As she sat by the campfire, Connie couldn't help reflecting how different their lives were. Kez looked much older than her twenty-two years. Her hands were calloused from potato picking and Brussels sprout harvesting in the winter. At this time of year, her fingers were already stained bright red from picking strawberries and raspberries.

As is the custom with Romani gypsies, Kez had married young. The strict ethics of their culture demanded that all girls marry between sixteen and eighteen. She had to be a virgin and according to the code, she was only allowed a maximum of four suitors. Any more and she would be considered too flighty. Simeon, Kezia's husband, had been her one and only suitor and she'd married him just before her seventeenth birthday.

As the baby finished feeding Kez looked up, giving Connie a shy smile. She sat her baby up to wind her and then handed her to Connie. 'What did you call her?'

'Blossom.'

'I don't recall a Blossom in the Bible!'

'Well, that's where you're wrong, Connie Dixon,' said Kez. 'The day my daughter first drew breath Pen told Simeon, "It shall blossom abundantly, and rejoice even with joy and singing," and that's in the Bible that is.'

'You're kidding,' Connie gasped.

'Isaiah 35, Verse 2,' said Kez adopting a superior tone.

Connie burst out laughing and Kez joined in. Looking down at this pretty green-eyed baby with wisps of bright red hair, her name suited her perfectly. She was small but sturdy. She would need to be. The life of a gypsy was hard. Kezia and her family were constantly on the move. They had always gone wherever there was picking to be done, setting up camp in some field belonging to the farmer in question. As each season came and went, they went on to the next place. It sounded idyllic, waking with the dawn and hitching the horse to the wagon to head towards the next source of work, but Connie didn't envy them.

Sam had found a ball and he and Pip began a game of toss and fetch. The gypsy dogs, tied to the fence post, could only look on enviously and the pair of them giggled and barked together. Connie sighed. If only life were always this simple, this pleasurable.

Connie had been around Kez and her family enough times to know that contrary to a commonly held belief, the true gypsy was not dirty. She watched as Kez scrubbed her little boy before getting him ready for bed. She worked so hard on him the child began to protest. After changing her baby's nappy, one of the other women took them both inside the long trailer to put them to bed, giving the two friends time together to catch up with their news.

As soon as he had eaten, Reuben was ready to sleep. He never slept inside the caravan because that was purely to house his possessions. Instead, he crawled inside a small tunnel tent pitched on the grass verge beside it and said his goodnight. As he laced the front of the tent, Connie listened to him coughing.

'He's not so good,' said Kez quietly, as if reading her thoughts. Connie nodded. What could she say? Life on the road was hard on them all. Sleeping out in the open when you're unwell wasn't ideal but it was no good suggesting that he should go indoors. The open air and the freedom of the road was all Reuben knew.

'Has he seen a doctor?' Connie asked.

'He won't go to a doctor,' said Kez with a shrug. 'He says all doctors are Gorgias and not to be trusted.'

'Doesn't it get any easier?' Connie asked. 'Being on the road, I mean?'

Kezia shook her head. 'Sometimes, even before we unhitch

the horse, the village bobby comes along on his bicycle to tell us to move on.'

'Couldn't you refuse?'

'If we do they threaten to take our children away and put them in a home.'

Connie was appalled. 'Can they do that?'

Kez shrugged. 'So they say.'

Connie shivered. The sweater only had short sleeves and she was getting cold now. She wished she'd brought a cardigan. 'I'd better be getting back,' she said.

'You didn't get your tea yet,' said Kez.

Connie sat back on the caravan steps and sipped the scalding hot tea. Kez must have noticed her shivering because she threw a shawl over her shoulders. As Kezia ate, Connie told her about life in the munitions factory and the WAAF. Kez told Connie about the day her mother died and the loss of her little Joseph. On a happier note, she told Connie about meeting Simeon and of their marriage. Simeon, who had joined up during the war, had only just returned to her. He had adjusted to life with the Gorgia and, she said proudly, 'He did his bit.'

'Simeon talks of buying land,' Kez went on. 'He wants us to settle down.'

Connie was sceptical. 'But you've always enjoyed moving around. Will you be able to settle in one place?'

'Simeon managed in the army right enough,' she smiled. 'The kids and I will get used to it. I want Sam to go to school. I want him to read and write.'

Connie nodded and the two friends looked at each other with the same unspoken thought in her head. Reuben coughed again.

'I want a better life,' said Kez quietly. 'The Frenchie says Simeon has a real talent.'

Connie was puzzled. 'The Frenchie?'

'I don't know his name,' Kez shrugged, 'but he says if I learn to read proper, we could go into business and I can help Simeon.'

She sighed. 'We never stayed long enough in one place for me to learn at school.'

'If you're going to stick around here for a while,' said Connie, 'I could try and teach you to read if you like?'

'Would you?' cried Kez.

They hadn't noticed Isaac coming up behind them. 'What's the point?' he glared. 'Waste of time, a girl learning to read.'

'I want to read books,' said Kez defiantly. 'There's some good things in books.'

'Pah!' said Isaac. He had some fishing gear in his hand. 'You can't eat books.'

They watched him walk away and Connie smiled. 'You stick to your guns, girl.'

'I intend to.'

'You said the Frenchie says Simeon has a talent but what does he do for a living?'

Kez shrugged. 'Odd jobs, scrap metal, driving, that's all that's on offer for the likes of us.'

'So what is his talent?'

Kez led the way round the hedge to where the motor trailer stood. Connie gasped as she saw the beautiful wooden carvings he had put on the side. It wasn't to Connie's taste, too garish for that, but she could see that he had a real eye for it. Fleurs-de-lys, scrolls and arches were everywhere and Simeon was up a ladder decorating them with gold leaf.

'This is amazing!' Connie cried.

'And he done the whole thing from scratch.' Kez smiled in a satisfied way as she touched her husband's leg and they exchanged a loving glance.

'What about you, Connie?' asked Kez. 'What do you do now?'

'Didn't I tell you, I'm going to be a nurse?' said Connie.

'A nurse,' cried Kezia. 'Don't you want to get married?'

Connie thought fleetingly of Emmett. 'Maybe. When the right man comes along.'

Kez grinned. 'Good for you.'

They went back to the fire and sat down to reminisce. It was getting dark by the time Connie made a move to go home. 'Are you sure you're going to be all right walking back on your own?' Simeon asked as he cleaned his brushes.

'Fine,' said Connie. 'I have Pip with me. He won't let anybody touch me.'

'Don't forget to put the clocks back an hour,' Kez reminded her. 'Double summer time ends tonight.'

'So it does,' Connie smiled.

As she said her goodbyes and left, Connie felt loved and accepted by all of them. Everyone except Isaac. He had been less pleasant. In fact, he seemed to have a giant chip on his shoulder.

The house was in darkness when Connie got back home. She gave Pip a drink of water and the few scraps her mother had saved him from the evening meal.

'Silly old dog,' she said softly as she fondled his ear. 'I didn't abandon you, you know. I still love you.'

Leaving him in his basket, Connie crept upstairs. She had thought everyone was asleep but then she heard Ga call her from her room. Connie only ever went in there when invited. It was a cluttered place with piles of leaflets and papers all over the dressing table and the chair. As soon as she walked in the door, Connie could tell by the expression on Ga's face that something was wrong. She was sitting up in bed, her handbag beside her and her bad knee resting on a pillow. She had a lacy bed-shawl around her shoulders and her hair was in steel pins. How on earth did she sleep in those? Connie wondered.

Olive motioned for her to sit on the bedside chair so Connie moved the mound of papers onto the floor.

'I want to talk to you about this nursing business,' said Ga. Connie opened her mouth straight away but her great aunt put up her hand to silence her. 'You might not be worried about how this will affect me . . .'

'And you don't seem to be bothered that I have a right to my own life,' Connie interjected.

'But,' Ga continued loudly and clearly not listening, 'have you thought of what this will do to your mother?'

Connie faltered. 'Mother? In what way?'

'Can't you see how she looks?' said Ga accusingly. 'The poor woman is exhausted.' She paused as if to let the words sink in. 'We need you, Constance. We need you to help share the workload. Gwen cannot carry on much longer.'

There was a short silence. 'But Clifford will be coming home shortly,' said Connie.

'And what sort of a state do you think he might be in?' Ga retorted. 'Besides, he's not getting any younger either. I already told you, we need a *young* pair of hands.'

Connie looked away. She felt sick with disappointment. She didn't want to admit it but Ga was right about one thing. Her mother did look worn out. And thin. Connie chewed her bottom lip helplessly. Did she really have to give up the idea of nursing? Surely there had to be another way? It was so bloody unfair. She had a right to live her own life but if she walked out on her mother now, she would just be plain selfish.

'You don't have to give me your answer now', said Ga. 'Just think about it.'

'All right,' she said quietly, loathing the look of triumph in Ga's eyes.

Ga nodded. 'Good girl.'

Biting back her tears, Connie stood up. 'If I do stay', she said stiffly, 'it will only be for a while. I intend to be a nurse, no matter what you say.'

Ga's mouth set in a tight line.

'Oh, one more thing', said Ga, as Connie turned to leave. She opened her cavernous handbag, and pulled out a newspaper cutting. Connie took in her breath. It was the picture from the *Daily Sketch*, the one of her and Eva standing in the fountain at

47

Trafalgar Square with the two sailors. The caption above it read, *Playtime for English Roses*. She remembered how she'd rolled up her slacks and stood in the water before the two sailors climbed in beside them. The picture was quite flattering too. Connie grinned.

'It's no laughing matter,' Ga snapped. 'I am absolutely disgusted.'

'Why?' Connie challenged. 'It was only a bit of innocent fun. You were young yourself once, Ga.'

Olive's face clouded.

'Come on, it was VE Day,' Connie protested mildly. 'We were all happy. The war was over.'

'And so you took it upon yourself to climb into a fountain with Eva Maxwell.'

For a minute Connie was thrown. She had thought she was going to get a lecture about flaunting herself with two strange men. She hadn't forgotten the rage she'd felt herself when she'd realised who Eva was, but it didn't seem that important now. 'At the time, I didn't know who she was,' Connie said with a shake of her head. 'She was a friend of a friend and she said her name was O'Hara.'

'Typical,' Olive sneered. 'They're all liars, that lot.'

For some reason, Connie felt the need to defend Eva. 'O'Hara is her married name,' she said haughtily. 'And just for your information, I met her family. It was all very sad. Her husband was killed in the war and I didn't know who she was until much later in the day.'

Their eyes locked together in a common challenge. Connie refused to look away but it was clear that Olive wasn't beaten yet. 'Perhaps that is why Emmett disappeared,' she said cuttingly. 'I wonder what he thought when he saw a picture of his fiancée *cavorting about* with other men? I should have thought you would have learned your lesson by now, my girl.'

Connie's heart began thumping in her chest. 'For a start, Emmett was never my fiancé,' she snapped angrily. 'And secondly,

I have never cavorted with other men, Ga, no matter what you think.'

'I have a long memory,' said Ga pointedly.

Connie froze. 'You always have to bring that up again, don't you,' she snapped. 'I was only a child. It wasn't my fault.'

Ga looked down her nose. 'Huh. Seems to me you haven't changed much,' she said, waving the newspaper cutting in the air. 'Most men can sniff out a loose woman a mile off and you've got Gertrude's blood in you, that's for sure.'

Gertrude Dixon had scandalised the family first by getting herself tattooed and then by running away with a man from the fairground. It might have only raised a few eyebrows now, but fifty years ago, it was so shocking the family had never spoken of her again. Only Ga was determined to keep her memory alive.

Connie felt her face grow hot. 'The whole of Trafalgar Square was packed with people,' she said from between her teeth, 'and they simply climbed in with us.'

'You've got your arms around them,' said Olive looking at the cutting again. 'Not to mention the fact that both of you were half undressed . . .'

'We were not! We rolled our slacks up so that they wouldn't get wet.' Connie's face was flaming with anger. 'Anyway, you never read the *Sketch*. How did you get this?'

'You're right. I never look at such trashy papers,' said Olive with a deep breath. 'And I certainly don't expect members of my family to be on the front page but you see, someone sent it to me.'

She pulled an empty envelope from her bag. Connie could see it was addressed to Ga and in the left-hand corner someone had printed in bold letters the words, CONSTANCE AND EVA MAXWELL.

That added insult to injury. Connie was furious but with one quick move, she snatched the cutting from her hand. It tore as

49

she did so but she still had most of the picture. Screwing it into a tight ball, she swept angrily from the room.

Olive lay on her bed staring at the ceiling. She couldn't sleep. She glanced at the clock beside her bed. One thirty. It wasn't her leg that kept her awake, it was Constance. How dare she cavort in that fountain with Cissy Maxwell's granddaughter? Everybody knew how she felt about that family. Constance should have known better.

Olive turned out the light and her mind drifted back some forty years ago, to a time when she herself was twenty, and the century was only five years old. Arthur was coming home. It had been a bleak time. The Boer War hadn't been as terrible as the Great War nor as bad as the one they'd just gone through, but war is war. The enemy may be different and the weapons more sophisticated, but being wounded far from home and facing the prospect of dying in a foreign field was just as terrible whatever the age. Damn these ambitious men and their thirst for power, she thought. Most people simply wanted to live their lives in peace and safety. Why couldn't they do the same?

She remembered how it was when the troops came back, all that marching in the streets, the parades, the flag waving and the cheers. She smiled when she thought of Arthur. Dear Arthur. How handsome he looked, so tall, so suave with his new moustache and smart uniform. It hadn't been easy for him. She could tell that the moment she'd looked into his eyes. There was a weariness there that belied his twenty and six years. He never talked about what he'd seen but Pa had read about the war and what was going on in the papers at the breakfast table. He must have had a terrible time.

Life for Olive and her family had gone on as usual while they were away. They had been well off. Pa's greenhouses were renowned for their beautiful grapes and cucumbers. There had been no need for her to work back then so she had grown up taking long walks on the downs where the musky scent of wild flowers, pink and blue and yellow mingled with the dainty call of skylarks and the curlew. She still recalled the spicy scent of honeysuckle and gorse and the more rancid odour of the sheep allowed to roam free. Back then, the silence of the countryside was only broken by the sound of bleating sheep or the occasional dog barking and on Sundays, the peal of church bells. How times had changed. When was the last time she had heard the sound of the coachman's horn as he entered the village bringing much needed goods from Worthing three times a week and in all weathers? Not since the 1930s. Now it was all army lorries thundering along the lanes and coupons and going without.

Arthur had been part of the final stages of the Boer War, a time of ignoble victory. Frustrated by the constant skirmishes and guerrilla tactics, the British had adopted a scorched earth policy, destroying farms, homesteads and poisoning wells to prevent the Boers re-mustering. Any women and children left behind on their farms by their menfolk were rounded up and put into camps and because the supplies were hard to come by, tens of thousands of them died of malnutrition and disease. Much to his disgust, Arthur and his unit were left to guard them. How he'd hated it. He had even written to say that he would have much preferred to fight the enemy rather than take it out on women and children. Peace came with the Treaty of Vereeniging. The irony was, just as he was about to embark for home, Arthur was terribly injured.

She'd carried on writing to him of course, but the thought of a man with half a leg missing turned her stomach. If she was his wife, she would be expected to look at it, or even worse, dress the wound. She had confided in Aggie and wept on her shoulder. Dear Aggie had been wise beyond her years and such a comfort. After a few months, Olive had put her mind to doing the best she possibly could. When Arthur came out of hospital, she would make herself love all that horror away. It was her duty. He would soon be better, strong again. She would do whatever he asked. This time she wouldn't hold back. She would give herself to him . . . even though the thought of that leg still made her shudder, she would nurse him back to health. But it wasn't to be and it was all that Maxwell woman's fault. It was humiliating enough having to stay an old maid all her life but having a grandniece jumping into fountains with the granddaughter of the woman who had caused her all that heartache was too much to bear. It wasn't right. A tear trickled down her cheek and she brushed it away angrily before she turned over to sleep.

Sleep didn't come easily for Connie either. She lay on her back, hot tears of anger, disappointment and frustration trickling down the sides of her face and into her ears. Anger because Ga made her so. There had always been a flashpoint between them and it didn't take much to make Connie flare. The woman was impossible. What did it matter if Connie had been in a fountain with Eva Maxwell? Ga treated the incident as if it were some sort of treason. The feud was between Ga and the Maxwells. Connie didn't fully understand what it was all about, so why should she be expected to carry it on? And why did Ga constantly make snide remarks about her morals?

The disappointment was because of Emmett. Life would have been so different if they had got married. It was a mystery to her why he hadn't contacted her again after the war. They had had some good times together and she'd done all the 'right' things to make him like her. She'd flattered him, laughed at his awful jokes, worn pretty clothes so that he would admire her – all the things other girls did to trap their men but Emmett hadn't responded the way he was supposed to. Now all her ex-pals from the WAAFs were married but she was still on the shelf. It wasn't fair.

The frustration was worst of all. She had taken a long time

to think about nursing and had been so excited to be accepted for training but now she was being asked to put it on hold. Of course, this time Ga was right. Her mother did look haggard and worn out and she was not yet fifty. Connie had seen the way it was but she had chosen to pretend it would be all right. Her mother was such a wonderful person. 'I'm pleased you're going to make a career for yourself,' she had told her. 'You'll make a good nurse.' How much must it have cost her to say that and yet Connie knew she'd meant every word. She had given her the freedom to make her own life but much as she wanted to go, Connie knew she couldn't walk out on her.

The door clicked open and she raised her head to see Pip come into the room. He came to her bedside and laid his muzzle on the sheet beside her. Funny how he always sensed when she was upset.

'You'll get yourself into a heap of trouble if Ga finds you upstairs,' she whispered and she heard his tail thump against the chest of drawers as he licked her tears away.

Four

The atmosphere between Connie and Ga remained frosty for a couple of days. They avoided talking to each other any more than they had to, although they made polite conversation whenever Gwen or Mandy were around. Left to her own thoughts, Connie went over and over what Ga had said until there came a moment when she told herself she had to stop. It was beginning to make her feel ill. If only she had a close friend she could confide in, but Rene Thompson was living in Scotland now and recently married. She would have her mind on other things, and besides, it was difficult to write everything down in a letter.

'Clifford is coming home,' said Gwen as she sat at the breakfast table with a letter. Her voice was choked with emotion. 'He's being demobbed at last.'

'Oh Mum, I'm so pleased for you,' said Connie. Pip was standing next to her resting his head on her lap. Connie fondled his ear as her mind went into overdrive. If he got back before September she could still go to nursing school.

Gwen pulled a handkerchief from under her watch strap and dabbed her nose.

'About time,' said Ga rather pointedly. 'You and I can't keep the place going forever on our own. And get that dog away from the table, Constance. You know I can't stand it.'

Pip slunk into his basket but Connie ignored the jibe. Ga

could be insufferable at times, making mountains out of mole-hills and keeping up her hostility for days.

'It'll be good for Mandy to have her dad back,' said Gwen. 'She's missed him dreadfully.'

Being an older man, Clifford wasn't called up until the final big push. His regiment ended up in Holland supporting the Canadian troops who had surrounded Amsterdam. After VE Day, he was sent to Germany itself.

'Do we know when he's coming?' Connie tried to sound casual but her voice was a little tremulous with excitement.

Gwen shook her head. '"Soon", that's all he says.'

Connie was aware of Ga's eyes boring into the side of her face. 'I can pick Mandy up from school when he comes, Mum,' Connie said. 'That way you can meet him at the station on your own.'

'Thank you, darling. That would be nice.'

'And what about the shop?' said Ga.

'We'll manage,' said Connie throwing her a look and Ga jutted her chin defiantly.

'Perhaps when he gets back, you and Clifford could have a little holiday, Mum. A bit of time to yourselves. I could look after Mandy for you.'

'I don't know about that,' said her mother coyly.

'Well, think about it,' said Connie. 'Wait until you've talked to Clifford before you say no.'

Ga stood up with a harrumph. 'People never bothered with holidays in my day,' she announced as she gathered her plate and cup and saucer and put them in the sink with a clatter. 'They just got on with it.' She didn't see Connie and Gwen share a secret wink behind her back. 'There's plenty to do today,' Ga said as she limped to the door. 'Connie, you can plant the leeks and some winter cabbage in the plot by the fence and Gwen, we need to get the carrots up for winter storage.'

The back door slammed as she left the room. 'No rest for the wicked,' Gwen sighed good-naturedly.

At the weekend, the pattern of life at home was slightly different. The shop closed at noon on Saturday and normally on Sunday the whole family went to church in the morning. They were Anglicans but preferred to go to the Free Church which, because the war had interrupted their building programme, met in the local school. The services were bright and cheerful and it had a large Sunday school.

'After Sunday school,' Connie had told Mandy when she'd tucked her up the night before, 'if you're good, I'll take you to see the gypsies.'

They ate their Sunday roast, and while Gwen sat with her knitting listening to the radio and Ga sat at her writing desk, Connie and Mandy and just about every other child in Worthing set off for Sunday school. In the main it was fun and the hour was precious to parents because it was the one time that they could have an hour to themselves with no interruptions. Pip went along with them but Connie made him wait outside. The class was held in a small room at the back of the church. The teacher, Miss Jackson, was a little older than Connie but they had both gone to the same school.

'Connie!' Jane Jackson, an attractive brunette, was now a librarian. 'How good to see you. Are you back for good?'

'Looks like it,' Connie smiled.

'We must get together sometime,' Jane smiled. 'No, William, stop hitting Eddie with that hymn book. That's no way to behave in church.'

The children sat in a semi-circle on a large mat on the floor. There were about thirty of them in Jane's class, nearly all of them the children of church members although there were a few who had been sent along by their parents so that they could have a bit of peace and quiet and a little time to themselves. They began with a prayer and then some choruses. Jane and her fellow teachers were ably assisted by Michael Cunningham, the son of the church treasurer, a pimply faced youth who was waiting to go to university. Michael hammered out the tune on the school piano.

The choruses brought back memories of her own childhood. They were as timeless and as meaningless as they had ever been. '*Jesus wants me for a sunbeam . . .*' '*Bumble bee, bumble bee, buzz, buzz, buzz, buzz, buzz . . .*' and '*I am H-A-P-P-Y . . .*' The Bible story was based around *the woman with the issue of blood*. Connie wondered if five- to seven-year-olds had any idea what 'an issue of blood' meant, but she was surprised to see that the children listened enraptured. Apparently Jane was a gifted story-teller. One more chorus, this time one relating to the story itself, '*Oh touch the hem of His garment and thou too shalt be whole . . .*' and Sunday school was over. At the end of the session, as they said their goodbyes, Jane produced a box of sweets. Each 'good' child, namely the ones who had sat still while they'd had the story, was allowed to take one. Connie permitted herself a wry smile. Clever old Jane. No wonder the children sat still and listened.

'There's a dance at the Assembly Rooms on Saturday,' said Jane as they were leaving. 'A few of us from the village are going. Sally Burndell comes. You know her, don't you?'

'She works part time in our shop,' Connie nodded.

'Do come to the dance,' said Jane. 'They're great fun.'

A couple of days slipped by but at the earliest opportunity, Connie climbed upstairs to the attic with a torch. It was hot and musty but she'd only been there for about ten minutes before Gwen came to see what she was doing.

'It's chock-a-block up here, Mum!' Connie gasped. 'I had no idea we had all this junk.'

Her mother looked a little surprised too. 'I suppose it's years of saying, "Oh . . . put it in the attic for now",' she smiled. 'What are you looking for anyway?'

'My old school books,' said Connie. 'I'm teaching Kez to read.'

'Try that box over there,' said her mother.

The first of the boxes contained an old photograph album. Connie flicked through and smiled. The box Brownie had recorded so many happy occasions but it was a shock to see her father's face again. Out of respect for her new husband, her mother had moved his pictures up here when Clifford came into the family. She turned a page and there was Kenneth. Her heart missed a beat and she sighed inwardly. He looked about twelve. He was bare-chested and wearing short trousers. His fair hair was tousled and he had obviously been looking for something in the pond. He was proudly holding up a jam jar tied with a string handle and something lurked in the water. She stared at her long lost brother and wished he was here. Memory is selective, she knew that. She'd forgotten the times when they had been at loggerheads, or the times when he'd thumped her for getting in his way. All she could recall were the picnics on the hill and her mother reading them endless stories, or fun and laughter at the beach and being pushed on the swings until she was so high it was scary. She ran her finger over Kenneth's face and slipping the photograph from its stuck-down corners, she palmed it secretly into her pocket.

Her mother was rummaging through a different box. 'These are all books,' she said.

Putting the album down, Connie went to join her. Her mother had found an old school book but it looked very babyish. Connie didn't want to embarrass Kez because she knew that she wouldn't bother to practise if the book looked like it was for a child. In the end she chose two of her own books to take. Grace Darling's *Tales*, a book she had been given by an aunt when she was about nine. It had two girls in swimsuits on the front cover. They were standing on the rocks with their dog. It was a bit more advanced than Connie would have liked but it was a start. The other book was her all-time favourite when she'd been a girl. She'd bought the *Stories from the Arabian Nights* for thruppence in a jumble sale. Connie knew she would enjoy hearing the stories again; The Porter and Ladies of Baghdad, Caliph the Fisherman and Ali Baba, who adorned the front cover. She'd always loved the romantic illustrations of the men in their flowing robes and dark smouldering looks. Now she and Kez could begin her long uphill journey to literacy.

As they pushed the box back against the wall, it was hindered by something underneath. Connie bent down and picked up a stuffed giraffe, Kenneth's toy from when he was a baby. It was in a sorry state now, lopsided and some of the stuffing had come out of one foot. The two women stared at it in silence.

'Do you ever think of him, Mum?' Connie asked quietly.

Gwen straightened her back. 'He is my son,' she said simply. 'There isn't a day goes by when I don't think about him.'

Connie could feel the tears picking at her eyes. She pushed the box right back and stuffed the giraffe down the side. That's when she spotted her old doll's pram. 'Oh, look! I bet Mandy would like to play with that,' she said deliberately changing the subject. She raised the hood and fingered the holes along the crease.

'It could do with a bit of repair,' said Gwen uncertainly.

'And I know just the man,' smiled Connie. 'Don't say anything and we'll get it done for Christmas.'

Armed with her books, Connie made for the stairs. Her mother hesitated. 'You don't know why Kenneth left like that, do you?'

Connie froze. Her face flamed. She dared not look back or her mother would have seen. 'Haven't a clue,' she said brightly as she ran down the stairs.

The nurse pulled the curtain around his bed and leaned over to undo the buttons on his pyjama top. Kenneth didn't look down. He didn't want to see the livid redness, the uneven skin and the scars. He'd looked at himself in the mirror once and it had turned his stomach. His own body and he couldn't stand to look at it. They had done what they could and the ice packs on his hand relieved the awful pain. Hands. That was a joke. He didn't have hands anymore. One of them was little more than a shapeless stump.

The doctor and his entourage swept in, each pulling the curtain closed until they were all cocooned together. Now there were six of them standing around his bed. Six and the nurse. Nobody spoke. He looked at each man in turn. He knew what they were thinking. Poor sod. Got right through the war unscathed and then, while the rest of the world is dancing in the streets, he comes down in flames to this . . . He thought of some of those who didn't make it. Pongo Harris and Woody Slade and little Jimmy. At least they'd gone out intact. He might be still alive, but look at the state he was in. It would have been better if he'd died along with the rest of his crew.

The doctor leaned towards him. 'I'm putting you up for transfer, Dickie,' he said.

Kenneth snorted and turned away. That's right, he thought. Out of sight, out of mind. Not my problem.

'Listen, son,' said the doctor. 'We've done all we can for you here, but there's a place where they are brilliant at helping boys in your position. It's in East Grinstead, the Royal Victoria Hospital. They've got this man there called McIndoe and he's pioneered some wonderful treatments for burn victims.'

'The chaps who've been there are proud of what they've achieved. They called themselves The Guinea Pig Club,' said one of the others.

Kenneth closed his eyes in disgust. 'I'm not going somewhere to be experimented on. Just give me a gun and I'll finish the job for good.'

'That's enough of that kind of talk,' the doctor snapped. 'Look,' he added softening his tone, 'what if I get someone to come and see you? Maybe even the big man himself. It's up to you, but surely it's worth a try.'

Kenneth sighed. He didn't want this but they'd keep on and on until they had their way and he was too tired to argue. 'All right,' he said wearily.

'Good man.' The doctor leaned towards him again. 'You know, it's time you thought about contacting your loved ones.'

His patient's eyes blazed. 'No, absolutely not. I'm not ready for all that.'

Connie kept herself busy for the rest of the day and did her best to avoid working with her mother. After tea, Connie worked in the shop with Sally. They usually had a bit of a laugh together but Sally wasn't her usual chatty self which suited Connie for now. Her mind was filled with thoughts of Kenneth. If all went to plan, she would join Kez in the evening and begin her lessons. Perhaps she should talk to Kez about Kenneth, and yet even as the thought crossed her mind she knew she wouldn't. It was embarrassing and shameful and she couldn't bear the thought of Kez knowing such awful things about her. She had struggled for years to put it all behind her, but what with Ga and her constant reminders and the fact that her brother was estranged from the family, what hope had she? At least by keeping busy, she wasn't thinking about having to lie to her mother. How she wished she could just up sticks and go for her training. Being a nurse seemed to be so right for her but by being stuck here in the nursery, she'd probably end up like Ga, an old maid with nobody to love. Life was bloody unfair sometimes.

Five

It didn't take long for Saturday evenings at the dance hall to become a routine. Connie joined up with Jane Jackson, Sally Burndell and a couple of other girls to go to the Assembly Hall in Worthing. Their dresses were all homemade. There was so little material to be had but Connie was good with a needle. She was wearing a pretty blue and white dress with a full skirt and a scooped neck with a trail of white muslin draped attractively across the shoulders. She'd found the material in another form in a jumble sale. The dress was far too big so she was able to take it to pieces and start again.

The dance was up some steps in the next road to the New Town Hall. The place was packed although as time went by, there were fewer men in uniform. Demob suits were very much in evidence. The Assembly Hall was a beautiful building. They entered a large foyer, bought their tickets and went to the cloakroom to hang up their coats. Connie loved the Art Deco reliefs, the star-shaped light fittings and the proscenium arch which was flanked by seahorses. It spoke of an age long since gone and yet somehow the building seemed as fresh and exciting as it must have done when it was built in the 1930s.

The band was already playing as they walked in and a small glass orb glittered from the ceiling. Connie and her friends found a table and sat down. The dances were done in threes. It might be a foxtrot or a rumba or a waltz when the lights were dimmed right down.

As the band struck up, the men circled the seated area looking for a partner. Jane was always popular but Connie and Sally had to wait a little while before someone asked them to dance.

It had taken Connie a while before she'd got to know the other girls. At sixteen, Sally's secretarial course was due to start towards the end of September. She may have been a lot younger than the rest of them, but she fitted into the group well. Jane was the joker. Having heard of Sally's ambition to be a private secretary rather than ending up in the typing pool, Connie had asked Jane about her ambitions. Jane had looked thoughtful and then said, 'I think I'll marry a man with one foot in the grave and the other on a banana skin,' and they'd all laughed.

'How's your boyfriend in the army?' said Connie making small talk while they waited.

Sally had just refused to dance with a tall, lanky man with buck teeth. 'Terry? Fine,' she nodded. She picked up her handbag and rummaged inside. 'He's still in Germany. He says he'll be stuck there until he's demobbed next year.'

'What rotten luck,' said Connie. 'A year is a long time.'

'I'll wait for him,' said Sally, pulling out a dog-eared photograph. 'That's my Terry.' He looked about twenty and was tall with round-rimmed glasses.

'He doesn't mind you coming to dances?'

'Well, he can't expect me to live like a hermit,' Sally retorted, 'but I shall always be faithful to him.'

A good looking man with slicked-down hair came up to the table and gave the girls a short bow. 'May I?'

'And what the eye doesn't see . . .' said Sally, taking his hand.

Connie went back to the gypsy camp whenever she had a spare minute. Kez was a willing pupil even though some of her relatives teased her when they saw what she was doing. She had been right about the books. Kez had loved the *Stories from the Arabian Nights* and who could blame her. All those handsome, dark-eyed men fighting for the women they loved and looking at the girls in their pretty Eastern dress made enjoyable reading.

'The way you two sit like that,' Reuben remarked one day, 'you could be sisters.'

Connie smiled. She would have liked to have had a sister like Kez. Simeon was a nice man too. He sat close to his wife and a couple of times, as Connie traced the words with her finger on the page, she caught him mouthing the words along with her. So he was illiterate too? Connie was amazed. He had created a real work of art in wood on the outside of the trailer. He clearly had a good eye because the few times she had watched him at work, she'd noticed that he didn't have a pattern to follow. It was all in his head. Eventually Connie plucked up enough courage to ask him about the pram.

'Bring it with you next time,' Simeon smiled, 'and I'll see what I can do.'

People labelled gypsies as stupid but Kez and her family were far from that. They may have lacked formal education but their skills and knowledge in other areas were second to none. Isaac was always turning up with a river fish or a couple of rabbits, and at one time a couple of pigeons for their supper. Kez invited Connie to stay but most times she declined, preferring to be home in time to read Mandy a bedtime story.

When Connie got back home on 24 July, her mother and Ga were glued to the radio. At the beginning of the month the whole country had been full of election fever. Most people thought it a foregone conclusion that Mr Churchill would get back into Downing Street but there was also a groundswell of opinion that the country couldn't go back to the old ways. It was time for radical change. All the same it came as an enormous shock when the final count was declared after the overseas votes had been collected by RAF Transport Command. The Labour Party headed by a rather weedy looking man called Clement Attlee had won a landslide victory.

'God help us all,' Ga said darkly as she turned the radio off. 'It's going to be just like Churchill said. We beat the Gestapo in Germany and now they'll come here, you mark my words.'

'I'm sure it won't be that bad, Ga,' said Gwen good-naturedly.

'And you can hardly blame us for wanting change,' said Connie tartly. 'Look what's on offer, full employment and a free health service.'

'Stuff and nonsense,' Ga retorted. 'Anyone with half a brain could see that's all rhetoric and empty promises. A welfare state from the cradle to the grave? It'll never happen in my lifetime.'

It had taken a bit longer than they'd thought but Clifford came home with the minimum of fuss. Connie and her mother were anxious about him because they had no idea what kind of state he might be in. Immediately after the war, the newsreels at the pictures showed some harrowing sights coming out of Germany. Whole cities flattened by Allied bombing, women and children picking their way through the ruins and of course the opening up of those terrible concentration camps. It was a lot to take in and it must have been even worse for those who saw it at first hand. Joan Hill from the village found a wreck of a man waiting on the platform when her Charlie came home and he still wasn't right in the head.

Clifford was due to come back on a Saturday and so Connie took Mandy out for the day in order to give her mother a little space. They went to Arundel on the bus and on to Swanbourne Lake. Pip invited himself too and had been as good as gold on the bus, lying by their feet until it was time to get out. Mandy fed the ducks with some crusts of bread and then they walked right around the lake. Pip loved it. He didn't chase a single duck but enjoyed his freedom to scent and smell as he pleased. They stayed until late afternoon and Connie treated them to tea in a little tea rooms while Pip lay on the pavement outside and waited for them.

As it turned out, Clifford had come through his experiences with little evidence of trauma. A clean shaven man with a strong jawline and firm resolve, he looked a little too small for his demob suit but he was still good looking enough to cut a dash. His Brylcreemed brown hair had retained its colour although there were a few grey hairs at either side of his ears. When he spotted Connie and Mandy walking up the road, he ran to meet them, and catching Mandy into the air he swung her up. Pip barked and jumped at his legs and Connie laughed. Clifford's daughter was a little more reserved in her greeting and wriggling out of his arms, as soon as he put her down she ran and hid behind Connie's skirts.

'She'll be all right,' Connie whispered when she saw the look of disappointment on his face. 'Just give her time.'

Clifford put his hand lightly on her shoulder and kissed Connie on the cheek. 'Is it good to be back?' she asked.

Her mother was standing by the front door, looking on. 'I'll say,' he smiled, adding out of the corner of his mouth, 'although your mother looks a bit pasty.'

'I've tried to persuade her to go to Dr Andrews,' Connie whispered as she smiled brightly, 'but she won't go.'

'I'll get her to make an appointment as soon as I can,' he said as they turned to walk back to the nurseries.

'She probably won't tell you,' Connie said while they were still far enough away from the door to be out of earshot, 'but I've offered to look after Mandy if you want to go away for a holiday.'

'Can I go on holiday too?' Mandy piped up.

'Oh my, what big ears you have,' laughed Connie and Clifford ruffled Mandy's hair.

'Was Ga all right with you?' Connie asked as her sister skipped up the garden path.

'Same as usual,' said Clifford grimly. 'I swear that woman looks more miserable than Queen Victoria with every passing year.'

Connie put her hand over her mouth to stifle a giggle.

The rest of the weekend was good because everyone was on their best behaviour. Clifford insisted her mother go to the doctor on Monday. A touch of anaemia, that's all it was, and she was prescribed a tonic. 'Take a rest if you can,' he advised and so Clifford went ahead with his plans for them to go to Eastbourne for a few days.

A week went by and slowly the family readjusted itself back into some sort of normality. Aunt Aggie turned up as usual and although she probed Clifford with questions, thankfully she wasn't too intrusive. It was obvious that he didn't want to talk about his experiences. He'd lost too many friends and three years of his life. Ga continued making her barbed remarks, the worst being one day when the four of them were in the shop.

'It'll be hard for you to settle down,' Ga told Clifford. She was smiling but her eyes were bright with insincerity. 'No pretty girls throwing themselves at the liberators here.'

'Ga!' said Connie, shocked.

'Don't tell me he didn't enjoy the attention,' Ga went on. 'Sailors have a girl in every port so I don't suppose the army is much different?'

'Not everybody is sex mad, Miss Dixon.'

They turned to look at Sally who was clearing overripe fruit from the display. They'd all forgotten she was there. Sally straightened up and blushed deeply, realising at once that she had overstepped the mark and been too familiar with her employers.

'And I'll thank you to keep your nose out of other people's conversations, Sally,' said Ga haughtily. The girl turned back to her work and said no more.

Clifford walked away, the door banging against the wood as he left.

'Pay no attention, dear,' said Aggie when she saw the crestfallen look on her friend's face.

'Some people just can't take a joke,' said Ga.

As Connie walked with Mandy to the gypsy camp the day after her mother and Clifford had gone away, she already felt more relaxed. She might not have met anyone at the dance, but each week she'd had a bit of fun, something singularly lacking in her life up to now. It was incredible that Kez and her family had spent so long in the lane and there was always that sinking feeling that they might be gone when she turned the corner.

'Susan Revel says gypsies are smelly and shouldn't be allowed here,' said Mandy, taking Connie's hand as they came to the lane. Pip came bounding along to join them. 'She said they steal people's babies and turn them to stone.'

'Does she now?' said Connie.

'And Gary Philips says they are short in the arm and thick in the head.'

Connie suppressed a smile. 'If I were you, I wouldn't repeat what someone else says,' she said gently. 'I'll tell you what, after we've been there, you tell me what *you* think.'

Mandy nodded gravely. 'Can I share my sweeties with Sam?'

So that was why Connie had seen her squirrelling away a couple of farthing chews from her sweetie box. Mandy hadn't asked if she could have one but Connie hadn't said anything. Why not let her have them? They were her sweets after all. She had no idea Mandy was planning to share them with Kezia's son. 'I'm sure he'd love that,' said Connie, 'but ask his mummy first.'

Somewhere along the lane, Pip joined them again. 'Where have you been?' said Connie, patting his side.

The two sisters were very close. Connie adored Mandy and it was plain to see that Mandy enjoyed being with her. Kez took to her straight away especially when Mandy began to mother little Samuel.

The women spent the rest of the afternoon rubbing down handmade clothes pegs and putting them into bundles. On Monday, Kez and some of the other women would take them around the big houses in Goring and sell them. As they worked, Pen told them tales about the old days . . . 'Little Mac took the tattooed lady's mare then Abe gave Little Mac a piece of bread and a quart of ale but there was none for 'e so he died . . .' Mandy listened spellbound and for Connie it felt just like old times. Peninnah always used the same form of words and if anyone interrupted her, she'd go back a bit and start again.

While Connie helped Kez with the meal, Reuben let Mandy feed the horse tethered in the field. By the end of the afternoon, they'd both had a wonderful time and it was time to go home.

'Where's Isaac?' said Connie, suddenly missing him.

'He's with Simeon and the Frenchie,' said Kez. She was putting Blossom to the breast.

'What are they doing?' Connie frowned.

'Go and see for yourself,' said Kez mysteriously. 'It's on your way home.'

Connie was curious. It was unusual for a gypsy to be working with a non-Romani. She wondered how the Frenchie got on with someone like Isaac who was so surly. They said their goodbyes and Connie and Mandy set off for home with Pip.

'I like Auntie Kez and Sam,' said Mandy as they walked towards Goring Street. 'And Uncle Reuben.'

'So what do you think about gypsies then?' Connie asked.

Mandy thought for a bit and then said, 'Just because you are different, doesn't mean you're bad, does it?'

Connie squeezed her hand. 'I think you've got the right idea, darling.'

'Can we sing my song?' Mandy asked.

Connie smiled. 'I'm amazed that you still like it so much.'

Mandy nodded and holding her sister's hand, they swung their arms as they sang 'You are my sunshine . . .'

The dog had run on ahead and was surprised to see them turn away from Goring Street and towards Jupp's barn. As Connie approached Sam Haffenden's blacksmith's forge, she craned her neck. So where were the men? Beyond the forge and the two thatched cottages, everything melted away into farm land. It was then that she noticed a corrugated iron shed to the right of the forge. She'd never noticed that before even though it was obvious it wasn't new. It was just off the road, and the only access was via a short lane entrance littered with old bits of wood. The potholed pathway opened out into a weed-filled yard. There was no sign of Isaac or Simeon but Connie heard the sound of raised men's voices coming from inside the shed. She reached for her little sister's hand and held on tight. Perhaps she should leave it for now and come back another time. She was about to turn around but Pip sped past her barking excitedly.

Six

The Frenchie's workshop, cluttered, untidy and littered with bicycle parts, doubled as an artist's studio. She and Mandy stopped singing as they went through the door. There were pencil drawings and paintings everywhere. Connie spotted a fantastic drawing of Reuben sitting on the steps of his caravan smoking his pipe. High on the wall she saw a watercolour of two local fishermen she recognised from the beach at Goring from where they sold their fresh fish from the jetty. She looked at their rugged faces and rheumy eyes and knew that whoever had painted them had caught their likeness exactly. Kenneth had been good at drawing but nowhere near as good as this. The room itself smelled of engine oil and paint.

As she and Mandy walked in, it was obvious that the men had reached a crucial stage of their work. There were about four of them in the large open area in the middle of the building, Isaac, Simeon and two other men. Which one was the Frenchie? They were all working together using a series of pulleys and chains to lower a large wooden frame onto a chassis on wheels.

Calling the dog to heel, Connie stood in the corner by the door and drew Mandy into a protective embrace. One man was acting as instructor and guiding their every move. 'Steady, steady. Keep that end nice and straight. Take your time, steady . . . Right, that's it.'

Someone let go of the chains and they clattered across the roof.

'Careful,' said the man. 'Don't damage the bodywork.'

Once the bulky frame was secure, Simeon began screwing it into place. It was a very solid piece of work and she could see that with the door at one end, it would be like a small house on wheels.

'Well, I'd best be off,' said an older man Connie had never seen before.

'Thanks for your help, Bob,' said the one who had been giving the orders.

Isaac grabbed his jacket and turned with a scowl on his face. 'What do you want?' he demanded when he saw Connie and her sister. Pip growled.

Connie jumped. 'I-I'm sorry,' she spluttered. 'Kez said you and Simeon were here and I thought . . . Sorry.'

'That's no way to speak to a lady.' The instructor had come out of the shadows and into the light. Connie's heart skipped a beat. He was broad shouldered and muscular. She could tell by the bulge at the top of his rolled-up sleeves that this man was used to heavy work and yet he moved fluidly and effortlessly. This must be the Frenchie. His brown hair was curled, not with tight curls but with more of an attractive wave. His face was streaked with perspiration. He glanced at her and Mandy and smiled. The smile transformed his whole face, revealing a long dimple on his left cheek. 'Good afternoon, Madam,' he said, bending to stroke the dog. His voice was like deep velvet, and he spoke like a Canadian with just a hint of a French accent. Connie felt her face flush and her heart began to beat a little faster.

'She ain't no lady, Frenchie,' said Isaac bringing Connie back to the here and now.

Connie's jaw dropped but Mandy interrupted before she could say something.

'We came to see where Simeon works,' she piped up.

The Frenchie waved his arm expansively and smiled. 'And here it is!'

Emboldened, Mandy started asking questions. 'What are you doing? What's that for? Why did you put that in there? Is that a picture of Mr Light?' He answered all her questions patiently and with good humour, explaining that they had just repaired the van and were reconstructing it onto a new chassis. 'That's a very solid looking thing,' Connie remarked.

'It used to be called a living van,' he explained. 'It was the sort of thing road menders used to use when they stayed on the job. This one dates back to the turn of the century.' He patted the wooden sides as he looked down at Mandy. 'Back then you would see a steam engine on the front, then the living van, followed by a cart with all the equipment and finally the water cart to top up the engine, so the old timers tell me. It was a bit like a road train.'

Connie was puzzled. 'But what are you going to use it for now?'

'This mush is full of ideas,' said Simeon coming around the vehicle with a smile. 'This is a travelling shop.'

Connie was impressed. She could see it now. They were obviously going to put shelving along the sides and with the driver's cab at the front, it would be ready to go.

'And these paintings,' Connie said with a wave of her hand, 'did you do them as well?'

The Frenchie glanced at Connie and gave her a shy smile. 'Yes, I did. A hobby of mine.'

'They're very good,' said Connie.

'Thank you,' he said, wiping his hands on an oily rag.

'And now I have to go,' he told Mandy. 'I have to get ready to go out. It was nice to have met you and your mummy. I hope you'll come again.'

Mandy glared at him crossly. 'She's not my mummy. She's my sister.'

The Frenchie turned to Connie. 'I apologise,' he said quietly. 'My mistake.'

Connie's heart was beating fast. She had never felt quite like this before. It was both alarming and exciting. 'That's quite all right,' she said feebly. 'I hope we didn't intrude.'

As Simeon reached for his coat, she and Mandy stepped back towards the door. The artist turned his head and their eyes met once again. 'My name is Eugène Étienne but around here they all call me the Frenchie,' he said extending his hand. Her small hand was all but swallowed by his. The grip was firm but gentle, warm and sincere. As he released her, he apologised and took a cleaner looking rag from a nail driven into the post and gently wiped her fingers.

'Why do they call you the Frenchie?' Mandy asked.

'Mandy,' Connie scolded.

'It's all right. You see, I never met him but perhaps you can tell by my name that my father was French,' he said without a trace of bitterness. 'I was brought up in an orphanage in Québec.'

'Where's that?'

'Canada,' he smiled. 'I came over here during the war and forgot to go back.'

Connie's eyes widened. 'They let you do that?'

'Not actually,' he laughed. 'I was ill and I decided to stay here when the army discharged me.'

'Nothing serious I hope,' said Connie.

The Frenchie shook his head. 'Enough to keep me at the military hospital in Shaftesbury Avenue for a few months. I ended up falling in love with Worthing. I've only been here a little while but I want to make it my home.'

A shadow fell over them. Someone was standing in the doorway. The Frenchie stepped back and looked up. 'Darling,' he said. 'I am sorry. Is it that late already?'

Connie was faced with the most beautiful girl she'd ever seen. She was blonde and tall and wore a pink floral dress with a straight skirt and a small white belt. She had the daintiest white peep-toed high heels and she carried a small clutch bag. Connie recognised her instantly. Mavis Hampton, the daughter of one of the richest men in town and Worthing's very own beauty queen. Pip wagged his tail and headed towards her.

'Oh no!' she cried. 'Don't let that thing jump up at me.'

Connie grabbed Pip's collar just in time and although he never would have jumped up, Mavis eyed the two of them anxiously. There was no mistaking the curl of contempt on her lip. As Simeon walked past her on his way out, she shrank away as if he was poisonous.

'I knew it,' Mavis said frostily. 'You're going to make us late.' The Frenchie had walked towards her to kiss her cheek. 'No,' she trilled. 'Don't you dare kiss me. You're filthy.'

'I'm sorry, darling,' he said again.

Connie took Mandy's hand and tried to slip away. 'Excuse me.'

Mandy turned her innocent face towards them. 'Bye, Mr Frenchie.'

'Goodbye,' he said.

Mavis only scowled and as Connie reached the lane she heard her saying, 'I know you like helping these ungrateful wretches but really darling, do you have to do it every day?'

'For me?'

Sally Burndell was surprised when her mother came into the shop and handed her a letter. 'I knew you couldn't wait,' she smiled. 'It's from them, isn't it?'

'In a minute, Mum,' said Sally drawing her mother's attention to the woman standing by the till. 'I've got customers.'

'Sorry, luv,' said Mrs Burndell stepping to one side. 'My Sally is going to college. The first girl in our family to get a real education.'

'Mum . . .' Sally protested.

'Well, I can't help being proud, can I?' said Mrs Burndell turning to go. 'See you later.'

The customer smiled indulgently and Sally rolled her eyes.

It was mid-morning before Sally had the chance to open the envelope. She had to wait until the old lady had gone back to the house and the shop was empty before she dared to take it from her apron pocket.

The letter from the college was brief and because of her tears, Sally had a job focusing her eyes properly to read it. Nine words stood out from the rest. '. . . *unable to offer you a position at this time . . .*' Why? What had happened? They'd seemed so sure about her at the interview. She wiped her eyes with the heel of her hand and began again. '*We regret that due to certain facts coming to light we are unable to offer you a position at this time . . .*' She pushed the letter back inside the envelope and sniffed loudly. What facts? Had somebody said something bad about her? She heard the back door of the house slam. Old Miss Dixon must be coming back. Could this be something to do with her? Had the old bag given her a bad reference? Sally looked up but it wasn't the old woman coming.

'Time for a cuppa,' Connie called as she walked into the shop with two cups of tea on a tray. Sally pushed the letter back in her pocket.

'You all right, Sally?' Connie asked casually.

'Fine,' said Sally a little too quickly but to Connie it was obvious she wasn't. Her eyes were puffy and she refused to meet Connie's gaze. She busied herself with the apple box, taking out the damaged ones and giving the good ones a bit of a polish with a duster.

'Coming to the dance this week?' Connie persisted.

'No.' Sally shook her head. 'I'm washing my hair.'

'Oh, come on,' she said. 'If you're feeling a bit down, it'll do you the world of good.'

'Terry's coming home,' said Sally. 'People might talk.'

Connie shrugged. If Sally didn't want to come anymore, there was little she could do.

*

The Japanese surrender came suddenly. When the announce-
ment came over the radio, Ga called from the back door.
'Constance, Sally . . . leave that and come inside.' They closed
the shop door and walked across the yard. The radio was turned
up enough to let the people in the next county hear it but when
Connie mentioned it, Ga said, 'Shhh. Listen.'

'This is London,' the announcer Alvar Lidell began. 'The Prime
Minister, the Right Honorable C.R. Attlee.' The radio crackled
and then his deep slow voice was followed by the more reedy
tones of Clement Attlee.

'Japan has surrendered. The last of our enemies is laid low . . .'

It all seemed to be a bit of an anti-climax but even though
she was still a little distant, Connie hugged Sally. It seemed that
the horrors inflicted on Hiroshima and Nagasaki by the atomic
bomb had brought a swift end to all hostilities. She took a deep
breath. This was the first day of peace in the world for nearly
six years.

As the day wore on, Ga insisted on listening to every news
bulletin on the radio. In the evening Connie took the bus into
Worthing to be with her friends. She'd asked Sally to come but
she was met with the same response. Connie shrugged inwardly.
There was clearly something wrong but Sally wouldn't talk about
it. Ah, well, if the girl wanted to be on her own she could but
after all the misery of the past few years, Connie wanted to let
her hair down. She met up with Jane Jackson near the pier. The
country had been given two days' holiday and there were to be
fireworks later on but there were fewer flags than on VE Day
and only the usual holiday crowd along the seafront. She was
missing Kenneth again. What sort of war had he had? Had he
survived? No, she wouldn't even think about that. Of course he
was alive . . . somewhere. Connie struggled to be glad. A grey
veil of disappointment seemed to hang over everyone until a
hastily formed band of amateur musicians gathered and the
young people took over. The two girls gave a wonderful display

of the jitterbug and before long, everyone was joining in. For Connie, it wasn't the same as being in the crowds in London on VE Day but she and Jane had made a valiant attempt to get the party going.

Despite their high hopes, the end of the war hadn't brought change. There were still petrol shortages, little in the way of coal and supplies and rationing had actually been increased. Aunt Aggie came to see Ga on the Thursday for their weekly game of whist but elsewhere there was little in the way of celebration at the nurseries.

'You should have seen the queue outside Potter and Bailey's today,' she told them at supper. 'Someone said there was a shipment of bacon but by the time I got there, there wasn't a rasher to be had.'

'I noticed that the butcher in the village has a sign in the window,' Aunt Aggie said. 'I can't remember the exact words but it was something like, "Wanted: magician for next week's stock".' And they all laughed.

'So much for the Labour government,' Ga muttered darkly.

When Clifford and her mother got back from their week's holiday, Gwen looked rested and actually sported a bit of a suntan.

'It was simply heavenly being able to walk along the seafront without all that barbed wire and concrete,' she said. 'The shops were a bit bare but we had fireworks when the Jap surrender was announced.'

They'd managed to pick up a couple of sticks of rock for Mandy, a perpetual calendar covered in shells and *a present from Eastbourne* on it for Ga, and a pretty headscarf for Connie.

Clifford had bought a roll of toilet paper. When he put it on the table Ga wrinkled her nose. Connie burst out laughing. It was called Nasti Toilet Roll and had a cartoon picture of Adolf Hitler on the wrapper.

'Guaranteed non-irritant,' grinned Clifford. 'Good, eh?'

Gwen had even thought of Sally Burndell and Sally seemed quite touched by the box of three handkerchiefs from Woolworths.

'They're very pretty,' said Sally, 'but you shouldn't have.'

'You look as if you need a bit of cheering up,' smiled Gwen. 'That boyfriend of yours will soon be home.'

August was drifting towards September. Double summer time finished its first stage in July when the clocks went back one hour. Clifford had eased himself back into position but there was a tension between him and Ga. Even so, the nurseries were being run efficiently and smoothly. The next time Connie went into the lane, Kez and her family had gone. There were no goodbyes. When she saw the pitch was empty, Connie wondered about the pram she had given Simeon. Nothing had been said about it and she was a bit annoyed that he'd apparently taken it with them. She'd trusted him and it would have been nice to give it to her little sister for Christmas.

Mandy and Pip had played outside with her friends during the long school holiday. Connie would miss the lazy afternoons when she took her little sister down to the beach for a swim. The rough ground at the bottom of Sea Lane was ideal for hide and seek and if it got too hot, they could sit among the bushes for a picnic. There were times when her heart ached for what might have been but she knew she was doing the right thing. She had to put her family first.

'When is it you start at the hospital?' Gwen and Connie were changing the beds together. It was the beginning of September and Mandy was back at school.

Connie couldn't look at her mother. 'I'm not going.'

Gwen was putting the bolster case on. It was always a struggle because the thing was the length of two pillows and very unwieldy. 'What do you mean, you're not going?'

'I thought I'd leave it a year, Mum,' said Connie trying her best to sound casual. 'By next year, everything will be back to normal.'

'Everything is back to normal now,' Gwen frowned. She stopped what she was doing and looked at her daughter. 'This sounds like Ga talking.'

Connie picked up the dirty sheets and made for the door.

'Connie?' said Gwen. 'You were so excited when you told us. What's this all about?'

'You looked a bit off-colour when I came home,' said Connie without looking round. 'It seemed best to wait a while, that's all.' Her hand went out to the door latch.

'Connie, look at me,' said her mother. 'Look at me.'

Connie turned slowly, knowing that there was no hiding the tears already glistening in her eyes. 'Oh Mum . . .' Connie said quietly. 'I really didn't want to come back to the smallholding. I had already enrolled at the hospital.'

'I know you had,' said her mother.

'But Ga thought . . .'

'That bloody woman!' snapped her mother. 'Why does she have to stick her oar in every time?'

Connie's jaw dropped. She'd never heard her mother speak like this before. Gwen smiled encouragingly. 'Connie, it's your life and we, Clifford and I, both want you to have the best you possibly can. The world is a much bigger place now. We all need to put the past behind us and start again. Don't let your opportunities pass you by.'

Connie's chest constricted. Her mother was an amazing person and she longed to tell her how much her approval meant to her. 'I wish you had a better life, Mum.'

Gwen carried on struggling with the bolster case. 'My life is fine,' she smiled. 'Now that Clifford has come home, we are making plans of our own.'

'Plans? What plans?'

'I can't talk about it yet but Clifford has some wonderful ideas for the smallholding,' said her mother. 'One thing is absolutely certain, you mustn't waste your life hanging around for us.'

Impulsively, Connie hugged her. 'Thanks, Mum.' As they parted, Gwen's eyes were bright with unshed tears. Put the past behind us . . . the words echoed in Connie's head. Ga never let her forget the past . . . but could she do it? Could she forget the shame and guilt *that awful man* had brought on her family and actually make something of her life? Could she make it up to her mother for her brother going away? Was there still time? 'I may not be able to do it now anyway,' Connie said uncertainly. 'I haven't replied to any of their letters.'

Gwen looked at her, horrified. 'When were you supposed to start?'

'On 10th September,' said Connie.

'Then you'd better leave that and get on the bus straight away,' she cried. 'Go down there in person. Blame the war, blame me. Say I've been really ill and now I'm better . . . say anything you like, but whatever you do, make sure you get that place again.'

Connie hesitated.

'Go on girl!' her mother cried. And Connie fled.

*

The bridegroom stood up and turned to see the small procession make its way down the aisle. The church was small and even in these difficult times, little used. It smelled dank and musty as he'd walked into the door. He would have preferred a registry office himself. All this preamble – the reading of the banns and talks with the Vicar made him nervous but she'd had her heart set on a proper wedding so he'd given in. The usher, some old fossil who looked as old as Methuselah, showed him to the front pew. His best man, a chap he'd met in the pub a week before, rose unsteadily to his feet as he arrived and gave him a watery smile. His teeth were tobacco stained but he had scrubbed up well enough. They sat down together and waited. After a while he said, 'Got the ring?' and the best man nodded. There was a rustling sound by the door of the church and the Vicar came down the aisle. 'Please stand.'

The organist struck up the tune, 'Here Comes the Bride' and his heartbeat quickened. No getting out of this now. He had made a decision which had surprised even himself. He had never really had a close relationship before. Only the one with his mother. Would he be able to cope with marriage? He swayed a little at the thought and wiped his open palms down the side of his suit as he slowly turned to look. The congregation, such as it was, was already standing; only one relative on his side and a spattering of people on hers. Every head was turned in anticipation of the coming bride but his eye was immediately drawn to her. She was wearing a white satin dress with a pretty pink bow at her waist. Someone had put her hair into golden ringlets and she had a halo of roses, the last roses of the summer, on her head. He took in his breath. She was nothing short of an angel sent from heaven. She carried a posy and she watched his face as she walked purposefully towards him. She returned his smile with a gappy grin and then closed her mouth as she remembered her missing milk teeth. He laughed softly and looked up at his bride, her mother, coming on behind her. Yes, he had done the right thing. Everything was perfect, just perfect.

Seven

It was weird. Pip had been following Connie around all day with his tail between his legs. It was as if he knew she was going.

'I'll be around until the 9th but after that I shall move into the nurses' home,' Connie told everyone at the tea table.

She had managed to see someone in management and after an hour of being moved from one person to another, had persuaded them that she was ready to start her training.

'Why can't you live here?' Ga sat tight-lipped and frowning at her great niece. 'You could catch the bus from the end of the road.'

Connie knew that was just a ruse to make her feel that they couldn't cope without her. Before long Ga would be dumping 'would-you-just jobs' into her lap. Oh, Connie while you're doing that, would-you-just pick out a few of those seedlings, or before you catch the bus, would-you-just take that into the shop for me.

'I have to be on the ward at seven and you know me first thing in the morning, Ga,' she said brightly. 'It'll be better if I'm in the nurses' home.'

But Ga wasn't about to give up that easily. 'What about all the books you're supposed to have? You needn't expect . . .'

'Don't worry,' said Connie, knowing perfectly well what was coming. 'I've already saved enough to buy everything.'

'Perhaps it's just as well things didn't work out for you and

Emmett then,' Ga remarked acidly. 'You wouldn't even be allowed to train if you were married.'

The mention of Emmett made Connie's heart lurch, but then Ga had meant to upset her, hadn't she? Why did she keep saying stuff like that? For the sake of her mother, Connie bit her tongue.

'Why can't you just be happy for the girl?' Clifford snapped, 'and for once, say something encouraging.'

'Well!' Ga glared.

'It's all right, Clifford,' Gwen soothed.

Clifford helped himself to some more potatoes. 'No, it's not, Gwennie,' he said.

'I'm only trying to make her see that it won't be easy,' Ga protested.

'I know it won't be easy, Ga.'

The atmosphere at the table soured. Her great aunt was probably right, or she would have been right if it was still 1939. The unwritten rule for nurses had always been that women who married would give up the profession but the war had left hospitals alongside many other institutions with severe shortages of manpower. Connie felt sure that by the time she'd gained her nursing badge, the 'no married women' edict would be a thing of the past anyway. Not only that, but the new government was pressing ahead with a country-wide health service which would be free to all, regardless of income or status, at the point of need. Things were changing. They were indeed entering a brave new world.

Now that she was really going, Connie was thrown into a hive of activity. She'd found the list of things she was supposed to bring with her to the hospital and set off into town. Ga said nothing when Connie came back with her purchases but she shot her one of her dark looks. As a child, they had terrified her and even now they made Connie feel a little uncomfortable, but she was determined not to let the old lady spoil her excitement.

'So you're going to run out on your mother after all,' said Ga when the two of them were alone in the kitchen. Connie was making a pot of tea and when Ga walked in she'd asked her if she wanted one.

'I'm not running out on anyone,' said Connie calmly. 'Mum's given me her blessing.' Her great aunt tightened her mouth disapprovingly. 'It's time to think about me,' Connie pre-empted. She hated herself for feeling the need to justify her own actions. She was a grown woman, for heaven's sake, but she knew what Ga was like.

'Me, me, me,' Ga taunted. 'Never mind about anyone else.'

Her cheeks flaming with anger, Connie shoved the cup in front of her, slopping some of the tea into the saucer. As she poured her own cup she could hear Ga rubbing her knee and letting out little sighs of pain and discomfort. It took everything Connie had not to stalk out of the room or to round on Ga with some cutting comment but she didn't want to give her the satisfaction of a fight. She wasn't going to allow Ga to spoil her last few days at home so there would be no more rows. Ga could harrumph and disapprove as much as she liked but Connie was going to be a nurse no matter what she damn well said.

Sally Burndell blinked at the piece of paper in her hand. She turned over the envelope and looked at the postmark. Worthing 6.30 p.m. Posted last night and locally. She could feel the tears pricking her eyes as she read it again. There was no name at the bottom of course, but whoever sent them seemed to know an awful lot about her. It had been bad enough when she'd got that awful letter from the secretarial college but when she'd applied to the one in Brighton and been refused there as well, she'd been devastated. As the panic rose within her chest, her heartbeat quickened. She lowered herself into a chair. And read it again. '*I do not wish to cast aspersions . . .*' What did aspersions mean? Sally wasn't sure but it didn't sound good. '*Do you think it wise to flirt with other men while Terry is away? If I wrote and told him what you were up to, he'd realise you are a tart.'* They were all signed '*a well-wisher*'. How could someone be a well-wisher and yet write such nasty things? What if this person wrote to Terry? Going to the dances had only been a bit of fun. She never even let another boy kiss her and she always went straight home after they'd finished, either with Connie or Jane. If only she knew who had written such hateful things she would have it out with them. The letter trembled in her hand and as she gave way to her sobs, she was so glad her mother was out shopping. She couldn't bear it. How could anyone be so cruel? It was all lies. Wicked, wicked lies!

Connie missed Kez. Jane was a good friend but there was something about Kez . . . She walked up to the lane with Pip most days in the vain hope that they might be back, but she was always disappointed. And what about that pram? Then it crossed her mind that Simeon might have told the Frenchie about it so on her way back from the shops, she headed towards his workshop. She knocked on the door even though it was already open. 'Hello . . .'

'Nearly done,' said a voice deep inside. He stood up from behind an upturned bicycle frame, and spun the wheel. 'Oh,' he said, 'I thought you were the owner come back for the bike. Connie, isn't it? What can I do for you?'

Already her heartbeat was gathering speed. His sleeves were neatly rolled up to his biceps and his shirt was open to the waist. She could see at once that he had an athletic build. He was as attractive as ever, despite his dirty clothes and oil-smudged face. 'I – I wondered if you knew when Kez and Simeon would be coming back?' she flustered.

He shook his head and taking a piece of rag from his pocket began to wipe his hands. 'I don't think they know themselves.'

Connie nodded and turned to go. 'It's just that I'm moving away for a bit.'

'If I see her, shall I tell her where you've gone?'

Connie quickly explained about her nursing. The Frenchie seemed impressed. 'Good for you. If I see them, I'll tell them,' he promised and their eyes locked.

'There seems to be no end to your talent,' she laughed nervously, waving her hand towards the mobile shop taking shape at last. 'Now here you are mending bicycles.'

'This is my proper job,' he smiled. 'I was only helping Simeon out. It was a good idea, wasn't it?'

'Your idea, so he said,' Connie grinned.

'Ah, yes,' he said. 'I'd forgotten. Brilliant, wasn't it?' and they both laughed.

Connie was suddenly distracted by her old doll's pram hanging on a hook by its handle on the wall behind him. It had been painted a lovely shade of maroon and the hood seemed new.

'Oh yes,' said the Frenchie following her eye. 'Simeon said you wanted that for your little sister. Simeon painted it and put on a new hood. I've repaired the wonky wheel and he asked me to paint something nice on the sides. I'm afraid I haven't got around to it yet. Sorry.'

'No, no,' she smiled. 'That's fine. I wanted it for Christmas, so there's plenty of time. How much do I owe you?'

'I'm not sure yet,' he said. 'I'll send the bill around to the nurseries if that's all right?'

She nodded.

'I suppose I'd better cover it up,' he said. 'In case your sister comes to the workshop.'

'That might be an idea,' she said. She was getting flustered again.

'Will you call for it?'

'I don't want to put you to too much trouble,' she said breathily. Their eyes met and the spell it cast was only broken when they both heard a footfall beside the door.

'Ready yet?' said a man's voice.

'Almost,' said the Frenchie, returning to his bicycle repair. Connie turned to go and as she reached the door he called after her, 'All the best, Connie.'

The hospital had a very distinctive smell, a cross somewhere between strong disinfectant and boiled cabbage.

Her first task when she'd arrived at the nurses' home was to go to the central stores and be kitted out with her uniform. She was given three dresses, all pale blue, with detachable buttons which were fastened through a button hole with a split pin. She had two belts the same colour as the dresses; three white aprons, stiffly starched, two plain white caps and two pink laundry boxes each with a leather strap. The sister giving out the uniforms, a gaunt looking woman with thin grey hair, explained that laundry day was Tuesday.

'The box has to be taken to the front hallway of the nurses' home by 8.30 a.m. for collection,' she said. 'Inside your box is a pink book. In it you have to record what you put into the box and when your clean laundry is returned, make sure that you check that everything is correct. Any mistakes have to be reported at once.'

Connie was given the keys to Room 13 on the first floor of the nurses' home, a room she would share with another girl she had yet to meet. 'After you have taken your uniform and your case up to your room, report to Room 6 in the main hospital.'

The room was better than she expected. It had two beds, each with a bedside locker, a chest of drawers and a sink in the corner. The other girl wasn't in the room but some of her things were. Some clothes were thrown untidily across the bed, a set of keys lay on the dressing table and a suitcase was standing on its heel beside one of the wardrobes. Connie put her single suitcase onto the bed and carefully laid the contents into the remaining empty drawers before putting the empty case on top of the other wardrobe. She stored the two laundry boxes under the bed, the same as the other girl had done. She had brought two photographs from home which she put on her bedside locker. One was of Mum and Clifford with Mandy when her sister was small. Pip sat on the ground between them. The other photograph was the one of Kenneth she'd taken from the album she'd found in the loft. Connie ran her finger across the glass. 'Welcome to your new home, Kenneth,' she smiled.

Connie took her time changing into her uniform. This was something to be savoured. It wasn't comfortable, everything was too heavily starched, but as she caught sight of herself in the mirror she felt a frisson of excitement. Her crisp white apron crackled as she walked along the corridor making her feel elated, as if she was walking on air. She now had a completely new identity. For the next four years, she would be student nurse Dixon. She liked the sound of that. It had a nice ring to it.

When she finally opened the door of Room 6, Connie felt as if she had stepped back in time. It was just like school. Four rows of desks, each with its own inkwell, stretched for the length of the room. There was a blackboard and a teacher's desk complete with a pile of books at one side and a register in the middle. The noise level in the room was extremely high and although a few people looked up as she came in, one or two sharing a shy smile, her entry made no difference at all. Hardly anyone was sitting down. The girls had draped themselves over the desks, or huddled together in groups, all talking nineteen to the dozen. Connie looked around. They appeared to be roughly the same age as her, although one or two looked younger.

One girl, plump with short dark curly hair and a ready smile stepped forward with a friendly greeting. 'Hello. You're number twenty. We're quite a big group, aren't we? Have you got any spare hairgrips?'

'I'm afraid not,' said Connie. 'My name is Connie, by the way.'

'Betty Wellman,' said the girl. 'I'm supposed to wear this hat thing but I can't put it on. I never use hairgrips.'

She was interrupted when a woman in a plain dark blue uniform with long sleeves sailed into the room on a waft of lavender water.

'Good afternoon, nurses,' she said with an air of authority. She was followed by two others dressed the same. They each wore a frilly cap but no apron. Everyone responded raggedly and sat down. Three other students hurried into the room behind her and sat right at the back with Connie.

'My name is Sister Abbott. Sister Brown and I are your home sisters,' the first woman announced. She extended her hand towards the woman next to her and looked around. 'In response to your puzzled expressions, let me explain that we supervise you throughout your training. If you have any questions, any queries about anything, Sister and I are your first port of call. Sister Hayes is your head tutor and will be in charge of your lectures.'

The third woman gave everyone a curt nod of her head.

Connie began to relax. Home Sister Abbott seemed strict but there was an air of fairness about her.

'You have all been allocated rooms in the nurses' home?' she said and there was a murmur of agreement. 'There is a cleaner on each floor, but I expect every nurse to keep her room clean and tidy. Laundry day is Tuesday. Strip your bed and put your dirty sheets in one of the pillowcases and leave it outside for collection.'

Should be easy enough to remember, thought Connie. It was the same day as the uniforms had to go out.

'You will find your clean sheets outside your door after 2 p.m.,' Home Sister continued. 'Failure to leave your dirty sheets outside means the cleaner will not leave any clean ones.' She began to walk up and down the aisles looking at each girl. 'The nurse's uniform is something to wear with pride. No cardigans.' She had drawn level with a girl wearing a pale blue knit. The girl blushed a deep red and took the cardigan off. 'No jewellery,' Sister continued and the girl beside her removed her engagement ring, 'and wear your cap at all times.'

'I haven't got any hairgrips,' Betty Wellman whimpered.

'I haven't got any hairgrips, *Sister*,' Sister Abbott corrected. 'Can anyone help this girl out?'

'I can.'

Connie's head spun round at the sound of her voice. The girl rose to her feet and walked to Betty's desk, handing her two Kirby grips. As she turned back to her seat, their eyes met and Connie's face flamed as she registered the same shocked surprise on the other girl's face.

It was Eva.

Eight

'Has anyone seen Pip?'

When Connie had walked to the bus stop that morning, they'd seen the dog following her but now he'd disappeared. Gwen picked up his dog bowl. The food was uneaten. Clifford shook his head and Ga looked blank. 'Isn't he down by the gate?'

It was getting dark but there was still no sign of him. Clifford and Mandy walked right round the nursery calling and calling while Gwen stood by the back door and banged a spoon on his dog bowl. Ga didn't join in but every time someone came back indoors she would look up from the letter she was writing at her desk and say, 'Any sign?'

The family ate their supper but there was little conversation at the table. Nobody wanted to voice their fears. When Gwen put Mandy to bed, Clifford went outside for one last time. The whole time she read her daughter's bedtime story, they could hear Clifford calling the dog's name.

Back downstairs, when Clifford came in, Gwen didn't need to ask. His face said it all. 'I do hope he hasn't run off altogether,' she sighed.

The new nurses had spent the rest of the afternoon putting together their timetables. Their day would begin at 8.30 a.m. and finish at 6 p.m. They would have an hour for lunch and two short tea breaks, one in the morning, the other in the afternoon.

Most of their first six weeks would be spent in the classroom but after a month, they would be spending some time on the wards. 'I'm sure that you all know you have to pay for your textbooks,' Sister Tutor said. 'If you haven't already collected them, please go to the office by tomorrow morning. It's twenty pounds. If anyone has a problem with that, we can make arrangements for it to be deducted from your wages.'

Connie had thought it was grossly unfair that she should have to pay for anything at all. There had been a vague possibility that she could have started her training straight after VE Day but by starting now it had given her enough time to save up. It had been a struggle because money was tight and Ga hadn't given her much money for helping in the nursery. Never mind, she was here now.

'You will be having lectures on various subjects,' Sister Hayes continued. 'Anatomy, nutrition, physiology and the care of patients.'

Connie shifted uncomfortably in her seat. It was beginning to sound rather daunting. What on earth was physiology? Was she up to this? Sister Hayes had been talking for some time and several of her fellow students looked bored. One girl had closed her eyes. 'You will be learning about hygiene,' said Sister. 'Especially personal hygiene.' She paused. 'For instance, as soon as I walked into this room I immediately knew that someone has not changed her knickers today.'

The effect of her words was electrifying. Everyone sat bolt upright, their faces speared by embarrassment and horror. Sister Abbot had singled out the girl wearing a cardigan, and the one without her cap. Surely Sister Hayes wasn't going to draw attention to somebody's lack of clean underwear?

'And what's more,' Sister continued relentlessly, 'someone in this room has underarm odour.'

Even though she had no reason, Connie, along with the rest of the girls was thrown into a blind panic as Sister Hayes walked slowly up and down the silent aisles, all the while heading in her direction. Even though Connie was always careful to wash and never left the bathroom without putting talc under her arms, she could feel her face heating up.

'There is nothing worse,' Sister Hayes continued, 'than a helpless patient having to put up with a nurse leaning over them if she has underarm odour.'

When she finally reached her desk and picked up the register, the class heaved a silent collective sigh of relief. 'You are all dismissed,' she said, 'be back here at eight thirty sharp tomorrow morning and your training will begin.'

Careful to avoid Eva, Connie headed for the door. The only remaining thing for them to do tonight was unpack, which she'd already done, and to find the dining room for their meal. Connie didn't think she could eat much. She already had a sinking feeling in her stomach. Not only did everything seem to be alien but there was the question of which girl was her roommate. Please God, she silently prayed, don't let it be Eva. What was she doing here anyway? She said she was going to join the GPO or the police, hadn't she? So why had she enrolled on this class?

They accidentally bumped into each other near the door. Connie heard the beginning of Eva's mumbled apology as it choked in her throat but she didn't look at her.

'Flippin' 'eck,' said Betty catching up with Connie in the corridor. 'That woman was a bit near the knuckle with her knickers and underarm stuff, wasn't she? My mum got the tin bath out for me before I came but I was terrified that she was going to point the finger at me.'

'She does it to get your attention,' said another girl. 'My sister did this training course a couple of years ago and she says she does it with every new group.'

Connie grinned. 'It certainly got our attention.'

Betty was going through her pockets. 'Oh, blimey,' she groaned.

'I've left my keys in my room. I've locked myself out. Anybody here in Room 13?'

'I found him, Mummy.'

Mandy had been tucked up in bed when she remembered that her favourite storybook was in Connie's room. She'd left it there last night when her sister read to her. When she opened the door, she'd found Pip lying on one of Connie's cardigans which had fallen to the floor. He looked the picture of misery.

With a little gentle persuasion, the family got him downstairs and in his basket, but only when they took the cardigan too. He wasn't interested in his food, although he did drink a little water before lying back down.

'Looks like he's going to pine for her like he did the last time,' said Gwen anxiously.

'He'll get used to it,' said Ga. 'She'll be back every week for her day off, won't she?'

'Perhaps,' said Gwen.

'What do you mean, perhaps?' Ga challenged.

'What she means is that the girl needs a life of her own, Ga,' said Clifford.

Olive scowled.

Mandy knelt by the dog's basket. 'Don't worry, Pip,' she said gently. 'Connie's coming back.' She stroked the dog's head. 'You don't have to be lonely. I'll be your special friend, if you like.'

Connie sat in the nurses' school room day after day, taking notes and trying to remember how to spell difficult names like Tincture of Guaiacum (used to test for blood in the urine), gonoçoccus (a bacteria which causes gonorrhoea) and encephalitis (inflammation of the brain). After lectures they got to spend an hour or two on the wards, usually doing the food trolley or the bedpan round. Some of her fellow students were a little disappointed to be doing such menial tasks but the ward sister had pre-empted any grumbling behind her back by stressing how important it was to make the patients feel warm, comfortable and safe when they were in difficult circumstances.

'All nursing care is of equal importance,' she told them.

So Connie learned to rub the stainless steel bedpan with a cloth before putting it underneath the patient because it could be very cold on the skin. She enjoyed helping the helpless to eat and when she was asked to do the temperature round, writing the results on the chart at the foot of the patient's bed, it made her feel like a real nurse.

She went home for her day off and pottered around in the nurseries. Pip followed her everywhere but after a while she noticed his growing attachment to her little sister. Connie had been worried when her mother told her the dog was pining, but perhaps he was adjusting to another change in his life. She certainly hoped so. Connie was having to make some big changes herself. There was little chance of going to dances with Jane Jackson. Connie could only have two late passes a month, and half the time, she was down to work part of Saturday evenings on the wards. They met for the pictures a couple of times which had to be a poor substitute for dancing with a real live man.

The tension at the house was sometimes palpable. Clifford and Ga couldn't see eye to eye about where the future of the nurseries lay and most of the friction between them centred around the use of the top field. Ga wanted to grow potatoes on a much larger scale but Clifford wanted to diversify.

'We haven't got the wherewithal,' Ga insisted. 'Not if we have to pay that dozy girl in the shop. I don't know why I bother to keep her on. She's always got a face like a wet week these days.'

'You know yourself the ground is poor,' he said. 'Potatoes don't bring in a lot so if we sold the land for building . . .'

'Over my dead body!'

'We could build something ourselves,' Clifford persisted. 'A factory or a shop. That would make a lot more sense than breaking our backs over a few stupid spuds.'

'So now you're calling me stupid?' Ga retorted.

'Did I say that?' Clifford challenged. The rows became more unreasonable as time went on and there seemed to be no middle ground.

Connie began her nursing proper on the men's ward. She was a little nervous when she reported for duty and the first day seemed extremely long, but she got through it without any mishap. She was working with another student nurse, thankfully not Eva.

Every day began with prayers on the ward. Sister would read the collect for the day from the Book of Common Prayer and they would all recite the Lord's Prayer together. Connie knew that some of the girls resented this but she found it a pleasant experience and it brought with it a sense of calm.

Her calm on her second day on the ward was soon shattered when she heard the night sister's report.

'The doctor has asked for a urine sample from Mr Dunster.'

Connie's heart sank. She wanted to say, whatever you do, don't ask me, but she knew a good nurse would never refuse to withhold treatment from her patient, no matter how obnoxious they were. She'd had a run-in with Mr Dunster when she was on the ward one day after lectures and he was nothing more than a lecherous old beast. She'd had to take a urine sample then and when she'd taken the bottle to his bed, he had pretended he wasn't feeling up to doing it himself. She'd had a suspicion that he was up to no good because as she drew the curtains around the bed, she spotted Mr Elliot and Mr Thomson nudging each other as they sat at the patients' table.

In the privacy of his bedside, Mr Dunster left Connie to undo his pyjama cord and he closed his eyes as she guided his flabby member into the neck of the bottle. As soon as she touched it, she felt it stiffen. Her hand was trembling and she was starting to feel hot and embarrassed. Don't think, she told herself. Don't think about it. Then she felt his hand creeping around her buttock. She'd hit him away angrily, her face flaming and glared at him, tight-lipped, until he passed water. When it was done, he smiled and sighed, 'Thank you, nurse. You've got a lovely touch.'

Connie had been furious of course, but she didn't say anything. She was convinced that if she'd made a fuss, especially on her first time on the ward, Sister would have made her life a misery, and the other men on the ward would have had a good laugh at her expense. But she simply couldn't face the dirty basket again.

As the day sister thanked the night sister for her report and the night staff left, Connie prayed a silent prayer. 'Oh God, please don't let Sister ask me to deal with Mr Dunster . . .' But before her prayer was even finished, she heard Sister Brown saying, 'After breakfast, Nurse Jefferies can do the drugs trolley with Staff Nurse Harris and Nurse Dixon, can you get the sample from Mr Dunster?'

Connie's heart plummeted. Alone in the sluice room she took a bottle from the shelf and put it in the autoclave. While she waited for it to sterilise, her gaze fell upon a treatment trolley some nurse had abandoned without clearing it up and an idea slowly formed in Connie's mind.

Sailing down the ward towards Mr Dunster's bed, Connie prayed her second prayer that morning. 'Oh God, please don't let Sister see me . . .'

'Good morning, Mr Dunster,' she said loudly and cheerfully as she reached his bedside. 'I'm afraid I have to ask you for another sample.'

'That's quite all right, nurse,' he grinned.

As she pulled the curtains around his bed, Connie was aware of the other patients watching and heard one of them whisper, 'Lucky dog.'

'I'm glad it was you who came to help me, nurse,' said Mr Dunster wanly. 'I just don't feel up to it today and you've got such lovely long fingers.' He closed his eyes and leaned against the backrest with a sigh.

'That's what I'm here for,' said Connie, tying on a face mask.

Someone on the other side of the curtain sniggered. Connie pulled on a pair of thick rubber gloves making sure that they snapped loudly against her wrists. Mr Dunster's eyes flew open.

'I'm afraid I owe you an apology,' she said crisply. 'I'm new here and the last time we did this, I didn't know the correct procedure. I'm sorry about that.' She whipped off the green cloth from the top of the tray to reveal a urine bottle and a large pair of flat bladed forceps. Mr Dunster's eyes grew large.

'Now I want you to relax, Mr Dunster,' said Connie brightly. She heard another snigger from the other side of the curtain. 'This won't hurt . . . much.'

The silence seemed to grow as she guided Mr Dunster's member towards the bottle, careful to keep a very firm grip to avoid any accidental spill. Moments later after sailing back down the ward with the sample, her head held high, she bumped into Sister by the door of the sluice room. Her heart went into her mouth. Oh Lord, now she was in trouble . . .

'Well done, nurse,' said Sister Brown and it was then that Connie noticed the twinkle in her eye. 'You're learning. He won't be doing that again, and while you're doing your own sterile tray, would you clear up this trolley? I think the night staff must have forgotten it.'

The door swung for a moment or two as she left and Connie set about clearing up the sluice room. How did Sister Brown know what she was up to? The woman must have the eyes of a hawk. One thing was for sure. Mr Dunster wouldn't be wanting her help again, especially as she'd held the forceps for a very long time under the cold water tap before she'd used them to hold his member.

Sally Burndell had had a letter from Terry. As soon as the letter fell on the mat, she'd recognised his writing. She'd planned to read it in her lunch break at work but she couldn't wait. She'd opened it on the bus. After that, she didn't remember much about the journey. The next thing she knew, she was at the terminus in Littlehampton. She'd been crying and she was as white as a sheet. The conductor had been so concerned he'd taken her to the First Aid room at the bus station.

'I think she might have had some bad news,' he told the nurse.

Sally heard them talking but it didn't seem important. She was still clutching Terry's letter in which he'd told her it was all off. The conductor put her off at the bus stop where she'd originally got on. She thanked him but she still seemed to be in shock. He worried as he watched her making her way back home again.

A couple of hours later, Mrs Burndell staggered up the garden path with her shopping.

'You look well loaded,' said her neighbour Mr Keen. He was on a stepladder and clipping the privet hedge.

'Donkeys go best well loaded,' she joked and he smiled. Her arms were nearly pulled out of their sockets and of course Sally wouldn't be there to help her. She was working her notice at the nursery. Next week she would be starting her secretarial course and she was so proud of her. Sally was the first girl in the family to have a proper career of her own. She was a bright girl, a bit lippy at times but she had a good head on her shoulders. Sally was destined to go far and Mrs Burndell could only hope she would give herself the chance to see a bit of the world before she settled down with Terry.

Mrs Burndell fumbled for her back door key.

'It'll be open,' said Mr Keen. 'Your Sally's home.'

Mrs Burndell frowned, puzzled. She put down her bags and

opened the back door. It was difficult bringing in the bags and keeping the door open at the same time. The door slammed and Mrs Burndell stumbled over something on the floor. As she looked down, all the colour drained from her face. Sally was crumpled up on the floor.

'Sally?' There was no response at all. Mrs Burndell fell to her knees and held her daughter's wrist. Thank God, there was a reedy pulse. She had to get help, but what had happened? Opening the back door again, Mrs Burndell screamed out, 'Mr Keen, Mr Keen help me! Get a doctor. My Sally's been taken bad.' She turned back into her kitchen and tried to make sense of what she was looking at. The washing pulley was in bits on the floor. Sally must have been hanging the washing and it all fell down. She pushed the bits of wood out of the way and glanced up at the huge hole in the ceiling. Mrs Burndell turned her daughter slowly and that was when she saw the rope around her neck.

Nine

Connie was on top of the world. By the time the last vestige of double summer time had been eradicated by the clocks going back the final hour in the middle of November, she had realised that she had truly found her vocation. There was a strong feeling of camaraderie between the student nurses. They supported each other when things went wrong and applauded each other when some milestone of achievement had been met. At first she and Eva avoided each other but things finally came to a head on their first night duty together and ironically, thanks to two dead men, the girls finally became friends.

Mr Ockley still hadn't been taken to the mortuary when Mr Steppings passed away. Sister Brown rang the porter's office only to be told that no one was available for at least another hour. There was a bit of a flap on somewhere.

'Nurse Dixon,' she said as Connie came by the night sister's desk with a full bedpan, 'when you've finished that, I want you and Nurse O'Hara to take Mr Ockley and Mr Steppings to the morgue. We'll be starting the morning round soon and I can't have the patients waking up to two dead bodies on the ward.'

Connie chewed her bottom lip anxiously.

'Yes, I know it's not very pleasant walking across the grounds in the dark,' said Sister completely misunderstanding Connie's hesitation, 'but if there are two of you, you can look after each other.'

Eva didn't look too thrilled when Connie told her. They put the two men on the trolley, one in the box underneath and the other on the top covered with a sheet. It was a tidy walk to the morgue and there wasn't time to do two trips.

They worked in silence until they got to the lift. As Connie pulled the trolley in, she bumped it and an arm slipped from under the sheet and bopped Eva on the bottom. The shock made her cry out and for a second Connie wondered if she'd be accused of doing it on purpose, but Eva clutched at her chest and said breathily, 'He scared me half to death.'

'I guess it was his last chance to touch a pretty girl,' Connie grinned and the atmosphere between them lightened.

The lift went down and shuddered to a halt. They opened the doors and walked along the corridor through the swing doors and out into the night. They were glad of their cloaks because the mortuary was at the other end of the hospital grounds. It was very cold. There was a light breeze and the moon was full. Even though she was with Eva, Connie felt nervous and a bit spooked up.

When they got to the morgue, there was only one porter in the office, having a tea break. He wasn't very pleased to see them, throwing his sandwich back into his lunch box and scraping his chair in annoyance as he stood up.

'No peace for the wicked,' he grumbled. 'We haven't stopped all bloody night and even when I gets five minutes to meself, you comes down.'

'Sorry,' said Eva, 'but Sister wants them out of the way before the rounds start.'

'Well, you'll have to help me,' he said grudgingly. 'I can't put him to bed on me own.'

He walked ahead of them, switching on the light. It was the first time Connie had ever been into a morgue. Inside it was almost as cold as out of doors. They laid Mr Steppings on the only free slab (someone else lay on the other one) and covered him again with the sheet. The porter turned to go. 'There's another one in the box,' said Connie matter-of-factly.

'You what?' the porter demanded.

'We've got two bodies,' said Eva. 'Mr Ockley is underneath, in the box.'

'But we ain't got no more room,' the porter said.

'Well, you'll have to put him somewhere,' said Eva, her hand on her hip. 'We can't take him back.'

The porter made a great show of his irritation and went back into the office to get a clipboard and another trolley. Together they checked the paperwork and laid Mr Ockley on the top of the porter's trolley and covered him with another sheet. 'Turn out the light when you goes,' said the porter going back to his sandwiches.

Connie flicked the switch and the two of them were just turning to go when Mr Ockley let out a long sigh. Connie froze.

'You all right?' said Eva.

Connie put her hand to her throat. 'Is he still breathing?'

Eva shook her head. 'It's only trapped air coming out of his lungs,' she said.

Connie put the light back on and stared at the sheet.

'You've gone deathly white.' Eva went back to the trolley and pulled back the sheet. 'Check for yourself, Connie, or you'll always wonder.'

Connie went back and looked at the old man. There was no doubt. Mr Ockley was definitely gone. Already rigor mortis was setting in. She looked up at Eva.

'Okay?'

Connie nodded and pulled her cloak around her. On the way back to the lift, she glanced across at Eva. 'Exhausting, isn't it?' Eva turned and gave her a quizzical look. 'All this not speaking to each other, it's exhausting.'

Eva nodded. 'You're right.'

'I really liked you that day in London,' Connie went on.

'And I you,' said Eva. 'It was good fun.'

Connie sighed. 'Whatever the quarrel is between our families, it's not ours.'

They had reached the lifts. Eva pressed the button. 'You know what? You're right.'

They smiled at each other shyly. 'I think Ga would skin me alive, if she knew,' said Connie. 'Someone sent her that newspaper cutting of us in the fountain with those sailors and she went mad.'

'Who would do that?' Eva frowned as they stepped out of the lift.

Connie shrugged. 'I thought she'd be annoyed that I was in the water with two strange men, but she was far more upset that I was with you.'

Eva giggled. 'Oh dear.' She linked her arm through Connie's. 'I'd better be careful not to let my bad reputation rub off on you then.' And laughing, they pushed open the ward doors to begin the morning rounds.

Jane Jackson wrote to tell Connie that Sally Burndell had lost her place in the secretarial college. Apparently she had been very upset about it and so her mother had sent her to stay in Oxford with her grandmother for a while. Connie told everybody at home, and Ga, after a little persuasion, agreed to have her back in the shop when she was well enough. Sally came back to work in the nurseries just before Christmas.

Connie had been dreading Christmas because she was so close to home and yet unable to be with the family but in the event, it turned out to be rather special. On Christmas Eve, she and her fellow students put on their blue and red cloaks and went round the wards singing Christmas carols. Eva managed to get hold of an old-fashioned oil lantern and the rest of them carried torches. Sister Curtis was wearing angel wings on the back of her uniform. On the women's ward, a patient who had spent most of the day in theatre had just come round from the anaesthetic for the first time. Seeing Sister Curtis and her wings, her eyes grew as wide as saucers.

'Bloody 'ell! Looks like I've died,' she whispered and then relaxing added, 'Well, at least I'm in the right place.'

On Christmas Day, every patient was given a gift from the management committee while Father Christmas (thanks to the hospital porter) turned up to give them out. He and the mayor toured the wards spreading their unique brand of goodwill. Throughout the hospital, the visiting hours were extended. Later in the day, the staff put on a concert and on Boxing Day the patients were allowed to invite their visitors to tea. The Hospital Bees Christmas party raised a much needed £29 for hospital funds and the week-long festivities ended on Saturday, 29 December with the nurses' dinner and dance. Connie loved every minute of it.

She managed to go home for the day on 30 December, her day off. Pip and Mandy were overjoyed when they saw her coming down the path, and to Connie's delight, the family had saved their Christmas meal to have it with her. Gwen had saved a few presents for everyone to unwrap and a box of crackers from Woolworths, so Connie felt very spoiled.

She discovered that late on Christmas Eve, the Frenchie had called by with Connie's old pram although it didn't look like her old pram any longer. Apart from Simeon's attention to the bodywork and the hood, the Frenchie had painted Snow White in her rags on one side and with her handsome prince on the other. The two pictures were linked together by trailing rose buds and Mandy had been thrilled to have it. She showered her sister with kisses. Before she left for the hospital again, Connie dashed off a note of thanks but when she went round to the workshop, she had to make do with putting it under a brick on the doorstep. There had been no bill sent so she put £3 in the envelope and asked the Frenchie to tell her if the work cost more than that.

'Are you enjoying nursing?' Gwen asked when she got back. They were alone in the kitchen doing the drying up.

Connie hugged her mother. 'Mum, I just love it,' she smiled. 'And this has been the most amazing Christmas of my whole life. The girls in my set are wonderful. It's hard work and there's a lot to remember, but honestly, Mum, I've never been happier.'

'I'm glad,' said Gwen. She sounded a little wistful and at once Connie knew why. Her mother was remembering the one person in the family nobody spoke of. She was thinking of Kenneth.

Connie slipped her arm around her mother's waist and gave her a squeeze. 'He'll come back home one day, Mum,' she whispered. 'I'm sure of it.'

He mother nodded. 'I just wish I knew where he was.'

The door burst open and Ga came into the room carrying some dirty plates. 'What are you two plotting?' she demanded.

'Nothing,' said Gwen. She turned back to the sink and began the washing up.

Ga stared at her for a moment. 'Don't spoil a lovely day,' she challenged.

Gwen and Connie shared a knowing look together as Ga threw the plates into the washing up bowl. Ga hated talking about Connie's brother, but no matter how strongly she felt, it didn't alter the fact that Connie and her mother missed Kenneth, especially at times like this.

It was easier for Connie and Eva to keep their friendship from both families for the time being. Connie was glad of a friend like Eva. Here at last was someone she could trust and confide in, although she wasn't ready to talk about Kenneth yet.

Eva, on the other hand, was desperate to talk about her problems. She had met and was greatly attracted to one of the doctors in the hospital but so far she had refused to go out with him. Through Connie's gentle probing Eva began to understand her own reticence to embark on a romance. Hadn't she loved Dermid and when she'd pledged her life to him, hadn't he died? It was irrational but she was angry with him for getting himself killed and she was afraid to risk having her heart broken again. But Connie had seen the way Steven Mitchell looked at Eva and was convinced she had no reason to fear another broken heart.

'If Dermid was here,' Connie told Eva one night when they were having a deep and meaningful conversation, 'don't you think he would tell you to grab life by the scruff of the neck and enjoy it?'

Eva sighed and stared down at her fingernails. 'Yes, but . . .'

'Supposing it were the other way around,' said Connie interrupting with another tactic. 'Supposing you had died and Dermid was still here. Would you want him to stay faithful to your dead memory until he died an old man?'

'Of course not!' cried Eva.

'Then let him go,' said Connie. 'He belonged to 1944 but you're still alive in 1946.'

Her counsel didn't fall on deaf ears. By Whitsun the following year, Eva and Steven were secretly engaged. That wasn't the only engagement. When July came, the town was buzzing with the news that Mavis Hampton had just got engaged. The local papers had her picture on the front pages and there was a feature article on the inside pages of the *Worthing Gazette*. The girls in the nurses' home drooled over the dress Mavis was wearing but Connie found her attention was on the man she was to marry, Eugène Étienne. The Frenchie looked so different in his formal suit and tie; like a different person altogether.

Sally Burndell carried on working throughout the year but she was a very different girl. She was much quieter and less cheeky but the customers still liked her. Terry still refused to answer her letters so by the middle of May she gave up trying. Connie encouraged her to apply for the secretarial course again in July, this time at a different college, and to her absolute delight, she was accepted. Ga was a little put out that once again Sally was leaving, but the family gave her a little leaving party and by 3 September, she was on her way.

The continuing blot on the landscape was the relationship between Ga and Clifford. It had never been an easy one but now it was full of angst and anger. The atmosphere at home was so bad, they could hardly bear to be in the same room as each other without a tetchy argument. Clifford had made plans for the nurseries but Ga disapproved of everything he suggested. With the advent of Worthing Borough Council's grand plan for the regeneration of the town, came the need of land for housing. Clifford still wanted to sell off part of the nurseries to raise capital. Using that money, he planned to build a series of glass-houses and intensify his growing power. Strawberries, tomatoes and cucumbers were the way to go, he was sure of it. With the close proximity to the railway, he could get his produce up to Covent Garden within a couple of hours and if they could establish themselves with the top restaurants in London, the world would be his oyster, but Ga, as holder of the purse strings, was having none of it.

'This nursery serves the people of this area,' she said tartly. 'We don't need to look any further.'

'Times are changing,' Clifford said. 'If we think small, we'll stay small and eventually we'll be swallowed up by a much bigger fish. We're only just scraping by as it is. You can't stand in the way of progress.'

'May I remind you,' said Ga getting onto her high horse, 'that this is *my* place, not yours.' And the argument ended in the usual slanging match. Whenever she came home on her day off, Connie could see how much it was getting her mother down, but what could she do?

The year hadn't been without its flash points between Ga and Connie. The old woman made a beef about her sore leg every time she saw Connie coming even though she was quite capable of digging potatoes, humping boxes and even running for the bus when she thought no one was looking.

'If you're not going to help in the nursery,' she told Connie in the summer, 'you should at least pay for your keep.'

Connie gasped. She was on her way to the post office on an errand for Clifford. 'Excuse me?'

'We can't afford freeloaders,' said Ga maliciously. 'Food is short and it costs money.'

Connie felt her face flame. Her great aunt put her nose in the air and walked into the house. As Connie stared at her receding back, for a moment she really hated her. She may not be putting money on the table but she paid them in kind. Wasn't the rabbit they'd all eaten last night for supper bought from a butcher in Worthing by her? And didn't she often put a few shillings in the electric meter when nobody was looking? Just because she didn't make a song and dance about it, didn't mean she wasn't helping out when she could. Ga was impossible. In fact, the only person who thought she could do no wrong was her old friend Aggie.

*

He came downstairs quickly. She was unloading the shopping onto the kitchen table.

'You're back early,' he smiled.

'I caught the earlier bus,' she said flatly. 'You been in bed?'

'No,' he said, offended.

'Your hair is all flat,' she said.

'Well, I did have a bit of a lie down,' he admitted. 'A bad head-ache. It's gone now.'

'Did you take an aspirin?'

'No.' He took out his cigarette case and tapped a cigarette on the closed lid.

There was a footfall on the stairs and the child came down one by one. His wife turned her head and stared at him uncertainly.

'She was playing in her bedroom,' he said defensively as he struck a match.

The child came into the room and without even looking at her mother, sat down by the fire. She drew her cardigan around her body and hugged herself tight.

'You all right, luv?'

'Yes Mum.'

'Well, I'll be off to the pub for a bit,' he said snatching his cap from the nail on the back door.

'What, at this time?' she said glancing at the clock. 'They don't open until six.'

He kissed his wife on the cheek and tapped the side of his nose. 'Christmas is coming and I've got to see a man about a dog.'

She grinned knowingly. 'Make sure it's a lovely surprise, won't you?' she whispered.

The child didn't move. The back door banged and she continued to stare into the fire as her mother carried on unloading the shopping.

Ten

It was a bit of a shock to see Sally Burndell on the ward. Connie, who was on a split shift, listened with growing alarm as the ward sister read the report.

'Miss Burndell is a seventeen-year-old female with no history of mental illness. She was admitted from the emergency ward where she was treated for an overdose of barbiturates.' Sister leaned forward to the junior student nurse sitting next to Connie and added, 'That means she's had a stomach wash-out.' Connie was feeling uncomfortable. Should she tell Sister that Sally was a friend of hers? As the report continued, she decided against it. If Sister knew, she might stop Connie from nursing Sally.

'Miss Burndell is to be kept in overnight for observation and then the police want to question her,' Sister added with a sniff.

As the report was finished and they separated to their various duties, the other student nurse touched Sally's arm. 'Why do the police want to speak to Miss Burndell?' she whispered anxiously. 'Has she done something bad?'

Connie shook her head. 'Probably not, but attempted suicide is a criminal offence. The patient is at risk of being charged and imprisoned.'

The junior nurse went on her way satisfied, but just saying the words had sent a chill through Connie's heart. At the earliest opportunity she went behind the curtain screen separating Sally from the rest of the ward. Her friend turned her head away in shame as she entered. Connie rubbed Sally's arm sympathetically.

'I'm sorry,' Sally choked.

'It's all right,' Connie whispered. 'If there's anything I can do to help . . .'

'My mum is so cross with me,' Sally wept.

'She's had a fright, that's all,' said Connie. 'She'll come round.'

Sally shook her head. 'I feel so miserable.'

'Why didn't you tell me?' said Connie but she quickly realised that this was neither the time nor the place. Explanations would have to wait a while. 'Look, you get some sleep and we'll talk again later.' Sally's temperature was slightly raised but her heartbeat was normal.

'Listen,' said Connie as she entered the results on her chart at the foot of the bed, 'I don't know if they've told you, but the police want to talk to you.'

Sally nodded.

'Is there any chance you made a mistake?' Connie went on. 'I mean, could you have taken an accidental overdose?'

'That's what Mum told me to say,' said Sally. 'The silly thing was, it really was a mistake, but because I tried it before, she thinks I've done it again.'

'You tried it before?' Connie gasped. 'Oh Sally, why didn't you tell me?'

'I was an idiot,' said Sally, 'but . . .'

The screen clattered back and the ward sister came in with a scowl. 'That's enough chattering, nurse,' she said tartly. 'I'll deal with this patient.'

'Yes, Sister,' said Connie and smiling encouragingly she left Sister to it. For some time afterwards, Connie found herself shouldering some of the responsibility. Sally hadn't been her usual self at the beginning of the year but she honestly thought she was all right now. Connie had no idea it was so serious. Why hadn't Sally told her what was troubling her?

Sister cornered Connie about an hour later on her way back to the sluice room after having shaved Mrs Tucker in preparation for her operation the next day. 'Miss Burndell tells me you are a friend of hers, Nurse Dixon.'

'Yes, Sister,' Connie nodded.

'Then leave her to the other members of staff,' said Sister. 'You know the rules. You should not nurse any relative or friend.'

Sister bustled away leaving Connie feeling even worse. She hoped Sally wouldn't think she was deliberately avoiding her. Some friend you were anyway, Connie Dixon, she told herself crossly.

Christmas 1946 was moving ever closer. In the Sty, as the patients of Mr McIndoe called their ward at East Grinstead's Royal Victoria Hospital, they were making a go of putting up the decorations. They were a motley crew, some with injuries which they had sustained during the war and others, like Kenneth, who had been wounded in peacetime. Membership of The Guinea Pig Club which had been formed by thirty-nine injured airmen in 1941 was now closed. Members could only join the club if they had had at least ten operations and it lasted until 1945, so Kenneth had been a latecomer. He had been in the Sty for just over a year and he still faced several more months if not years of further treatment. Fortunately, the Royal Victoria wasn't as rigid as most hospitals. Kenneth was allowed to wear his own clothes or his service uniforms instead of 'convalescent blues' and he was able to leave the hospital whenever he wanted to. The trouble was, he never wanted to, and that was giving cause for concern.

'You never come to the pub with us, Dickie,' said Bunny Warren.

'Why bother when there's a free barrel on the ward?' Kenneth joked. He looked away. He knew what his companion was thinking. Bunny had overcome his disabilities but Kenneth still struggled with

114

his own appearance. He'd never get his face back although the Maestro, as they called McIndoe, had made a valiant attempt. He had eyelids now and the eye sockets had been strengthened by bone from his thigh. He had no eyebrows but a couple of operations around the eyes had given him a small ridge on his forehead. Although he had been left with a slightly surprised expression, it was a lot better than before. Now that the area had settled down, the next step was to rebuild his nose and as soon as Christmas was over, Kenneth would be back on the operating table. The state of his hands meant that the RAF had no further use for him which came as a bitter blow during the year. It took all the help he could get from the other chaps to pull him out of the black depression which threatened to engulf him. And even though East Grinstead had gained the reputation of being 'the town that did not stare', Kenneth still couldn't bring himself to venture out.

Bill Garfield had been coming back to the Sty for almost three years. A dashing pilot at twenty-two, he'd crashed in flames but the Maestro had rebuilt his eye socket, both cheekbones and his jaw. If anyone knew how Dickie felt about himself, it was Bill. Hadn't he gone through just the same? And yet this chap couldn't seem to lift himself up out of the pit. Dickie's reluctance to go out was more than simply because he'd lost his looks. It was as if he was carrying some great weight on his shoulders. Bill had probed and hinted but it was hopeless. Dickie kept himself to himself. He never had visitors or letters. Could he have been brought up in an orphanage? Bill fancied himself as a bit of an amateur sleuth and so he and Bunny decided to try and find Dickie's family.

They got into the office fairly easily. Of course they knew they'd be for the high jump if they got caught, but it was worth the risk for a pal. While Bunny kept watch, Bill riffled the patients' notes and then bingo, he'd found something.

Sally Burndell was discharged later that day. Her parents came to take her home and Connie made a point of asking if she could visit her. She went in her next off duty, taking a couple of apples with her. Sally was in her bedroom and her mum had lit a fire in the grate. She had dark circles under her eyes and as Connie came into the room, she pulled herself into a sitting position. Connie helped her put a bed jacket around her shoulders and they made small talk until finally Connie had to say something.

'Why did you do it, Sally?'

'I told you,' said Sally. 'It really was an accident this time.'

'I didn't even know about the last time,' cried Connie.

Sally's eyes filled immediately. Connie leaned forward and squeezed her hands. 'Tell me. You can trust me. I can keep a confidence.'

'In the end, they got me down,' she said brokenly.

'What got you down? I don't understand.'

'The letters,' said Sally. She leaned over and, opening a drawer in the dresser beside the bed, she took out a couple of envelopes. 'Mum burned the others,' she said. 'She doesn't know I've still got these.'

Connie opened one already torn envelope. *Some go with one man but a whore like you would entertain a football team. What will your boyfriend say?* The other contained a picture of a delicious looking apple tart cut from a magazine. Someone had scribbled, *'I'm still watching you, tart'* across the top.

'This is awful,' said Connie. 'Have you told the police?'

Sally shook her head. 'At first I thought it was someone's idea of a sick joke,' she said, 'but now I think whoever sent these has been writing to my college and to Terry. He stopped answering my letters ages ago. I didn't do anything wrong, Connie.'

'I know,' Connie soothed. 'You must show this to the police.'

'I can't,' said Sally. 'If I do, they'll think I intended to kill myself and I'll end up in prison. I know I was being dramatic but you see I tried to hang myself about a year ago.'

Connie was appalled. 'Oh, Sally . . .'

'I know,' Sally said dejectedly. 'I just felt so miserable. I made

116

a complete mess of it anyway. I tried to do it on the clothes pulley but of course as soon as my whole weight was on it, the screws came away from the ceiling. I knocked myself silly and then Mum found me.'

'Thank God she did,' Connie gasped.

There was a footfall outside the door. Sally said 'Shh,' and quickly shoved the letters under the eiderdown as Mrs Burndell brought them some tea.

'I've just been telling Sally that as soon as she's better,' Connie said brightly, 'we'll be off to the Assembly Hall dance again.'

'That'll be nice, dear,' said Mrs Burndell. 'It'll do her good to get out and about again.'

Kez decided to move her pitch. She had been selling holly wreaths by the market cross in the middle of Chichester. Made from Caen stone, the octagon structure was built four hundred years before at the junction of four roads and in plain sight of the cathedral. It was still doing what it was intended for, namely to provide shelter for poorer people as they sold their wares. Had she bothered to read the inscription above her head, which thanks to Connie's help she was now well able to do, Kez would have seen that it was put up by Edward Story 1477–1503, who was at one time bishop of Chichester.

Kez and her family had been in the area for about a fortnight. They'd camped near Slinden where she had trudged through the woods to find holly and mistletoe. The holly she'd made into wreaths and the mistletoe into bunches. They had sold like hot cakes and she only had six wreaths left but by now the crowds of Christmas shoppers were beginning to thin out. Simeon wouldn't be bringing the trailer back to pick her up until six so there was still time to try and sell them.

By now, people were heading back towards the station so Kez gambled that if she sat by the entrance, a few might buy a last minute holly wreath once they were sure they still had plenty of time to catch the train. She had just put the few she had left in her basket, when someone in a tearing hurry bumped into her and everything fell back onto the cobbles. The person who had done it was full of apologies but didn't stop to help. One wreath went into the road and a passing car ran over it. When she picked it up, it wasn't too badly damaged so Kez sat on the stone bench inside the cross to repair it.

A man and woman were arguing behind a pillar on the other side of the building. She could see them but it was obvious they didn't know she was there.

'It wasn't like that,' the man said angrily. He began tapping his cigarette on its case and Kez froze. No, it couldn't be . . . could it?

'Oh, I think it was,' the woman snapped. 'Even on our wedding day, you couldn't take your filthy eyes off her.' She threw back her head and laughed sardonically. 'Dear God in heaven, what a fool I've been.'

'Eleanor,' the man said, trying to placate her. He put the case in his pocket and put out his hand.

'Don't touch me!' she cried. 'Admit it. You only wanted me to get your hands on my Rosemary, didn't you?'

'How can you even think such a thing?'

'That's what you were doing the day I came home early, wasn't it?' the woman insisted.

Kez stood to leave. Her stomach churned and she felt sick.

'Don't be ridiculous!' The man was getting annoyed.

'They tried to warn me, but I wouldn't listen,' the woman snarled. 'Well, you won't get away with this, Stan. I'm going to the police.'

'No one will believe you,' he said coldly and behind them Kez was struggling to breathe normally. Her heart was pounding and she was shaking.

She shoved the repaired wreath into her basket and stepped away. There was a bus coming so she was forced to wait until it passed. Kez didn't intend to look back but her eye was drawn to him. And that's when she saw what happened next. Stan made what looked like a grab at the woman. A grab and then a push. The woman flung her arms into the air and fell into the road. The next few seconds were horrific. First a squeal of brakes and then a sickening thud. Kez was rooted to the spot, her heart pounding, her mouth dry and gaping. People came running from all directions but from where she stood, Kez could already see that it was far too late.

The bus driver climbed ashen-faced out of his cab. 'What did she do that for? She jumped right out in front of me. I didn't stand a chance. Is she all right?'

'She's dead,' said a voice, and the driver staggered backwards holding his head and dislodging his cap to the back of his head. Someone caught him and made him sit down inside the market cross. The poor man was shaking his head and he'd begun to cry. 'Oh God, Oh God, why did she do it?' he wept. 'One minute she was on the pavement and the next she was under me wheels.'

Kez glanced at the man who had been with her. Stan was staring down at the woman's lifeless body, partially hidden under the wheel of the bus. He held his gloved hand to his mouth. Someone in the crowd turned towards him. 'Was she with you?'

He nodded. 'She's my wife.'

Immediately the crowd turned its attention towards him, each person doing his or her best to comfort a man who had just seen his wife die. Kez could hear the whispers all around her. 'He's in shock.' 'Someone get a doctor.' 'What a dreadful thing to happen.' 'And on Christmas Eve too.'

Kez turned away. She had no stomach to sell holly wreaths now. No one would want them anyway. Christmas was spoiled. She'd never be able to get the image of that poor woman out of her mind. She wouldn't forget the woman's husband either. Even though she hadn't seen him since she was a little girl, she'd recognised him at once. He wouldn't have known her of course.

She was all grown up now. A married woman too. She hurried away, only glancing back the once. That's when she noticed that the gloved hand Stan kept so close to his mouth hid a small smile on his lips.

Eleven

That second winter of her training, beginning on 21 January 1947, the weather deteriorated. Outside the relative warmth of the hospital wards, the country was at a virtual standstill. The bitingly cold winds which came to the south moved up country and brought blizzard conditions which in turn caused huge snow drifts. In the chaos which followed, schools were closed and because it was impossible to get around, just about every business in the country was hit hard. It seemed that every news bulletin on the radio was even gloomier than the last. Old people, particularly those living alone, died of hypothermia in their own homes. Livestock had been found frozen to death in the fields, wild birds and animals fell to the ground and starved to death.

Connie had nearly always gone home on her day off. She enjoyed helping around the house and looking after Mandy while her mother and Clifford went out for the afternoon. Sometimes she would have a lazy day and lie in bed until mid-morning (much to Ga's disgust) and then take Pip for a long walk up to Highdown Hill. It was lovely up there and if she was well wrapped up, Connie didn't mind the cold winds. As the relationship between Clifford and Ga had soured and following her own disagreement with Ga, going home wasn't nearly as pleasant. Her great aunt was still a bit frosty towards her but Connie pretended not to notice. Kez was still on the road but Connie did manage a couple of Saturday dances at the Assembly Hall with

Jane Jackson when she had the night off duty. Sally Burndell was still convalescing with her aunt in Hampshire. Connie enjoyed herself at the dances even though she didn't meet anybody special but she loved the twinkling globe and the swishing of the dance dresses. Whenever someone asked her to dance, as she walked onto the dance floor, Connie was whisked away on a dreamy cloud of romance, usually until the man in question opened his mouth.

Once the snow came, she had made no attempt to brave the bus journey to Goring. She knew her mother would understand why. Even if she had found a bus going that way, there was no guarantee she would be able to get back to the hospital. Several nurses were stuck at home, unable to get back and three of her set had heavy colds, making the wards very short of staff. The intake was already down to twelve, seven of the girls already having decided that nursing wasn't for them, or they wanted to get married and stop working altogether.

By February, with the weather conditions terrible the hospital was bulging was at the seams, mostly with people breaking legs, hips and arms, all with complications, after falling in the icy conditions. When a serious road accident added to the problem and five people were admitted in one night, extra beds had been put down the middle of the wards. After that, everyone had their fingers crossed that the stores wouldn't run out of beds, or the wards run out of space.

With such awful conditions outside, Connie was surprised to find three letters in her pigeonhole in the foyer of the nurses' home. She couldn't imagine how the GPO managed to deliver any letters at all! As she sat on the stair to read them, Connie heard a low rumble in the distance. She frowned. Not thunder, surely? It was far too cold and yet it had been a very distinct sound. Perhaps it was a movement of snow somewhere, maybe falling off the roof. She drew her nurse's cloak around her body and sighed. What next?

Someone came down the stairs and she had to move over to let them pass.

'Off out?' she said to the girl.

'Going to phone my mother if I can,' came the reply. 'I haven't heard from her for a week.'

Connie sympathised. Finding out what was happening at home was difficult. The Dixons weren't on the telephone at Belvedere Nurseries but in the case of a real emergency Connie knew she could always make a call to the Frenchie and he would pass any message on. Connie hadn't heard from her family for a couple of weeks either. She'd written herself but she had no real hope of her letters getting through. There were power cuts, with domestic electricity reduced to nineteen hours per day and industrial supplies were cut completely. Radio broadcasts were reduced, and television, only owned by the wealthy few anyway, was suspended altogether. Even the newspapers were a lot smaller in size. To add insult to injury, the country faced another food shortage because the vegetables were impossible to get out of the ground.

Connie shivered. The treacherous road conditions not only prevented food supplies getting through, but also much needed coal. Stocks had been low since the end of the war but now there was a chronic shortage. Even though the authorities used some of the remaining German POWs still in the country to shift the snow on the railways by hand, the coal stored at railway depots was frozen to the ground and impossible to move anyway. When coal supplies did get through, naturally the Hospital Committee put the patients first. That meant there was precious little left for the nurses' home. Someone had put a blackout curtain over the back of the door in the staff sitting room and they were still at the windows of the room, but even so, the fire in the grate struggled to bring the temperature anything close to cosy. The radiators were switched off in the bedrooms which meant that Connie and the other girls woke up to frost on the inside of the windows and icicles, some as long as three inches or more, hanging on the outside. She already had three blankets and sometimes she had to throw her winter coat over the bed to keep warm. She hated getting up in the morning. Her bed felt warm and cosy and it took every ounce of courage to throw back the covers and wash and dress in such freezing temperatures. It was hardly surprising. Snow had fallen on twenty-six consecutive days and as the temperatures plummeted, Worthing managed to get in the record books with 23 degrees of frost with the sea frozen too!

She was surprised to see that one of her letters was from Ga. It was dated a week ago . . . a week to get from Goring to Worthing, a distance of about four miles.

'*Your mother had blisters on her hands, even though she'd worn thick gloves when she and Clifford tried to lift some turnips,*' she wrote. In view of the way Ga behaved when she was at home, Connie was surprised that the letter was both friendly and chatty. '*Clifford says it will take a pneumatic drill to get them up.*'

Connie shook her head despairingly. If they couldn't get the food out of the ground, they couldn't eat. They couldn't sell anything either. Whatever were they going to do?

The lack of everything from food to fuel made everyone so depressed it came as little surprise to hear that Manny Shinwell, the Minister for Fuel and Power, the man who had allowed the stockpile of coal to dwindle to only four weeks' supply at the beginning of winter, had received death threats and had to be put under police guard.

Did Mum and Clifford have enough coal?

'*Of course,*' Ga went on, '*if we had some young blood, a stronger person to help us, perhaps we could manage to get something out of the ground, but Clifford does the best he can.*'

At this point, Connie was tempted to screw the letter into a ball and chuck it into a bin. Why couldn't the woman let it drop?

She'd been nursing for fifteen months now and still Ga was doing her best to make her give it up and come home. Taking a deep breath to calm her nerves, Connie began again.

'*Mandy is off school*,' Ga's letter continued, '*because there's no heating. Clifford's friend, the Frenchie, has been helping people out with logs but he's given that much away, I don't think he can do it much longer.*'

Connie shook away the memory of the Frenchie and yet, she was glad he was keeping an eye on everyone in the village.

'*Take care of yourself*,' Ga said on the last page. '*As soon as you can, let us know how you are.*'

With that last statement, it sounded as if she was mellowing at last and surprisingly Connie was left with a twinge of guilt. Of course, she'd thought about her family every day, but what with her studies and the crisis which seemed to go on and on, the thought of struggling to the postbox again with a letter which might never get there, was too much. Connie decided there and then, that even if it took hours and hours, she would try to get home on her next day off.

There was a PS. '*You mustn't go worrying about us*,' Ga wrote. '*We're all alright. Everyone is well. We have plenty of logs if the coal runs out and your mother has a good store cupboard so we won't starve.*'

Connie smiled. That was a relief anyway. She folded the letter only to find another postscript. '*I put my teeth in the glass by my bed and when I woke up in the morning, they were frozen solid.*'

Connie chuckled. Perhaps Ga had forgiven her at last.

The second letter was in one of Ga's special envelopes. Connie knew the old lady only used her best writing paper occasionally and only for important letters which was why she was so surprised to see it. Why not put the letter in with the one she'd just read? She tore open the envelope and gasped. It contained what looked like a newspaper cutting. Connie spread it out and the fury rose in her chest. The cutting had come from *Tit-Bits* and was about a female dancer whose body was covered in tattoos. At the top of the page, Ga had printed the words *Like Gertrude?* Damn Ga and her nasty insinuations. She hadn't changed one bit.

The wartime spirit hadn't died. People did their best to help each other so Clifford and the Frenchie were not unique. As the weather conditions grew worse, neighbours banded together, sharing their meagre supplies whenever they could. Most people could only afford to heat one room in their house anyway so the whole of family life was reduced to that. The blackout curtains came in useful again. If they weren't at the doors or windows, they were sewn together and used as draught excluders. The power cuts compounded everything. The Frenchie and Clifford took what extra candles they could find to the old, the sick or the frail who couldn't get out themselves. Of course, they couldn't help everybody and Aggie's nose was out of joint when the Frenchie refused her some logs even though he had pointed out that she had the best part of ½ cwt. of coal in her bunker while other people had nothing at all. She eventually accepted the decision with tight-lipped resignation and the Frenchie kissed her on both cheeks.

All this took time. No one was earning any money and as the weather conditions continued to deteriorate, everyone had a sense that the whole country was in the grip of a catastrophe.

'Some Valentine's present,' said Ga turning off the radio.

'What's that?' Gwen was trying to dry the washing. She hung a clothes horse by the fire and she was busy turning things around. Staying damp for too long and there was a danger it would start to smell.

'It's now illegal to use electrical appliances,' said Ga.

Gwen gasped. 'They can't do that can they?'

'They can and they have,' said Ga grimly. 'I just heard it on the radio. Failure to comply can result in a £100 fine or two years imprisonment.'

'For switching on an electric fire?' Gwen gasped. 'This place is getting more like a police state every day.'

Mandy was under the table playing with her dollies. She liked it under there. Sometimes the adults forgot she was there and talked about things she wouldn't normally be allowed to hear. Of course, she didn't always understand what they were talking about . . . a police state, for instance, what was that?

Pip was with her. He was lying with his head on his front paws. She'd put a dolly's hat on his head and he swallowed against the ribbons under his chin.

'He's nice, that Frenchie,' her mother mused.

Ga harrumphed. 'If you say so.'

'Come on, Ga,' said Gwen. 'You must admit he's certainly got us all helping each other and that can't be bad. Poor old Charlie Walker would have been a goner if he and Clifford hadn't checked up on him. The poor man didn't have a stick of food in the house.'

Mandy peeped through the fringes on the tablecloth and saw Ga's mouth tightened. 'It's that Mavis Hampton I can't stand. The way she bosses everybody about. What he sees in her, I'll never know.'

'He rents that workshop of his from Councillor Hampton,' said her mother, 'and he's a very talented artist. I think the Frenchie is going places and she knows it.'

'Changing the subject,' said Ga, 'have we got any more spuds out of the ground?'

Her mother shook her head. 'The ground's too hard. Shame really. Everyone is complaining about the supplies. Apparently, they had some in the greengrocer's but they were all diseased and there was half a ton of dirt in the sack as well.' Mandy watched as her mother wiped the condensation on the window with a dry cloth. 'And there's us with a field full of them and we can't get them out!'

'Never mind,' said Ga, 'once the thaw comes we'll have a gold mine out there.'

'But when is it coming?' said her mother. 'That's what I want to know. It's been like this since January.'

The two women stopped talking. In the distance they could hear a speaker van coming. 'We'd better listen to what that says,' said Ga. 'It wouldn't be able to go much further than the bottom of the lane. The council only clears the main roads.'

They reached for their coats and opened the back door. The sudden draught of cold air made Mandy lift the heavy tablecloth which hid her beneath the table, but she didn't come out. Pip did. He seized the opportunity of freedom and pushed between the two women and bounded outside. Luckily for him, Mandy's mother had the presence of mind to snatch the doll's hat from his head as he went.

'You are reminded that it is your duty to clear the front of your premises of snow,' said a disembodied voice in the distance. 'Please do not use any electricity for domestic purposes between the hours of nine and twelve and two to four. Failure to comply . . .'

'I really don't want to hear any more of that,' said Mandy's mother shutting the door. 'At least Connie's all right. They'll be nice and warm in the hospital.'

'It would be nice to hear from her,' Ga grunted. 'Surely it wouldn't take five minutes to drop us a line?'

There was a pause and her mother sighed. 'I wonder where Kenneth is. Don't you ever want to know what happened to my boy?'

'Now, now,' said Ga firmly. 'Don't go upsetting yourself over him. He's not worth it.'

'I wish you wouldn't keep saying that,' said her mother. 'I know he was a bit of a tearaway but what young lad isn't? I never understood why he went off like that without so much as a by-your-leave.'

Under the table, Mandy held her breath as she heard her mother choke back a small sob. She knew she had a brother called Kenneth but she'd never seen him. Connie told her about him sometimes, about the games they'd played when Connie was young and the things he'd got up to. Her favourite story was the one when Kenneth and his friend pulled up all the For Sale notices in the village and stuck them in the vicarage garden. Apparently the vicar was furious. Connie showed her a picture of him once but this was the first time she'd ever heard her mother and Ga talking about him.

'It was for the best,' said Ga.

'What was for the best?' said Gwen rounding on her. 'Did you see him go then? You never told me. Do you know more than you're telling me?'

'No, no of course not,' said Ga. 'What I mean is that the boy gave you nothing but grief all the time. Without a father's hand, he was running wild.'

Mandy could hear her mother blowing her nose. 'I suppose so. All the same, I wonder where he went, what sort of war he had and where he is now.'

'Perhaps it's just as well we don't know,' said Ga.

'What's that supposed to mean?' her mother snapped.

'Well,' said Ga uncertainly, 'he could have been injured or killed.'

Mandy heard her mother take in her breath. 'No, no,' she said pressing her hand on her chest. 'If he was dead, I would know it.'

'He could have been injured,' Ga insisted.

'I don't want to think of him that way,' said her mother.

They could hear Pip barking, and then Clifford called from the lane. 'Gwennie love, come and give us a hand will you?'

'Well, if you'll take my advice,' said Ga, as Mandy's mother reached for her coat again, 'you'll forget all about him.'

'I can never do that, Ga,' said Gwen. 'However old he is, he's my child.' And opening the door, she called, 'What is it?'

Mandy went back to her tea party until she heard a rather odd scrabbling sound. She peeked again and saw Ga searching through her cavernous handbag. A second later, she took out some papers and looked at them. Then using the portable handle, she lifted the lid on the range and dropped them onto the fire. One fell to the floor and floated under the table. Mandy picked it up and put it into the dolly's cradle.

'It's for the best,' Ga whispered as bright red and yellow flame leapt above the hole and she slipped the lid back over it.

Connie put Ga's letter back in the envelope and looked at the third. She expected it to come from home as well but the headed envelope told her it was from another hospital. The Royal Victoria Hospital, East Grinstead. Her stomach tightened. Had her mother been taken ill? No, it couldn't be that. The postmark was even older than the one from Ga and she'd finished up by saying everyone was well. So who was in hospital?

The girl who had pushed past her on the stairs was back. 'All right, luv?'

Connie nodded. 'Did you contact your mother?'

'Nah, her telephone line is down,' she called. 'But I got through to a neighbour and they're all right.' In the distance a door banged and it went quiet again.

Connie stood up. This wasn't the best place to read bad news, if it was bad news. Shoving the unopened letter into her pocket, she made her way upstairs to her room.

Connie was halfway up the stairs when Sister Hayes burst through the door. 'I need three nurses immediately,' she called out. 'There's been a serious accident and we're expecting a great many casualties.'

Connie turned round and ran down the stairs after her. Two other girls were coming into the nurses' home.

'What happened?' Connie called.

'An unexploded bomb has gone off,' said Sister. 'Quickly now, girls. Go straight to the main entrance.'

And as she flew out of the door, Connie could only imagine what horrors lay before her.

Twelve

Stan sensed something was wrong as soon as he came in through the front door. He turned sharply as he went to close the door as if someone was watching him but there was only the inky darkness of night. A cat ran across the path behind him and he jumped. Pull yourself together, he thought, and he slid the bolt across.

He'd spent the evening in the pub. He'd sat in the corner by the bar and drank alone. They refused to talk to him but they were whispering behind his back. Part of him was annoyed and the other part thought to hell with the lot of them. He knew they were upset about the inquest but he had no regrets. He swirled his glass and thought back to the events in the week before Christmas, or to be more exact, the day his wife died.

'She was walking in front of you?' the coroner had asked.

He'd looked down at the floor. 'Yes.' He had thought it best to say as little as possible. The less people knew, the better.

'What happened then?'

He shrugged. 'She suddenly rushed out into the road.'

'Have you any idea why?'

'No.' There had been a murmur in the court room but he'd kept his head down. Let them think what they bloody well wanted to. There was no proof.

'You see, I can't understand what made her run out like that,' said the coroner. 'Surely she must have seen the bus coming? The previous witness said that he thought her action was part of a joke.

132

He thought that you and your wife could have been indulging in some kind of horseplay when she fell. You, on the other hand, say it was deliberate.'

Stan had raised his head and looked the silly old fool right in the eye. 'That's right, it was deliberate. She meant to do it.'

The whole place erupted as her relatives shouted down from the back of the room. 'Liar!' 'Bastard.'

The coroner struggled to make himself heard over the din. 'Any more disruptions like that and I shall have no other alternative than to have you all forcibly ejected from this room.'

Stan knew perfectly well why they were upset. They were Catholics. She couldn't be buried in consecrated ground and there would be no Mass said in her memory if the verdict was suicide. He didn't believe in all that mumbo-jumbo, but they did. She did too and she was planning to tell the whole world about him. That wasn't right. A wife should never betray her husband. He did his best not to let them take the kid away from him but now that the grandparents had got hold of her, they were fighting tooth and nail to keep her. Never mind, he would have his revenge.

The coroner had been very thorough in his summing up and it had been music to his ears when he finally said, 'It had been suggested that what happened could have been caused by laughing and joking, but her husband's testimony flies in the face of that. There is no reason to believe that the deceased had intended to take her life, but I can only draw my conclusions on the circumstantial evidence.' There had been a howl of protest from the seats at the back when the verdict was announced. 'Suicide while mentally unbalanced.'

The police had advised Stan to stay within the court until the family had gone. They were baying for blood. Perhaps he should move again. They'd never let him forget. They'd already poisoned half the town against him.

*

Connie was sent to the medical ward so that the more trained staff could be in Accident and Emergency. In the event, there were few casualties because the weather had kept most people in their homes. Connie had finally come off duty at ten past midnight. She was dog tired and hardly able to put one foot in front of the other. Sister Curtis had given both her and the other two nurses extra off duty but it didn't amount to much.

'You can come back on duty at twelve noon tomorrow,' she told them. 'I'll clear it with the day staff. You can have a bit of a lie-in.'

They were grateful of course, but it would have been better if they'd had the whole day off. If she had, she might have risked going home.

Connie got undressed without putting on the light and crawled into bed, careful not to wake Betty who was snoring nicely. As soon as she hit the pillow she went out like a light and only woke up at 10.15 a.m. Starving hungry, she was too late for breakfast and too early for lunch.

Betty had tidied the room and Connie's laundry box was gone. Good old Betty, she thought. She'd have to have the same sheets for another week but at least her uniforms had been sent to the laundry. It was only then that she remembered the letters. Connie searched everywhere, hoping against hope that Betty had looked in the pockets and taken them out, but she couldn't find them anywhere. Why, oh why hadn't she opened that third letter? Connie had tried to take a sneaky look on the ward a couple of times, but Sister had spotted her and made sure she had something else to do.

One look out of the window told her that the snow was as bad as ever but she had to find Betty and ask her if she'd put them somewhere safe. If Betty hadn't found them, they would have gone to the laundry and that didn't bear thinking about. Connie decided if she couldn't find the letter, she would have to ring the Frenchie after all. Perhaps there had been some sort of emergency at home and someone had ended up in hospital.

What other explanation was there? She looked at her watch. She had exactly one hour to do all that and get back on duty.

When she found Betty, she was full of apologies. 'What a stupid clown I am,' she said, looking around to make sure Sister hadn't seen her creeping outside the ward doors. 'I should have gone through your pockets but I never gave it a thought. The letters must still be there. Were they very personal?'

'It's not that,' Connie said. 'Where do they take the laundry boxes?'

'Oh, they'll be long gone now,' said Betty. 'The laundry is round the back of the hospital. You could try and see if they'll let you look for your things, I suppose.'

Connie groaned. If she went there right now, she'd probably have to get permission in triplicate before they would even let her in. She hadn't a hope of managing all that before her shift began.

'I'm really sorry,' said Betty.

'It's not your fault,' said Connie. 'I don't know why I didn't just go to the toilet and read them. Everybody seemed to be in such a flap what with the bombing and all I didn't want anyone to think I was skiving.'

The ward door burst open almost knocking them over. 'What do you think you are doing out here, nurse?' said an angry voice. 'This is no time for a mothers' meeting.'

Betty hurried back into the ward with a, 'No, Sister, sorry Sister . . .'

*

Stan had been jumpy, opening doors cautiously and looking around the rooms before he went in. The fire was almost out in the sitting room. He threw on another log and poked the embers back into life. Reaching for the whisky bottle, he'd poured himself a stiff drink and flopped down in the chair. He must have slept soundly and only woke when he heard a sound in the hallway. His heart began to thump wildly in his chest. He got up and opened the sitting room door. A vivid tongue of flame leapt to the ceiling and a rush of hot air came towards him. He felt it burn his skin. He made a dash towards the kitchen and the back door but he couldn't open it. The handle was wedged in some way. The flames were coming towards him. He couldn't stay here. He glanced wildly at the stairs but even if he could make it, it would be the height of stupidity to go up. He had to get out. He made his way back to the sitting room and immediately slammed the door, took off his coat and threw it across the doorway. Somewhere inside his head he remembered someone saying that fire feeds on oxygen. Cut off the supply and it would be contained. He'd obviously fed the fire as he opened the door but he could stop the steady draught of air under the door adding more fuel. He ran to the window and tried to open it but someone had nailed it shut. It was only then that he realised that his only way of escape was cut off. His hands hurt but he managed to grab a chair and smash the window. He laid cushions over the jagged edges and hauled himself coughing and gasping for air, into the garden.

The eight minutes it took the fire brigade to get to him seemed like a lifetime. He'd lain in the garden listening to the small explosions beyond the window as his beautiful home burned.

The firemen did what they could but he had lost everything. The hallway was a shell and elsewhere the walls were streaked and the carpets sodden. The smoke damage was everywhere. Everything stank and the whole house was grimy, smudged and blackened.

Of course the police asked a lot of questions. It was clear that someone had tried to murder him, but he was in a difficult position. He didn't want them probing too deeply. Who knows what they'd find out? He'd move away. Back to his mother's or something.

'You'd better get that face seen to,' someone said.

That's when he'd looked down at his hands. They were burned. The skin hanging from his fingers as if he'd been peeled like an apple. Now that he thought about it, his face was beginning to throb. 'It's off to hospital with you,' said a voice and all at once, the ground rushed up to meet him as he fainted clean away.

*

Belvedere Nurseries wasn't on the telephone but Clifford had made an arrangement with the Frenchie, the only person in the area with a telephone, that if there was an exceptional emergency, Connie could ring the workshop and he would pass on the message. Connie hurried to the public telephone box. There had been talk of the GPO putting a phone box inside the nurses' home but so far it was only talk. The call box was on the main road but at least someone had cleared the footpaths of snow and thrown salt down to prevent it from re-freezing.

When she picked up the receiver, Connie was relieved to hear the operator ask, 'Number please.' She heard the dialling sound and then the pips went. Connie pressed the money home and a deep velvet voice said 'Goring 529.'

She felt her knees go weak. 'Oh, hello.' Her voice sounded ridiculously high. Connie cleared her throat and began again. 'This is Connie Dixon. My mother lives at Belvedere Nurseries. I don't know if you remember me.'

'I certainly do, Connie Dixon. How are you?'

'I-I'm fine,' said Connie, 'but I'm worried about my family. Do you know if they are all right?'

'As a matter of fact, Clifford is here,' said the Frenchie. 'I've got a bit of an emergency and I have to go. Do you want to speak to him?'

Connie was so relieved but why on earth was Clifford there? 'Oh yes, yes please.' As she waited she remembered that Ga had told her they were helping the neighbours.

'Everybody is fine,' Clifford assured her and went on to tell her what they had been doing. It was much the same as she remembered from Ga's letter. 'We're organising ourselves to go

137

round to some of the old folks and the people with very young families to make sure they are okay,' he went on. 'Mandy has her sled and we've got blankets and spare hot water bottles and some food. We're having to dig some of them out. Nobody can remember snow as bad as this.' She heard someone calling in the background and Clifford said, 'There's a small bottle of brandy in that brown bag, just in case.'

The money didn't last long but Connie didn't mind. Everybody at home was well and that was all that mattered. The letter from East Grinstead must have been about somebody else entirely. But who? If it wasn't about Ga or Mum or Mandy, who else could it have been? Her mind drifted to old friends. What about Irene Thompson? No, she told herself, don't be ridiculous. Why would a hospital contact her about Irene? She was as fit as a flea, and living in Weston-Super-Mare, a million miles from East Grinstead, and besides, there was no reason to contact Connie, she had her own family.

Then the thought hit her like a sledge hammer. There was only one other person it could be. Emmett Gosling.

'I'm afraid you've drawn the short straw,' Sister said when Connie finally got back on the ward. 'There's a private patient in Room 2 who has just been admitted and I've assigned you to look after her.'

The accident ward was still overflowing with people, mostly with broken legs, ankles and wrists from falling on the ice. On the whole, their patients took it in good spirits, probably glad to be in the warm for a bit and so long as the Friendly Society or the assurance company picked up the bill, they didn't have to worry about the cost.

Connie recognised her patient as soon as she opened the door. Mavis Hampton had a bandage on her ankle. She lay back on the pillow with a lace handkerchief to her lips. She had been doing her make-up.

'Good afternoon, Miss Hampton,' Connie said pleasantly. 'I'm

Nurse Dixon and I shall be looking after you until the night staff come on duty.'

Mavis gave her a cold stare. 'Then get me some tea. I'm dying of thirst in here.'

Connie bristled with indignation but she had no alternative but to go. Room 2 was usually reserved for Mr Nankeville's private patients and he was very particular. When she came back with the tea tray, the Frenchie was sitting beside Mavis' bed. Connie put the tray down and turned to go.

'Thank you, nurse,' said Eugène and Connie gave him a shy smile. Already her heart was racing. 'Oh, it's you, Connie. How nice to see you.'

As he stood up to open the door for her, Mavis burst into tears. 'No one cares that I'm in such awful pain.'

Connie was surprised. Mavis had seemed all right when she'd first come into the room but then she realised that she disliked the woman so much she hadn't really given a thought to her nursing needs. 'Would you like me to ask the doctor to see you again, Miss Hampton?'

'Well . . .' said Mavis fluttering her eyelids at the Frenchie, 'I hate to be a nuisance . . .'

Connie let the door close quietly behind her as Eugène went back to his fiancée's bedside. Her first port of the call was the Sister's desk where she reported Miss Hampton's pain and Sister sent for Mr Nankeville.

The rest of Connie's shift was a complete nightmare. Mavis rang the emergency bell for her flowers to be put in water, for Connie to rearrange her pillows, for more tea when her visitors came and for a bedpan. Connie struggled to keep smiling and to be pleasant especially when there were patients who were far more seriously ill on the ward.

'That woman,' Sister complained when Connie came to tell her Mavis said her bandage was a little too tight, 'I'll swing for her, so I will.'

The bell rang again. 'Remind her that bell is only for emergencies,' Sister called as Connie dashed down the ward.

'But this is an emergency,' Mavis snapped when Connie relayed the message. 'I asked you ages ago to put my flowers in a vase and you still haven't done it.'

Eugène smiled apologetically which set Connie all at sixes and sevens again. Oh why did he have to be so gorgeous looking? she thought bitterly. And why were all the nice men taken?

Clifford seemed preoccupied about something. Gwen put Mandy to bed and suggested he take them to the Bull for a drink. It was the only place where they could be sure of being alone. Gwen was grateful to Ga for giving them a home and the business, but the trouble was, she was always there. She never went out with friends, Gwen wasn't even sure she had any, apart from Aggie and even she only turned up once a week. Ga never went to Aggie's house. Ga had become more and more demanding and the atmosphere between Ga and Clifford was getting worse all the time. They had little money from the nurseries because Ga was always talking about investing everything in the future.

'When I'm dead and gone,' she would say, 'it'll all be yours.'

Gwen sighed. She was tired of waiting for jam tomorrow. She wanted to live for today. Who knew how long they would have to wait? Ga was hale and hearty and besides she didn't like to think about somebody dying before they could enjoy their lives. How much longer they could put up with it, Gwen didn't know. She and Clifford never had a moment to themselves. Gwen wouldn't have minded so much if Ga had offered to babysit now and again, but the thought never seemed to cross her mind. The only chance they had to go out was when Connie came home and since the bad weather started, they hadn't been out at all. Usually Worthing was well protected by the South Downs. The terrible weather they had in the east of the county and Kent seldom reached Worthing and the surrounding villages, but this year the town had enough snow to cover the top of a wellington boot.

Mandy was asleep and Ga downstairs so rather than *ask* her to babysit and have her refuse, Clifford *told* her they were going out. She looked a bit put out but Gwen and her husband wrapped up warmly and made their way to Goring Street. The Bull Inn had been built around 1770 and was near the old post office. Because of its thick walls, the building had been used as a mortuary and an extension built in the late eighteen hundreds was used as a butcher's shop. In a more sombre mood, Ga had a picture of a funeral procession leaving the Bull in 1907 when two of her acquaintances, Sid Orchard and Fred Wadey were killed by a bolt of lightning on Highdown. They were only nineteen and twenty-two years old.

They opened the door and were greeted by a warm fire and an equally warm welcome from a few of the locals gathered at the bar. After swapping a few snowbound stories, Gwen and Clifford made their way to the fire, sat next to each other and held hands. As bad as things were, Gwen thanked God every day that Clifford had made it through the war. They all had. At least, she hoped they had. Whatever happened to Kenneth?

Clifford pushed her glass of sherry towards her. 'Drink up,' he smiled, seeing her sad expression. 'A couple more days of mild weather and maybe I can get to those root vegetables still in the ground. That'll bring in a bit of an income.'

'We still have a bit of savings,' said Gwen. She kept the books and she was a shrewd woman. 'I've always put a bit by in case of bad times and this is the first time we've used it.'

'I should be paid a proper wage,' he said acidly.

Gwen looked away. He was right and she was embarrassed for him. 'I wish I'd never persuaded you to stay,' she said.

'It's not your fault, Gwennie,' he said squeezing her hand. 'If the old lady would only agree to sell the end plot, it would make all the difference.'

'She doesn't like change,' said Gwen.

'We have to move with the times,' said Clifford. 'The nursery is too small to make a decent living. We have to diversify if we're going to make a go of things.'

'I know.'

'I want to provide well for you and Mandy,' Clifford went on, 'not pinch and scrape all our lives.'

'I know, darling.'

'If she won't sell it,' Clifford went on, 'the Frenchie suggested putting up a workshop on the land. If we rented it out, that would bring in a good income. Regular too.'

'Do you want me to try and talk to her?' said Gwen.

Clifford looked uncertain. 'I'd like to say yes, but I don't want her sending you to Coventry as well. One person in the family is enough.' He took a sip of his beer and sighed. 'You and Mandy deserve better than this, Gwennie.'

'We're fine,' she said reassuringly.

The lapsed into silence and then she said, 'You're worried about something else, aren't you?'

'Me? No.'

Gwen looked him in the eye. 'Clifford, we promised we would never lie to each other or hold anything back. What is it you're worrying about?'

He sighed. 'Not much gets past you, Gwennie,' he smiled. He took another swig of his drink as if to give himself some Dutch courage. 'We've been helping a lot of people since the snow came . . .'

'Yes.'

'And now it seems that some things are going missing.'

Gwen frowned. 'Gone missing?'

'Aunt Aggie told me that Mrs Wright has lost a pearl brooch, Granny Morrison says her late husband's watch is missing and Reverend McKay in St Mary's says someone has tampered with the collection box at the back of the church.'

Gwen took in her breath. 'But who would do such a thing?'

'It's not always the same people who go out at the same time. That leaves us with three distinct possibilities,' said Clifford. 'The Frenchie, Isaac Light and me. The only certainty is that it wasn't me.'

'I can't believe either of them would steal.'

'Nor can I,' said Clifford, 'but it leaves a nasty taste in the mouth.'

'And you are worried that if this gets out it could ruin our reputation?' said Gwen.

'I think it may already have damaged the Frenchie,' said Clifford. 'Two of his biggest customers have gone elsewhere.'

'That could be down to the weather,' said Gwen.

'Could be, I suppose,' said Clifford but he looked far from convinced.

'What are you going to do?' said Gwen.

Clifford drained his glass. 'I don't know,' he said with a shrug. 'Thank God the thaw is on its way.'

As he made his way back to the bar for another drink, Gwen chewed her cheek thoughtfully. What sort of person took advantage of people in dire straits? These were hard times and they couldn't afford to lose the goodwill they had built up over the years. She'd better tell Clifford to steer clear of the Frenchie and Isaac until this had all blown over.

Thirteen

As soon as Connie came off duty, Eva drew her attention to the notice board in the nurses' home. 'Have you seen this?'

Home Sister had stuck a memo on the board. *Staff will please note that because of the present situation, the hospital laundry is operating a three day week. This means delays in getting clean uniforms and sheets are inevitable. Nurses may be required to wash their own dresses if necessary. Collection of pink boxes are as follows* . . . There followed a list of numbers. Connie's box wasn't due for collection until next week.

'At this rate, I'll never get my letter,' she groaned.

'What letter?' asked Eva and Connie explained.

'You might be in luck,' said Eva. 'What with all the power cuts, they might not have got around to washing the nurses' uniforms yet.'

'I suppose,' said Connie cautiously.

'I'm on an early tomorrow,' said Eva brightly. 'I could go over there in person and ask for you if you like.'

'Better still,' smiled Connie. 'We could both go together. I'm on an early too.'

As soon as they'd finished their duty they'd met up at 2.15 p.m. and wrapping up warmly, set out for the laundry.

'When the laundry comes in,' said the supervisor after Connie told her why they'd come, 'the girls go through every box.' She led them into a heat-filled room. There were several large presses and a long bare wood table. In the middle of the table was a large pile of sheets. Two girls were folding the sheets while a third woman eased them through the press. Every time she brought the heavy pad down to press the sheet free of creases, a hiss of steam filled the air.

'You'd be surprised what we find in the pockets,' the supervisor said, not stopping for any introductions. The women looked up as Connie and Eva walked through the steam room but nobody smiled. 'Bus tickets, hankies, pocket books, pens,' the supervisor was on a roll now. 'We found a bottom set of teeth once,' she cackled and turned around.

'What did you do with them?' Connie asked anxiously.

'Everything gets sent back,' said the supervisor with emphasis. 'It gets put into a brown paper bag and left in the laundry box.'

'That's why Betty had that half a sandwich in her laundry box,' Eva said behind her hand and into Connie's ear.

Connie smiled. They'd all had a laugh when Betty showed them. It was rock solid and going mouldy. Betty binned it.

'The trouble is,' said the supervisor going deeper and deeper into the building, 'everything has got out of kilter. We've got far too many boxes and not enough room.'

They had arrived beside a brown door. The supervisor flung it open and Connie took in her breath.

'Lummy Charlie,' gasped Eva.

The room was packed floor to ceiling with pink boxes. 'We not only do the laundry from this hospital but Swandean and Courtlands as well,' said the supervisor. She took a tally book from a shelf. 'What was your number?'

'Triple seven,' said Connie faintly. It would take hours to go through all this lot.

'It's in here somewhere,' the supervisor said cheerfully. 'I'll leave you to it.'

It took them twenty minutes before Eva found Connie's box because the number was facing the wall but a second later, all her letters were in her hands. Connie tore open the envelope while Eva rearranged the boxes back into place. 'Why don't you wait until we get back to the nurses' home?' she cautioned.

'Because I can't wait a second longer,' said Connie turning the upside down paper the right way up. As she read, she could feel the colour draining from her face.

'Connie? Whatever is it? You've gone as white as a sheet.'

The supervisor walked back into the room. 'Ah,' she smiled. 'You've obviously found it. Not bad news, I hope?'

'Not exactly,' said Connie, knowing that the woman was concerned that there had been a death in the family. 'Someone I thought I would never see again has been terribly injured.'

They walked back to the nurses' home in silence. Connie was desperately trying to absorb what the letter had said.

'Come to my room,' said Eva. 'I've got some cherry brandy. It's not much but you look as if you could do with something.'

Connie sat on the bed and took out the letter again while Eva found a glass and washed her tooth mug. 'If there's anything I can do . . .' Eva began.

Connie swirled the dark liquid a couple of times and then downed it in one. It was heavy and sweet, not exactly pleasant to her palate and it burned on the way down. She shuddered involuntarily.

'I know,' said Eva. 'It tastes pretty ghastly but it does the trick.'

'*Dear Miss Dixon,*' Connie read aloud, '*I am writing to you about your brother Kenneth Dixon. I am sorry the writing is so lousy, but it's the best I can do. I know the hospital has been in contact with your mother but she has never replied. We made contact through a local charity which helps ex-servicemen and they gave us your address.*'

'What on earth does that mean?' Eva interrupted.

Connie shrugged. 'I can't believe that Mum has never replied to their letters. She wants nothing more in the world than to find my brother.'

'I remember you said you'd lost touch,' said Eva sitting on the bed beside her.

'It's a long story,' said Connie, 'suffice to say that he walked out of our lives in 1938 and we've never heard from him since.'

Eva pulled a face. 'Do you think this letter is on the level?'

Connie shrugged again.

'Go on with the letter,' said Eva jerking her head.

'*We are both at the Queen Victoria Hospital in East Grinstead,*' Connie continued. '*We are looked after in an ex-army Nissen hut at the back of the main building. It's not as bad as it sounds. Matron is a thoroughly good egg and turns a blind eye to our grogging parties and Mr McIndoe, or the Maestro as we call him, gives the chaps their lives back again. We enjoy the Sussex countryside and those who are well enough can play tennis and squash. Your brother hasn't quite made it to the courts yet. He still has a bit of work to be done on his hand. He is making really good progress but I know he longs for some contact with you or any member of your family. The Skipper on our ward seems to think it would speed up his recovery if you could find it in your heart to forgive him. We have no idea what it's all about but the guilt he carries weighs him down. If, for any reason, you find it too hard, I should like to offer myself as a mediator. Could you please contact me at the above address? Kenneth has no idea that I have written to you. Yours Sincerely, William Garfield.*'

'East Grinstead,' Eva mused. 'That's where they nursed badly burned airmen during the war.'

'The Guinea Pig Club,' said Connie. She had seen the story in the *Tit-Bits* magazine, how a young New Zealand surgeon had pioneered skin graft operations on young men who had escaped from burning bombers and Spitfires. 'I wonder if that means Kenneth was in the RAF during the war?'

'You'll go, of course,' said Eva.

147

Connie stared down at the words again. 'I want to but I'm forbidden even to speak his name.'

'Good Lord!' cried Eva. 'What on earth did he do?'

'It didn't seem so dreadful at the time,' said Connie, 'but Ga insists no one is to mention his name.'

'The more I hear about your great aunt,' said Eva, 'the worse she sounds. She must be a real tartar.'

Connie sighed. 'It's never really bothered me before. When you grow up with someone, you sort of accept that that's the way things are but I know she'll go loopy if she finds out.'

'So what happened?' Eva persisted.

'He let someone into the house and I was attacked,' said Connie cautiously. She still wasn't comfortable talking about it.

'Blimey,' said Eva. 'Were the police involved?'

'It was all hushed up,' said Connie.

Eva shook her head. 'But you can't hold grudges forever, can you? Your brother wasn't very old, was he? I'm sure he didn't do it on purpose.'

Connie hesitated. Eva was right. Kenneth couldn't have done it on purpose. He was little more than a child himself when it happened. Somehow, the fact that he'd always been her big brother had made her forget that.

'Are you going to see him?'

'Too right I am,' said Connie, suddenly finding courage. 'He's my brother.'

There was a sharp knock on the door. 'There's someone down-stairs wants to see you,' said a timid voice when Eva opened the door.

'Send them up then,' said Eva.

The girl looked this way and that before whispering conspira-torially, 'I can't. It's a man.'

Eva pulled a face at Connie. 'I won't be a minute. Help yourself to another cherry brandy if you want.' The door closed softly as she left.

Connie didn't want any more brandy so she read the letter again instead. It was wonderful and worrying at the same time. Wonderful to know Kenneth was alive and where he was but worrying that he might be horribly injured. Mum would be pleased to have news of him ... or would she? He had been such a handsome young man. How would Mum feel if he was permanently disfigured?

She thought back to that last day, the day Kenneth left home. She had blanked it out for so many years now that it was hard to think about it again. She remembered afterwards and the point when her head had finally stopped spinning and she was in her bed with a clean nightdress on. Ga was by her bedside sponging her hot forehead with a cold flannel.

She remembered that she'd moaned a little and Ga had said, 'How do you feel?'

'Awful. I want to die.'

Then Ga had said something really odd. 'Good. Constance, I want you never to forget how you feel right now.'

And that's exactly what she'd done. She had never forgotten that her mouth felt like gravel and her tongue seemed far too big. She remembered that her head was pounding and her stomach felt as if someone had hit it with a fence panel. She could recall that the light in the room was subdued and yet it was too strong for her eyes. She could also remember Ga lifting her head as she took a sip of water from the glass she was holding. It was one of the very few intimate moments she'd ever had with Ga.

Eva bounced back into the room. 'You'll never guess what?' she cried. Her eyes were alive with excitement. 'This is so weird. *My* brother is downstairs. He's offering to take both of us out for a meal.'

'Oh, no,' said Connie. 'You'll want to be alone, to talk.'

'Come on,' said Eva, taking her uniform off. 'It'll be fun. You'll like him. He's very dashing.'

'Is he the bomb disposal man?'

'The very same,' said Eva. She was standing in her petticoat as she went through her wardrobe looking for something to wear. 'I didn't realise that he was the one they sent for when that bomb went off.'

Connie shook her head. 'I need to be on my own for a bit. I need to do some thinking.'

'Rubbish,' said Eva pulling on her high heels. She pulled Connie to her feet and pushed her towards the door. 'You'll only brood and get depressed. Go. Get changed. I'll call for you in ten minutes.'

Connie walked down the corridor to her own room with mixed feelings. Eva was probably right. She would have brooded and made herself feel miserable about Kenneth, but she wasn't sure she wanted a jolly night out either. When she got to her room, Connie picked up the picture of Kenneth on her locker and stared at his face. She put her finger to her lips, kissed it and then placed it over her brother's cheek. Brushing away a tear, she opened her wardrobe and surveyed the contents. She had nothing to wear. Even her uniform looked better than some of the stuff hanging there. She opened Betty's wardrobe. Most of her things looked as dull as Connie's, except for one dress. It was a brightly coloured paisley dress in pinks and purple with a sweetheart neckline. Connie pulled it out and held it against herself. Would Betty mind if she borrowed it? She should really ask her first but there wasn't time. Connie slipped it over her shoulders and it fitted her perfectly. She fluffed up her hair and put on a bit of make-up. She felt a bit guilty about Betty's dress, but she looked fabulous even if she said so herself. What was Eva's brother like? Heavens, she didn't even know his name.

Fourteen

Roger Maxwell took them to Mitchell's in the Arcade. The restaurant which was on two floors had become a symbol of resilience during the war. Its sister restaurant near the New Town Hall in Chapel Road had been bombed out in September 1940, the direct hit also taking out the shop next door. Mercifully, the New Town Hall got off lightly with no structural damage and only minimal damage from two other bombs which fell in the car park at the back and in the road at the same time.

Mitchell's in the Arcade was hugely popular. Food was rationed but not in restaurants and cafés. At lunchtimes they often had a queue of people reaching out into Montague Street, but at this time of day, 4.30 p.m., there were few customers. Eva, Connie and Roger sat next to the window so that they could enjoy watching the passers-by. It was a bit early for tea but they were all hungry and hadn't eaten since lunchtime so they ordered the fish and chips.

Once the waitress had gone, Connie had a chance to have a good look at Eva's brother. He wasn't exactly handsome but he had a pleasant face. He looked about thirty, with long fingers, some heavily stained with nicotine. His eyes were grey and he had the same laughter lines on his face as his sister. He took out a packet of Players Navy Cut and offered them round. Connie shook her head.

'You smoke too much,' said Eva.

'It helps me with my nerves,' Roger smiled playfully and pretended that he had the shakes. 'It keeps me steady when I do the bombs.'

'Don't,' said Eva looking down at her hands.

'I'm sorry,' he said remorsefully, 'and you're right. I should give up. I'll try. I will, I promise.'

Placated, she smiled again.

'So tell me,' he said stubbing out the half-finished cigarette, 'how's the training going?'

Eva and Connie spent the next few minutes telling him about the events of the past year and a bit and Roger laughed heartily at some of the tales they had to tell. 'I'm surprised that you have such fun,' he said. 'I always thought of nursing as a demanding and difficult job.'

'It is most of the time,' said Connie, 'but we can have a laugh now and then.'

'We're the same as you,' said Eva. 'We have a black humour too. It's the only thing that keeps you going at times.'

Roger nodded sagely.

Their tea arrived. The portions were small, but they all enjoyed their meal and a round of bread and butter served with it made it go a little further.

'Are you staying with the bomb squad?' said Eva and Connie could tell she was dreading his reply.

'It suits me at the moment,' said Roger. 'I've no ties, no family, and no children to worry about if anything should happen . . . so why not?'

Eva avoided eye contact.

'I am very careful, sis,' he said.

'Mum and I worry about you,' she said dully.

'Well, don't,' he said firmly.

'Will you stay in the army?' Connie asked.

He smiled. 'At the moment, I like what I do. In fact, the day

I start worrying about myself is the day I pack it in. Changing the subject, when can you girls get an evening off?'

'Saturday,' said Connie glancing at her friend to confirm it. 'With a late pass we can be out until 11 p.m.'

'Why?' said Eva.

'Do you enjoy dancing?' he said looking directly at Connie. Connie grinned.

He looked thoughtful. 'Ah, but do they have any decent dances around here?'

'There's one every Saturday in the Assembly Hall,' Connie said. 'They're quite good. I used to go with Jane Jackson but I haven't been for ages.'

'Good,' said Roger. 'Then it's all settled. We'll do it this coming Saturday.'

'You're a fast worker,' Connie laughed. 'Can I ask you something?'

'Go ahead,' said Roger taking a sideways glance at his sister. Eva was giving Connie a quizzical look.

'Do you know anything about the burns unit at East Grinstead?'

Almost as soon as the words were out of her mouth, Eva shot her a wounded look and Connie realised she had been thoughtless and crass. Thankfully, Roger seemed completely unfazed.

'I'm told it's the best damned unit in the country,' he said. 'Why?'

Connie took a deep breath and told him about the letter and Kenneth.

'You'll go and see him of course,' said Roger.

Connie nodded. 'My family won't like it but, yes, I will.'

'If you're nervous about seeing him,' said Roger, 'I'll take you.'

Connie was surprised to realise her heart had skipped a beat.

'That's all right, Roger,' said Eva. 'I've already offered.'

Roger looked concerned. 'Some of the chaps look a bit odd,' he said. 'I don't know about your brother but you must be prepared that you might see some terrible injuries.'

Connie nodded gravely.

'Having said that,' Roger went on, 'you'll be amazed at their courage. They don't let what's happened to them stop them enjoying life and the whole town has taken them to their hearts. They go dancing, and to the pubs and pictures just like anybody else. The doctors do their best to get them back to normal. There's no question of shutting them away somewhere.'

The waitress came and offered them ice cream. They didn't take much persuading and she hurried away to fetch some.

'Right,' said Roger when she'd gone. 'After ice cream the night is still young. Who fancies coming to the pictures with me?'

'What's on?' Eva shrugged.

'*Great Expectations* with John Mills at the Rivoli, *Notorious*, that's an Alfred Hitchcock film with Cary Grant at the Odeon and *The Postman Always Rings Twice* at the Dome, with Lana Turner,' said Roger reeling them off.

'*Notorious*,' said Eva and Connie together.

'Cary Grant it is then,' Roger grinned.

Their ice cream was delicious and the bill came to a whopping £1/13/- but Roger wouldn't hear of taking anything from them. As they settled into their cinema seats, although Connie was glad she'd asked him about the hospital at East Grinstead, a deep sense of foreboding had settled onto her shoulders. She would write to William Garfield when she got back to the hospital and arrange to go and see Kenneth on her next day off.

It wasn't until lunchtime that Connie realised something was wrong. It had been two days since she and Eva had gone to the pictures with her brother. The film was excellent and Cary Grant was wonderfully handsome. When Eva popped out to the toilet, Roger had asked Connie again if she would like him to go with her to East Grinstead. She dearly wanted to say yes but was afraid of offending Eva.

'I can't get away until next week,' she said.

'Well, let me know,' said Roger quickly as he saw Eva coming their way, 'and I'll drive you there.'

Connie remembered thinking how kind he was and wishing it was Eugène, the Frenchie asking her. She'd have jumped at the chance to be alone in a car with him and as soon as the thought ran through her head, a wave of guilt washed over her. What was she thinking about? She wasn't going to East Grinstead on a jolly for heaven's sake. She was going to see her brother and who knows what sort of a state he'd be in. And besides, Eugène wasn't available. He belonged to Mavis Hampton.

Right now, she had other concerns. Eva hadn't come onto the ward this morning and nobody seemed to know where she was. Connie kept looking over her shoulder as the staff did morning prayers together and after Sister had read the night report but still there was no sign of Eva.

Connie began her day by getting the remaining bed-bound patients washed. Without Eva, she had to manage the breakfast trolley on her own but luckily there were only two patients who needed help with eating. She couldn't help looking at the ward doors, because she thought that at any minute Eva would fly through them all apologies and embarrassment, but they remained firmly shut. Although she had to hurry her patients a little more than she would have liked, Connie was able to get everything done before the ward round. Sister was on her tail to make sure all the beds were tidy and the lockers wiped before Matron appeared, so what had happened to Eva had to wait.

It wasn't until her mid-morning break that Connie had time to ask around. Nobody seemed to have any idea where Eva was and by now Connie was getting worried. She knew Eva had gone out with her boyfriend for a drink but she hadn't got a late pass so she should have been in by ten. Connie also knew Phyllis had gone to the pictures last night but when she asked her if she had seen Eva, Phyllis looked blank.

'When I got in,' she said, 'I heard the porter say, "You're the last one," so she must have come in before me.'

Connie frowned. 'So why didn't she come on duty?'

Phyllis shrugged. 'Perhaps she has a hangover.'

Connie's morning dragged slowly. As soon as Sister sent her to lunch, she headed for the nurses' home and tapped lightly on Eva's door. No one came. Where was she? Standing close to the wood, Connie could hear an odd rattling sound. Eva must be in there, she thought. So why doesn't she answer the door?

'Eva?' Connie knocked a little louder. But still no one came. She tried the door handle and the door wasn't locked. As she opened it, she was hit by the rank smell of vomit.

Eva was still in bed. She made no attempt to get up and the iron bedstead was rattling violently against the wall. Connie moved anxiously towards the untidy heap of bedclothes and saw at once that Eva was far from well. Her face was ashen and there was dried vomit all over the pillow, on her face and in her hair. She had her eyes half open but they were unfocused. When Connie said her name, there was no reaction at all. She looked as if she was frozen to death but when Connie touched her forehead, she was burning up.

Connie raced from the room and downstairs where she rang Home Sister on the internal phone. By the time Sister Abbott arrived, Connie had already fetched a bowl of warm water from the bathroom and was washing Eva's face. Sister Abbott took charge immediately and Connie was told to go for a doctor.

Dr Greene came straight away. Connie hovered by the door but Home Sister shooed her away. 'There's no need for you to stay, nurse,' she said curtly.

'Is she going to be all right?' Connie was really worried. Dr Greene was listening to Eva's chest.

'It's nothing,' said Home Sister. 'A touch of flu, that's all. Off you go now.'

Outside in the corridor, Connie looked at her fob watch. It

was too late to go to the canteen; she had to get back on duty. She'd have to go without lunch. She stayed outside until Eva was stretchered to the nurses' sickbay and then ran all the way back to the ward.

Connie's first thought when she came off duty was Eva but the nurse on duty in the sickbay was reluctant to let her come in. 'Sister will kill me,' she said looking nervously over her shoulder. 'She said no visitors.'

'But she's my friend,' Connie protested mildly. 'I was the one who found her.'

The girl relented. Eva was just as pale but she had stopped trembling and looked more rested.

'How are you feeling?' Connie whispered.

'Terrible,' Eva croaked. 'My head is banging and my mouth feels like the bottom of a parrot's cage.'

'I thought you might be suffering from a hangover.'

'Fat chance,' she said. 'We're saving every bean we can to get married.'

'Does he know you're here?'

Eva shook her head. 'Don't tell him. He'll want to come and nobody must know about us.'

'He'll be devastated if I don't tell him.'

Eva sighed. 'Then tell him not to come.'

Connie nodded and thought that there was no way Steven would stay away once he knew. He was potty about her. 'Get some sleep,' she said touching Eva lightly on the shoulder. 'I'll come back tomorrow.'

'Connie,' Eva whispered as she turned to go. 'Tell my mum I'm here. I want . . .' her eyes filled with tears. 'I want to see my mum.'

Connie's heart constricted. Talk to the Maxwells? Being best friends with Eva was one thing but making contact with the family was quite another. But one look at Eva's face and she knew she couldn't refuse. The girl looked so ill.

157

'Have you got someone I could telephone in an emergency?'

Eva shook her head. 'We're not as organised as you are.'

Connie swallowed hard. So she'd have to go in person. A tear rolled down Eva's cheek and Connie's heart went out to her. The poor girl had already suffered so much losing the love of her life and it was obvious that for just this once, she wanted to be a little girl again. She wanted her mum.

'Don't you worry about a thing,' said Connie. 'I'll get the bus over there as soon as I've changed.'

'Thank you,' Eva mouthed.

Connie patted her arm. 'Now you get some sleep. I'll come back tomorrow.'

Connie went back to her own room and changed quickly. She put on a smart hand-knitted twinset her mother had made and livened it up with a string of pearls from Woolworths. She wanted to create a good impression. As soon as she was ready, Connie wrote a note for Steven telling him to be cautious. '*Eva will be fine with rest,*' she told him. '*She sends her love.*' After that, Connie left the note in the pigeonhole Eva and Steven used.

The snow was receding all the time now and the bus services were back to normal. She didn't have to wait long. The house was part way up Durrington Hill, a Victorian cottage with grey flint work on the walls. The garden, although bare at this time of year, was neat and tidy and as she walked up the tiny path, she could hear someone playing the piano. Eva knocked on the door. When it opened a small rotund woman who looked like a much older version of Eva stood on the step.

'Mrs Maxwell?' Connie began cautiously.

'Yes.'

'I'm a . . .' she almost said friend but drew back in case Mrs Maxwell took exception, 'a work colleague of Eva's.'

Mrs Maxwell's face broke into a wide and welcoming smile. 'Come in, come in, dear,' she said hurrying ahead of Connie. 'Please excuse the mess.' She led Connie into the front room, taking off her wrap-over apron as she went. 'Can I offer you some tea?'

An older woman came out into the hallway and followed them to the door.

'This is one of the nurses Eva works with,' Mrs Maxwell said and turning back to Connie she said, 'Sit down, dear. Would you like some tea, or I can make coffee if you prefer it. I know you young girls prefer coffee, don't you? We never had it much in my . . .'

Her words died on her lips as the older woman put her hand on her arm. 'Something's happened, Vi. That's right, isn't it, something's happened to our Eva?'

Mrs Maxwell's hand flew to her mouth.

'It's not that bad,' Connie said quickly. She pulled her scarf away from her neck and lowered herself onto the chair. 'But you're right. Eva's not well. She's in the nurses' sickbay.'

The older woman came right into the room and sat opposite Connie. She was about the same age as Ga but she looked a lot fitter. Her white hair had been cut in a bob and she had deep finger waves. Her lined face was full of concern but she made no sound.

'This is my mother, Eva's grandmother,' said Mrs Maxwell.

'Cecilia,' said the older woman, 'but everyone calls me Cissy.'

'How do you do?' Connie flustered. 'I don't know exactly what's wrong, but I think she may have the flu.' She went on to describe how she'd found Eva and what had happened.

Mrs Maxwell sat down. 'Is she going to be all right?'

'I'm sure of it,' said Connie, 'especially as Home Sister didn't see the need to inform you. She would have told you if it had been something serious.'

Their relief was almost palpable but Mrs Maxwell frowned crossly. 'She should have told me anyway. I'm her mother.'

Connie couldn't argue with that.

'Would you like me to take your coat?' said Cissy.

'I'll get the tea,' said Mrs Maxwell suddenly as if remembering her manners. As she left the room, the older woman rearranged her cushions to give herself more support.

'You're Gwen Dixon's girl, aren't you?' Cissy spoke casually and when she saw the alarm in Connie's eyes, she put her hand up. 'It's all right. I know how your great aunt feels about this family.' She paused and added thoughtfully, 'It must have taken quite a bit of courage for you to come here. I appreciate what you have done.'

Connie felt her face flush as she looked down at her hands.

Mrs Maxwell brought in a tea tray and the best china cups. 'What time are the visiting hours, dear?'

'Six thirty until seven fifteen,' said Connie automatically glancing at the clock. It said ten past six. She would never make it tonight. 'But Eva's not on the wards. She's in the nurses' sickbay. You could take a chance if you wanted to. They'll probably let you in if you ask.'

'I shall go to see her tomorrow,' said Mrs Maxwell.

'Did you come on the bus?' the old lady asked.

Connie nodded.

'Have you had your tea?'

Connie took her cup. 'Not yet. I'll get some fish and chips on the way home.'

'You'll do no such thing,' said Mrs Maxwell. 'You can have your tea with us. I was just about to dish up when you knocked on the door.'

'I don't want to put you to any trouble,' said Connie realising for the first time just how hungry she was and remembering that she hadn't had a thing since the mid-morning break.

'No trouble at all, dear,' said Mrs Maxwell getting up and going back out of the room. There was an awkward silence. Connie looked around the room and was startled to see a picture on the dresser. It was an identical picture to the one Ga had in her bedroom. A handsome young man in army uniform stood sedately next to an aspidistra plant in a formal pose. Without stopping to think, Connie blurted out, 'Who's that?'

'Arthur,' said Cissy. 'My late husband.'

Connie was stunned into silence. The old lady scrutinised Connie's face. 'How is Olive, by the way?'

'Fine,' said Connie brightly but she could see that the brevity of her answer wasn't enough so she added, 'She has trouble with an arthritic knee but apart from that . . .'

'She and I used to be best friends, you know.'

Connie blinked in surprise. No, she didn't know that. Ga had never once told her they'd been friends.

'Agatha, Olive and Cissy,' the old woman mused. 'We were inseparable.'

Connie frowned. If they were all such good friends, what on earth could have happened to pull them apart? It must have had something to do with Arthur. And if he was Cissy's husband, why would Ga keep his picture by her bedside and put a red rose next to it twice a year? She was about to ask when Mrs Maxwell returned to tell her dinner was dished up. They both stood up and as Connie stepped back to let the old woman go first, she noticed that Cissy had put her bony finger on her lips. She obviously didn't want Eva's mother to know what they had been talking about, so Connie knew the questions would have to wait.

161

Fifteen

Eva made slow progress. Her mother came to see her the next day, much to the annoyance of Sister Abbott who was hoping to get her back on the wards as soon as possible.

'You had no right to interfere,' Sister Abbott told Connie. 'It's my responsibility to speak to parents. You're getting above yourself, nurse.'

'I only did what Nurse O'Hara asked me to do, Sister,' Connie protested mildly.

'And don't answer back,' snapped Sister Abbott.

Someone with a car had brought Mrs Maxwell to the hospital so she took her daughter home. As Connie watched her friend go, she had no regrets. Sister Abbott might give her a black mark and Ga would have an apoplectic fit if she knew Connie had gone to Eva's house, but Eva would be in the best place.

Alone in her room that night, Connie found herself going over a few of life's puzzles. What could have happened between Aunt Aggie, Ga and Cissy Maxwell to break their friendship? And why did Ga have the same photograph of Cissy's husband in her room? Could it be that they were both in love with the same man? Ga had never married. Surely two women in love with one man was hardly enough to split two families?

Her thoughts turned inevitably to the Frenchie. He was engaged to someone else but Connie couldn't stop thinking about him. Over time she'd realised that she was hopelessly in love with him but of course she would never act on it. He belonged to Mavis. She was very beautiful but if he married that awful woman . . . well, it didn't bear thinking about. How simple life would have been if she'd stayed with Emmett. Funny, but she could hardly remember what he looked like now, except that she'd once told Rene that he was very handsome and reminded her of Gary Cooper.

The evening before she went to see her brother, Connie took the bus up to Durrington. Eva was already looking rested and relaxed after being pampered by her mother. The three women greeted her warmly.

'I wish I could come with you tomorrow,' said Eva. She was lying on the sofa with her feet up. 'I feel badly letting you down like this.'

'Don't be silly,' said Connie. 'You can't help being ill and besides, I think you should know, your brother has agreed to come with me.'

'Roger?' cried Eva. 'Connie Dixon, you are a dark horse.'

'Oh, it's nothing like that,' Connie protested. 'He telephoned to check when I was going and said that although he couldn't come and fetch me, he'd meet me off the train.'

'Who is meeting you off the train?' Mrs Maxwell interrupted them with a tray of tea.

'Roger,' teased Eva.

Vi Maxwell beamed. 'That's nice, dear.'

The same scenario was repeated with Eva's grandmother, Cissy. 'It would certainly be a turn up for the books if you and Roger get together,' she smiled.

'He's only meeting me from the train,' cried Connie. Heavens above, they were hearing wedding bells already!

'Does Olive know?' and when Connie shook her head, Cissy added, 'I didn't think so.'

They were interrupted by a knock on the door and Eva's fiancé, Dr Steven Mitchell stood on the doorstep. He was tall with a lean body and long artistic fingers. He wore glasses and his hair was slightly receding. After introductions, Connie, Vi and Cissy went into the kitchen and left Eva and Steven alone. 'Don't bother with the bus back,' she called to Connie. 'Steven says he'll drive you.' Connie was secretly pleased. A car ride was always preferable because it was door to door. She was tired after the long day and didn't fancy the walk from the bus stop especially when she had to be up early the next day. While they waited, Vi offered her some sponge cake and they sat at the kitchen table.

'Can I ask you something?' Connie ventured, her cheeks bulging.

'What happened between Olive and me?' Cissy pre-empted.

Connie nodded and pushed a stray crumb back into her mouth with her finger.

'It was because of Arthur,' Cissy sighed. 'He was the love of my life, but he was with Olive to begin with.'

Connie raised an eyebrow. 'So that's why she has his picture on her dressing table,' she blurted out. A hurt look flicked across Cissy's face and Connie immediately regretted what she'd said. 'Oh, I'm sorry. I shouldn't have told you that. Please forgive me.'

'There's nothing to forgive,' said Cissy. 'When Arthur came back from the Boer War, he only had one leg. It never bothered me, after all, he was the same person. She tried to make a go of it but Olive couldn't bear him to touch her. We were all friends together. We grew up together and when he turned to me for comfort, I fell in love with him.'

'I see,' said Connie.

Cissy shrugged deeply. 'I don't regret what I did and I did my best to make him happy. We had a good life together.'

'He always loved you, Mum,' said Vi.

Connie was still struggling to understand. 'Is that why Olive, I mean Ga, is still upset with you, because you married Arthur?'

Cissy nodded. 'But there was something between our families

long before then. She and I went against the grain by being friends.'

'A bit like Eva and me, then,' said Connie.

'Exactly like you and Eva,' smiled Cissy.

'So what was it that tore the families apart in the first place?' said Connie, intrigued.

Cissy shrugged. 'I never knew what it was but it went all the way back to the last century. Something to do with Little Mac.'

Eva frowned. 'Little Mac? Who was that?'

Cissy pouted her bottom lip and shook her head. 'Some long-dead relative or other.'

*

'I've got nowhere to go, Mum.'

Stan was standing on the doorstep in the pouring rain with only the clothes he stood up in.

Her heart was already racing but how could she refuse? He was her son. She knew the rumours, she'd heard the gossip and she'd read the newspapers but she couldn't turn him away, could she?

'I did everything properly, just like you wanted. I looked after her, Mum. She was happy, I swear it.'

'If she was happy,' she snapped, 'how come she did what she did?'

'We can't talk on the doorstep, Mum,' he said looking around. 'Let me in and we'll talk about it.'

She hesitated. A woman walking her dog peered in at the gate.

He glanced behind him and then leaned towards his mother and whispered, 'You don't want all the neighbours hearing our business do you?'

She stepped back and let him through. He made his way to the only warm room in the house and flopped into a chair. 'Make us a cup of tea, Mum?'

Reluctantly she filled the kettle and put it onto the New World gas stove.

'If you could let me have my old room,' he was saying, 'just for a while. I'll keep out of your way.'

She kept her back to him. 'I can't go through all that again,' she said cautiously.

'You won't have to, Mum,' he said rising to his feet and putting his arm around her shoulder. 'I've changed. Doesn't the fact that I got married prove that I have changed?'

She said nothing.

'I'm sorry I hurt you, Mum.' He had both arms around her now. 'It won't happen again, I promise.'

She found herself relaxing. He wasn't a bad boy. That first time he didn't realise what he was doing. That stupid girl was just as much to blame. Mud sticks, that's all. And he'd kept out of trouble since, hadn't he?

The kettle whistled and he let go of her so that she could make the tea.

'I've got to start all over again, Mum. These past few weeks have been awful.'

Her heart constricted. She turned towards him. He was sitting back at the table with his head in his hands. His shoulders were shaking. She sat opposite him and took his hands in hers. 'Oh! What happened to your hands?'

'Burnt.' He looked up at her, his face streaked with tears. 'Someone set fire to my house, Mum. I've only just come out of hospital. I've been in there for nearly two weeks. What did I do to deserve all this?'

She was so moved she almost cried with him. Her boy. Her poor boy.

'Help me, Mum,' he said brokenly. 'Please.'

'Promise me,' she began, 'promise me that what your wife did had nothing to do with you.'

'Absolutely not, Mum. How can you even think . . .' he broke off and reached in his pocket for a handkerchief. He blew his nose noisily. 'What can I say to make you believe me?'

166

'I want to, son,' she earnestly. 'I really want to.'

'We were happy,' he said. 'We were trying for a baby. I have no idea why she ran out in front of that bus but I swear if I could have stopped her I would have done. They torched the house because they don't want me to have Rosemary.'

She looked up sharply. 'You really think someone burned your house deliberately? But who? Who would do such a thing?'

'Her family of course. I know Rosemary is not my child but I'm the only father she has ever known. She loved me, Mum,' and seeing her expression added quickly, 'like a father. Her grandparents don't want me to have custody, so they set fire to the place, hoping to get rid of me too.'

She'd put her hand to her mouth. 'What do the police say? Surely . . .'

'They're investigating,' he said with a shrug. 'But there's no doubt, Mum. Someone poured petrol through the letterbox and if I had been asleep, I would have been a goner.'

'What will you do now?' She was putting a knitted cosy over the teapot.

'Claim on the insurance and then fight them through the courts to get Rosemary,' he said.

She handed him a cup and saucer. 'Do you think it's wise, considering your past history . . .?'

'I've changed, Mum,' he snapped. 'I keep telling you that. Dear God, when your own mother . . .'

'I'm sorry,' she cried, reaching out for him. 'You're right. This is not your fault. You're not a bad boy.'

'So I can stay?'

'You can stay as long as you like.'

He sighed. 'Thanks, Mum.'

When he'd finished his tea, he yawned. 'I'm dog-tired, Mum.'

'Your bed is all made up,' she said.

He went upstairs. As she watched his receding back, all the old nerves came flooding back. Had he really changed? She'd have to keep a close eye on him until she was absolutely sure. But then he turned at the top of the stairs and smiled and her heart was lifted. He was such a good looking boy, just like his father had been. It wasn't his fault girls threw themselves at him. She made her way back to the kitchen to wash up the cups. Stan was back. Her precious boy was home at last.

Sixteen

Connie stared out of the window of the train. Her only travelling companion, a middle-aged woman was engrossed in a book. It was a week since she had had a reply from William Garfield and she was already on the way to the hospital. It was a shame Eva still hadn't fully recovered from that very nasty bout of flu. Much to Sister Abbott's disgust, Mrs Maxwell told her that Eva was still under the weather because she had a bad chest and wouldn't be back at work until next week at the earliest.

Connie hadn't told the family what she was doing. Ga would have forbidden her to go and her mother would have wanted to go with her. Connie wanted to see her brother first. She had no idea how badly injured he had been and she couldn't let her mother go unprepared.

Connie had dressed carefully. Under her winter coat, she wore a grey pinstriped dress with a white peter pan collar. Her dress had maroon piping down the side seam and so she had matched it with maroon shoes and a maroon bag. The bag, which had come from a jumble sale, was a bit ancient but it made an attractive ensemble. Her hair was caught up in curls and she wore a grey beret on the side of her head.

The English countryside looked beautiful at this time of year. After the terrible winter, the signs of spring were on their way. The snow had been followed by severe floods in some areas, but along the south coast, the weather was much milder than up country. The fields were newly ploughed and the spring lambs frolicked on the downs. The sun glistened on the rivers and already the birds were beginning to nest. Whenever they went through a village or hamlet, Connie saw children playing, ramblers in country lanes and mothers pushing their well wrapped up babies in their coach-built prams. At one railway crossing, three boys on bicycles waited for the train to pass and at another, two children leaned over the crossing gates and waved to the train. Every now and then she would catch sight of something which would bring back a stark reminder that the country had just come through five years of war and misery. It may have been a man with only one leg getting about on crutches, or someone in a wheelchair or a bombed-out building. The scars were ever present.

She leaned against the headrest and closed her eyes. It was a miracle the letter had reached her. Connie could only suppose that Ga must have intercepted all the others. She had always been adamant that they should have nothing more to do with Kenneth.

Connie relaxed and let her mind drift back to that day, the day Kenneth left home. She didn't mind thinking about the stiffness of clean white sheets and the smell of the lavender talc Ga had put on her body afterwards. What she didn't want to remember was the fact that her arms hurt and that for a time she had been held against her will. Not that she'd had much sympathy.

'Don't you ever,' Ga had said angrily and through gritted teeth, 'ever let a man get you drunk again.'

Connie's eyes flew open. At the time, she'd been too scared to say anything but now she realised that it wasn't her fault. She'd hardly had anything to drink. There must have been something in that cider he'd given her. It made her feel funny almost as soon as she'd tasted it. Kenneth had had some too. In fact he'd had so much he'd passed out but he wasn't drunk like everyone said.

She became aware that the woman sitting opposite was giving her a concerned look. 'You all right, dear?'

Connie took a deep breath and smiled. 'Yes, thank you,' she said.

'You look as if you've had a bit of a shock.'

'Really,' said Connie shaking her head. 'I'm fine.'

The woman went back to her book and Connie looked out of the window. She'd never really bothered to analyse what happened that day but Ga had been so wrong, hadn't she? And because of what she thought had happened, she had hated Kenneth.

Her mother was different. Kenneth had always been her blue-eyed boy. She didn't talk about him but Connie knew her heart was broken. She never gave up hope that he would come sailing back into her life again. Every Remembrance Sunday her mother would put a red poppy next to his photograph in her bedroom. Kenneth had always wanted to join the RAF and Connie supposed that when the war came he had done just that. Nobody was too fussy about age back then and she liked to think of him over the skies, protecting the country. It was a bit scary when the Battle of Britain was raging but seeing as how they had never been informed that he had been shot down or anything like that, Connie had always supposed he had survived the war intact.

The journey took less than an hour. From the station she had to find her way to Holtye Road and the Queen Victoria Hospital. East Grinstead was famed for two things, one which was horrific and the other brought a ray of hope to the victims of war. On a Friday evening in July 1943, a German bomber had targeted the Whitehall Cinema. It was early evening and schoolchildren were enjoying a Hopalong Cassidy film when the bombs fell. As well as the cinema, several shops were hit and then the plane returned to machine gun survivors. In total, 108 were killed and 235 people were injured, a large number of them being the children in the cinema. The whole town, indeed the whole country was devastated by the pictures of helpless fathers searching the rubble for their lost boys and girls. Everyone in East Grinstead knew someone who had been affected by the terrible loss of life.

The other reason why East Grinstead was on the map was because of the pioneering work being done at the East Grinstead burns unit, the place where Connie was heading. After the Battle of Britain, hospital wards were littered with young men in their early twenties who, in their heroic efforts to save the country, had suffered horrific burns. Modern medicine meant that they survived their ordeal but the consequences were unimaginable.

The building itself turned out to be two storeys and long. It had a round tower at one end and was set in green lawns. Roger was waiting by the double doors and shook her hand warmly as they met. His hair was slicked back and he looked smart in a dark blue suit, white shirt and grey tie. She'd noticed his eyes before but today they looked particularly kind and friendly making her feel much more relaxed now that he was here. Connie was shown into a small visitors' room and after a short wait, a well-dressed man with an open face and enigmatic smile entered the room. He introduced himself as Mr Archibald McIndoe. He had a clean shaven face and wore round glasses. He was tall with thinning hair and looked for all the world like a college lecturer.

He shook her hand. 'Have you seen your brother since his accident?' He had the faintest trace of an accent but Connie couldn't quite place it. Australian or South African? She shook her head.

'Then I think you must brace yourself for a shock, Miss Dixon,' he said indicating that they should all sit down. 'We are keen that our boys come to terms with what's happened to them but until they do, we do our best to help them feel as comfortable as possible. Do you understand?'

Connie nodded but she wasn't really sure that she did understand.

'It is important that you try to behave as normally as possible,' the doctor went on. 'Please don't register your shock or surprise when you see him.'

Connie's heartbeat quickened. What was he saying? What exactly was wrong with Kenneth?

'Has he been badly affected, sir?' Roger asked.

'Flying Officer Dixon was trapped in his aircraft when it caught fire,' the doctor continued. 'He had extensive burns to his face and arm.' He paused. 'I'm afraid you may not recognise him.'

Connie felt sick. Oh Kenneth . . . Roger reached for her hands resting on her lap and squeezed them.

'Are you all right, Miss Dixon?' Mr McIndoe asked not unkindly.

'I'm fine,' Connie smiled.

'The men here have already had several skin grafts,' Mr McIndoe continued. 'Flying Officer Dixon, we call him Dickie, has had a few more than most. He's been here over a year and we've already given him new eyelids and new cheekbones. We now have to restructure his nose. I understand you are a nurse, Miss Dixon.'

Connie nodded. 'I'm training to be a nurse.'

Mr McIndoe looked at her thoughtfully. 'Your brother has got what we call a walking stalk skin flap on his nose.'

Connie looked puzzled.

'It's skin and soft tissue which we have formed into a tubular pedicle,' said Mr McIndoe waving his hands from his nose to his chest. 'It's joined to two parts of his body, his nose and his chest, so that it retains the blood supply from the source, his chest, until it's fully taken. I'm afraid he looks as if he's got an elephant's trunk at the moment.'

There was a pregnant silence and then Roger asked, 'Is that all that needs to be done?'

Mr McIndoe shook his head. 'It's his hands that are the problem. I'm afraid it's going to take a few more operations before he can use them again.'

Connie was numb with shock. She had guessed it must be bad but she had never expected anything as bad as this.

'As a matter of fact, he's out there on the terrace,' the doctor went on. 'You can see him from here and I should like you to do that. I warn you again, it may be a shock. Once you have recovered yourself, I will take you to see him. I hope you will find it in yourself to treat him as if he is perfectly normal. Although in the early days we tried our best to persuade him otherwise, we had to respect his wish not to inform his family. It's taken him a long time to pluck up the courage to agree to see you.'

'Does he know I'm coming today?' Connie asked.

'I have to confess I was annoyed when his friends told me what they had done,' he said. 'But Dickie has come round to the idea. You must know that we wrote first to your mother but she chose not to reply.'

Connie rose to her feet and walked unsteadily to the window. 'I'm sure if my mother had known Kenneth was here,' she said, 'she would have been on the very first train. I think my great aunt, for reasons best known to herself, must have intercepted the letters.'

Roger came to stand with her. There were several men on the terrace. Some were playing cards, one had his arm in some sort of brace which held it extended outwards and another was apparently practising some lines from a play.

'The men have come on in leaps and bounds since we formed The Guinea Pig Club,' Mr McIndoe continued and he came to join them at the window. 'Of course when the war ended they stopped taking on members but it helps them no end to feel that what we do here is of great help to others.'

'I can't see my brother,' she said eventually.

174

Also as soon as she said it, a Lancaster bomber rumbled overhead in the sky and the man with his back to the window turned around and looked up. Connie gasped in horror and stepped back from the window. Her eyes immediately filled with tears. Half of his face was a mass of livid scars. His left eye drooped and part of his nose was an odd shape. The doctor was right. He did look as if he had a long skinny elephant's trunk. The hair on the left side of his face stood up in untidy tufts. Now that he had moved, she could see the hand that held his cards was also damaged. The fingers were no more than stumps although the other hand, his left, was not nearly so deformed. His card playing companion said something and Kenneth turned back to the table. Laying down his cards he laughed heartily. Clearly, he had won the game.

Connie reached for Roger's hand and he held her tightly.

The doctor glanced at Connie who was wiping her eyes. 'I'm sorry,' she said stiffly, her voice thick with emotion. 'Just give me a minute, will you?'

Roger produced a clean white handkerchief.

'It's a perfectly normal reaction,' said Mr McIndoe. 'I'll arrange for you to have some tea.'

Connie sniffed. 'No, no. I'll be fine. In fact, I should like to take tea with my brother if that's all right? After all, that's what I came for. Is there somewhere I could powder my nose?'

Alone in the ladies room, Connie allowed herself a short cry and then splashed her face with water. 'Pull yourself together,' she told her reflection. She was a professional. A nurse. She dealt with this sort of thing every day, but, oh dear, it was so very different being on the other side of the fence. This was agony . . . her chest hurt and her eyes were stinging with unshed tears. She shivered involuntarily. On the wards, she could be sympathetic but remain detached. She had a reputation for being a gentle and considerate nurse, someone people could talk to, but this was different. This was her brother. Her Kenneth. Connie took a deep breath, several in fact. After that, she powdered her nose and put on some lipstick. Her last move was to rearrange a curl or two and then taking one last look at herself in the mirror, she practised a bright smile and then she knew she was ready.

Seventeen

The police were outside the Frenchie's workshop. Had he seen them before he came down the little lane, Isaac would have ridden straight past the entrance and gone back to his caravan still parked behind the hedge in Titnore Lane, but one of them had spotted him. Isaac had never liked the police but if he made a run for it now, whatever they'd come for, they'd decide it was him. He'd have to take a chance.

Isaac had enjoyed the winter months. For the first time in his life he felt he had a purpose. He'd stayed because his father had wanted to stay. The old man had become nostalgic in his old age. He wasn't well either. The rest of the family had moved on but Isaac had decided to take up the Frenchie's offer to learn about motors. Actually, it wasn't the Frenchie who taught him. An ex-soldier from REME was in one end of the workshop helping ex-servicemen get on their feet and the Frenchie had persuaded the bloke to take Isaac on as well. Isaac had had little formal schooling but young as he was, he had a sound business head on his shoulders. Since the end of the war, there were a lot of ex-service vehicles available. Plenty of people were buying and he had a shrewd idea that before long, once things started to pick up, everybody would want their own car. Reuben had worked in the fields, his uncle was a dealer in scrap metal, and his brother-in-law was good with wood so Isaac decided to become a mechanic. To his surprise, he found he enjoyed it. That was a bonus.

The freezing cold weather had put a bit of a dampener on things. He had no income and had to rely on his wits for a few weeks, trapping the odd pheasant and fishing in the river Rife, but he avoided anything illegal and stuck with it, knowing that it wouldn't be long before they could get back to fixing motors.

Isaac parked his bike against the wall and sauntered into the garage whistling a tune. Perhaps the police car had come in for repairs. The Frenchie and the two burly policemen turned towards him and Isaac's whistle died on his lips. 'What's up?'

'Someone has complained,' said the Frenchie.

'Complained? About what?'

'There have been some thefts,' said the copper with the sergeant's stripes. All three of them stared at him hard.

'This is Sergeant Palmer,' said the Frenchie. 'He wants to ask you some questions.'

'Why me?' Isaac protested.

'Oh, I know all about you lot,' said the sergeant with a sneer, 'so don't you go getting on your high horse, my lad.'

Isaac felt a rage creeping up into his chest. For the first time in his life he'd done nothing wrong but he knew what was coming. He was the gypsy. The man of 'no fixed abode'. If somebody was thieving, it had to be him. His eyes narrowed. It wouldn't matter what he said, they'd pin it on him anyway. He made a split decision, one he would forever regret. Turning on his heel, he legged it. He didn't get far. The copper he'd seen just outside the door stuck his foot out and Isaac went flying.

'Looks like we've found our culprit,' said the sergeant with a satisfied smirk.

The Frenchie shook his head. 'No, no. I cannot believe it. He wouldn't . . .'

'When you've been in the job as long as I have,' interrupted the sergeant, 'you get a nose for this sort of thing.'

The police officers had dragged Isaac to his feet and cuffed him. 'It wasn't me,' he cried helplessly. 'I ain't done nothing.'

The Frenchie watched him being bundled into the police car and turned back into the garage. Isaac had been at the workshop every day helping out and learning whatever he could about motors. They slipped Isaac the odd pound or two and gave him a pie at lunchtime but there wasn't enough money coming in to pay him a wage. True, Isaac had helped them with the old folks when the weather was really bad, but stealing from them? Eugène couldn't believe it. But what had happened to Isaac wasn't the end of his troubles. Because he had few customers, the mechanic who shared part of his workshop couldn't pay his share of the rent. The terrible weather had meant that Eugène was losing money hand over fist and he couldn't keep going much longer. Nobody was buying luxuries like Simeon's carvings or his own paintings and the bicycle repairs he usually did completely dried up because of the bad weather. He'd got a few odd jobs but even though he was engaged to his daughter, Councillor Hampton was already breathing down his neck for a good return on his investment. Mavis didn't seem to care that he had no money. She spent it anyway. Eugène had ploughed everything he'd got into the workshop. He had built up a sizeable bit of goodwill by helping the locals in the snow, but now the thefts had left an unwelcome blight on his good deeds. All that mattered now was racking up some more business. Pity about Isaac. The boy could have made his way in life. He was a damned good mechanic, a natural. Then it occurred to him that the police would be searching Isaac's caravan before the day was out. The boy's father didn't look too good the last time he saw him and would be needing a hot meal. He'd better get up there and check on things.

'Hello, Kenneth.'

As he heard Connie's soft greeting, Kenneth leapt to his feet knocking his chair over in the process. 'What are you doing here?' He had flung his arm across his face. 'No, I don't want you here. Go away, Connie. Leave me alone.'

Roger righted the chair and Kenneth sank into it, his head in his hands. His shoulders were shaking.

'Shhh,' Connie soothed. 'It's all right, Kenny.'

The rest of the men melted away. They'd seen reunions like this before. Some of them had even had their own. They were painful, but once everyone got over the terrible shock, they were usually therapeutic.

Someone tapped Roger on the shoulder. 'Fancy a drink, mate?'

'I thought he'd agreed to her coming,' Roger accused.

The scarred man looked a little sheepish. 'He'll be fine in a minute. You look as if you need a stiff one and this place is famous for its grogging parties.' His benefactor was about twenty-three with a deeply scarred face. His eyebrows were missing and his hairline began somewhere near the crown of his head. 'So, what's your poison?'

Roger followed the others indoors.

Connie was crouched down in front of Kenneth, with one hand on his knee and the other on his arm. 'I'm here now, Kenny,' she said softly. 'I'm here.'

Eventually he regained control of his emotions and lifted his head. Connie stood, bending over him with her arms around his shoulders, her forehead to his forehead.

'Oh, Connie,' he wept, 'I'm sorry, I'm so sorry.'

It took a while before either of them could talk. She drew a chair close to him and put her hands over his poor scarred hand and the stump. She kissed his cheek and smiled up at him as if he were the same handsome brother who had left home all those years ago. To her, he was. To her he might be damaged but he was her perfect brother, her Kenny, and she had him back at last.

A nurse put a tea tray on the table beside them. Connie looked up and mouthed a thank you.

'Is there anything else I can get you?' she asked.

Connie shook her head. Kenneth tried to get something out

of his pocket and the nurse anticipated his movement. Pulling out a neatly folded handkerchief, she shook it and handed it to him. 'Do you want me to ask someone to come and look at your pedicle?'

It was only then that Connie really looked at the long trunk-like skin hanging from his nose. She guessed crying must make it feel uncomfortable.

'You do it,' Kenneth told the nurse, and while the nurse busied herself cleaning him up, Connie turned her attention to the tea. There were three cups and saucers on the tray but Roger had disappeared. She could hear the sound of laughter coming from inside. No need to worry about him. He was obviously all right.

'How did you find me?' said Kenneth when the nurse had gone. 'Did Mum ask you to come?'

Connie shook her head. It took a while to explain that most likely Ga had prevented their mother from knowing where Kenneth was. 'You know we've moved to Goring-by-Sea?' she said.

'No, I didn't,' said Kenneth. 'Was that because of me?'

Connie grasped his fingers. 'Of course not!' she cried. In truth she'd never put the two things together but this wasn't the time to go into all that. 'Mum got married again and Ga bought the nurseries.'

Kenneth was staggered. 'Mum got married?'

'To Clifford Craig,' said Connie. She wished she hadn't blurted it out like that. It must have been a shock to hear their mother had married again.

Kenneth beamed. 'I remember him. He was a really nice bloke.'

'He still is,' Connie laughed in relief. 'They have a little girl now. Mandy.' She opened her bag and took out the photographs she had brought especially to show him. Kenneth studied them carefully. 'You can keep them if you like,' said Connie. He gazed lovingly at the family picture with unshed tears glistening in his eyes. They talked for ages. Kenneth wanted to hear all about the WAAFs and now her nursing experience.

'I love it,' smiled Connie. There was a lull in the conversation and then Connie said, 'What happened to you?'

'You may not think so to look at me,' he said, 'but I'm lucky to be alive. I lost the undercarriage in '45. We thought we'd be all right but as soon as we realised we were on fire, God alone knows how it landed. I can hardly remember what happened except for the bloody flames. They came between my legs and were twenty feet above me. My hand was burnt straight away and it seized up altogether. Funnily enough, I didn't even feel my face.'

'Oh, Kenny,' said Connie.

'I vaguely remember them dragging me out of the cockpit,' he went on. 'I was on fire and they rolled me in the grass to smother the flames. The rest of the crew . . .' he faltered and swallowed hard. Connie squeezed his hand again and he took a deep breath. 'They took me to the local hospital and they did the best they could, but eventually, I got sent here. Best thing that ever happened to me.'

'Mum will be so relieved to know you are still alive.'

His head jerked up. 'You mustn't tell Mum,' he said.

'But Kenny . . .'

'No,' he cried. 'Absolutely not. I don't want her to see me like this. Please Connie, you've got to promise me you won't tell her.'

Connie stared at him helplessly. 'She wouldn't care, Kenny. So long as you're alive and on the road to recovery, she'd look past all this.'

'No!' Kenneth insisted. 'I'd sooner top myself than let her see me like this.'

'I'm sorry,' Connie cried. 'Please don't say such things. I can't bear it. All right, I won't tell, but please don't ask me to keep it a secret forever. Mum would never forgive me.'

'Just let me get this thing sorted out first,' said Kenneth pointing to his nose.

Connie nodded bleakly. This wasn't what she was expecting. She'd wanted a fairy-tale reunion and for Kenneth to come home. He looked exhausted.

'Do you need to rest?' she said. 'I'll go if you're tired.'

'I am a bit,' he said.

'I have a train to catch anyway,' she smiled.

Kenneth rang a little bell the nurse had placed on the tea tray. 'Who's the chap you came with? Is he your beau?'

Connie shook her head. 'Just a friend.' Out of the corner of her eye she could see Roger hovering near the doorway. She nodded for him to come out on the terrace.

'I'm glad you've got someone, Connie,' smiled Kenneth. 'I did wonder after that business with Stan Saul.'

Connie shot to her feet. Hearing that name again after all this time still made her feel physically sick. She staggered and would have fallen had not Roger reached her and grabbed her arm. Kenneth had risen from his seat as well. 'I'm an absolute idiot,' he said. 'I never should have mentioned him . . . sorry.'

Connie's mind was a complete jumble. Those horrible memories she'd spent so long pushing away came rushing back. Stan kissing her on the mouth, sucking her lips into his own mouth and pushing his tongue between her teeth. It was horrible and his smoky breath was disgusting. She hated it. Her head was spinning. Now she could still see Stan flying down the stairs dressed only in his shirt, his hands covering his modesty and when he reached the bottom, his clothes hit him on the back of his head. Then he'd looked up at her and pointed his finger. She shuddered. Even now, just the thought of him scared her half to death.

'She's going to faint,' cried Kenneth. 'Do something. Dear God, I never meant for this to happen. I only said his name.'

Roger forced Connie back onto the chair and the nurse who appeared in answer to the bell took charge. 'Breathe slowly,' she told Connie as she made her put her head between her legs.

Roger stood over her with quiet and puzzled concern. Someone gave Connie a glass of water and she gradually stopped trembling and regained her composure.

'We've put Kenneth on his bed,' the nurse said eventually. 'It's probably best if you say goodbye to him now. He's very upset about what happened.'

Now recovered and leaning on Roger's arm, Connie went to say goodbye to Kenneth. Roger waited at the foot of the bed as brother and sister whispered together.

'It was because of Stan that you left home, wasn't it?' said Connie.

Kenneth hung his head and nodded. 'Ga blamed me for what happened,' he said, 'but I promise you, that bastard hoodwinked me just the same as he did you.'

'I know,' said Connie. 'It wasn't your fault.'

Kenneth squeezed her hand. 'You have no idea what that means to me,' he said. 'Thank you for coming.'

'Let me tell Mum . . .'

'No,' said Kenneth, his eyes blazing once more. 'If she comes here, I shall make them send her away.'

Connie sighed. 'I'll come and see you when I can,' she said, pushing her hospital address into his hand. 'I'll write but I can't come every week. Mum expects me to go home on my days off.'

Kenneth nodded. 'But you will come?'

'Just try and stop me,' she smiled.

Roger took her to a small café in the town. They were the only customers and as they walked in the radio was playing 'You Are My Sunshine'. Connie was emotionally exhausted and was glad of a few minutes in which to gather her thoughts and relax.

'My little sister's favourite tune,' she smiled at Roger.

'I like that one too,' he said. In truth he didn't know what to say.

The waitress, a rather bored looking girl with plain straight hair and buck teeth, took their order. Connie stared out of the window. She was glad of Roger's company but she wished she was with someone she could talk to. He was kind and considerate but she didn't know Roger well enough to offload her family secrets. He reached for her hand on the table and gave it a squeeze.

'This has been one hell of a day for you,' he ventured.

Connie nodded. 'Thank you for coming. It made it a lot easier having someone with me.'

'My pleasure,' he smiled.

'I never got around to telling you that Eva has been unwell.' She told him about his sister's illness and meeting his family for the first time. 'Your grandmother and my great aunt used to be friends.'

'Apparently,' he agreed. 'I think Gran always wanted to patch it up but Olive and Agatha wouldn't wear it. They never forgave her for marrying my grandfather.'

Connie was curious about the man loved by two women. 'What was he like?'

Roger smiled. 'Just about the best grandfather a chap could have.' By the time their pie and mash meal arrived he had waded into childhood memories ranging from catching tiddlers in the local pond to ferreting for rabbits and bareback riding on the downs, all done with a dearly loved grandparent.

'I greatly admired him because he never let his war wound hold him back,' said Roger.

'Oh yes, his war wound,' said Connie faintly.

'He only had one leg and he'd lost the sight in his right eye,' said Roger. 'They were a tough lot back then. Once they set their minds on something, they'd go for it.'

'What did your grandfather do for a living?'

'He carried on with the family tradition,' said Roger. 'He was a stonemason.'

Roger looked thoughtful as he played with his spoon on the table. 'Connie, who was Stan Saul?'

'I don't want to talk about him,' Connie said quickly.

Roger nodded. 'Well, if ever you do . . .' he began.

'I won't,' said Connie firmly.

After their meal, Roger took her to the station and they said their goodbyes. When he kissed her, it was as soft as a butterfly's wing brushing her lips and something within her was aroused. Connie closed her eyes waiting for the next kiss but it never came. He had left her wanting more.

'Even though it was a difficult day for you, Connie,' he smiled, 'I've enjoyed being with you.'

'And I with you,' she said shyly. 'Thank you for being there.'

'Take care,' he said kissing her on the cheek. 'I'll write.'

She leaned out of the carriage window until the train moved off. He waved and then he was gone. She liked Roger. He was a kind man.

Eighteen

Eva was dying to hear all about it. She was fully recovered from her bout of flu and as soon as she'd checked back into the nurses' home, she came looking for Connie who was in the laundry washing her smalls. Connie dried her hands and the two friends embraced warmly.

'Are you sure you're well enough to come back?' Connie asked anxiously.

'There's only so much soup and chocolate cake a girl can have,' she laughed. 'It was lovely to be home, but Mum drove me nuts with her fussing. Your friend Jane Jackson came with an orange. Did you tell her I was ill?'

Connie nodded and turned her attention back to the sink.

'She tells me she's met someone. He goes to her church and she says he's lovely.'

'I'm glad,' said Connie. 'She deserves someone nice. Did she say anything about Sally Burndell?'

'Only that she's staying with her aunt for a bit longer,' said Eva, making herself comfortable on the laundry table. 'She found out that her boyfriend has left the army but he's never got in touch. She thinks he had some poison pen letters.'

'Yes, I heard that too,' said Connie. 'I ask you, who would do a thing like that?'

'There are some really sick people out there, Connie,' said Eva. 'Now, tell me about your brother.'

Connie was glad of someone to talk to about Kenneth. Roger had wanted to know all about him but she was reluctant to say too much. She had written to Kenneth a couple of times since she'd got back and she was due to go home to Belvedere Nurseries on her next day off. 'I've never been good at keeping secrets,' she told Eva, 'and he flatly refuses to let me tell Mum he's alive and well.'

'Why doesn't he want her to see him?' Eva asked.

As Connie wrung her things out and put them on the draining board she explained about the walking stalk skin flap and Kenneth's ongoing rhinoplasty. 'To be honest,' she said, 'it makes him look as if he has an elephant's trunk and he hates the idea of Mum seeing him like that.'

'Perfectly understandable,' said Eva.

Of course it was. How silly of her not to realise. Connie hadn't really thought about it from Kenneth's point of view. Her whole focus had been on how difficult it would be keeping the secret. Yes, Kenneth was right. It would be much better to wait for a while and then see Mum when he had some semblance of a normal face. 'He must be an amazing man to work for,' Connie observed.

'Who, Kenneth?'

'No, Mr McIndoe,' said Connie plunging everything back into the rinsing water. 'In the way he's pioneered the way people with terrible burns are treated. They say he even got the Ministry of Aircraft Production down there to see what damage their aircraft can do to the men trapped inside.'

'Whatever for?'

'He was trying to get them to build safer aircraft.'

'I can't say I would have even thought of that,' Eva nodded. 'I wish I'd brought my ironing down while we talked.'

'How is Steven?' Connie was surprised that Eva hadn't yet mentioned the love of her life.

Eva grinned and looked a little coy. 'He's lovely. Oh Connie, he's such a wonderful man. I never thought I would say this about anyone after Dermid but I love him so much.'

'I know you do,' Connie laughed. She tipped the rinsing water away and took her things to the mangle. 'It's in your eyes.'

'Oh dear,' said Eva. 'Does it really show? It's so important to keep it a secret. You know going out with the junior doctors is strictly off limits. Sister Hayes would go loopy if she found out.'

Connie squeezed her friend's hand. 'Your secret is safe with all of us,' she said. 'You two were made for each other so just enjoy it.'

Eva mouthed a silent thank you. 'I've made arrangements to go and see Queenie. I hope she won't be too upset.'

'She'll be fine,' said Connie and her friend nodded.

'Your brother was so kind,' Connie said and Eva listened starry eyed as she told her of Roger's gentleness when she had collapsed. 'He took me for a meal afterwards. I'm afraid I wasn't up to much by the end of the evening but he had me laughing.'

'He's like that,' Eva smiled. 'Could there be . . .?'

'Eva, don't,' Connie interrupted. 'What with training and worrying about Kenneth . . .' She hung everything on the overhead pulley. She didn't say so, but with all this Stan business being raked up, Connie was in two minds about everything. She didn't tell Eva that Roger had already written to her. It was a chatty letter, telling her that he was going up to Yorkshire for a refresher course for a few days and asking her to write. '*It gets a bit lonely for a chap in a strange place*,' he'd written, '*so it would be nice to have the odd letter from a friend.*' She hadn't replied but it sounded as if he was keen on her. 'I don't even want to think about romance right now . . .'

Eva put her hands up in mock surrender. 'All right, all right, keep your hair on,' she laughed.

While Connie cleared up, Eva told her about her illness. 'My granny had me inhaling Friar's Balsam and Mum kept me in bed for ages . . .' But by now, Connie was only half listening. She was thinking about her nightmare journey home from East Grinstead. She'd been totally exhausted, both physically and mentally drained and yet every time she'd tried to relax, that awful face would push its way into her thoughts. She hadn't really thought about Stan Saul for years but ever since Kenneth said his name, she could almost smell his sweaty body above her and feel his breath on her cheeks.

Eva jumped down from the table. 'Connie, you're miles away. Something is wrong.'

'Umm? Oh, sorry,' said Connie. 'Go on. I am listening.'

'No,' said Eva. 'I can tell by your face that you've got something on your mind. Come on, out with it.'

'I was thinking about something that happened when I was thirteen,' she began, 'and it's not a pretty story.'

'Go on,' said Eva uncertainly.

'It's the reason my brother left home.'

Eva sat back on the table and gave Connie her full attention. 'I'm listening.'

'I was with my brother at a place called Long Furlong near Patching where we used to live and we'd met up with another lad called Stan Saul,' she said leaning against the wall. 'Kenneth and I had been out on our bikes all day with a few other boys and girls from the village. We'd taken a primus stove and cooked some sausages in the frying pan.'

Eva smiled. 'Nothing like cooking out of doors. Go on.'

'Kenneth is two years older than me but Stan was already grown-up. He was seventeen and nobody could understand why he hung around with us kids all the time.'

'Does sound a bit odd,' Eva agreed.

'Anyway, he'd brought some bread and he had some sweets which of course made him everybody's mate that day,' Connie went on. 'It was a lot more fun having a slice of bread to wrap around a boiling hot sausage, although it did pose a bit of a problem having to cut the slices with only Curly Bishop's penknife.' She laughed briefly.

Eva listened as she recalled what happened. She told Eva that she wasn't very happy when Stan had invited himself back to their place afterwards and was even more anxious when she'd realised that no one else was at home. Mum and Ga were out but she'd consoled herself that Pip, although still only a pup, was there to protect them.

'That's when Stan produced the cider.'

'Cider?' Eva remarked.

'It was very strong and the bubbles gave me hiccups. Stan told me to "Drink up," and he kept tipping the glass back every time I put it to my lips.' Connie put her trembling hand to her forehead as she remembered. The gathering gloom outside gave the window a mirror effect and she studied herself in the glass. The jumble in her mind was clearing and she shuddered as she remembered Stan running his tongue over his dirty teeth.

'Connie?' Eva jumped down and put her hand on Connie's shoulder. 'Did something awful happen?'

Connie thought of Roger again. He was a nice man but if Eva told him about Stan, would he want to write to her again? As she felt her eyes smarting, Connie pulled herself together crossly. The past was the past. She couldn't alter it and the only way it could hurt her was if she dwelt on it. Stan was out of her life forever and the chances of ever seeing him again were remote. They'd just come through a war for heaven's sake. There was a fair chance that Stan Saul had perished on the battlefield anyway. She picked up her empty laundry basket. 'Nah,' she said brightly. 'A silly memory of a rubbish first kiss, that's all.'

*

His mother wouldn't like it but he'd have to tell her. No point in beating about the bush. He'd come right out with it. Best way.

'I'm changing my name, Mum.'

She almost dropped a stitch. 'Change your name. Whatever for?'

191

'I told you, didn't I? I want a new start. As soon as people hear my name, they remember what happened to my wife and they've already made up their minds, haven't they?'

She had no answer to that.

'I'm going to use my second name instead,' he went on. 'It might bring me better luck.'

'Oh, son,' she said cautiously. 'I'm not so sure it's a good idea. People are bound to think you've got something to hide.'

She saw something flicker in his eyes and his mouth took on a sinister sneer. 'I didn't ask for your opinion, Mum,' he said coldly. 'I told you what I'm going to do, so you'd better get used to it.'

As he left the room, he slammed the door so hard the cups rattled on the sideboard. She could feel the panic rising inside her chest. It was starting all over again, wasn't it? He hadn't changed at all.

*

Matron was doing her ward rounds and Sister had asked Connie to clean Room 1 in preparation for an incoming patient. She had spent the morning wiping the locker, the iron bedstead and the mattress with disinfectant. She'd checked the curtains on the screen and changed one of them because it had a splash of some sort on it. She'd cleaned the thermometer holder on the wall and changed the mouthwash solution. When she had finished, Sister deemed it a job well done.

As Matron sailed onto the ward, Connie was just taking a bedpan to Mrs Meyer in bed four. She whipped the curtains round and hidden from view, she dealt with her patient. Mrs Meyer was lovely. She'd come in for an operation on her stomach but when the surgeons had opened her up, they'd found out that there was nothing more they could do. They'd stitched her back up again and when she came around, told her the bad news. Mrs Meyer knew she didn't have long to live but it never seemed to dampen her spirit.

Connie had just taken the full pan from under Mrs Meyer when Matron swept the curtain aside. 'Everything all right here?' she bellowed.

The sudden movement made Connie jump and she accidentally spilled a little urine on the bed sheet. Matron's eyes narrowed. 'Scandalous waste of bed linen, nurse.'

'Yes, Matron, sorry Matron.'

'You cleaned Room 1, didn't you, nurse?'

'Yes, Matron.'

'Then when you've cleaned that up come and stand outside.'

When Connie had finished changing Mrs Meyer's sheet, she stood outside the door of Room 1 and waited. A minute or two later, Matron came and took a pair of white gloves out of her pocket. Putting the left one on, Matron went inside and closed the door. They could hear her moving around and then it all went quiet. A couple of seconds later she came out with her hands in the air. On the right hand, the index finger of her white glove had a black smudge on it.

'Not good enough, nurse,' she said curtly. 'Do it again.'

'But where did you find it?' Connie blurted out.

'That is for you to find out, nurse,' snapped Matron sweeping out of the ward. 'I shall be back in one hour.'

Connie could have wept. Her face was flaming with rage. She went to the sluice room to fetch her cleaning things again. She was supposed to be off duty in half an hour.

As she hurried to Room 1 for the second time, Mrs Meyer called her over. Pulling Connie down to the bedclothes she whispered conspiratorially, 'Don't let the old witch get to you, darling. Remember we all look the same with our knickers around our ankles first thing in the morning.'

Connie laughed and somehow that thought kept her going as she began again.

*

The reporter yawned. Not much excitement in court today, a couple of non-payments of fines, a chap accused of harassing his ex-wife and someone being prosecuted for not having a gun licence. It was all pretty boring stuff, only fit to go on page nine and column four. What he wanted was a page two or three piece or better still, a juicy front page story.

The last case of the day involved a gypsy. Who cares about gypsies, he thought as the boy stood in the dock, and then he realised he'd seen him before. As the case unfolded it dawned on him that this was the kid who had been in the paper a few weeks ago. He was the do-gooder who had been helping people out in the cold weather. Helping himself more like. The headlines were already turning over in his head. *Good neighbour turns bad.* That sounded quite good. Or, bearing in mind the boy's name, how about, *Light-fingered Light.*

Isaac Light stood glum-faced in the dock as the judge passed sentence. 'You will go to prison for six months.'

He had expected no less; after all, the police had found some stolen items, a pearl necklace and a valuable ring, in his caravan. The prosecution made much of the fact that there was other stuff missing and even though the police had searched the caravan thoroughly, it was still missing. Isaac was told to come clean and say where it was if he wanted a lighter sentence but how could he? He hadn't stolen it in the first place. Everything seemed very circumstantial until the crown produced its most damning piece of evidence, eighty-six pounds they'd found under the floorboards. 'No doubt the proceeds from your ill-gotten gains,' the judge decided as he confiscated it for police funds. 'Take him down.'

His father, Reuben, had leapt to his feet to shout but instead struggled to control his cough. As Isaac was escorted down the steps, the reporter's lip curled. The old man was in no fit state to look after himself. It was obvious to everyone in the courtroom that he was on his last legs. Another man, vaguely familiar but the reporter couldn't place him, was sitting next to the old man.

'I'm innocent, Dad,' Isaac called from the bottom of the stairs. 'I didn't do nothing.'

There was another case coming up but the reporter dashed out to get to the telephone and the news desk. With a bit of luck, the story of Light-fingered Light would be in the morning paper.

The other spectators in court shrugged and exchanged sceptical looks as Isaac called out from below the dock but Reuben was a broken man. Everyone in his family cut corners and bent the rules a bit, but this was the first time anyone had been jailed for theft.

'It wasn't him,' he croaked.

Sitting next to him, the Frenchie patted his back. 'I, for one, don't believe it either, Reuben,' he whispered and the old man looked up at him with hope in his eyes.

Nineteen

Connie had the weekend off and on her way back home, she planned to post another letter to Roger. He'd only written a couple of times but she wasn't too worried. He'd told her in one of his letters that he wasn't very good at letter writing.

As soon as she walked in the door, the family showed off their new telephone. It had been a mammoth task to persuade Ga to have it installed and Connie was thrilled.

'We'll be able to take orders over the phone now,' said Gwen.

'A great deal of expense for nothing if you ask me,' Ga murmured.

'It's time to join the twentieth century, Ga,' Connie said light-heartedly and was rewarded with a cold stare.

Connie had hardly settled in the door before Clifford wanted her to come and see Reuben. To her surprise, the old man wasn't in his caravan in Titnore Lane. Clifford took her instead to the Frenchie's workshop. Eugène opened the rickety door and stepped back to let them in. He looked as handsome as ever and Connie's heartbeat quickened as soon as she saw him. He smiled and held his arm out to indicate where Reuben was. Connie looked up and saw the old man lying on an old horsehair sofa at the back.

'What's he doing here?' she asked. She hurried to him and touched his forehead. It was cold and clammy. His skin was grey and he was struggling to breathe. She listened with mounting horror as Clifford told her about Isaac going to jail and the police search of his caravan. 'I'm really annoyed that they did nothing to help him,' said Clifford. 'They must have seen the state the old boy was in.'

'Then it's a good job he has friends nearby,' said Connie, taking Reuben's pulse.

'That was all down to Pip,' said Clifford. 'He kept sloping off and we couldn't find him for hours. Then a couple of nights ago we could hear this dog howling in the distance. Mandy knew it was him straight away so I went to look for him.'

'No sign of Kez and the others then?' said Connie.

'Moved on some time ago.' Clifford shook his head. 'I found Pip outside Reuben's canvas tent howling his head off. If I hadn't turned up, the poor man would have been dead by now. He hadn't even had a drink for God knows how long.'

'But Kez usually turns up this time of year,' said Connie, clearly puzzled.

Clifford nodded. 'And when someone's ill, somehow or other, they all turn up from nowhere but not this time. With Isaac locked up, the poor old boy was on his own. He refused to let us take him to the doc. We didn't know what to do for the best.'

Reuben's eyes were fixed on the wooden wall and it didn't take Connie long to realise he was staring between the planks where the daylight made its watery way inside. His chest sounded awful and she could see that he had been coughing up blood. One thing was obvious. He couldn't stay here. The Frenchie stood beside him with his hands in his pockets and chewing his lip anxiously. Connie willed her heart not to pound so when he was so near.

'Eugène, I know you mean well,' Connie began, 'but we really must get him to hospital.'

'He knows he is dying,' Eugène said quietly. 'He doesn't want to be indoors.'

Connie moved a little closer to him and laid her hand on his arm. 'I'm afraid he has no choice,' she said. 'There's nothing I can do and especially not here.'

Eugène shook his head. 'But I promised.'

'The authorities will make it difficult for you if he dies here,' Connie went on. 'They may decide that your failure to get him medical help is neglect . . . or something far worse. After all, you have no written proof that this was his wish, and Reuben won't be around to explain.'

Eugène's nostrils flared slightly and he nodded his head reluctantly.

'Go and ring for an ambulance, Clifford,' Connie said taking charge, and then looking at Eugène, she said, 'Can you get me a bowl, a towel and some water please?'

By the time the ambulance came, Connie had cleaned Reuben up a bit. He'd managed to go to the toilet which was outside, but the two men had to virtually carry him. When they laid him back down, his breathing was laboured and clearly painful. Connie went with him in the ambulance and he was admitted straight away into isolation on the men's ward. She sat with him for a while and even though he was definitely more comfortable and had less pain because of the drugs they'd given him, Connie couldn't help feeling guilty. Reuben had been denied the one thing he had always wanted – to die under the open sky.

As she sat in the peace and quiet, Connie chewed over what had happened to Isaac. It was hard to believe. It was true, he was surly and bad tempered, and he had a chip on his shoulder. He was sometimes guilty of illegal fishing or shooting the odd deer for food, but stealing from old ladies? Somehow that wasn't his style and yet Clifford had told her the police had found stolen goods in his caravan. After all the Frenchie had done for him, she didn't know whether to be angry or to pity him.

Towards the end of the evening, the door flew open and Connie leapt to her feet with a cry, 'Kez!'

She had the baby on her hip. Connie took Blossom from her

arms and Kez went to her father's bedside. Outside the door, Connie could see the corridor was swarming with people. Dressed in black, the gypsies had come to say their farewells. Ward Sister was frantic. 'Only two visitors at a time,' she was shouting, but the endless stream of people totally ignored her. She appealed to Connie, but there was nothing she could do, except to implore Sister to let them do what they came for and then they would go. By ten o'clock there was only Kez and Connie left. Someone had taken the children so that Kez was free to be with her father during his final hours.

'How did you find out?' Connie asked.

'Pen has the gift,' she said mysteriously and seeing Connie's raised eyebrows, she grinned. 'The Frenchie came to look for us.'

Eva turned up as soon as she'd finished her duty. 'Someone in the canteen said you were here,' she said. 'Anything I can do for you?'

There was nothing but Connie was glad to have her two best friends meet at last although she wished it could have been under less difficult circumstances. The two girls seemed to get on well. As the rest of the ward settled for the night, Connie motioned to Kez and Eva and between them they manoeuvred Reuben's bed towards the window. Connie pulled back the curtain but of course it was pitch black outside. She opened the window a crack and he seemed to know that he was breathing fresh air. At midnight, Eva left, promising to come back first thing in the morning.

As the night wore on, Reuben's death rattle was very loud. The nurses kept an eye on him and plied Kez and Connie with cups of tea, but they made their appearances as unobtrusive as possible. Connie's heart went out to Kez. Her friend behaved with dignity but it was obvious that she loved her father deeply. They didn't talk much. Somehow it was enough to be together. Reuben Light passed away just as the dawn was breaking on Easter Sunday, 6 April, 1947. He was fifty-six years old.

Eva telephoned and Clifford came to take them both home, Kez to her own trailer parked next to Reuben's caravan and Connie to Belvedere Nurseries. 'Makes a hell of a difference having a car,' he told Connie. Clifford had seen it in an old lady's garage when they were helping her out with some coal during the cold snap. It had belonged to her late husband and no one had driven it since 1937. Clifford paid her a fair price and, before he'd left the workshop, the mechanic had fixed it up.

The family had planned to have a day out but Connie had been up all night. Mandy couldn't hide her disappointment. 'It's not fair,' she complained. 'We never do anything together anymore.'

'I'm sure you'll have a wonderful time with Mum and Dad,' said Connie. 'We'll do something another time.'

'But I wanted to be with you,' Mandy pouted.

'How would it be if Connie slept this morning,' Gwen suggested, 'and then we go out this afternoon?'

Connie was desperate for some sleep but even she didn't want to be in bed all day, so it was agreed that they'd wake her at two. It took her a while to come round. Her head felt heavy and she felt a little sick. She couldn't stop yawning either but once she was in the car, Connie felt a lot better. The family motored onto the South Downs using the London Road which went past Sompting church. It was a bit of a squash in the car especially as Pip had squeezed himself in as well. When they got there they parked on the hill and taking out the picnic things, set off for some trees in the distance. Even though it was early in the year, it was a beautiful day. Pip ran on ahead, scattering wild pheasants hiding in the hedgerows.

Connie looked up at the big sky and felt small. The rolling Sussex downs with their patchwork fields dotted with sheep made a beautiful backdrop. Coming here was a good choice. The sadness of yesterday was somehow put in its place. Reuben was gone, but others, his children and grandchildren would take his place. Life moved on. Nothing stayed the same. She was in maudlin mood. She thought of the brevity of life, of the people she'd nursed in hospital, cut down in the prime of their lives. She thought of the importance of friendships, especially of her friendship with Kez. They didn't see each other for months, sometimes years on end and yet they were able to pick up exactly where they'd left off as if there had been no time between. She thought of Eva and the friendship they'd had to keep under wraps in case they upset the family and she wondered again about Ga and Cissy. They had both loved the same man but Cissy had said the family were at loggerheads long before she married Arthur. Something about a man called Little Mac. Connie knew she'd heard that name before, but where? It seemed so sad that for all these years, Ga had denied herself a friendship, because of someone else's fight. Why hold a grudge for all that time? Apart from Aggie, Ga had no friends now. She relied on the family for her socialising, which was why she was with them now, but she had little in common with any of them. It occurred to Connie, for the first time, that Ga wasn't actually related to any of the people who still lived at Belvedere Nurseries. She and Kenneth were her great niece and nephew, but Ga was only related to her mother through marriage. How different it had been for Reuben. It seemed like he was all alone in the world and yet all those people had turned up as he lay dying. What was the point of that? How much better to enjoy a friendship or relationship with that person while they were still alive. Then there was Sally Burndell. Rumour had it that Sally was coming back home. Connie purposed to drop her a line and find out how she was doing. Thinking of Sally made her think of Jane Jackson. Their friendship was more casual and yet she valued Jane as a friend. She smiled to herself. She still hadn't met this wonderful man of Jane's yet!

'You're quiet, dear,' said her mother, breaking into Connie's thoughts.

'Sorry, Mum,' she smiled. 'Just enjoying the peace and quiet.'

Mandy ran on ahead of them all, picking the first of the wild flowers as she went. Primroses danced along the pathway and Connie could hear skylarks and stone chats calling in the open. A grey partridge ran across the field making his grating sound as he went and Pip looked up, sniffing the air as he sensed the presence of rabbits. There were a few other families around and occasionally they would nod to a passing rambler going along the same pathway.

Her mother had chosen a lovely spot for their picnic. Connie helped her put the blanket down and get out the food. Ga sat on a nearby log until Clifford had returned from the car with her folding stool. A few minutes later they were all eating egg sandwiches and drinking tea from the thermos flask. Mandy had found a tree she could climb and so she made the fork in the branches her table and chair.

'I suppose they'll give Reuben a right royal send off,' Ga remarked. 'The rest of the world and his wife turn up when a gypsy dies.'

'There were loads of them in the hospital last night,' Connie remarked.

'What did I tell you?' said Ga. 'At least they were spared having that little toe-rag Isaac around.'

'Can't we all talk about something a little more cheerful?' said Gwen.

'Sorry, Mum,' said Connie. She stretched herself out and took some writing paper from her bag. She penned a quick note to Roger and then lay back and looked up at the sky. Her mind drifted towards Eugène Étienne and the way he had got everyone pulling together during the bad weather. He was so much nicer than Mavis Hampton. Connie frowned. Was her leg all right now? Yes, of course it must be. Poor Eugène. She was probably still leading him a dog's life. How handsome he was. She loved the way he'd stood with his hands in his pockets as she talked about Reuben. With his tousled hair flopping over his forehead he looked like a schoolboy. Her heart lurched with desire. Now if only Eugène was hers . . .

'Ah, now you're smiling,' said her mother. 'Penny for them.'

'I like doing this sort of thing,' Connie said quickly. 'If Reuben's death has taught me anything, it's been a timely reminder that family is important.'

'It would be even more lovely if we were all here,' her mother remarked and Connie felt her face burn. She rolled onto her stomach in case anyone noticed. How she wished she could tell her mother about Kenneth but he'd made her promise to say nothing.

Her mother passed around some of her sultana apple cake and Connie sat up. They could hear someone shouting in the distance. 'Help me, oh help me please . . .' It was a woman's voice. Pip, who had been resting with his head on his paws, leapt to his feet and growled. Clifford, who had been lying with his newspaper over his face, sat up too. 'What was that?'

Gwen shrugged. 'I've no idea.'

'Shall I go and see?' said Connie, jumping to her feet. Pip ran ahead of her and disappeared.

'I'll come with you,' said Clifford.

'Me too,' cried Mandy from the tree.

'No,' said her father. 'You stay with Mummy.'

The two adults hurried towards the clump of trees. A woman, frantic and panicking, ran around like a headless chicken imploring the other walkers in the area, 'Have you seen a little girl? She's seven. She's got blonde curls and blue eyes. She's wearing a pink polka-dot dress?' A man, clearly the child's father was running through the trees calling, 'Janice, Janice, where are you?'

The woman saw Connie and Clifford coming and hurried towards them. Pip bounded towards the trees and in a short while, they could hear him barking furiously and presently they heard him yelp. Connie caught a glimpse of another person running and then a voice called to them from the pathway. Connie's heart lurched. The child. Someone had found the child.

'Excuse me,' Connie shouted towards the woman who was walking away from them. 'I think she's here.'

He had come out onto the path holding a little girl's hand. The child spotted her mother and ran to her. Connie's throat constricted as she watched the child's mother scoop her up into her arms and burst into grateful tears. The child clung to her. Then Connie's heart did a somersault as she turned back and saw the child's rescuer. It was Emmett Gosling.

The child's father ran up to him and pumped his hand. 'Thank you. We've been looking everywhere. One minute she was there and the next she was gone. Where was she?'

'We heard a dog barking,' said Emmett, 'and then all of a sudden she came stumbling out of the undergrowth. I don't think any harm is done.' He turned and saw her for the first time. 'Connie!'

'Hello, Emmett,' she said shyly. Her throat had gone dry and her heart was bumping. This has to have been fate, she thought. I never thought I would see you again and now here you are appearing right out of nowhere. He wasn't quite as handsome as she'd remembered but he still had that gentle look in his eyes. He was dressed in tweeds and was wearing knee-length socks on the outside of his trousers and heavy walking boots.

'How nice to see you again,' said Emmett rather formally.

A woman came up beside him and slipped her arm through his. 'Was she the missing child?' she purred.

'Yes, darling.' Emmett smiled down at her and turning to Connie he added with a cheesy grin, 'You must meet my wife, Lucy. We were married Easter Saturday.'

Married? Connie almost choked. 'Congratulations,' Connie

smiled as graciously as she could. 'I hope you both will be very happy.'

'Oh, we will,' Lucy assured her.

'Connie and I went out together a few times during the war,' Emmett told his new wife. 'It was good to have someone to help while the time away.'

Connie's heart sank. Someone to help while the time away? Surely she meant more to him than that?

He turned back to Connie. 'Lucy was an absolute brick when Mother died.'

'I'm sorry to hear she died,' said Connie, regaining her composure. 'I know you were fond of her.' So fond of her that you stood me up on VE Day, she wanted to say.

'Is this your husband?' Emmett asked.

Connie and Clifford laughed. 'Heaven forbid,' Clifford said. 'But I am married to her mother.'

The other walkers had already dispersed. In the distance, they heard a motorbike starting up. The tearful family were packing up their things. Clearly losing their daughter albeit for a short time had affected them deeply.

'I didn't like the nasty man, Mummy,' said Janice.

'He isn't a nasty man, darling,' said her mother glancing at Emmett. 'He's a nice man. He brought you back to us again.'

The parents shook Emmett's hand again and they left.

'Well,' said Emmett awkwardly. 'We'd better be off too.'

Clifford called Pip and he came to them, although he seemed a little subdued. Connie went to pat his side and the dog yelped again. 'Must have fallen over or something,' said Clifford.

Connie and Pip walked back to the others side by side. How could she have got it so wrong? She had truly believed she and Emmett were important to each other, but clearly he had other ideas. 'Someone to help while away the time . . .' That had hurt her deeply. How could she have been so stupid? Up until now, Connie had always prided herself that she understood people but perhaps she wasn't so clever after all. As they packed the picnic things away, she caught a glimpse of the letter she'd just penned to Roger waiting to be posted. Perhaps she was wrong about him too.

Twenty

Reuben had a fantastic send-off. Friends and family had been 'sitting up' with Kez ever since her father died which meant that she'd had someone with her day and night. According to the Romani tradition, Kez had fasted the whole time. Connie hadn't seen her friend since Clifford took them both home that Easter Sunday and she was concerned to see her looking so drawn and tired. Connie had managed to get time off to go to the funeral by swapping her off duty time with one of the other student nurses. She dressed in black with a white blouse as was the custom for women going to a gypsy funeral.

It seemed the gypsies had come from the four corners of the earth to pay their respects but Isaac wasn't among them. He was still serving his time. They walked from Titnore Lane behind the hearse all the way to Broadwater cemetery, a distance of some three miles, holding up the traffic and creating a staring crowd as they went. The women who normally sold their flowers from coach-built prams parked along the Broadwater Road weren't doing any business today. Instead, they stood in a silent line near the cemetery entrance. Reuben was in a glass-sided horse-drawn hearse with a lorry full of wreaths and flowers following behind. Kez had put a Gates of Heaven wreath which she'd made herself at the side of his coffin; a tall archway of green foliage, peppered with Love in the Mist and a dramatic spray of mimosa, daffodils and Queen Anne's Lace on the left-hand side. As was the custom, the little black gates beneath the archway were permanently open.

The service, in the chapel at the cemetery itself, was beautifully done and to Connie's surprise, Isaac was already waiting in the pew, a prison officer next to him. The officer's coat hid the hand-cuffs on both their wrists until the Vicar, Rev McKay from St Mary's, had a word with the man and Isaac was allowed to sit next to Kez without the cuffs. They had chosen the place to lay Reuben to rest with care. It was a sunny spot, halfway up a hill, overlooking the Findon Valley. It was peaceful and as they walked towards the open grave, the birds sang in the warm April sun and rabbits scurried into the undergrowth. Reuben would have loved it up here, Connie thought. As soon as the graveside cere-mony was over, Isaac was taken away again and Connie couldn't help voicing her disgust over his treatment. 'Anyone would think he was a murderer, the way they're treating him.'

Everyone got lifts back to the caravans in Titnore Lane and once they were all gathered, Reuben's caravan was towed into the middle of the field to be set alight. Connie knew for a fact that he had many valuable things inside. 'Aren't you going to keep anything of his?' she asked Kez before the thing went up in flames. 'Something to remember him by?'

Kez seemed surprised. 'We never touch a dead man's things.'

'Perhaps there's something Isaac would want?' Connie insisted. 'Some of his own things.' She couldn't bear the thought of Isaac coming back to nothing.

'All Isaac's things are in his own tent,' Kez said wiping her eyes. 'The Roma believe touching a dead man's things would bring bad luck.'

Connie watched the flames leaping into the air as a perfectly good home went up in smoke. She couldn't understand it. All that lovely china and glass, his pots and pans, the watches he repaired . . . and nobody wanted anything. Even the caravan itself was valuable. Simeon had used gold leaf rather than paint when he'd decorated it and Reuben had always kept it up to date so far as repairs went.

As the flames died down, the gypsies took to the road again. Connie stayed to say goodbye. 'What will you do now?'

Kez shrugged. 'Move on, I suppose. This was the place where Reuben wanted to be. Simeon is talking to some mush about buying a piece of land over Slinden way.'

Connie kissed her children and hugged her friend. 'How will Isaac know where you are when he gets out of prison? Shall I send him to Slinden?'

'He knows we'll be at the horse fairs,' Kez said. She swallowed hard. 'He'll find us.'

Connie walked away with a heavy heart. Something had changed. It wasn't just losing Reuben. Perhaps something in Kez had died with him. She seemed troubled, as if something was playing upon her mind. Whatever it was, Connie was worried about her.

When she got back to the nurses' home, Connie found another letter from Kenneth in her pigeonhole. It had been penned using his left hand so the few lines were shaky and a little difficult to decipher. '*My nose is better. It's still a little . . .*' (Connie couldn't make out that word) '*but the Maestro says it will improve with time.*' Connie's spirits leapt. Maybe now at last she could tell her mother. She wrote back immediately to ask.

It was the end of the week and the girls were going to a dance but Connie had been asked to do a short spell of nights because they were short staffed. She was a bit disappointed as she watched Betty and Eva getting ready. Although they were meeting up with Jane Jackson, Sally, back home from college and with her mother again for the Easter holidays, had declined to come. She was better, but still hadn't quite got over losing Terry. Connie wished with all her heart she was going with them. In fact, she

209

wished she was going herself. After all the angst of the past few days, she could have done with a bit of light relief and a good laugh.

Betty had some lovely things. Her mother was good with a needle and spent a lot of time making the latest Butterick or Simplicity pattern. Everyone still needed coupons but she managed to pick up some nice material on the market. The room was filled with excited chatter. Avon's Wishing and Evyon's White Shoulders perfume filled the air as Connie helped Eva with her hair and lent Betty the pearl earrings she had bought in H. Samuels.

'Oh, I wish you could come too,' said Betty, 'especially as we're meeting your friend Jane. She's lovely, isn't she?'

'She tells me she's got a new boyfriend,' said Connie. 'I haven't met him yet. Tell me what he's like, won't you.'

'Leave it to me,' said Betty conspiratorially. 'I'll dish the dirt.' And they all laughed.

'Roger will be disappointed to miss you,' said Eva, patting her hair in place.

'You didn't tell me he was coming,' Connie cried.

'You didn't tell me you were doing nights,' Eva countered.

Connie slumped on the bed. 'I didn't know until yesterday,' she said. 'Honestly, I sometimes think Ward Sister has it in for me because I swapped duties to go to Reuben's funeral.'

'You always let your imagination run away with you,' said Betty. 'Has anyone seen my stole?'

Connie was stunned into silence. Betty's remark made her bristle but Connie let it go. Starting a row would spoil their evening. Betty found her stole and the girls were ready. Some of the other nurses were already gathered in the corridor. Connie stood at the door to wave them off, their high heels clacking along the linoleum floor. It was seven o'clock and she had an hour and a half before she had to be on duty. It was time to try out the new family phone.

'Belvedere Nurseries. How can I help you?' Connie's mother sounded very efficient and when Connie told her so, they both giggled. It was lovely to hear her mum's voice and it made Connie feel ever so slightly homesick. They chatted about Mandy and school. 'She's doing maypole dancing in the vicarage summer garden fete. Ga? She's fine. Oh, and we took Pip to the vet.'

'Why?' Connie was alarmed.

'You remember how he didn't like anyone patting his side after we'd been on that picnic where the little girl went missing?' said Gwen. 'Well, the vet thinks he was hit with something.'

'I don't understand,' said Connie.

'His side has been badly bruised. He was lucky not to have a broken rib, apparently.'

Connie vaguely remembered Pip barking as he rushed into the wooded area where the child was and then hearing a sharp yelp before he came out again. Everyone was so taken up with little Janice being reunited with her mother that Connie hadn't given her dog a thought. Could he have been hit by a falling log or something?

'The vet thinks he was hit or kicked,' her mother went on.

'Kicked!' Connie was horrified. 'Who on earth would have done that? Is he going to be all right?'

'Yes,' said her mother. 'It's just going to take time, that's all.'

'Poor old Pip.'

When she'd put the phone down, Connie thought back to that day. Something was niggling away at the back of her mind. Something that was connected to all this, but what was it? She felt like she was grabbing at something only just out of reach.

When she reported for duty, Connie was sent to the antenatal ward. She was working with Sister Neil and she wasn't looking forward to it. Connie had already had an altercation or two with her since she'd begun her training, once when Connie had been asked to tidy the linen cupboard and didn't get the sheets in a perfectly straight line and another time when Connie had burst through some swing doors when Sister was coming in the opposite direction, causing her to drop a bottle of distilled water. Everyone said she was an excellent nurse but Connie thought her hard-nosed and unfeeling. Still, it might not all be bad. Connie had never actually seen a baby being born and this was a golden opportunity. Sadly, once again she was doomed to disappointment. It was a very quiet night with only one woman in labour with her first baby. 'She'll be hours yet,' said Sister after she'd examined the patient. 'It probably won't come until the day staff are here.'

At two in the morning, a bell sounded near Sister's desk. Connie was making cotton wool balls and putting them into huge jars at a table nearby. Sister Neil looked up anxiously. 'That's the patients' bathroom on antenatal. Who would be having a bath at this time of night?'

Connie was just as puzzled.

'Nurse Dixon,' said Sister, 'you come along with me. I'm not going on my own.'

Taking torches, they walked purposefully along the dimly lit corridor to the bathroom. The light was on, the door slightly ajar and they could see movement inside. Glancing back at Connie, and taking a deep breath, Sister pushed the door and strode in. Afterwards, Connie wasn't sure which of them had been the most surprised, Sister, herself or the bearded man standing stark naked in the bath, drying himself with the hospital bathmat. While he was washing his feet and legs, he must have bent a little and accidentally pushed the emergency bell with his bottom. As soon as he saw Sister and Connie, he used the mat to cover his modesty.

'It's okay, missus,' he said gruffly. 'I ain't gonna hurt nobody.'

Sister Neil puffed out her chest. 'What on earth do you think you are doing?' she demanded.

The man held his hand out in surrender. 'I'm sorry, missus.

This is the only place I can get cleaned up. I've got an interview for a job in the morning.'

Sister Neil strode towards the bundle of clothes on the floor. Her mouth was set in a tight line. Oh, you're in for it now, my lad, thought Connie. Even from where she stood, Connie could see that his body was covered with clusters of little red dots, not unlike the German measles rash. The man obviously had body lice. His clothes were probably alive with them. He stepped out of the bath and stood on the tiled floor.

'Please, missus,' he begged. 'Don't call the police. I'll get dressed and be out of here in two minutes. You won't even know I was here.'

Sister Neil tut-tutted. 'Well, you're not walking out of here with those clothes.'

'I have to,' he said. 'They're all I've got.'

Sister Neil turned to Connie. 'I hope I can trust you to say nothing about this, nurse,' she began. 'Go to the porter's office and ask him for a complete change of clothes from the lost property box.'

Connie couldn't believe her ears but she said, 'Yes, Sister.'

'But first of all,' said Sister, 'go and get a brown paper bag from my office and take those things with you. Tell the porter to burn them in the boiler and then ask him to come up here in about half an hour.' She had taken a cloth from the cleaning cupboard and was rubbing Gumption onto the side of the bath. 'As for you, my lad,' she said addressing the astonished midnight bather in a far more gentle tone of voice, 'when I've cleaned this scum from the sides, you can have a proper bath. In fact, you can have a good long soak.' Sister turned and saw Connie standing in the doorway. 'Are you still here, nurse?' she said sharply and Connie fled.

Down in the bowels of the hospital, the porter's lodge was empty. Connie was just wondering what to do when a fresh-faced young man came towards her. He looked familiar but Connie couldn't work out where she'd seen him. He was younger than her, tall, average looking with round rimmed glasses and a small moustache.

'Can I help you, nurse?'

Connie handed him the bag of clothes and explained what Sister wanted. He seemed surprised. 'You've left her alone up there,' he said anxiously. 'Is she going to be all right?'

Connie grinned. 'If you knew Sister Neil,' she began, 'you wouldn't ask me that.'

'Oh, it's Sister Neil,' he said with a knowing grin. 'Why didn't you say?'

'I think I know you,' said Connie as they searched the lost property box for a new set of men's clothing. 'Have you always lived in Worthing?'

'I'm from East Worthing,' he said. 'How about you?'

'Goring,' she said. 'Where would we have met?'

'I don't think I have met you before,' he said candidly.

Connie wasn't about to give up just yet. 'Did you go to the dances in the Assembly Hall?'

He shook his head. 'I've been abroad serving King and country for two years,' he said. 'I only got demobbed four months ago.'

It was then that it dawned on Connie where she'd seen him before. 'Did you have a girlfriend called Sally?'

His expression clouded. 'I might have done.'

'Sally Burndell,' Connie persisted. 'I seem to remember seeing your photograph in her handbag.'

'What do you know about her?' His voice was hostile and it was obvious he didn't really want to talk about Sally.

'Did you know, for instance, that Sally has been having poison pen letters?' She could see that he had been brought up sharply so Connie went on. 'Someone has been accusing her, quite falsely as it happens, of being a loose woman. We've been quite worried that someone who didn't know what a lovely girl Sally was might actually believe all that stuff.'

Terry had paled but he said nothing.

'I just thought as a friend of hers, you might like to know that.'

They continued pulling clothes from the box until Connie was sure that she had something suitable for the man upstairs. 'Sister wants you to give us half an hour and then come up to chuck the man out,' she said.

Terry nodded.

When she came back with the clean clothes, Connie was amazed to find the man clean shaven and sitting on a chair, wrapped in a bath towel while Sister cut his hair. She had obviously put Dettol in the bath. The smell pervaded the whole bathroom. Once he was dressed in the clothes Connie had brought, he looked quite presentable. 'Good luck,' said Sister Neil. 'I hope you get that job.'

There were tears of gratitude in his eyes and he snatched her hand and kissed it.

'That's enough of that nonsense,' she said stiffly. Terry had appeared at the doorway and Sister Neil changed her demeanour. 'Escort this man off the premises,' she said tartly. 'He is trespassing.'

The man followed the porter, stopping only for a second as he reached the stairs to turn and mouth 'thank you' to Sister Neil. She straightened her cap and went back into the bathroom.

They cleaned up the room, scrubbing the bath and putting his tramp's cut hair in another brown paper bag for the incinerator. Outside in the corridor, another nurse advanced towards them. The woman in labour was in the second stage and Sister was wanted in the labour ward. It had been an eventful night and to her absolute delight, Connie saw baby John Charles Dare come into the world about forty minutes later.

Twenty-One

When the night duty came to an end, Connie had three whole days off. It was absolute bliss. She slept for part of the first day and then went home to Belvedere Nurseries. She especially wanted to see Pip. He greeted her warmly but she noticed that all of a sudden he seemed a lot older. There were even more grey hairs around his muzzle and he had white in his eyebrows.

'I wish you could talk,' she said softly as she fondled his ears. 'What happened to you in that wood?' She racked her brains to remember. She and Clifford had heard the mother shouting and they had joined the other walkers searching for the child. All the while, Pip had been barking and then she'd heard that yelp. Then she remembered somebody running out of the undergrowth just before Emmett brought the little girl out. She froze. 'I don't remember seeing that bloke afterwards,' she whispered to Pip. 'Was it a bloke or a girl?' She thought some more and decided it must have been a man. 'Did he do something to you? Where did he go?' She tried to recall his face, but she couldn't. She wasn't even sure she'd seen it because he was running away from everybody, and besides, she had such a shock seeing Emmett, everything else went out of her mind.

Her mother came downstairs with a couple of shirts that needed mending. The two women embraced. 'Connie, I don't want you to worry,' said Gwen drawing her to one side and looking round anxiously, 'but Clifford and I have been thinking about something.'

Connie lowered herself into a chair. This sounded serious.

'Where's Ga?' said Gwen.

'Serving in the shop when I came in,' said Connie.

'Clifford and I both want a new start in life,' her mother said. 'This past winter has made us both realise that we want more than this for Mandy and Clifford is positive that we'll never get it here.' A shadow moved in the hallway. 'We'll talk later,' whispered Gwen.

'What are you two whispering about?' Ga demanded as she walked into the room.

'Hello, Ga,' said Connie. 'How are you?'

'Overworked,' snapped the old woman.

Give it a rest, thought Connie. 'Oh, dear,' she said taking her bags upstairs to her room.

Connie brought up the subject of the man running in the woods as they ate their evening meal.

'I don't recall him at all,' said Clifford pulling the corners of his mouth down.

'Does it really matter?' Ga challenged. 'What's done is done.'

'That's true,' said Connie, 'but it's been puzzling me.'

'You mean you think something happened to that poor child?'

Connie shrugged. 'I don't know, Mum.'

Gwen and Clifford shared an anxious look.

'I think we should change the subject,' said Ga. 'Little ears are flapping.'

'That's not true,' Mandy retorted. 'I'm not listening.'

Connie grinned. 'Tell me what you've been doing at school,' she said. Her sister was pouting because they'd stopped talking. 'I hear you're going to dance around the maypole at the school fete.'

Mandy nodded vigorously. 'It's ever so hard. You have to keep counting.'

217

'Tell me what day it is and I'll see if I can get the day off,' said Connie.

'Will you help with the Sunday school outing?' asked Mandy. 'Miss Jackson says she needs lots of helpers.'

'I'll see what I can do,' Connie smiled. 'When is it?'

'Whit Monday,' said Gwen. 'The maypole dancing is on the Saturday before.'

'I may not be able to do both,' Connie cautioned. She didn't tell the family she had two more days off when she went back to the nurses' home that night because tomorrow, she was going to see Kenneth.

Her brother looked so much better. He had lost his elephant's trunk and the skin over his nose looked pink and healthy. He was more excited about his hands and proudly showed her that Mr McIndoe had created a ridge along his palm at the base of where his fingers used to be. This would eventually give him the ability to grip, once the swelling had gone down.

'Not quite as good as fingers,' Kenneth smiled, 'but it will certainly help.'

They both examined his hand and then Kenneth said, 'Where's your chap today? Couldn't he come?'

'He's not my chap,' Connie protested. 'He's the brother of a friend of mine.'

'Oh,' said Kenneth in an all-knowing way. 'He seemed to like you though.'

Connie blushed and changed the subject. 'I want to ask you something,' she said. 'It's about the day you were sent away.'

Kenneth shot out his bottom lip. 'Are you sure you want to talk about that? The last time I mentioned it you almost fainted.'

'I'll behave myself this time,' she said. 'You don't mind me talking about it?'

He shook his head. 'Not at all. If Ga was here she'd have something to say about it, but no, I don't mind.'

'You see,' said Connie sitting closer as if talking in confidence, 'I can remember some stuff but not everything.'

He looked puzzled. 'You mean to do with Stan Saul?'

Hearing the name made Connie want to shudder but she tried not to let it show. 'Over the years, I've blocked out so much of that day. I remember him kissing me and that I didn't like it. I remember him giving us cider and then I remember him running away when Ga came.'

'I reckon there was something in that cider,' said Kenneth. 'I didn't drink very much of it but I felt really ill. Ga accused me of being drunk.'

'So what did happen?' said Connie.

'All I remember is Ga coming in and giving me hell. She bashed me half to death with a hair brush. I could hear you upstairs being sick and she was telling me I was a pimp. I had no idea what the word meant but she was hopping mad.'

'I know she told you to go,' said Connie, 'but why did you stay away?'

'I was about ready to go anyway,' said Kenneth. 'I was coming up to sixteen and it was just the excuse I needed. The only trouble was, just as I was going out of the door, she told me she'd tell Mum about you and Stan if I came back. I kept away because I didn't want to ruin your reputation.'

'Me and Stan?' said Connie. 'There was no me and Stan. He was horrible. I hated him.'

'She said he'd got you pregnant,' Kenneth said quietly.

'What!' Connie stood up. 'That's awful. How dare she? Nothing happened, Kenny, I swear.'

The two of them fell silent and Connie sat back down. 'He was nothing but a creepy little maggot.'

'I knew if Ga told Mum she would skin me alive,' said Kenneth staring at the floor. 'Ga said she would protect you and that no one would ever know what you two had been up to. She made out as if it was all my fault.'

'How?'

'Because I had invited him,' said Kenneth. 'She even accused me of taking money from him.'

'What money?' Connie shook her head. 'You mean the money on the table?'

Kenneth took in his breath. 'How did you know about that?'

'I don't know,' said Connie. 'I can't remember exactly. Kenny, I tried to tell Ga it was nothing to do with you, but she wouldn't listen. Who did the money belong to anyway?'

Kenneth shrugged.

'But Ga said Stan had paid you to take me to bed.'

'That's a barefaced lie!'

'And I was thirteen, for goodness' sake,' said Connie. 'What did I know about stuff like that?'

'So I stayed away all this time for nothing,' said Kenneth.

Connie's heart went out to him. 'Well, we've found each other now, Kenny. We have to tell Mum that you're alive. I can't keep this up much longer.'

'Not yet.'

'But why?'

'There's something else,' he said. 'I've met someone.'

Connie was completely taken aback. 'Met someone?'

'I know,' said Kenneth. 'I find it pretty amazing too.'

'It's not that,' Connie said quickly and her brother laughed as her face flushed. 'Who is she?'

'One of the nurses,' he said. 'Her name is Pearl.' His eyes misted over. 'She's wonderful.'

'Do I get to meet her?'

'She's on duty today,' he said. 'She'll be bringing the teas around in a minute.'

Connie was totally gobsmacked. What a surprise! She hadn't expected that, and yet why not? Kenneth was still a young man. She rubbed his arm affectionately. 'I'm really happy for you,' she smiled.

'Ah, here she is.'

Connie looked around as a small woman with her mousy blonde hair pushed back in a French plait walked towards them. She was smiling.

'Darling,' Kenneth called, 'I want you to meet my sister.'

Connie stood up and Pearl reached for her hand. Her handshake was firm. 'Pleased to meet you,' she said.

She sat with them on the lawn as Connie and Kenneth drank their tea. With a little gentle probing, Connie found out that Pearl had nursed her brother from the beginning of his stay at the Royal Victoria and somewhere along the line, they'd fallen in love. Certainly when Pearl looked at Kenny, Connie couldn't help being aware that she gazed at him as if he was as handsome as Tyrone Power or James Stewart.

'About Mum?' Connie asked as she was leaving. 'I should tell her.'

'Soon,' promised Kenneth.

On the way home, as she dozed on the train, she finally pieced together the events of that day. The only thing that eluded her now was why. Why did Ga send Kenny away for good? What possible motive could she have?

For her third day off, Connie was going to Chichester with Eva. They knew there was a market there and it would make a lovely day out on the train. Connie had to be careful not to spend too much. All these train fares were beginning to eat into her money but she'd never been to Chichester before and the long journey meant that she and Eva could talk.

'Steven is taking me to meet his parents at the end of the month.'

Connie grinned. 'Does that mean your romance is no longer a secret?'

Eva nodded. 'It's getting harder and harder to deny it,' she said candidly. 'I'm about to enter my third year of nursing and he's got another two. We're planning to marry as soon as he graduates.'

'How exciting,' Connie enthused. 'Did you go and see Queenie? Was she all right about it?'

'She was fantastic,' said Eva. 'She said she couldn't face coming to the wedding . . .'

'Understandable,' Connie interrupted.

'But she wants to help me with the reception. Will you be my bridesmaid when the time comes?'

'Oh Eva, I'd be thrilled.' Connie paused. 'It looks like your romance won't be the only secret out in the open at last.'

They spent the rest of the journey talking about Emmett and his wife and Connie's visit to Kenneth the day before. The one person they didn't talk about was Roger. Every time Connie went into Eva's room, she'd look at the photograph of Roger she kept on her dressing table. It wasn't very big, and Roger was standing a long way from the camera, but Connie's eye was always drawn to it. She had to be careful Eva didn't see her looking, because she didn't want to give her ideas. In the end Connie had to ask. 'How's Roger?' she said, trying to sound as casual as possible.

Eva grinned knowingly.

'Only asking,' Connie said quickly. Because Roger hadn't written for some time, Connie found herself thinking about him all the time. She'd started worrying that something may have happened to him. Had he been injured by a bomb? Had he been . . . no, if he had, Eva would have told her. Eva seemed unconcerned about her brother but Connie knew they wrote to each other at least once a week, so he must be all right. She didn't want Eva jumping to conclusions. Roger was a friend.

'He's doing some sort of training course,' said Eva. 'They have to keep up-to-date with things. One of his mates was killed last week.'

So that was why he hadn't written. The revelation hit Connie hard. Roger was a nice man. She hated the idea that his life was in danger all the time.

'Are you all right?' Eva asked. 'You look a bit pale.'

'How can you stay so calm about it?' Connie accused.

Eva gave her a long hard stare. 'Years of practice but inside I'm screaming.'

They were sitting opposite each other and as her friend turned her head to look out of the window, Connie moved to sit next to her and hold her hand. 'I'm sorry,' she said. 'I was being crass and stupid. It must be hell for you.'

'And you?' said Eva.

'I don't want to think of him that way,' said Connie. 'He's just a friend. I'm done with men.'

'Oh, Connie . . .'

'I mean it. I was so wrong about Emmett.'

'There's plenty more fish in the sea,' said Eva.

'Now you sound like my mother,' said Connie, resuming her usual seat.

*

Stan had put it off long enough. It hadn't come as a shock this time. He'd had the clap before but this time he was frustrated. That slut had virtually offered herself to him. If he hadn't been so weak this would never have happened. It didn't take much to work out who had given it to him this time. He smiled grimly. She wouldn't be giving it to some other mug; he'd make sure of that. She'd looked so young that he'd felt sure he was the first but she obviously wasn't as unsullied as he'd thought. It was unfortunate that he'd had to go to his mother's doctor, but there was no alternative. Still, the man was close to retirement, and he still knew his stuff. Of course, he had insisted that he hadn't been with anyone.

'It must have been on the lavatory seat. Those public toilets down by the seafront leave a lot to be desired,' he'd said and the doctor didn't argue. He knew and the doctor knew he was talking out of the back of his head, but so long as his mother never found out, he didn't care. It began with an itch, but as soon as the discharge

223

came, he knew what it was. Damn it and he'd been so careful. He'd never liked going to one of those tarts, but there were times when the need was so strong and no one else was available. He didn't want to wear a rubber and the girl had looked very young. She'd looked cute in that gym slip. His mouth tightened. Next time he'd put something over her mouth. Not that there would be a next time. He couldn't stand women prattling away all the time. He had enough of that from his mother. She never shut up.

'Venereal disease is much easier to treat these days,' the doctor told him.

He was glad. The last time he'd had a dose of the clap, he was in hospital and had to miss the whole of the VE celebrations because by then he was on his third day of treatment. Thirty-four grams of sulfathiazole by injection over a period of five days. It was bloody painful but it had done the trick.

According to the doc, the VD clinic was at the back of the hospital and down a lane. Apparently, they were very careful about privacy and made sure that no one would be able to see him arriving or identify him. It was open Monday, Wednesday and Friday evening and from nine till noon on Thursday. He decided to go as soon as possible.

Twenty-Two

Chichester was wonderful. Connie and Eva strolled around the shops for a while and in among the market stalls. They had decided to make a day of it and although there was little money to spend, she and Eva enjoyed browsing.

'Connie!'

Connie spun round when she heard the voice and a second later, a bemused Eva looked on as Connie and Kez hugged and danced with each other in the middle of the pavement.

She was selling lovely handmade dollies' clothes, beautifully crafted wooden trains, rattles and rockers. Connie could see Simeon's amazing talent straight away. They browsed among the things and Connie bought Mandy some lovely wall-mounted letters which spelt her name. There was a peg on the 'a' so she could hang her dressing gown up if she wanted. Connie loved the bright jazzy colours. After living for so long with dull browns and creams and woodland green, it was so much fun to see reds and yellows and bright blues. Connie wondered where Simeon had found them but the market stall was so busy, there was hardly any time to speak to Kez.

'Where are you camped?'

'We're keréngro now,' Kez beamed in between customers. 'Simeon bought a piece of land over Slinden way and we've got our trailer there. My kids can go to school and learn to read.'

'These things are fantastic,' said Eva after Connie introduced them. 'I'm sure you'll do a roaring trade.'

Kez was wrapping another sale in newspaper. 'She is already!' laughed Connie.

'Simeon is talking about getting a shop,' Kez told them during another brief lull. 'He's talking with the bank mush right now.'

Another customer interrupted them, giving Connie another chance to admire more stock, some lovely skittles and a small train.

'Does Simeon make all of these?' Connie asked.

'He makes the wooden stuff,' said Kez. 'I dress the dollies.'

'Where are your kids?' said Connie, looking around.

'Pen looks after them while I works,' said Kez.

'You look like a real business woman,' Connie laughed.

'Thanks to you helping me to read,' said Kez, giving her arm a grateful squeeze.

Eva wandered off to the next stall. 'Have you heard from Isaac?' Connie asked. Kez shook her head.

'His time must be up soon.'

Kez sold a toy farmhouse and wrapped it in newspaper. As she put the money in her pouch, she sighed. 'He should be out in a week or so,' she said. 'We went up to Portsmouth, but he didn't want us to see him.'

'He must be very angry and upset,' Connie remarked.

''Course he is, 'cos he never done it,' said Kez fiercely. 'Isaac is a lot of things, but he ain't no liar. If he says he never took the stuff, then he never.'

'Clifford told me they found the stuff in his caravan,' Connie said cautiously.

'And that's another thing,' said Kez. 'That weren't his caravan. They found it in Reuben's caravan.'

She moved to serve someone else leaving Connie to digest what she had said. She hadn't really thought about it before but Kez was right. Isaac slept behind the hedge in his own tent. In recent times he had progressed into a small touring caravan dating back to the 1930s. It wasn't at all like Reuben's traditional gypsy caravan. It was a bit battered but he was doing it up. He also had a small lorry which was why he'd been learning about motors. Connie frowned. Having seen how independent the gypsies were, there was no reason for Isaac to put his stuff in his father's caravan. What was the point? Reuben was on his last legs and Isaac would have known that when the old man died, everything would go up in smoke, so why hide valuable booty there? Of course he had no idea *when* the old man would die, but it would be one hell of a risk, wouldn't it?

'Did your dad have a lot of money?' Connie asked.

Kez shrugged.

'You said Simeon has gone to the bank,' Connie persisted. 'Did Reuben have a bank account?'

'You know Reuben never trusted Gorgia,' said Kez. 'If he had money, he hid it somewhere.'

Connie looked away with a frown. Like under the floorboards of his caravan, for instance? With no one around to direct them (Isaac in jail and Reuben too ill to protest) the police had searched the wrong caravan, hadn't they. The money they'd found was Reuben's and somebody must have planted the missing jewellery in his caravan thinking that's where Isaac lived as well. So Isaac was innocent after all. She didn't like him all that much, but nobody deserved to be framed for something they didn't do. The revelation left Connie with more pressing questions. Who could have done it and why?

'Ready to move?' Eva cut across Connie's thoughts and she nodded. Kez was dealing with a steady stream of customers anyway. She called her goodbyes and Kez gave her the thumbs up. Connie was upset but there was little point in making waves now. Isaac would be out of prison soon.

'Fancy going to the pictures before we catch the bus back?' said Eva.

'Why not?' said Connie breaking into a trot. 'Race you there.'

'How do you test the patient's urine for sugar, nurse?'

It was two days later and Connie was doing her best to appear calm and controlled while shaking in her shoes. Matron always made her feel inadequate and she hated it. She couldn't forget the white glove incident in Room 1. Connie had been so sure she had cleaned every speck of dirt from that room and when she went back, she couldn't find any other smudges similar to the black on Matron's glove, so how come she had missed it? It was a complete mystery.

'Come along, nurse, speak up,' said Matron tetchily.

'Um . . .' Connie hesitated. 'I pour 5cc of Bendict's solution into the test tube and add . . .' The words died on Connie's lips because she could see by Matron's expression that she'd said something wrong. What had she said? 'Umm, 5cc of Benni . . .'

Behind Matron's head she could see Betty mouthing *Ben-e-dick.*

'I mean Beniprick solution . . .' Connie began again.

'For heaven's sake, nurse, you have been here long enough to know this,' came the reply. 'This should be routine by now.'

'Yes, Matron.' Connie could feel her face flaming.

'Routine!' said Matron turning on her heel.

Aggie relaxed deep into the armchair. It wasn't very often that she and Olive had the place to themselves but today the rest of the family was out. Clifford had gone up to London. Aggie didn't know why but she was sure Olive would get around to telling her. It was the second time he'd been up there on business in as many weeks. Her thoughts clouded. She hoped he wasn't pretending to be working when all the time he was running around with some floozy.

Gwen had gone to school to see Mandy dancing around the maypole as part of the school summer fete. There had been great excitement this year because she was one of the children chosen but numbers were restricted to one parent so Olive wasn't invited. Not that she would mind, of course. Her friend ignored children unless they were doing something they shouldn't.

Left alone while Olive was in the kitchen getting the tea things, Aggie stood up to admire Olive's nice ornaments and pretty pictures. She wouldn't dream of touching anything of course, that would be deemed as nosy, but looking was all right. Aggie kept her own home fairly plain. It cut down on the dusting. With no birthday or Christmas cards to catch her attention, Aggie satisfied her curiosity by looking at the bookshelf and trying to make up her mind which family member had chosen which book. Mandy was the easy one with a well-thumbed copy of Enid Blyton's book *Five on a Treasure Island*. There was a C.S. Forester book about Lord Hornblower which Aggie guessed belonged to Clifford and another called *The Egg and I* by Betty MacDonald which, because it was about the wife of a chicken farmer, Aggie supposed belonged to Gwen.

As she turned to sit down, she noticed that Olive had been writing letters. The bureau was open and Aggie gazed longingly at the paper rack. She remembered a time before the war when Olive had paid the absolute earth for some pretty sheets of creamy paper with a watermark. At the time, although Olive had given her a couple of sheets, Aggie had thought she was quite mad but now she was of the opinion that in these austere times the paper added a little distinction to a letter. There wasn't much left now. With one ear open for the sound of the tea trolley, Aggie thumbed through the pile of letters waiting to be posted. Nothing of interest except for one addressed to Sally Burndell. Why would Olive be writing to her?

By the time the rattling tea trolley came into the room, Aggie was sitting in the armchair just as Olive left her.

'I've made some sardine sandwiches,' said Olive as she backed through the door pulling the trolley behind her.

'Oooh, lovely,' said Aggie although she couldn't stand sardines.

She had the toaster from the kitchen and bending to put it in the hearth, slipped in a couple of crumpets. Aggie licked her lips. The crumpets were delicious eaten with butter and some of Gwen's homemade greengage jam.

'Of course, you've heard about Sally,' said Olive handing her a plate.

'What's she done now?' Aggie took a bite of her sandwich.

'She's getting married.'

'No!' Aggie took a sip of tea to swill away the taste. 'Well, that's a turn up for the books. I thought you said her gentleman friend didn't want her.'

'That's what I thought,' said Olive matter-of-factly. 'I can't keep up with her. First it's on, then it's off. Then she's going to be a secretary and then she's not. Next she's free to work in the shop and now she's not.'

Aggie frowned. 'Her poor mother must be at her wits' end.'

'Anyway,' Ga continued, 'she hasn't bothered to send us an invitation to the wedding.'

They sipped tea, each left to her own thoughts.

'I was looking in your bookcase,' Aggie eventually confessed. 'Mandy must enjoy reading. I noticed *Five on a Treasure Island* . . .'

'Oh, that's Connie's,' said Olive. 'She picked it up in a jumble sale. I think she's read it to Mandy but it's a bit old for her yet.' Olive stood up and went to the bookcase. 'This is my favourite,' she said pulling down *The Egg and I*. 'It's so funny. I love it. Have you read it?'

'No,' said Aggie feeling a bit miffed. 'I don't get much time to read.'

'I'm sure they're up to something again,' said Olive. She took Aggie's cup and emptied the dregs into the slop bowl before pouring her another cup of tea.

'Who?'

'The family. There's a lot of whispering and Clifford is always writing letters.'

'Maybe they're planning something nice for the summer holidays?' Aggie suggested.

Olive gave her a withering look. 'I don't think so. That Clifford always was a devious one. I wouldn't trust him as far as I could throw him.'

'And after all you've done for them,' Aggie tut-tutted sadly. 'I don't know why you put up with it, dear.'

'What choice do I have?' said Olive sourly. 'Give him his due, he is a good worker.' She sighed. 'We'd get along just fine if he wasn't always trying to change things.' She pointed to her friend's chin and Aggie wiped away some melted butter with her napkin.

'Perhaps you should just come out with it and ask them what they're up to?'

'I wouldn't give them the satisfaction.'

'What about Connie?' said Aggie. 'Couldn't you have a word with her?'

'Constance!' Olive snapped. 'That little minx. She'd only stick up for Clifford, wouldn't she. I still can't bring myself to forgive her for running out on us like that when she left the WAAFs.'

'I think it's terrible the way they treat you,' said Aggie. 'Especially when you've been so good to them.'

Ga smiled bravely. 'Have another crumpet, dear.'

This was Connie's first Saturday off for some time but it meant that she was lucky enough to help with the church jumble sale. The church held several jumble sales during the year. They were a good way of raising funds for the building they hoped to have one day. Connie loved them and collecting jumble could be just as much fun as the event itself. Connie's duties at the hospital had stopped her from taking part in that, but as soon as she'd heard Connie was free on the day, Jane Jackson didn't waste time in asking her to help. Connie was at the hired hall in Mulberry Lane by half past seven.

'Glad you could make it,' said Jane, giving her arm a squeeze.

'Wouldn't miss it for the world,' smiled Connie.

'Have you heard about Sally . . .?' Jane began.

Connie held her breath. Not more bad news?

'Terry turned up,' said Jane. 'It's all on again and they've even set a wedding date.'

Connie grinned. 'Oh Jane, that's wonderful news!'

'It certainly is,' said Jane. 'Her mother is looking a bit bewildered but everybody is thrilled of course.'

'Of course,' said Connie. She was so glad for Sally. The poor kid had had such a rough time and Terry had looked a decent sort. She'd drop her a line to congratulate her when she got back home. 'Jane, I've brought Mandy along too.'

Connie's sister stood beside her beaming.

'Hello Mandy,' smiled Jane. 'You can help with the children's toys, if you like.'

The arrangements were almost always the same. The men would put a line of trestle tables along each side of the church hall, and some more tables in front of the stage. Books and children's toys were on the left-hand side near the door with women's clothing on the next two tables. The bric-a-brac was always on the end tables with any big items like an old pram or washstand on the stage itself. On the other side of the hall the tables were divided in two halves with shoes and handbags on a small table just before the hatch where teas and coffees were served from the kitchen, and then the other side of the hatch the tables were for men's clothes – not so many of those.

While the men were putting up the tables, Connie and Jane

joined the other women in dragging the bags from the cupboards where they had been stored, into the main hall.

'Is your boyfriend here?' said Connie giving Mandy a toy soldier to put on the children's table. 'I'm the only one who hasn't seen him yet.'

Jane shook her head. 'He's working today but he'll be coming to the outing on Whit Monday.'

They had plenty of helpers and any time someone found something they'd like, they would put it on the stage behind the curtain until the end of the 'sort out'. The perk for helping was being able to buy what you wanted before the sale. The jumble came from a cross section of the village. Sometimes Connie was handling stuff from the upper crust and at other times she was dealing with things that had obviously been handed down several times already. And it didn't always follow that the good stuff came from the rich either. Connie knew it was often the roughest looking people who gave good, complete, unbroken and clean jumble while the obviously affluent might fob them off with rubbish.

'I was half expecting Reverend Jackson to be here,' Connie remarked to one of the other women as she handed her a welcome cup of tea.

'He'll be along later,' she said. 'This morning he's interviewing somebody to play the piano for the Sunday services.'

'At last,' cried Connie. 'It's ages since Michael Cunningham left.'

They were about halfway through their sorting when a well-heeled woman in a big car drove up to the door. 'I've brought you some things for your sale,' she announced in an all too loud plummy voice. Several heads looked up but everyone carried on with the job in hand. Eventually she spotted Connie. 'Hey, you. Miss. Fetch them from the car for me.'

Reluctantly, Connie followed her out of the door.

'I don't want anything for them,' she said handing Connie a rather large and heavy box.

As soon as she'd gone, Connie sorted through the boxes she'd left. They were filled with broken toys, cracked plates and cups with no handles.

'She's just dumped her rubbish on us,' Connie said in disgust.

Rev Jackson had just arrived in the hall. He came over to look. 'Put it all in the hallway, Connie,' he said shaking his head. 'We'll put it in the pile for the rag and bone man at the end of the sale.'

Connie dragged the box into the hallway and then noticed an old tea caddy. When she opened it, it was full of green mouldy tea. She couldn't resist taking it back into the hall to show Jane.

'How vile,' said Jane, jerking her head back as the musty smell filled the air. 'Ugh.'

Something caught Connie's eye. She looked around and found a bent spoon.

'What on earth are you doing?' cried Jane.

Connie fished around in the tea and pulled out a silver caddy spoon. 'Voilà!'

Rev Jackson took it from her and looked at it a little more closely. 'Well done, Connie,' he said. 'This is hallmarked. It could be worth a bit. We'll take it to the jewellers after the sale.'

'Ha!' laughed Jane. 'I bet she doesn't know it was in there.'

'And I bet she wouldn't have given it to us if she had,' Connie grinned.

Everything was ready by nine forty, so someone made them all another cup of tea. Mandy was going to stand with Connie on the children's clothing section.

'Tell everybody, whatever it is, it's thruppence,' Connie told her.

Mandy nodded gravely, aware of her responsibility to make a lot of money for the church.

The queue outside was already snaking around the hall. At ten o'clock, Rev Jackson called out, 'Ready everybody?' and a moment or two later having paid him sixpence to get in, the people rushed into the hall like a stampede of wild elephants and the sale was underway.

The first half an hour was manic. Most things were going for a song but sometimes people would barter.

'How much is this shirt, love?'

'A tanner.'

'I'll give you fourpence.'

People pushed and shoved, some even snatching their bargains out of the hands of another. Connie was terrified that they'd get to the end of the morning and find somebody's flattened child under the table but even though a few children disappeared under the frenzy of shopping bags and mothers in search of a bargain, nobody was hurt. A few ended up with a clip around the ear if their mother missed a bargain because they were in the wrong place and getting under her feet.

Mandy was chuffed every time she put another thruppenny bit in the money tin and Connie could see the coins were mounting up. By eleven o'clock the worst was over. A few women stayed doggedly sorting through the mountain of clothes for something they could wear or remake into something else. Another cup of tea came round and it was most welcome.

And at the end of the sale, the remaining jumble had to be piled up and stuffed into bags ready for the rag and bone man who was coming at twelve thirty. They cleared the hall, the men put the trestles back under the stage and Mandy helped Connie sweep the floor. Battle-scarred and weary, some helpers were promising themselves 'never again' until Rev Jackson said, 'Thank you everybody. It's been a good morning. Not only do we have a new church pianist called Graham, but we have made seventy-two pounds three shillings and five pence,' and everybody applauded.

When they collected their things from behind the curtain, Connie gave Mandy the toy typewriter she'd seen her admiring as she put the toys out.

'You were brilliant,' she said, giving her a kiss.

'Is that for me?' said Mandy, her bright eyes shining.

'Of course,' said Connie. 'I want you to type me a letter one day.'

'Oh, I will,' said Mandy. 'You're the bestest sister ever.'

By the time they got back home, Gwen had lunch waiting for them, macaroni cheese, Mandy's favourite. Afterwards, while Mandy played outside with Susan Revel and Sarah Bawden, Connie sat on the sofa in the little sitting room exhausted but happy. It was good to have this little oasis of calm available any time she was able to be here.

Her mother walked in with two cups of tea.

'Where's Ga?'

'Gone into Worthing for something,' said Gwen. 'I'm glad because I want to talk to you about something.'

'Sounds serious,' Connie joked.

'It is,' said her mother. 'Oh bother, I forgot you like sugar in your tea, don't you?'

She hurried out of the room leaving Connie worried. Serious? What could that mean? Was her mother ill again? She didn't look ill and she had boundless energy since Clifford came back. Perhaps there was something wrong with Clifford. He certainly seemed pretty miserable at times and once she had caught him looking at some papers, papers which he stuffed under a cushion as she'd come into the room. Was he in trouble with the business? No, Ga would have said something if the nurseries were failing. Maybe there was something wrong with Mandy. She could hear her playing outside with Susan and Sarah. They were skipping.

'Raspberry,
strawberry,
apple jam tart.
Tell me the name of your sweet heart.'

No, it couldn't be Mandy. She'd been full of energy at the jumble sale and listen to her now. If it wasn't Mandy, it had to be something about Ga.

Until her mother had pre-empted the moment, Connie had decided that this was the moment to tell her about Kenneth. Whatever Kenneth said, it wasn't right keeping his whereabouts from her any longer. She'd be cross enough that Connie had known where he was for almost two months now and that she'd been writing to him ever since and not told her. It would soften the blow a bit when her mother found out about his fiancée, but she still had to tell her about his terrible injuries.

Her mother reappeared with the sugar bowl and put it on the little table next to the sofa. 'Sorry I was so long,' she smiled. 'It was empty and I had to get some more from the cupboard.' She flopped into her chair and arranged the cushions.

'Come on, Mum,' said Connie. 'You've got me worried.'

'This is going to come as a bit of a shock,' said Gwen, 'but Clifford and I are thinking about leaving.'

Connie's brain was a little slow to catch on. 'Leaving? Leaving what?'

'The nurseries are hard work for little return,' said Gwen. 'We don't mind hard work, but we want a better future for ourselves and Mandy. We've decided to leave Belvedere Nurseries.'

'Is that all?' Connie laughed. 'That's fine. What will you do? Buy a shop?'

Gwen took a deep breath. 'Clifford read an advertisement in *The Times*,' she said getting to her feet. She went to find a tin box under the sideboard. Unlocking it with a key, she searched until she found a particular envelope and handed it to Connie. Inside was a cutting. *Calling all able bodied and skilled workers. Australia needs you. The Australian government is setting up assisted passages for British families. For only £10 you could have a brand new life for you and your family.* It was followed by a telephone number.

Connie's heart thudded. Her mother was staring at her anxiously. 'Australia?'

Gwen nodded. Connie re-read the cutting. Her mouth had

gone dry. Australia was thousands of miles away. It took six weeks to get there. It was on the other side of the world. She would never see her mother or Mandy again. She wanted to burst into tears, to shout and rant, 'No, you can't go, I don't want you to go, don't leave me please . . .' She wanted to say, 'Wait, you can't go, I haven't told you about Kenneth yet. Would you really leave him as soon as you've found him again?' She wanted to call her mother selfish and horrible but as she looked up again, something else kicked in.

'That's amazing, Mum,' she smiled although her voice had developed a distinct wobble. 'What an opportunity. All that way for just £10?'

'You don't mind?' Gwen asked anxiously.

'Of course I do,' said Connie brightly, 'but if you and Clifford want to do it, who am I to stop you? Don't let your opportunities pass you by, Mum.' Her voice had become thick with emotion as she repeated the very words her mother had said to her when she'd talked about nursing.

Gwen flung her arms around her daughter. 'Oh, Connie. You're such a wonderful daughter. You don't know what it means to me to have your blessing. I've been dreading telling you.'

As they let each other go, they both had tears in their eyes. 'I shall miss you,' Connie smiled brokenly.

'Why don't you come too?' said her mother.

Connie blinked. 'To Australia?'

'Why not?'

'I can't, Mum. My training.'

'You could enrol over there,' said Gwen, clearly excited by her own suggestion.

Connie shook her head. 'Mum, I need my SRN.'

'I wish it didn't have to be this way,' said Gwen, taking a hanky out of her apron pocket and blowing her nose, 'but Clifford . . .'

'I know,' said Connie, drying her own eyes. 'Clifford is a good man and he wants the best for you both.'

'There are such wonderful opportunities out there, Connie,' said Gwen. 'And after what happened to poor Sally . . . those terrible letters. I can't wait to get away from here.'

'Is anyone any closer to finding who sent them?'

Gwen shook her head. 'There are some sick people out there.' She paused. 'Oh darling, when you've finished your training please come and join us. We'd be settled by then.'

'When do you plan to go?' Connie was dreading the answer and when it came it was worse than she thought.

'The middle of September.'

'September!' Connie cried. 'So soon?'

'The assisted passage is only for younger people,' said Gwen. 'We have to be among the first to go. If we leave it any longer, Clifford will be too old.'

Connie's whole world was crashing down around her ears. 'What does Ga say?'

'We haven't told her yet,' said Gwen. 'I wanted you to know first.'

'Do you think she will go with you? I mean, she's got the money to pay her fare, hasn't she?'

Her mother's expression darkened. 'We want to do this on our own.'

'But what will she do?' Connie cried.

Gwen sipped her tea. 'Sell up and move into a luxury flat I should imagine. She's never paid us a proper wage the whole time she's lived here, so I imagine she's loaded. She'll land on her feet. She always does.'

'She kept you and Clifford short as well?' Connie gasped. 'I thought it was only me.'

Her mother shook her head. 'I shouldn't have told you really, but it's true. That's why Clifford gets so upset. She won't let him expand. She's stopped him from putting up more glasshouses, and she won't let him sell any of the land. He even suggested using the rough patch at the bottom for static caravans or building a few prefabs to help people with housing. The rent would have supplemented the nurseries but she won't have any of it and although we get by, he wants to be free to do what he wants without having to ask her first.'

By the tone of her mother's voice, Connie finally understood just how difficult it must have been to live with Ga. After she had packed up the WAAFs, Connie had been away from home for so long, that the thought of being forced to live with Ga again was what drove her towards nursing. The only reason she came home on her days off was to see her mother and Mandy. Certainly not Ga.

'I had no idea it was so bad, Mum.'

Gwen sat next to her daughter and put out her arms. 'I'm torn, Connie,' she said. 'I don't want to leave you, but I must go with my husband. He's a good man but he's so unhappy.'

Connie could see that this was going to be a wonderful release for her mother, Clifford and Mandy. They could be a family in their own right at last. It was only the sinking feeling in her own heart that reminded Connie that she would be on her own too.

Twenty-Three

When she got back to her room in the nurses' home, Connie sat on her bed and stared dejectedly at the wall. She had heard the water running in the bathroom as she came in. Betty's things were on her bed but her dressing gown was gone from the back of the door so she must be in the bath.

Connie's chin quivered and she let her tears fall freely. Everything was going wrong. She knew she was a good nurse but every time Matron was around, she got so flummoxed she did stupid things and now that her mother and her sister were leaving her for good, she felt really depressed. How could she survive without them? And what on earth was she going to do about Kenneth?

On her way in, she'd been to her pigeonhole and collected a letter from Roger. '*Thanks for both of your letters,*' he wrote. '*I think our letters must have crossed in the post. I've been kept quite busy. It seems that as soon as things get back to normal, someone uncovers another UXB. I reckon we'll be carrying on with the unit for some time to come.*'

She didn't know what to do about him either. She liked him. He was a good friend but did she really want more? Not that he'd intimated anything else but friendship of course. She sighed. It was hardly the end of the world but it was one of those moments when you wonder what it's all about.

There was a soft knock on the door and Eva came in. 'Hello.

Had a nice day? I saw the light was on.' Her voice faltered. 'Connie, whatever's wrong?'

Eva sat on the bed beside her and as soon as she put her arms around Connie's shoulders, she broke down altogether and once she started crying, she couldn't stop. Eva let her do it, plying her with clean handkerchiefs until she was done, and Connie told her everything. Some of it, Eva already knew. She knew about Kenneth and Connie's dilemma about telling her mother, but Connie's run-ins with Matron and the family's move to Australia was news to her.

'Dear life,' said Eva, 'you've obviously had one hell of a day.'

'What am I going to do?' Connie wept.

'Well,' said Eva blowing out her cheeks, 'as far as Kenneth goes, I think you should tell your mum. She'll be angry of course but she will hate you forever if you let her go all the way to Australia without seeing him.'

Connie nodded. 'You're right. I've been so anxious to please him, I haven't really thought about how it would affect Mum. Going to the other side of the world changes everything.' She burst into tears again as Betty came into the bedroom wearing her dressing gown. Her towel was over one shoulder and she was carrying her wash bag. 'Whatever's wrong?' she gasped.

'Connie has just discovered her family are moving to Australia,' said Eva.

'Oh, you poor love,' said Betty sitting on the other side of Connie. She smelled deliciously of Yardley's French Fern bath salts.

'I don't think I can do this anymore,' said Connie. Deep in her heart she knew she didn't really mean what she was saying but she was hurting so much. She couldn't do anything about Australia, and she knew whatever she decided Mum was going to be upset about Kenneth. Nursing was the one part of her life over which she had complete control.

'Do what?' said Betty.

'Be a nurse,' Connie wailed. 'I'm lousy at it. For some reason, Matron's got it in for me and she gets me in such a state I can't do anything right.'

'Don't be silly,' said Eva. 'You can't let the old bat ruin your life.'

'But she always picks on me, Eva,' said Connie blowing her nose. 'You remember how I was when she asked me about the Benedict solution. I knew what it was, but she got me in such a panic my mind went a complete blank.'

'She does that to everyone,' said Eva.

Connie was calming down but she wasn't ready to let go yet. 'Then there was that day when she found the dust in the room I'd just cleaned . . .'

'The old cow has been doing that one for years,' scoffed Betty. 'She had a pair of white gloves on, right?'

'Yes,' said Connie slowly.

'Some of the older girls have told me about it,' said Betty. 'She makes a big thing of putting on one glove and keeps the other in her hand, right?'

'What *are* you talking about?' said Eva.

'And when she comes out of the room,' Betty went on, 'she's got both gloves on and one of them has a dirty finger. Am I right again?'

The two girls looked at her with blank expressions.

'That's because she's already blacked it with shoe polish.'

Neither girl spoke.

'It's a set-up,' cried Betty. 'There was nothing wrong with the room you cleaned.'

Connie was trying to recall everything that happened and Betty was right. She had searched that room from top to bottom but she'd never found the source of that black smudge. No wonder if it was boot polish!

243

'I don't believe it,' gasped Eva. 'That's an awful thing to do.'

They looked from one to the other and burst out laughing. 'The crafty old cat!' cried Connie.

Betty got up from the bed. 'I've got a bottle of sherry in the wardrobe. Fancy something to drink, girls? Connie?'

Connie blew her nose noisily.

'She's up for it,' said Eva. 'Is that a letter from Kenneth?'

Connie blushed. 'From Roger, actually.'

Eva grinned. Betty poured the sherry into the one glass she had stashed in her wardrobe and some more into the lid and a third lot into her tooth mug. Eva got the glass, Connie the tooth mug. Connie sipped slowly. Even though the mug was clean, the sherry still tasted vaguely of toothpaste.

'Ga always pulls me up on my shortcomings,' said Connie. 'She was convinced from the start that I'd never make the grade. Do you honestly think I can do it?'

'Absolutely,' cried Eva. 'You're a really caring person, Connie. Just the sort of nurse the new NHS will need.'

'Don't let Matron see that you're getting into a flap,' advised Betty. 'Find a way to bring her down to size.'

'She's pretty small if she has to resort to such mean tricks,' said Connie.

'Atta girl,' said Eva, giving her a hearty pat on the back.

'Anyway, enough of that,' said Betty. 'Have I got a juicy bit of gossip for you!'

Connie and Eva looked up.

'Sister Hayes is leaving,' said Betty. 'She's pregnant.'

'But she's not married,' Connie blurted out.

'Exactly,' said Betty. She puffed up her chest and imitated Sister Hayes as she was on their first day. 'This hospital has a good reputation for clean living gels with fine upstanding morals. We don't allow men in the nurses' home under any circumstances.' Betty paused for effect and then lifting the lid of the

244

sherry bottle to her lips added, 'Sound advice if you don't want to get in the family way, gels.'

And all three of them roared with laughter.

It was supper time and Matron made a surprise visit to the women's ward. 'We are short of nurses in the special clinic,' she announced to Sister Wayland.

'We don't usually send the students,' Sister reminded her. 'Dr Saunders prefers the older nurses.'

'Needs must, when the devil drives,' Matron said coldly. 'Who have you got on duty?'

Sister Wayland read out the names on the duty roster.

'Give me Nurse Dixon,' said Matron.

Connie put Mrs Meyer's meal on the locker and with an apology left her chewing a morsel of fish. Mrs Meyer had little appetite these days and she knew she hadn't got long to live. It had taken a while to trace her daughter who lived in Kenya but she was now on her way. They'd told Mrs Meyer she was coming, and somehow it kept the old lady going. As Connie did her best to encourage her to eat a little more she couldn't help wondering how she would feel if her mother was taken ill when she was twelve thousand miles away. She could only hope and pray that Mrs Meyer's daughter got here in time to say her last goodbye.

'You will report to the special clinic,' said Matron. 'Have you any objections to that?'

Connie shook her head. 'No, Matron.' What was the special clinic? Connie was dying to ask but she couldn't bring herself to say the words. Matron turned and walked away. A couple of seconds later, she came sailing back down the ward, her mouth looking as tight as a cat's bottom. She was holding up a stocking. Connie braced herself.

'What's the meaning of this?'

Connie stared at her blankly. 'I don't know, Matron.'

'I found it attached to the cupboard door,' said Matron. 'You have just come from that cupboard, haven't you?'

'I needed to get Mrs Meyer a new gown,' said Connie.

'Don't answer back,' Matron snapped.

Connie thought about protesting but what was the point? The woman had already made up her mind Connie was responsible for putting the stocking there and nothing would change it. 'No, Matron.'

There was a loud bang and Sister came running. 'Who has been messing around with the cupboard door again? I thought I told . . .' The words died on her lips as she saw Matron. 'Excuse me, Matron. I thought you'd gone.'

Matron puffed out her chest. 'I had until I saw what this stupid nurse had done.'

She threw the stocking in Connie's face and turned on her heel saying, 'Please remember that this is a hospital ward, nurse, not a changing room.' And with that she swept out.

There was another loud bang. Sister bent to pick up the stocking. 'Someone spilled some cleaning fluid on the floor,' she said. 'I kept the door open with the stocking to assist the drying. If it's not tied back, it bangs all the time.'

Biting back her tears, Connie returned to her patient. 'I'm sorry, Mrs Meyer, but I have to go. I am needed elsewhere. I'll get Nurse Frances to help you.'

'You're trembling, dear,' the old lady said with effort.

Connie smiled even though she was struggling to keep a lid on her emotions.

'Take no notice of that miserable dried-up old prune, dear,' said Mrs Meyer. Connie felt a bony hand patting hers. 'Remember what I said and think of her with her knickers around her ankles.'

And despite everything, Connie laughed.

*

Stan almost missed the lane, it was so well hidden by undergrowth. At the end he was faced with two doors. They were unmarked but the doctor had said one was for women and the other for men. For a second, he panicked. Which one was which? All at once, the door opened and he was face to face with another man. Keeping his head down, he went in. As the door closed behind him, the man was lighting up and he could see his hand was shaking.

The reception area was small with seating around the walls. He went to the hatchway and he was handed a card with a number on it. X527. The nurse on the other side, some old bat with grey hair, smiled and asked him to take a seat until the doctor called him. This was the worst bit. He was in mortal fear that he would see someone he recognised.

*

Connie discovered that the special clinic was for patients with vene-real disease. Patients accessed the clinic by a back entrance and the nursing staff used an internal yellow door. She was dreading this but she also realised that as unpalatable as it might be, a good nurse had to deal with all patients with all sorts of problems and from all walks of life. Her first lesson was not to judge a person. She had been assigned to look after two women, X65 and X495. X65 was about thirty-five, a brassy looking woman who smoked incessantly. Her language was crude and according to her notes, she had been to the clinic several times. X495 was much younger. A respectable looking woman dressed in a smart suit and a faded fur, she had only been married a couple of years. Although no one asked for details, she made it clear that she was mortified to be in the clinic. She told Connie she had only just discovered that her husband had been visiting what she called a house of ill repute and that he had passed something unmentionable on to her. Connie's heart went out to her and she did her best to make her feel at ease.

After the doctor had seen them both, he said he was popping

out for a fag. As soon as she was dressed, Connie walked X495 to the door.

'Do I have to come again?'

'I'm afraid so,' said Connie sympathetically. 'The treatment is for six days.'

'Don't waste your sympathy on that witch,' muttered the doctor as he came back in and the door closed. 'She might look like the cat's whiskers but she runs a brothel just outside the town centre. I pity the man who gave her that. He'll probably have no chance of fatherhood by the morning.'

'But I thought . . .' Connie began.

'That X65 was the worst?' said the doctor. 'Raped when she was six, and used by her mother's men friends until she left school. I wouldn't say she's got a heart of gold but no one deserves what happened to her in life.'

Connie was stunned. A nurse called another number. 'X527. X527.' There was a movement on the other side of the screen and the nurse said, 'Right this way, sir.'

Connie followed the doctor back into the women's section.

*

Stan had been sitting in the corner until she called his number. He had reached for a magazine from the table but then it occurred to him that someone else might have already picked it up and he changed his mind. You never knew what filthy disease they might have. Instead, he leaned back in the chair, closed his eyes and tried not to think about the itch that was driving him mad.

When the nurse called him into the other room, he had to go behind a curtain and undress. While the doctor took a swab, he stared at the top of the man's head. He had a wart in the centre. It didn't have hairs on it like his mother's wart on her top lip, but it made him shudder. Thinking that his examination had hurt him, the doctor apologised.

'Does it hurt you to pass water?'

'It burns.'

'I think that without doubt, X527, you have gonorrhoea,' said the doctor, returning to his seat and writing up his notes. 'The swab will ascertain whether or not this is so, but you will commence treatment straight away. You will need to come back for daily injections.'

'Daily?' he spluttered.

'I think six days should do the trick,' the doctor went on. 'This new Penicillin therapy has had some very promising results.'

'But every day?' he complained. 'It will be hard. I have commitments.'

'If you cannot manage the night clinic,' said the doctor, 'we can put you down for the day clinic. It starts at ten o'clock but of course there is always the risk that you might bump into someone you know. Would that be better?'

'I think I'll stick to the nights.'

The doctor motioned to the nurse and she brought a small tray with a glass syringe. 'I cannot stress the importance of maintaining the full treatment,' he said. 'Drop your trousers again, X527.'

On the bus on the way home, he sat on the edge of the seat. Now he had an unbearable itch and a sore backside.

*

Connie went home as soon as she'd finished her late duty and caught the last bus back to Goring. The house was in darkness when she walked in. Everyone was already in bed. Her heart was heavy. If Ga moved as well, this place would soon be a thing of the past. Pip greeted her lavishly and it occurred to her for the first time that he would soon be without a home. What was going to happen to him? Ga wouldn't keep him. She'd never liked him. He was far too old to go all the way to Australia and she certainly couldn't look after him in the nurses' home. That

249

realisation added another layer to her heartache. She went to bed and cried herself to sleep.

She was dreaming that she was eating an ice cream, but for some reason the cone kept slipping into her ear. It was so cold she woke up to find Pip with his head on the pillow, breathing into her ear. She pushed him away sleepily but a second or two later, he was back. She opened her eyes and he made for the open door and looked back, his tail wagging. Obviously, he wanted to go out. Connie groaned. Swinging her legs out of the bed, she groped for her slippers.

As she was pulling on her dressing gown, Connie heard an unexpected noise. Someone was downstairs. Why didn't Pip bark? She crept out onto the landing, Pip padding along just ahead of her. Should she wake Clifford? If she did, the whole house would be awake and she'd feel a right idiot if it was nothing. She didn't put on the light as she went downstairs. Afterwards, she wondered why she hadn't. It would have been far more sensible and a lot safer. A light would have sent the burglar running.

She and Pip padded along the passageway to the sitting room door. As she walked in and turned on the light, she wasn't sure which one of them was the most surprised, herself or Isaac Light. Pip had stopped right next to her and she grabbed his collar.

There was a canvas bag on the sofa and Connie could see a couple of silver picture frames sticking out of it. Isaac was riffling through the contents of the roll top desk and he had found some cash. There were several pound notes in his hand and he held a letter opener. As soon as he saw Connie, he held the letter opener at arm's length and advanced towards her. Pip growled and he stopped in his tracks.

'Put it down, Isaac,' said Connie quietly, 'or I let the dog go.'

Isaac dropped the letter opener and the money.

'Why are you doing this?' Connie asked. 'My family has shown nothing but kindness to your family. Is this how you repay us?'

'Kindness,' he spat. 'Is that what you call it? You sit here in your cosy little house with all this . . .' he waved his arm extravagantly, 'this stuff, while we get shoved from pillar to post. We're not all dirty gypos you know. Some of us want to make an honest living.'

'When did you get out of jail?'

'Yesterday.'

'Yesterday,' said Connie, 'and here you are today, robbing the very people who tried to help you.'

'I've got *nothing*,' he said baring his teeth. 'Even my bloody van's been taken away.'

'I'm sorry,' said Connie. 'If it's not there, that's only happened recently. It was there a couple of weeks ago because I saw it. Kez has moved over to Slinden.'

He looked surprised.

'Kez and Simeon have a place over there,' she went on. 'They've set up in business together making toys. They're doing quite well.'

'While I'm left on the rubbish heap.'

'No, you're not,' said Connie. 'They want you back. Half of this is your fault anyway. They went all the way to Portsmouth to see you but you wouldn't see them.'

'That's right,' he said sulkily. 'Blame me. Everybody blames me.'

'Oh, stop feeling sorry for yourself,' said Connie crossly. 'And keep your voice down unless you want the rest of the family to hear you.'

'I never done what they said,' he hissed.

'I know you didn't,' said Connie. 'And what's more important, Kez knows that too. She believes you and so did Reuben. I know how much you've suffered.'

At the mention of his father's name, Isaac's face coloured. 'What do you know about suffering?'

Now Connie was furious. 'What do I know about suffering?' she hissed. 'I work in a hospital where half the people who come there have come far too late to get help because they can't afford

251

to pay the doctor's shilling. What do I know about suffering? My family are going to the other side of the world and I'll never see them again. My own brother is in a hospital with half his face blown away and only a stump for a hand. What do I know about suffering? I work bloody hard to make a living, so why can't you get off your backside and do the same?'

She had surprised herself with her own passion and Isaac's cocky attitude was somewhat deflated. 'Are you going to call the coppers?'

'I think I should,' said Connie. 'They'd come and take you down to the station straight away. Of course, you'll be locked up again. Remember how small the cells are? But of course you do. You must be really keen to go back seeing as you only got out yesterday.'

Isaac's face had gone white. 'Please,' he said faintly. 'Don't tell.' He went to the bag and took out the photo frames. 'I won't do it again.' He dug deeper and took out Clifford's silver cigarette case, her mother's best teapot, several other items, including her mother's silver thimble. 'Please don't tell,' he kept saying. 'I'm sorry. I'm sorry about your brother too. I don't want to be locked up again. I can't stand it.'

'You should go and see the Frenchie,' said Connie, her voice softening. 'He'll give you another chance, I'm sure. He helped your father.'

'He can't help me,' said Isaac, the old belligerence coming back. 'I went there. The place is all locked up.'

Connie frowned. 'All locked up?'

'He's gone,' said Isaac. The bag was empty and Isaac backed towards the French doors.

'Have you had anything to eat?' Connie asked.

'I've already helped myself to a pork pie . . . thanks.'

Pip growled again. Isaac put his hand up in a defensive gesture and slipped out into the night. She let the dog go and closed the French doors.

'You wanted to give him a second chance, didn't you?' she said patting Pip's side. 'Let's hope we made the right decision.'

The dog licked her face and Connie felt strangely emotional. She bent down and put her arms around his neck. 'Good boy,' she said quietly. 'Good boy, Pip.'

As she stood to her feet, Connie knew she wasn't alone. There was someone in the hallway. Dear God, had Isaac brought someone else with him to the house?

'Who's there?' she said cautiously and her mother stepped into the room. She was in her dressing gown, her hair in a long plait at the side of her head. Her eyes were red and she had obviously been crying.

'How could you?' she said coldly. 'How could you keep such a secret? Why didn't you tell me about Kenneth? You've done a wicked, wicked thing, Connie, and I don't know if I can ever forgive you.'

Twenty-Four

They sat up most of the night. There were tears aplenty but Connie told her mother everything.

'I wanted to tell you, Mum, I really did, but Kenny had a funny bit of skin dangling from his nose and he didn't want you to see him like that. He told me that if you came, he would tell them to send you away.' Pip came and put his head on Connie's lap.

'Tell me again what happened,' said Gwen.

So Connie told her mother about the crash and the flames that came up between Kenneth's legs. She told her about his burnt hand and how it had seized up until Mr McIndoe had managed after four operations to get some limited movement back into it. 'He couldn't even feel his face,' Connie explained. 'He said he vaguely remembered them dragging him out of the cockpit and rolling him on the ground, but he'd been burnt on the whole of his right side and they've had to rebuild his nose.'

'So what was the elephant trunk thing?' asked Gwen, clearly alarmed.

'A skin graft,' said Connie. 'They've taken skin from another part of his body and put it on his face. It was still attached to the place where they've taken it from because they don't want the skin to die.'

There was a brief lull in conversation and then Connie said, 'The hospital wrote to you several times but you never replied.'

'What are you saying?' said Gwen crossly. 'Do you really think that I would abandon my own son? I never had any letters, Connie.'

'That's what I told them,' said Connie. 'I felt sure that if you knew where Kenny was, you would have moved heaven and earth to be with him, but they insist that they definitely wrote to you.'

'Maybe they wrote to the old address,' said Gwen.

'They had the right address,' said Connie shaking her head. 'When you didn't reply, they tried my address at the hospital.'

'So why didn't I get the letters?' said Gwen, puzzled. 'I don't understand.'

Connie said nothing. She still had her suspicions but she didn't want to be the one to point the finger at Ga. After all, she had no proof.

'Mum, please forgive me for hurting you,' said Connie, her eyes filling with tears again. 'This has weighed heavily on my mind for so long. I wanted to tell you . . .'

Her mother leaned over and took Connie in her arms. 'I think from now on we have to promise each other that no matter how difficult a thing is, we mustn't keep secrets from each other,' she said.

Connie nodded. 'But Ken . . .'

'Shh, shh, shh,' said Gwen. 'I shall tell Kenneth the same thing, don't you worry. Now tell me where he is.'

'I'll take you in the morning, if you like,' said Connie. 'I'm not doing anything much.'

'No,' said Gwen. 'I want some time with him on my own. Tomorrow is Ascension Day. Mandy goes to school then they all go to the Anglican church for a service and she's got the rest of the day off. You'd be doing me a great favour if you would look after her.'

Connie nodded again. 'There's one more thing, Mum.'

Her mother's face paled and she groaned. 'Oh Connie . . . now what?'

'No, you'll like this,' Connie promised. 'Kenny is engaged.'

'Engaged?' Gwen gasped. 'But I thought you said . . .'

'She's his nurse, so she knows all there is to know about him. She's a lovely girl. Her name is Pearl. I think you'll like her a lot.'

'But what sort of a marriage will they have if he's so badly burned?'

'You wait until you see her, Mum,' said Connie. 'Yes, he's scarred but that doctor has worked wonders. I think once he's finished all the treatment, Kenny has every chance of having a good life.'

Gwen shook her head in disbelief. 'When I was a young woman, I saw men come back from the Great War,' she sighed. 'They had horrible open wounds . . .'

'Kenny's not a bit like that, Mum.'

Her mother yawned and stood up. 'Not a word of this to Ga,' she warned.

'I thought you said no more secrets,' Connie remarked.

'I don't want her sticking her oar in,' said Gwen fiercely. 'So please Connie, say nothing.'

The first grey light of dawn was coming through the window. Pip stretched and yawned before returning to his bed and flopping down although there was only about two hours left to sleep.

'Night, Mum,' Connie said wearily as they made their way back to bed. As she lay between the sheets, her head was pounding. It was a weight off her mind now that her mother knew about Kenneth. Connie knew that it was the stress of the past few weeks that had made her work in the hospital suffer. If only she could take a break, a holiday and give herself a chance to wind down and have a bit of peace and quiet in her life, but it was impossible.

Her mother left before anyone was up. Connie decided that while Mandy was in her Ascension Day service, she would take the opportunity to go to the Frenchie's workshop. She wanted to see if he knew what had happened to Isaac's caravan.

256

'You do know he's virtually closed down,' said Clifford at the breakfast table.

'Yes,' said Connie, 'I had heard that. What happened?'

Clifford shrugged. 'It might have something to do with breaking up with Mavis Hampton.'

Connie's heart jumped. Eugène had broken up with Mavis? Connie forced herself not to think about it as she deliberately changed the subject. 'Clifford, do you know what happened to Isaac's caravan and his old jalopy?'

'Isn't it still in the field?'

'Apparently not,' said Connie.

'Then the Frenchie must have moved it,' said Clifford. Connie was about to ask where but they both heard Ga taking her boots off by the back door. Clifford's chair scraped along the stone floor as he stood up and left the table. As she watched him go, it suddenly occurred to her that he couldn't even bear to be in the same room as Ga. Clifford had always been a quiet man but he was avoiding Ga as much as he could these days.

'Where's your mother gone so early in the morning?' said Ga sitting down at the table. 'I hope she's not expecting me to look after Mandy when she gets back.'

'I'm looking after Mandy,' said Connie, 'and Mum's gone to East Grinstead.'

'East Grinstead?' said Ga. 'Whatever for?'

Connie just looked at her and then she saw Ga's face colour as the realisation dawned. 'Oh, I think you already know that, Ga,' she said pointedly.

The old woman straightened herself with a sniff. 'I have no idea what you're talking about,' she said haughtily. At the same moment, Mandy came thundering down the stair so Connie had to let it go. It would be better not to pick a fight in front of the child.

'Mandy, sit up straight,' Ga snapped as Connie's sister slid onto her chair. 'You're late. It's nearly time to go. In fact, you'll

257

have to go without breakfast this morning. Go and put your shoes on.'

Mandy's face crumpled.

'It's all right,' said Connie. 'She doesn't have to be there yet. She's only got to be in time to be in the crocodile to go to the service.'

Mandy slid back onto her chair and Connie pushed her boiled egg in front of her. 'When the service is over,' she said, 'we'll come back and change, and then I'll take you out.'

'We could do with some help around here,' said Ga. 'Especially with Gwen off somewhere . . . gallivanting.'

'Sorry,' said Connie brightly. 'I'm afraid we're busy.' Her heart was thumping and she willed her voice not to quiver. Mandy stared at her wide-eyed.

Ga stood up from the table. 'Really, Constance, I have never known anyone quite as selfish as you.'

Connie ignored the barbed comment and her great aunt left the room banging the door behind her.

The door to the workshop was open. Connie walked inside and called. Her voice echoed around the empty void that had once been a busy workshop. She couldn't believe how different it was from the last time she was here. All the bicycle paraphernalia was gone. Last time she'd been there, there had been several cars and vans in various stages of repair, but they'd all gone too. She turned to leave and saw Isaac and the Frenchie walking up the path together.

'Connie,' cried Eugène, 'how nice to see you.'

'The door was open,' she said apologetically. She studied his handsome face and was worried. He seemed tired . . . no, haggard and drawn even and she longed to run her hand down his cheek. 'I'm so sorry,' she said indicating the workshop.

He shrugged.

'How is Mavis?' Connie fished. 'Is her leg better?'

258

'I no longer care,' he said angrily. 'She has ruined me.'

'Where are all your things?'

'The bailiffs took them in lieu of my debts,' he said bitterly. 'They left me one box of tools, that's all. And wouldn't you know it? All my friends are suddenly very busy. Fair-weather friends the lot of them.' He spat on the ground.

She couldn't blame him for feeling bitter but this was a side to him that wasn't very attractive.

'You've still got me,' said Isaac.

'A penniless man and an ex-jailbird,' he scoffed. 'We should go far.' He laughed bitterly 'A fat lot of good you are to me.'

Isaac's face fell and Connie saw a darkness fill his eyes. Something inside her rose up. 'That's not fair,' she said crossly. 'You have every right to feel angry and betrayed, but no right whatsoever to take it out on him.'

'But he has such unrealistic expectations!' cried Eugène. 'I am not God, you know. We have no money and no premises. How can we service vehicles when we have nowhere to work on them? How can I repair bicycles with nowhere to keep stock? I don't even have a motor to move my caravan.'

'You told me once that you had bought some land,' said Isaac.

'A postage stamp,' said Eugène. 'I now discover that it had been up for sale for years but nobody wanted to buy. Even if I could sell it again, it's worthless.'

'Couldn't you build a new workshop there?' Connie suggested.

'The guy who sold it to me saw me coming,' said Eugène bitterly. 'It might be beside the sea but apparently you're not allowed to build on it. All I have is a dirty pond and a few overgrown bushes.'

'Can you at least put the caravan there?' she said.

'Where?' he challenged. 'In the middle of the pond?'

Connie felt helpless. She couldn't leave them as they were but what could she do? All she had was a couple of quid which she was going to use to buy Mandy lunch out. She thought about all the people Eugène had helped when the snow came. Perhaps they hadn't really turned their back on him. They would have helped if they could, but they were as poor as the next man. And what about Isaac? Left to his own devices, he'd be back in jail in no time. Then Connie remembered Kez.

'You've still got Isaac's car, haven't you?'

'I told you,' said Isaac, 'I went there and it's gone.'

Eugène ran his fingers through his hair. 'I forgot to tell you. I moved it further into Titnore woods for safety. Sorry.'

A wave of relief spread over Isaac's face.

'Isaac, go and see Kez,' said Connie as she secretly stuffed the two pounds into his hand. 'She's doing well. Simeon started a business and I know he's bought some land over Slinden way. Take Eugène with you. They know how kind he was to Reuben. It's time to call in a favour or two. Go and see Kez.' And then before either of them could protest, she walked away.

Gwen Craig waited nervously in the little office. She was dressed in her Sunday best suit, white blouse and she wore a brown hat. She had no stockings but her legs were fairly brown so she felt she could get away with it. Just in case, she tucked her legs under the chair as she sat primly holding her handbag on her lap.

She had spoken with Kenneth's doctor and listened with mounting horror as he described what her son had been through. She bristled as he told her of what he'd suffered because the previous hospital didn't know how to deal with his injuries, and she relaxed a little as he told her of the progress Kenneth had made since being at the Royal Victoria. She appreciated that the doctor and his team were doing the best they could for her son, but she'd heard enough explanation . . . now she just wanted to see him.

'We have to respect his wishes,' said the doctor. 'I think you must brace yourself, Mrs Craig. He may refuse to see you.'

It was a sentiment completely incomprehensible to Gwen. 'But I'm his mother,' she said tartly.

'Precisely,' said the doctor, a seasoned diplomat. 'Sometimes our boys find it hardest to face those who are their nearest and dearest.'

So she'd been left in the office while he went to find her son and ask him.

The room was sparsely decorated. The walls were cream at the top and evergreen below the dado rail. There was a desk and chair, a clutter of papers and folders on the top of the filing cabinet and a wastepaper basket, chock-a-block full, next to her. A doctor's white coat hung from a hook on the back of the door. Not a very tidy place but she noted with some gratitude that it was spotlessly clean. She had seen a ward cleaner mopping the floor as she came in, a tired looking woman with grey hair and a lined face, who looked as if she felt unappreciated and probably taken for granted. Gwen determined that she would compliment her on the way out.

The door opened and a pleasant-faced nurse walked in. 'Good morning, Mrs Craig,' she smiled. 'I'll take you to see your son now, if you would like to follow me.'

Gwen had rehearsed in her own mind everything she would say when she saw Kenneth but all her romantic speeches evaporated when she saw her son. Thank God, her wartime stoicism kicked in. Fixing a bright smile on her face, she walked towards him. *Oh God, look at your poor face.* 'Hello, darling.' She put her arms out and he struggled to his feet. *Dear Lord, what happened to your fingers? They never said you'd lost all your fingers on that hand.* 'Don't get up, dear. It' all right.'

'Hello, Mum.'

Your eye is drooping.

'It's lovely to see you again.' She felt the warmth of his body as he put his arms around her but she didn't squeeze. Who knew what was lurking under that uniform of his? He was taller than she remembered. He'd grown up. Grown up and been shot down.

Oh Kenneth, Kenneth. They released each other and the nurse had put a chair in place for her. Gwen turned to thank her.

'Mum, this is Pearl.'

Gwen looked up at her. Pretty . . . well-rounded figure, a trustworthy open face. *Oh Kenneth, you've lost all the hair on one side of your head, and your ear . . . it looks almost as if it has melted.*

'Hello, dear.'

Kenneth put his hand out and Pearl went to his side and grasped it. 'Pearl and I are to be married.'

'That's nice, dear.' *Connie was right. She looks like a nice girl. She'd look after you but what sort of marriage will you have? Didn't Connie say the flames came up between your legs? What about . . . down there?*

'I'm sorry I refused to see you, Mum,' said Kenneth. 'I didn't want you to worry.'

'That's all right, dear.'

Gwen was aware that she sounded like an automaton but it was the only way she could keep the smile on her face and the tears at bay.

'You obviously must have a lot to talk about,' said Pearl. 'I'll get you some tea.'

She's so young. Too young. Why would she want to saddle herself with a cripple?

'Isn't she wonderful?' said Kenneth as he watched her go inside.

'Yes dear, she's very pretty.' *I don't want her hurting you. She might love you here in this setting but what happens when you are both in a little flat on your own and you can't give her babies?*

'Mum,' he began. 'It's all right. You don't have to be brave. You can have a cry if you want to.'

If I start, I won't stop.

'I don't know what to do,' said Gwen brokenly.

'You don't have to do anything, Mum. I'm fine. I'm getting better and Pearl will look after me.'

'Oh, Kenneth,' said Gwen. 'She's so young. Are you absolutely sure . . .'

'Yes, Mum, we are. Don't you think I haven't already gone over and over all this? I did my best to put her off, but she is determined.'

Gwen could see Pearl coming through the doors with a tea tray. 'Forgive me, son, but can you be a proper husband to her?'

Kenneth gave her a sheepish grin. 'Don't you worry on that score, Mum,' he whispered. 'We've already tried the equipment and it works just fine.'

Gwen felt her face colour but at the same time a sense of peace flooded her body. 'I still have a dilemma,' she said.

Kenneth frowned and then as Pearl poured the tea, she told them about Australia.

When Eva and Roger strolled into the Lyon's Tea Room on South Street, everyone sitting at the table seemed a little awkward and embarrassed. Steven was busy ordering afternoon tea while Vi and Cissy Maxwell and Mr and Mrs Mitchell sat primly in their seats. As Eva approached, Steven rose to his feet and kissed her cheek. Roger gave him a firm handshake as the waitress, neatly dressed in her nippy uniform and cap, hurried away with their order.

Once all the formal introductions were complete, everybody relaxed a little and started off with small talk.

'The traffic on the A24 was horrendous.'

'The bus was late too.'

'Looks like we'll be having more rain.'

Steven winked at Eva across the table.

The waitress came back with a pot of tea and the cake stand. Vi Maxwell elected herself as 'mother' and poured the tea. The cake selection was wonderful. Butterfly cakes, Victoria sponge and some jam tarts.

'I'm sure Eva is a lovely girl,' Mr Mitchell began, 'but Mother and I think this is all a bit quick.'

'Eva and I have been seeing each other for over a year now, Dad,' said Steven stoutly. 'We just didn't tell anyone, that's all.'

'Crafty devils,' muttered Roger.

'We hear that you've been married before,' said Mrs Mitchell. Her tone was a tad accusatory.

'Her husband was killed after only six weeks,' said Cissy.

'Oh,' said Mrs Mitchell, the wind clearly taken from her sails. 'How sad.'

'Yes, it was actually,' said Roger.

Eva talked briefly about Dermid adding, 'His family knows about us and have given us their blessing.'

'That's nice,' said Mrs Mitchell absently.

'Queenie is a big-hearted woman,' said Vi.

'Very generous,' Roger agreed.

The tension was rising so Eva kicked him under the table. Roger looked surprised and mouthed, 'What?'

'You're a lot older than my son,' said Mr Mitchell.

'She's only three years older than me,' said Steven. 'That's all.'

Mr Mitchell was unrepentant. 'One has to think of these things, especially where having children is concerned.'

'I hardly think the late twenties is too old, Dad,' said Steven crossly.

His father turned his attention back to Eva. 'And what did you do during the war?'

'I was in the WAAFs,' said Eva sweetly.

'You travelled around?' asked Mrs Mitchell.

'Yes,' said Eva. 'I was stationed in Poling but I had a couple of brief sorties to Blackpool and London.'

'Blackpool,' said Mrs Mitchell wrinkling her nose.

'It's where I trained,' said Eva.

'But you were brought up in Worthing?'

'Dad,' said Steven again. 'This is beginning to sound like the Spanish Inquisition.'

'I'm sorry,' said his father. 'I don't mean it to. I just want to get to know Eva.'

'Is this going to be a long engagement, dear?' asked his mother.

'We have to wait until Eva finishes her training,' said Steven.

'So it'll be at least a year,' said Vi Maxwell wiping her jammy fingers on the snowy white napkin. 'Plenty of time for you to get to know my lovely daughter.'

Eva's heart sank. They'd only been together a few minutes and already the parents were in competition with each other. She glanced helplessly at her grandmother.

'Pardon me for saying so, Mrs Mitchell,' said Cissy, 'but I can't help admiring your splendid hat.'

"You know I was thinking exactly the same thing,' said Roger. 'It's quite the best thing I've seen in ages. Such a beautiful colour.'

'More tea anyone?' said Vi. Mrs Mitchell, her face glowing a delicate pink of pleasure, passed her cup across.

'Perhaps you might all like to come and have Sunday lunch with us,' said Mrs Mitchell. 'When Eva and Steven can get off duty, of course.'

'Thank you,' said Eva, much relieved. 'I'd like that.'

'Sounds like a great idea,' said Roger. 'You're right on the doorstep for me. My unit is in Horsham.'

At the door as they said their goodbyes, Eva hugged her brother gratefully.

'I think that went very well,' he grinned.

'Thanks to you and the hat,' whispered Eva.

'Looks like a dead ferret, doesn't it?' Roger whispered in her ear.

'What about you and Connie?' said Eva laughing.

'Stop matchmaking, sis,' Roger grinned. 'I'm still thinking about it.'

'Don't take too long,' said Eva. 'She's an attractive woman. It won't be too long before somebody snaps her up.'

Twenty-Five

By the time she was halfway down the lane, it had started to spot with rain. She had put Mandy to bed but Mum wasn't back home yet so she couldn't ask about Kenneth and she had to go back to be on duty the next day. Connie toyed with the idea of going straight to the bus stop and back to the hospital but she was really worried about the Frenchie. She wondered if he had gone with Isaac to Slinden to see Kez the previous week and the minute Clifford mentioned that he was back in his caravan next to the workshop, Connie was anxious to see him. There was no doubt that Eugène had been dealt a bitter blow but she didn't like the thought of him being on his own. The past few weeks had been awful for her too. What with Reuben's death, meeting Emmett and his new wife, and then her mother announcing that she was leaving the country, even though her friends had helped her get a more rational approach to life, Connie still felt as if everything was changing too quickly. Her mother had returned from East Grinstead so everyone knew about Kenneth. As a result, Ga wasn't speaking to her, which was no hardship but if that wasn't enough to contend with, there was the problem of Roger. Roger who seemed to like her so much but stayed away days and weeks at a time, with hardly any contact at all. She quickened her step. The cloud burst long before she reached the door and knocked. A second later it opened and the Frenchie stood in front of her.

'Connie,' he cried as he pulled her inside. 'You're soaked.'

She stood inside his caravan for the first time. They stared at each other for a second and then he sprang into life. Pulling open a drawer, he handed her a clean towel. 'You must dry yourself,' he said, the words dying on his lips as he spoke. He touched the side of her face with the towel, his large dark eyes fixed upon her. He wasn't drunk but Connie could smell whisky on his breath. Her heart was pounding as a tendril of her wet hair fell across her cheek and he moved to brush it away.

'I was worried about you,' she said lamely.

She should go. She shouldn't be here. He was still getting over Mavis and she was feeling bruised and vulnerable, but then he touched her hair with the towel and Connie shivered.

'You must take off your things,' he said. 'You will get a cold.' He went back to the drawer and pulled out a crisp white shirt. Connie gave him a quizzical look and he shrugged. 'Mavis kept me well supplied with clean shirts. She insisted I was clean when she came.' His voice was full of regret and sadness.

'She gave you a bit of a hard time,' Connie observed.

'I like strong women,' he said unashamedly. 'I liked it when she was difficult. It was exciting.'

He handed her the shirt but they both knew she wouldn't be putting it on.

Connie unbuttoned her wet blouse slowly and as she slid it from her shoulders, he was waiting with the towel to pat her dry. She could feel his warm whisky breath close to her cheeks and she was the one who was drunk. Drunk with pleasure and desire and love. She began to pull her wet hair down and as it cascaded onto her shoulders, he rubbed it gently between his fingers and then put it to his lips. His slightly stubbly cheek brushed next to hers and she heard the sound of his breath against her ear. She trembled again and he put the towel right around her shoulders, drawing her closer.

'I shouldn't be here,' she said and their eyes locked. Connie could hardly breathe.

'But I am glad you are,' he said huskily.

He let go of the towel and pulled a chair towards the oil stove and put her wet blouse over the back of it to dry. 'I should go,' she said feebly.

The rain on the caravan roof was gathering pace as he cupped her face in his hands and kissed her. The first kiss was as gentle as if he'd brushed her lips with a feather, but when she didn't resist him, he looked at her again and then kissed her with passion. Connie moaned with delight. This was what she'd always dreamed of. Every cell in her body was electrified. She leaned into him, willing him on. She was conscious of only two things, the sound of the rain pounding on the roof, and her awakening desire. As the one grew louder, the other grew stronger. All at once he caught her by the tops of her arms and held her gently away from him. Connie opened her eyes.

'What?' she said. 'What is it?' Her voice sounded shrill, almost panicky and she hated the sound of it.

'Are you sure?'

This was the moment to say no. This was the time to come to her senses. To stay would be madness. Connie drew a breath and for a nanosecond took in her surroundings. She was in a battered old caravan with a broken man and yet as she looked at Eugène's face she saw a hunger in his eyes. Mavis Hampton, the most beautiful girl in Worthing, had ditched him and she'd been so wrong about Emmett and confused about Roger. They were both broken . . . kindred spirits.

'Connie?' The sound of his gentle whisper brought everything into focus. All at once, Connie didn't care if this was the one and only time he was with her. She wanted him, like she'd never wanted anyone before, not even Emmett and certainly not Roger.

'I am sure.'

He moved quickly hurling a whole lot of things away from the cramped little sofa and Connie chuckled as he led her to it and presented it to her as if it were a beautiful marriage bed. They undressed slowly and by the time every garment had fallen to the floor, Connie was awash with desire. As a last act before they lay together, he reached into his jacket pocket and drew out a rubber johnny. Connie wasn't aware of it, but her face must have registered surprise.

'I was engaged,' he shrugged. 'I want to protect you.'

She wished he hadn't brought up the fact of his engagement. It dampened her resolve but when he was ready and he'd taken her into his arms, he melted every other thought away.

He was so gentle, so controlled. She knew he was holding back, every move calculated to give her maximum pleasure. When he entered her, every fibre of her being was yielded to him. 'I am the first,' he said in mild surprise.

When it was all over and he lay on her, Connie smiled. He rolled onto his side and looked at her, tenderly playing with her hair as she drifted towards sleep.

'The first time I ever saw you, you were singing,' he said.

Connie frowned. 'I was?'

'You came into my workshop with your little sister and I heard you.'

'Oh yes,' she smiled. 'You are my sunshine, my only sunshine . . .'

He kissed her again. 'Connie . . .'

She woke in the early morning with the sun streaming in the caravan. Eugène was gone and her heart sank. He had covered her nakedness and she threw the blankets aside to look for her clothes.

The caravan was small but it was clean and reasonably tidy. Her blouse was still by the stove although that was no longer lit. A stack of pictures leaned against the wall. They were facing the wrong way. Connie glanced around and then began to look through them. She recognised a couple of them from when she'd seen them on the workshop wall, the two fishermen and a seascape. Even with her untrained eye, Connie could see that he was good. She pulled the next one towards her and Mavis Hampton smiled up at her. The shock was so great, Connie almost dropped the pictures leaning against her legs. The picture was amazing. He had caught the woman's expression perfectly and yet it was greatly romanticised. Anyone else would have interpreted Mavis as the self-centred girl she was, but there was something about this picture that told another story. As she scrutinised it more fully, Connie suddenly realised what she was seeing. He was still in love with her, wasn't he? It was his love for her that shone through the canvas. Dear Lord, what had she done? If he loved her this much, there was every chance that they would get back together again.

She already had her bra and suspender belt on and she was pulling on her stockings when the door opened. Connie grabbed her blouse and held it against her. Eugène came in with a loaf of bread, a bottle of milk and some cheese.

'I have to go,' she said and he nodded. 'I have to be on duty at one,' she said desperate to justify herself.

He nodded again and taking her hands in his he gave her that same grave look he'd given her the night before. 'Connie,' he said, his voice trailing.

'I know,' she said quickly. 'This was a mistake. A terrible mistake.'

'A mistake,' he repeated.

'I'm sorry, Eugène,' she blurted out. 'I didn't mean to . . . I'm sorry.'

He nodded grimly. 'It was my fault, Connie. I was drunk and I was angry. I took advantage of you.'

She put her finger on his lips and turned her head to hide her own embarrassment. What an idiot she'd been. How could she have let herself get carried away like that? He was being kind and she was the one who had taken advantage. She could only hope she hadn't ruined their friendship.

'Have some breakfast before you go,' he said and she nodded

270

but they were awkward with each other now. The bread stuck in her throat and she couldn't look him in the eye.

'What will you do now?' she asked.

He shrugged. 'Start again I suppose. Isaac will stay in Slinden. He'll be all right.'

'I took the liberty of looking at your paintings,' said Connie. 'You should sell them.'

'Sell them?' he said modestly. 'Do you think they are good enough?'

'Good enough!' she cried. 'They're brilliant. You have a real talent.'

Eugène shook his head. 'I am not trained,' he said.

'Maybe not,' she said. 'And I'm no expert on art but you have the gift of capturing the real essence of a person onto canvas. You paint with feeling.'

'Why, thank you, Miss Connie Dixon,' he smiled. 'That's very encouraging.'

As she left he squeezed her hand. 'You're a good person, Connie. I hope I shall always be your friend.'

On the bus on her way back to the hospital, she couldn't stop thinking about him. That silly Mavis had a gem of a man and she'd let him go but he still loved her. As soon as he made good with his paintings, she'd want him back.

*

A Sunday school outing. What luck! The notice on the church noticeboard said they needed helpers. Even better. It was a bit late in the day, but why not volunteer? Stan smiled to himself as he approached the door. Rev Jackson was there, shaking hands with everybody who had come to the early morning service. There was no time like the present.

*

Mandy had used up all the paper in her book. She wanted to make her mother a birthday card. She knew exactly which picture she would draw, a house with red curtains and a green door. She would put *Haqqy* over the top but she wasn't sure how to spell birthday. Susan Revel's mummy was coming to take her to Susan's house to play, so it would be the ideal time to make the card without anyone knowing what she was doing. Mrs Revel would help her with the spelling too. Mandy knew birthday had a 'b' but she wasn't sure how to write the rest. Until she'd had the idea, it had been a real problem because of course, she couldn't ask Mummy. Daddy was out for the day and Connie wasn't here. This way, it would be a real surprise. She went to look for Ga because she had some paper in her big bureau, but she was working in the shop and didn't like it if you interrupted. Mandy sighed in frustration. Grown-ups were never there when you needed them.

She stared at Ga's writing desk. Mandy knew she wasn't supposed to touch it and that Ga would be very cross if she got caught but she also knew there was plenty of paper inside. Sometimes other people took some. Mummy took a bit when she wanted to write to Connie and she'd seen Auntie Aggie take a couple of sheets once while Ga was getting her a cup of tea in the kitchen. Surely Ga wouldn't mind when she told her it was for Mummy's birthday. She wouldn't touch anything else. She wouldn't look in the drawers where Ga kept her stamps, but she'd go to the narrow slots which looked a bit like a toast rack and take a sheet of the pretty paper. She knew it was there because one wet afternoon when she had little to do, Ga had shown them all to her. The lid was up and locked but Mandy knew exactly where Ga kept the key. It was in the kitchen on the big hook. She had to stand on a chair to reach it. She did it easily but it was a bit scary when the chair wobbled a bit as she stretched up. Mandy unlocked the bureau and remembered to put the long rests down before she put the lid down. It was very heavy and it fell with a loud bump. Mandy stood on Ga's chair and leaned over. She was just reaching for the paper when Ga's booming voice made her jump.

'And what do you think you are doing, young lady?'

Mandy lost her balance and knocked several things out of the bureau onto the floor. At the same time, Ga's broad hand struck her bottom and the tops of her legs with a stinging force. 'How dare you?' she cried. 'This is private. It has nothing to do with you so you shouldn't be snooping into my affairs, you naughty little girl.'

By now Mandy was in floods of tears. Ga dragged her unceremoniously from the chair.

'I wanted some paper for Mummy,' Mandy wailed.

Ga picked up the letters Mandy had accidentally pushed onto the floor, put them all into one of the slots and slammed the lid of the bureau with great force. Then she rounded on the child once again.

'Go to your room this minute,' she bellowed.

'I only wanted to make a card for Mummy's birthday,' Mandy said again, but Ga wasn't listening.

'God punishes people who steal,' Ga said as she pushed Mandy towards the stairs. 'You wait until I tell your mummy what you did.'

'Please don't,' Mandy begged. 'It was a surprise.'

They had reached her bedroom door and Ga pushed her inside. 'Mrs Revel is here and I'm going to tell her that you can't come to her house to play with Susan,' said Ga, slamming the door. A second later, the door opened once again. 'And I shall also tell your mummy that I don't think you should go on the outing the day after tomorrow. I'm sure Miss Jackson wouldn't want to take a *thief* to High Salvington.'

As soon as she'd gone, Mandy threw herself across the bed and sobbed.

It was the day of the Sunday school outing and Connie was assigned to look after the patient behind the curtains. It

273

was Mrs Meyer. The end was very close but she seemed peaceful. Connie cleaned her eyes and swabbed her mouth. The old woman smiled as Connie offered a sip of water and laid her head back on the pillow. Connie reached into her locker and pulled out her hairbrush.

'There we are, Mrs Meyer,' she said brushing her hair gently. 'Sister's got a little surprise for you.'

'Not ice cream,' joked Mrs Meyer. 'I hate ice cream.'

Connie grinned. 'Better than ice cream,' she promised. She could hear voices on the other side of the curtain. 'Your daughter is here.'

'My Judy? Here?'

'That's right.'

Mrs Meyer shook her head. 'Oh no, dear. My Judy lives in Africa.'

'And she's here to see you,' said Connie as the curtain opened slightly and a middle-aged woman stepped beside the bed. Connie manoeuvred the chair, and Judy Meyer sat down. 'Hello, Mum.'

A lump formed in Connie's throat when she saw tears glistening in her patient's eyes. 'Oh Judy. I never thought I'd see you again. How are you, love?'

By midday it was all over. Judy and Mrs Meyer had said their goodbyes and her mother had gone peacefully. Connie was asked to perform one last duty for her. As she washed her poor thin body, Connie reflected that her whole life was dedicated to the care and treatment of her patients but there came a time when it was time to let them go. She'd liked Mrs Meyer. She'd often told Connie about her faith and explained that she was ready to go.

'I'm so tired,' she once told Connie. 'I'm ready for a bit of peace and quiet, although I don't suppose it'll be that peaceful up there. All that singing . . . Never mind, I've had a good life.'

To Connie's way of thinking, Mrs Meyer had had a hard life. Orphaned at a young age and stuck in a children's home for years, she'd married a fellow inmate almost as soon as they'd left it. He'd left her a widow with two small children so she'd had to take cleaning jobs to survive. Her son had been killed somewhere over Germany in 1940 and her daughter was a missionary in Kenya. Not an easy life at all and yet Mrs Meyer made the best of everything even when it came to dying. 'I'm lucky to have a clean bed and all you lovely nurses to look after me,' she'd once said.

Connie wiped a tear from her eye and blew her nose. She'd done the last thing for her and Mrs Meyer was ready for the undertaker. She left the curtain closed and went to clear up her trolley. When she came back to the desk to report her completed duty, Matron was sitting there looking at the patient's notes. Connie felt the old nervousness come back.

'Mrs Meyer is ready, Matron,' she said quietly. It was policy to speak in hushed tones when someone had died. Nobody wanted the rest of the ward to be upset.

'What's that supposed to mean, nurse?' Matron snapped. 'When you give a report, for heaven's sake speak clearly and precisely.'

Connie chewed her bottom lip anxiously. She gave Sister a helpless look. 'I have laid out Mrs Meyer,' Connie said in the same hushed tones.

'Speak up, girl,' Matron insisted.

'Mrs Meyer is ready for the undertaker,' said Connie.

Matron stared at her for a couple of seconds and then said, 'Why didn't you say so in the first place?'

'Thank you, Nurse Dixon,' said Sister. 'You can go off duty now.'

Matron made a point of looking at her watch.

'Nurse Dixon should have gone off duty an hour ago,' said Sister. 'She kindly stayed on to lay out the patient because we are short-staffed.'

Connie walked down the ward, conscious of Matron's eyes boring into her receding back. She was late, very late. In fact she wasn't at all sure that by the time she'd got back to the nurses' home and changed, there would be time to catch the bus. As she walked down the ward, Connie could see Nurse Boiling doing her best to comfort Mrs Jenkins. A very nervous woman, Mrs Jenkins was convinced she wouldn't survive her operation anyway. Really, it was too bad of Matron to make her talk about the undertaker like that. And why was Matron so aggressive towards her? Connie couldn't understand it. As she reached the swing doors, she thought she could heard Mrs Meyer's voice. 'Don't forget she's just the same as us with her drawers around her ankles first thing in the morning.'

Connie turned as she closed the door. Matron was still sitting at the desk, her giant legs akimbo and Connie could just imagine the biggest pair of bloomers imaginable draped around her ankles.

'Thanks, Mrs Meyer,' Connie whispered as she turned for the nurses' home.

It was a bit of a mad rush but if she ran all the way, she still might be in time for the 2.10 bus. That was supposed to arrive near the pick-up point at 2.30. Exactly the same time as the coach was leaving.

It was unusual for Olive to come to her house and Aggie's surprise must have shown as she opened the door. By the look on Olive's face, her friend was furious. Aggie stepped back to let her in.

'She's found Kenneth,' said Olive, taking off her coat. 'I've been trying to get up here for days but what with one thing and another . . . Anyway, I've found out that she's been going up to East Grinstead to see him.'

'How?' Aggie gasped.

'I don't know exactly,' said Olive. 'What are we going to do? Supposing she brings him home?'

'She's got to be stopped,' said Aggie, her eyes widening with fright. 'It'll only cause more trouble, you know it will.'

'I know that!' snapped Olive, 'but what can I do about it? I told them never to speak of that day but they're not children anymore. It's kept them apart for years but it's bound to come out now.'

The two friends stared at each other for a second and then Aggie's face softened. 'Sit down, dear. I'll make a cup of tea and then we can decide what to do.'

'Connie?'

As soon as she heard his voice, Connie's heart leapt. 'Roger!' He was leaning against his car. She had never seen him looking so handsome. 'What on earth are you doing here?'

He stood up straight. 'You seem to be in a tearing hurry. Can I give you a lift anywhere?'

'Oh, could you?' she blurted out. 'I'm terribly late. Sister made me stay on to lay out a patient and then Matron came onto the ward unexpectedly and . . .' She paused and smiled. 'Listen to me prattling on about nothing. Yes, please, I would love a lift.'

He opened the passenger door and gave a bow. Laughing, Connie climbed in.

'I don't understand,' she said as he climbed in the driver's side. 'Why are you here? How did you know I'd be coming off duty?'

'Eva told me,' he said starting the engine. 'Where are we going?'

'Goring,' she said. 'With a bit of luck I can still be in time to catch the coach.'

'Goring?' He frowned. 'What coach?'

He didn't even flinch when Connie told him about the Sunday school outing.

Twenty-Six

The day couldn't have been more perfect. Jane Jackson stood by the coach door checking her clipboard as the children climbed aboard and her cousin Jeanette Luxton who had travelled all the way from Taunton to help her, made sure everyone was sitting down. As always, it was hard to find helpers. People were glad to get rid of their children for an afternoon but reluctant to come along for the trip. Jane couldn't really blame them. Most of the families, even in this well-heeled area, worked hard. It was difficult to get free time and when they did, there was always the garden or the allotment to do or aged parents to visit. Mothers and fathers had little time to themselves and so Sunday school from three till four on a Sunday and the outing from two thirty till five once a year made a welcome break and a time to be alone.

She had the usual stalwarts she knew she could always rely on. Mrs Stevens, Mrs Hawks and Mrs Ibbotson never let her down and they could drum up support in the way of cakes and sandwiches even if they couldn't persuade people to come along. Jane watched tin after tin going into the boot of the coach and smiled. As usual, there would be plenty to eat. Mr Hawks loaded the big urn and Mr Stevens had made sure the camping stove was all cleaned up and ready to use. The two men kissed their wives goodbye and waved as they climbed aboard the coach. Arnold had volunteered to come too. This was the first time Jane had introduced her new boyfriend to her church friends. He was a bit 'last minute' but her father was happy for him to come along. Jane knew he loved children. 'I've brought along a little bit of magic,' he said as she checked him off the list. He opened his jacket and she saw a bulging bag of sweets. 'Just in case we need to bribe them to be good,' he added with a wink.

'I think you only need to stand up to persuade everyone to behave, darling,' she teased and he nodded ruefully. Arnold was very tall.

Her father came out of the hired hall. 'Graham has kindly offered his services too,' he said, pushing the new pianist forward. The man nodded shyly as Jane thanked him profusely, explaining how difficult it was to retain helpers as he climbed aboard.

'Connie said she'd be here in time to catch the coach,' said Jane, turning to her father, 'so that gives me three people to do the teas, and five of us to play the games with them. With twenty-eight children that should be enough, shouldn't it?'

'You are wonderful, my dear,' Rev Jackson said, giving his daughter a kiss on the cheek. 'I don't know how I would manage without you.'

'Time to get going,' said the driver irritably. He was looking at his watch. 'I've got another job at three.'

'There's one more person to come,' said Jane. 'She won't be long.'

It was wonderful sitting beside Roger as they sped on their way but Connie's mind was full of unanswered questions. They travelled east chatting about their various jobs and the things they had been doing since they'd last met. As they pulled up outside the pick-up point a dog barked and jumped up at the car, his tongue lolling.

'What the . . .' Roger began.

'Oh, it's Pip!' cried Connie. 'He must have come down to see Mandy off.'

She opened the door and Pip scrambled in, greeting Connie in his usual exuberant way, his wagging tail swinging Roger across his face. 'Hey, old fella,' he laughed. 'Get that tail into the back seat, will you?'

'Looks like we've missed the coach,' said Connie, looking around.

'Do you still want to go?' asked Roger.

'I did promise to help,' said Connie. 'Jane doesn't have that many helpers.'

'Then tell me where to go,' said Roger, starting the car again.

'Are you sure?' said Connie. 'A Sunday school outing is hardly a man's idea of fun.'

'Believe me,' said Roger. 'Right now a Sunday school outing is right at the top of my 100 things to do before I die list.' And laughing, they set off for High Salvington.

As soon as the children were off the coach, the driver turned his vehicle and sped away. Jane organised everybody into a crocodile and they walked the last few yards up the hill and into the meadow. As soon as she gave the word, the children ran freely like calves leaping from their enclosure after the long winter months. Jane watched them jumping and running, shouting and chasing each other and smiled. Even though it was such hard work and she'd be exhausted by the time they all went home, to see them as happy as this made it all worthwhile. They had such energy, such a joy of life and up here in the late summer sunshine, they were carefree and happy and it didn't matter how much noise they made.

Jane blew her whistle and called everybody together.

Once the groans and complaints had died down, she laid down some ground rules. 'In a minute,' she told them, 'we are all going to play rounders but first of all, I have a little competition for you.' She handed each child a piece of paper. 'On your paper, you will see a list of things to find. I want the older ones to be with the little ones who can't read. There is a prize for the people who bring back everything on the list.' Already some of the children were standing up and ready to go. 'Wait a minute,' Jane said firmly. 'You will find everything you have on the list in this meadow. I do not . . . I repeat, I do not want anyone to wander off in the woods on their own. Understood?'

There was a collective, 'Yes, Miss,' and the children set off on their treasure hunt.

Mrs Hawks and Mrs Stevens had found the ideal spot to set up the picnic and Arnold and Graham put up the trestle table. Once Jeanette had the snow white sheet pulled over the bare board, the table already looked grand. She then looked around for some large stones to weigh it down at each corner. Arnold had gone back for the crockery, left in boxes at the side of the narrow lane, while the women returned for the sandwiches. Jane left them to it. It was a well-oiled machine and Mrs Ibbotson who had waited in the lane to make sure nobody pinched anything, soon joined them.

Jane turned her attention to the children. She enjoyed watching them. Little Patrick Rivers had been ill most of the winter, but now his cheeks had colour in them. Jenny Wright had had a brush with polio and although her legs were not quite back to normal, she was making a valiant attempt to keep up with her big sister. Jack Albert had always been a bit of a loner, but now he had plenty of friends. Jane thought back to the Christmas party when they had been playing hide and seek. She and Jack Albert had been searching for the others. 'Let's see if anyone is in the toilet,' she'd suggested. Jack hurried to look and she'd chuckled when she'd found him lifting the lid and peering into the bowl. Little Elsie Anderson came up to her and gave her a gappy smile. 'Thank you for inviting me, Mith,' she lisped and then ran off again.

Jane sighed happily. Up here on High Salvington, they were

as safe as houses and with Arnold by her side, what more could a girl want?

'I know a really good place to find what's on your list,' he said, stepping up beside her. 'Here, take my hand and I'll show you.'

Mandy looked up at him trustingly and slipped her hand in his. Her hand fluttered a little in his and he felt his pulse quicken. See? She wanted him as much as he wanted her. He smiled down at her angelic face, loving her pretty blonde curls and the two red ribbons she wore in her hair. He led her away from the others, keeping close to the wooded area, where they could be alone. Gradually, the excited shouts of the other children faded.

Mandy spotted a bird's feather and bent to pick it up but he egged her on.

'No, not that one. I know a much better place where you can get loads of them.'

'But Miss Jackson said we shouldn't go into the woods,' Mandy protested mildly.

'It's all right,' he said soothingly. 'She said don't go alone, didn't she? Well, you're not alone. You're with me. I'll keep you safe. Besides, Miss Jackson knows where we are. She knows where the best bird feathers are.' She looked up at him trustingly and he stroked her lovely blonde curls. One of her ribbons came off in his hand. 'Whoops,' he laughed. 'Sorry.'

'I want to go back now,' she said but he wasn't listening. What a pity they'd cut her hair short but the red ribbons on either side of her head had made her attractive. No, he decided, she'd look even prettier with it long. He could feel himself harden. Just a little further and then she'd be his. 'Shall I tickle you and make you laugh?'

He tickled her neck and Mandy giggled.

'Shall I? I'm coming, I'm coming, I'm coming.' The child did her best to wriggle from his grip but he held on tight. He tickled her under her arms and down her body and she laughed. She *enjoyed* it.

'I've got something to show you,' he said, his voice tight with the thrill of it. 'I've got a little friend I want you meet down here.' She stared at the button on his trousers where he was pointing with a puzzled expression. 'Would you like to meet him?'

He could feel her tugging at his hand again and smiled. His head was buzzing. His heartbeat speeded up. She was only pretending to pull away. She wanted it too. She was as eager as he was. Keeping a tight grip on her, he unbuttoned his trousers deftly with the other hand.

'You're hurting me,' she whimpered.

'Don't you want to meet my friend? Come with me and I'll show you. His name is Mr Charles.'

Connie and Roger parked in the lane. It narrowed to the point where the ground was too soft for vehicles. Pip leapt out barking joyfully and began his sniff and mark routine.

As Connie headed towards the hill, Roger caught her arm. 'I owe you an explanation, Connie,' he said. 'I've been avoiding you.'

'I had noticed,' Connie laughed nervously and her throat tightened. Oh, now he was going to say he didn't want to see her again. She glanced at his firm jawline. Please give us one more chance? she said in her head. I've missed you, Roger. You've been a real friend to me and I need you even more now Mum and Clifford are leaving me.

'I've been making difficult decisions,' he began again.

Her heart sank a little more. Her mind was racing ahead of him and she wanted to say, Roger, I've made a stupid mistake. I shouldn't have let Eugène make love to me. I let my feelings run away with me. I was unhappy and he was unhappy because he's just lost the love of his life. You won't want me now, will you, Roger? Not when you find out I'm damaged goods . . .

Roger had pulled her in front of him and was looking directly at her. Connie blushed. Could he see it in her face? What she'd done with Eugène? Did it show, that first time?

'I once told you that I would carry on with my job until such time as I found something I cared for even more.'

She nodded.

'Well, the time has come to pack it in,' he said. 'I can't keep my mind on the job anymore, Connie. I'm distracted all the time.'

Connie didn't know what to say. Was he asking her to talk him out of it? Did he want sympathy? She didn't think she could do that. She knew he loved what he did but it was dangerous. She couldn't bear the thought of something awful happening to him even if she never saw him again. How Eva and her mother put up with it all for all these years she never knew.

'I don't know what to say,' she said quietly.

'You could say you feel the same way.'

'The same way?'

'Oh Connie, you silly goose, this is my God-awful clumsy way of telling you that I've fallen in love with you.'

She was stunned. She should say something but all at once, her mouth wouldn't work. Love? He loved her? The revelation hit her somewhere in the pit of her stomach but it wasn't a pleasant experience. She felt herself begin to panic.

'Oh, I should have booked a table somewhere romantic and given you flowers,' he groaned. 'What a fool I am, but I couldn't keep it inside any longer. Please say something, Connie.'

'Oh, Roger,' she said. 'I didn't think . . . I mean, you didn't reply to my letter . . . so I thought . . .'

Connie was confused. When he'd told her she should have been on top of the world but she felt numb. Now that the initial shock had gone, she felt . . . nothing . . .

He leaned over and pulled her closer and then his mouth searched for hers. As he kissed her she was thinking that this should have been the most wonderful moment of her life, but it wasn't. Roger Maxwell loved her but she didn't feel a thing. Connie took a step back and looked up at him. 'Roger,' she began. 'We have to be careful. The children . . .'

'Yes, yes of course,' he smiled.

As they began to walk towards the meadow, they could hear the children's voices and the occasional scream of excitement. 'Sounds like everyone is having a great time,' said Connie weakly.

Pip raced past them. Roger reached for her hand and smiled. 'Where's he off to in such a hurry?'

'Probably scented a rabbit,' she said and he had to stop and kiss her again.

Jane was overjoyed to see them. 'We could do with another man around,' she said when she saw Roger. 'Some of the boys are a bit boisterous.'

'I thought you had men,' said Connie.

'Arnold is around somewhere,' said Jane. 'Oh, there he is. You haven't met him yet, have you?' She called his name and a tall lanky man walked towards them coming from the direction of the woods. He towered over Jane and Connie noticed how much her face softened when she looked up at him.

'Where have you been?' Jane asked. 'You're all covered in scratches.'

'I went on a call of nature,' he said, dusting down his trouser leg. 'I thought I'd better walk quite a way inside in case one of the children saw me but on my way out, some dog went flying past me and I fell over a tree root.'

'Oh dear,' said Connie. 'That might have been Pip. He'd probably caught a scent of something. Are you all right?'

Arnold brushed the sleeve of his jacket and put out his hand. 'Fine,' he said, 'pleased to meet you both.'

'We've just got to get the blankets spread out,' said Jane,

handing them to Roger and Connie, 'and then I can blow the whistle for tea. Arnold, can you and Graham organise the boys on one side and girls on the other. Where is Graham?'

'Who is Graham?' asked Connie.

'The new pianist,' said Jane. 'To be honest, he's been a bit of a dream this afternoon. Dad asked him to come just to swell the numbers but I don't think I'll ask him next year. He hasn't helped much at all.'

The ladies from the church had got the water boiling, so tea was ready. Jane blew her whistle long and hard and the hungry children came running.

The first touch was always the sweetest. He groaned with delight.

Mandy was terrified. She didn't like this one bit. He had taken her away from the others even though Miss Jackson had said they should keep close together. The whistle had gone. She was supposed to run to Miss Jackson when the whistle went but he wouldn't let go of her hand and she certainly didn't like Mr Charles. Mummy always said that things down there were private. She had tried to pull away but he kept pressing her hand onto him. The man was pulling a funny face and making a funny noise and then to her horror Mr Charles began to move. The more she struggled to get her hand back the bigger it seemed to get.

'No,' she protested. 'I don't like it.' She was crying now. Big tears and sobs which racked her whole body. 'I don't want to.'

'That's a pity,' he said huskily, 'because Mr Charles likes you and he wants to look at you.'

'No!' cried Mandy. 'I want to go back with the others.'

'If you go back now,' he said harshly, his voice taking on a slight edge, 'I shall tell Miss Jackson that you've been a very naughty girl.'

The child froze.

'I shall tell her you wouldn't hold my hand when I told you

to. I shall tell her you made Mr Charles very cross. Do you want me to tell Miss Jackson that?'

Miserably, Mandy shook her head.

'Now let me show you my friend Mr Charles,' he said, his voice softening again. 'He wants to be your friend too.'

They both heard a dog barking in the distance but the man ignored it as he fished in his open trousers. Mandy stared in horror as Mr Charles emerged.

The children were sitting on the two blankets. 'Sit crossed-legged,' Jane told them, 'and then we'll say grace.'

Out in the fresh air, the smell of egg sandwiches was overwhelmingly good. So were the children. They put their hands together and as Arnold said grace, Jane, diligent as ever, was busy counting heads.

'Somebody's missing,' she announced as the first tin of sandwiches was handed around. 'There's only twenty-seven.'

Connie counted with her and realised who the missing child was. 'It's Mandy,' said Connie.

'Has anyone seen Mandy?' Jane demanded. The children looked from one to the other and shrugged.

'I saw a little girl walking towards the woods,' said Jeanette.

'Why would she be doing that?' said Jane. 'I told everyone to stay out here in the open.'

As the adults looked from one to the other their anxiety levels rose.

Connie frowned. 'It's not like Mandy to wander off.'

'You stay here with the children,' Roger told Jane. 'We'll go and look for her.'

The barking dog was coming closer. 'Pip,' she whispered and he came rushing out of the copse at full pelt and hurled himself at Stan. In the ensuing panic, Stan let go of Mandy's hand but the child remained frozen to the spot. Stan lashed out with his foot and the dog backed off and bared his teeth, a low threatening growl coming from his throat. Mandy stumbled backwards.

'Stay there!' Stan shouted at the child and once again she froze.

Pip put himself between Mandy and Stan and began backing into her until Mandy was forced to move backwards. Stan looked around desperately. If he didn't know better, he would say it was exactly the same dog he'd encountered the last time. He'd been forced to let the little girl go that time. Well, it wasn't going to happen again. Mandy was crying hard. He had to shut her up. Too much noise and they'd draw attention to themselves.

'And stop that bloody racket.'

The child sucked back her sobs and wet herself.

Stan launched his foot at the dog again but it missed its mark. The dog was snarling and growling fiercely. He had to find some way to get this wretched animal out of the way. Looking around he picked up a solid looking piece of wood. The dog knew what was coming and rushed at him, trying to get there first. They hurled themselves at each other several times before the wood caught Pip on the side of his head. There was a shrill yelp and the dog fell to the ground. Mandy stared at him in horror. Stan stood over him gasping for breath. 'That's sorted you out good and proper,' he snarled and he booted the dog in his side for good measure, but Pip didn't respond.

When the man turned back to Mandy, something kicked in in her mind. He had just kicked her dog. He was a bad man, a very bad man. Mandy turned and ran, screaming her head off as she flew.

'Come back here,' he shouted.

But for once she wasn't listening. She ran deeper into the coppice and he relaxed. The stupid brat didn't know it but she was running away from the others, into an area where the trees hadn't been thinned out. With a bit of luck, she'd reach a wooded wall and be trapped. He changed his tactic again. 'Mandy, come back at once or I shall have to tell Miss Jackson what a naughty little girl you've been. You know you shouldn't be running about in the woods. Miss Jackson told you not to do that, didn't she?'

He was quite close to her when he tripped over an exposed tree root. At the sound of his fall, she screamed again and ran in another direction. Damn it, now she was heading back towards the meadow. He couldn't let her go back in that state. There was no telling what she might say. Ignoring the painful bruise on his side, he jumped up as quickly as he could and ran after her again.

The ground in this part of the coppice was uneven. Small hillocks fell away into quite deep ruts and the place was littered with fallen trees and broken branches. The child ran wildly missing the overhanging branches which bothered him and made him slower.

'If you don't stop this minute, I shall slap your bottom,' he shouted. That usually did the trick. On the whole, children were anxious to please and by nature obedient to the voice of authority. He slithered and slid after her and almost caught up with her when all of a sudden, she fell with a scream and vanished.

She's gone down a rabbit hole, he told himself. I've got her now. I'll pull her out and be nice to her. She'd wet herself, hadn't she. That would make things really simple. He'd say, 'Take your knickers off, darling. You don't want to be walking around with wet knicks on do you?' But when he reached the spot where she had fallen he couldn't believe it. This was no rabbit hole. It was much deeper. He could see the top of her head and when she looked up at him, she was a long way down. He could have lain on the ground, leaned over and pulled her out but the ground alongside was unstable. It creaked and small clods of earth were still falling. He stood over the hole with his hands on his hips and looked down. 'You see what happens to naughty little girls who won't do what they're told?' he said cruelly.

'Please,' she sobbed. 'Please Mr Graham, I don't like it here. I will be good, I promise.'

'I would like to help you,' he said, shaking his head slowly, 'but Mr Charles is very upset with you. You weren't very nice to him, were you?'

'I will be,' she pleaded. 'Please get me out. I don't like it down here.'

But then he hesitated. Her face wasn't angelic anymore. It was dirty and bleeding from lots of little scratches. She had nettle stings under her eye and her lovely blonde curls were a mess and she'd lost both of her red ribbons. Her peachy cheeks were streaked with tears and there was yellow snot hanging from her nose. Ugh. She wasn't his little cherub anymore. His lip curled. She might as well stay there for all he cared. She was nothing more than a dirty little slut and he didn't want her anymore.

He stamped his foot a couple of times and she began to slide again. He smiled. Then he heard someone calling. He looked around frantically and the stupid kid began to shout back. He grabbed an exposed tree root and shook it. The earth fell away quickly and he only just stopped himself from going into the hole himself. He scrambled backwards, then one more stamp on the ground and she was gone.

Twenty-Seven

'Has she come back yet?' Connie and Roger had returned to the group sitting on the blanket.

Jane Jackson shook her head. 'I've got a couple of the helpers looking down the bottom of the meadow,' she said. 'I don't understand it. Why would she go off on her own?'

'My dog has gone missing too,' said Connie, struggling not to give way to the panic rising up inside her. 'I can only hope he's run off and Mandy has chased after him to bring him back.' Even as she said the words, she wasn't convinced that she even believed what she was saying. She looked around at the children on the blanket eating their sandwiches. 'Were any of you playing with Mandy? Did you see her going into the woods?'

The children looked from one to the other shaking their heads.

'You were with her, weren't you, Graham?' Jeanette Luxton said.

Connie turned towards the direction of the question and frowned. Jeanette was talking to a man in a brown suit. Connie hadn't noticed him before and she couldn't see his face because he had his back to her and yet there was something vaguely familiar about him.

'With who?' said Graham, tapping a cigarette on his cigarette case.

Connie grabbed Roger's arm. She had recognised the voice

immediately, but it was that tapping sound that sent a chill down her spine. It was *him*. How could she ever forget?

'What?' said Roger. 'Darling, what is it?'

'I know you,' Connie shuddered. 'Your name isn't Graham. You're Stan Saul.'

Everyone turned towards the man sitting on the corner of the blanket. Stan Saul turned slowly towards Connie. Earlier in the afternoon, when nobody was looking, he'd pocketed a ball. On his way out of the woods, he'd pretended to pick it up in case someone wondered what he was doing. There was no reason to fear that they'd find Mandy and he had hoped no one would notice him until the time the coach came. Bluff it out, he told himself as he turned to face her. He didn't recognise her and yet she knew him. 'Do I know you?' he smiled.

'Connie Dixon,' she said coldly.

He smiled affably but his heart sank. 'Connie Dixon,' he said brightly. 'I had no idea it was you. How are you?'

Connie could feel her face heating. Her heart began to thump in her chest and the old fear crept back. Don't be ridiculous, she told herself angrily. She was a grown woman now. A grown woman with a man beside her and her friends all around her yet Stan Saul still had the ability to instil a wave of sickening fear into her heart. Her hands felt clammy but she was unaware that she was wiping them up and down the side of her skirt.

'What were you doing out there?' she accused.

He looked surprised, wounded even. 'Me?' he said softly. 'I just went to look for this ball.' He held it up. 'Why? What's happened?'

'One of the children is missing,' said Jane.

'Missing?' said Stan. 'How awful. Which one?'

'My little sister,' said Connie. 'Mandy Craig.'

'Oh, dear,' said Stan softly.

'Why have you changed your name, Stan?' Connie accused.

'It's a long story,' said Stan, rolling his eyes innocently.

Jane frowned. 'Connie, is this relevant? Shouldn't we send someone back into the woods to look for Mandy?'

'Where is Mandy?' Connie asked Stan coldly.

Roger laid his hand on Connie's arm but she was too focused on Stan. She hadn't noticed that the whole Sunday school was staring open-mouthed.

'My dear girl,' said Stan, 'I have absolutely no idea.'

'Perhaps,' Roger said taking charge, 'if Jeanette and Graham . . . er, Stan saw Mandy going into the copse, it stands to reason she must still be in there. Where exactly did you see her?'

'She said she was looking for a feather,' said Stan casually. 'I left her by that stile down there.'

'That was one of the things on the treasure hunt list,' Jane groaned. 'Oh, I wish I hadn't done that now.'

Arnold put his arm around Jane's shoulders. 'Don't get upset, darling. She'll turn up, you wait and see.'

'What was she doing down there in the first place?' Jane wailed. 'I told everyone *not* to go into the woods.'

'Look, this isn't getting us anywhere,' said Roger. 'I'm going back to look for her again.'

'I'll come with you, if you like,' said Stan.

'No!' Connie cried.

'Connie, the more people we have out there looking for her,' said Roger, 'the quicker we'll find her.'

'But not Stan,' Connie insisted.

'That's all right,' said Stan, seeing the shocked expression on some of their faces. 'I'm quite happy to stay here and help look after the children and free up somebody else to go.'

Connie was about to say something else when Jane said, 'I think the rest of us should all stick together now. I've got a pass the parcel that we can play until the coach comes back. Mrs Stevens, did you say we had some cakes?'

The three ladies produced their cake tins and the children were happily occupied choosing them. Arnold emptied his pockets of sweets announcing that there would be one sweet for every *very good* boy and girl. 'I'll go with Roger and Connie, darling,' he told Jane. 'Between the three of us, we should find her quite quickly.'

Roger was asking Stan exactly where he'd last seen Mandy. He pointed to an area well away from the clearing where Pip lay and the place where Mandy had disappeared.

'She was definitely walking east,' he said in a considered tone of voice.

'I'm sure Stan has something to do with this,' Connie said as she and Roger walked back towards the trees. 'I don't trust him one bit.'

'Listen, Miss Jackson,' Stan said to Jane. 'I really ought to be getting back.'

'The coach will be here in half an hour,' said Jane.

'My mother is a sick woman,' he went on. 'I should have said something before but your father said you were desperate for helpers and I didn't like to let him down.'

Jane touched his shoulder. 'Of course,' she said. 'You must go. There's a bus that goes to town on the hour from the top of Salvington Rise by the shops if you'd rather not wait for the coach.'

'You don't mind?' he asked pleasantly.

'Not at all,' smiled Jane. 'I'm sorry about Connie.'

He nodded sagely. 'She's upset. I understand that.'

Jane patted his arm. 'You're a very understanding man.'

He said his goodbyes and struck out. 'I wonder if you would be good enough to call in to the manse and tell my father what has happened?' Jane asked.

Stan hesitated.

'If you don't have time to call in, could you perhaps telephone?'

'Of course,' Stan agreed amicably. He turned to go.

'The number . . .' Jane began.

'Beg pardon?'

'You'll want the number.' She was writing it down on a piece of paper torn from the list on her clipboard. 'It's Goring 458.'

He took the number and stuffed it into his pocket.

'And call her name on the way back,' Jane suggested.

'Beg pardon?'

'Mandy's. You never know, she could have gone in the opposite direction.'

'Good idea,' he said waving cheerfully.

Calling her name, he headed down Honeysuckle Lane until he was lost to view, then he stopped. It would be so much easier and quicker to go in the opposite direction. He could walk to Long Furlong and straight home but he wanted to avoid the searchers at all costs. He couldn't afford to be trapped into staying in the woods to help them. He was in luck. The bus was parked right by the shops and because he ran, he caught it comfortably. As the bus sped down Salvington Hill, he saw the coach coming up. He smiled to himself. They could search until the cows came home but they'd never find her. Served her right, little tease, egging him on like that and then running away.

Of course they'd keep trying to find her even when it got dark. Once the children were safely back home, someone in the village would organise a search party. Not the minister, because he wouldn't bother telling him. And when they complained, he'd tell them he was so concerned about his poor old mother that he'd clean forgot. He chuckled. Oh dear, oh dear. Everyone was going to have an awfully long night.

'Roger, I'm scared.'

Roger put his arm around Connie's shoulders. They'd been calling and searching for about fifteen minutes and there was still no sign of Mandy or Pip.

295

'I know,' Roger said quietly, 'but there a good chance she's simply got herself thoroughly lost.'

'That Stan . . .' she began.

'Yes,' said Roger. 'What was all that about?'

Connie wanted to tell him but somehow the words got stuck in her throat.

'I don't know,' said Connie. 'He always was a bit creepy and like I say, I just don't trust him.'

Roger's face darkened. 'But he's the church pianist, isn't he? Surely they would have checked his credentials.'

'Reverend Jackson is very trusting,' said Connie.

'You mentioned something in the past . . .'

'It was because of Stan that my brother was forced to leave home.' Now she was being economical with the truth.

Arnold had come to join them. 'Still no sign then?'

Roger shook his head. 'I think we should start working our way back to the lane,' he said. 'It's the only area we haven't looked at and perhaps if something frightened her, she may have thought she could make her own way home.'

'But if she was in the lane,' Connie reasoned, 'she would have had to walk right past the meadow where we all were.'

'True,' said Roger, 'but we are trying to get into the mind of a child here. I know it's not logical but she may have been looking for houses, civilisation, or running blindly to reach her mother.'

'It's worth a try,' said Arnold. 'You two go to the right. I'll cover the left side of the track.'

They turned back and began calling again, looking carefully through the trees for any sign of life. In the distance, Connie had spotted Stan running down the hill and her blood chilled. She recalled another man running towards the road the day she and the family were on the downs and that other little girl got lost. It was the same gait. She stopped walking and froze. Oh God . . . oh God . . . she thought as she turned to see where Roger and Arnold were. Her gaze went to the ground and she suddenly cried out. The two men came running. From where she was standing she could see that the grass in a small clearing was trampled down. In the centre of the area, there was a bright red stain.

'What is it?' said Roger.

Connie pointed and Roger bent down. He touched it with his fingers and bringing it to his nose, he sniffed. 'Definitely blood,' he said gravely and Connie took in her breath.

The search had now taken on a new sense of urgency. If Mandy had lost this much blood, what could have happened? Had she been attacked by someone or something? Had she fallen or got a nosebleed? Whatever the reason, surely she would have run towards the meadow and help. Connie's mind was racing ahead of all that. Supposing she was unable to run and get help? Supposing someone had stopped her. It was Stan Saul, wasn't it! She shuddered. Why else was he running away if he had nothing to do with this? She could feel herself beginning to panic. Where was her little sister? She called desperately. 'Mandy, where are you?'

Then Arnold found more blood. 'Whoever was bleeding was going in this direction,' he said.

Connie kept close to Roger and together they stepped over brambles and fallen branches following the trail of blood.

All at once Connie looked up and saw a dog lying on the ground. She could see at once that it was Pip. He was lying beside what looked like a fox's earth. She called his name and he tried to lift his head but flopped back down again. She ran as fast as she could and threw herself on the ground beside him. As he looked up at her there was no mistaking the adoration in his eyes and he managed to make his tail give a couple of painful and exhausted wags. He had been horribly injured. His side was torn and bleeding and his mouth was badly cut. She could see he was missing several teeth as well. Connie burst into tears. 'Oh,

Pip. Pip, what happened?' She looked helplessly at Roger. 'What was he doing here? He's an intelligent dog. He would have known to drag himself along the path if he needed help. Why come right down here in the thicket?'

They looked at each other, no one daring to actually say what they feared the most. Connie leapt to her feet. 'Mandy,' she screamed. 'Mandy, where are you? Mandy?'

They waited a couple of minutes, hopes rising once again but all they heard was the sound of the wind sighing through the trees. 'Mandy . . .' It was hopeless.

'Connie,' Roger began cautiously. 'Is it possible the dog attacked Mandy?'

Connie's eyes grew wide. 'Never in a million years. He adored her. If anything, he would have risked his life to save her.'

They stared at each other as the full import of what she had said dawned on them both.

'What do you want us to do?' said Roger. They were all on the horns of a dilemma. The dog needed the help of a vet, but Mandy couldn't be forgotten. Connie put her hands on either side of her head and tugged at her hair in desperation.

'I think we'd better get the dog to a vet straight away,' said Arnold, taking his coat off. He laid the coat on the ground and then he and Roger gently lifted Pip onto it. As they lifted him, the dog whimpered and yelped in pain.

'Get him to my car,' said Roger. 'We'll drive him there as soon as we can.'

They hurried towards the lane again, with Connie running behind them.

'Connie, we've got to get more help,' said Roger. 'We need others to help us cover the ground. We could be searching for a month of Sundays if we try to do it on our own.'

They'd reached the car. Connie fondled the dog's ears and kissed his muzzle. 'Thank you for trying,' she said, her voice strangled by a terrible sense of loss and anguish. 'I love you.' She felt his body quiver as he tried to lift his head and lick her face. The two men laid him on the back seat. 'I'll find her,' Connie promised and Pip managed one last wag of his tail.

'What do you want me to do?' Roger asked. 'I could take the dog to the vet, then go back to the village for some more bodies, or we leave the dog here to take his chances.'

'Go,' said Connie. 'You're right. We need help.'

'Coming?' asked Roger as he sat in the driver's seat.

Connie shook her head. 'I can't,' she said. 'She's in there some-where and I've got to find her.'

Roger got out of the car again. 'Do you drive?' he asked Arnold.

Arnold nodded. 'But not since I left the army two years ago.'

Roger tossed him the keys. 'That's good enough for me,' he said. 'I don't know the area so without someone to guide me it would take an age to find a vet.'

'Tell Jane where I've gone,' said Arnold, climbing in the driver's seat.

Roger watched Arnold reverse flawlessly and drive back down the hill. He was just about to walk back up the hill when he saw a coach coming up the hill and then he heard a chatter of excited voices as a crocodile of tired but happy children and their helpers came out of the meadow.

Connie drew Jane to one side and told her what had happened. 'We'll be back as soon as possible,' Jane reassured Connie and Roger.

'Bring as much help as you can,' said Roger. 'And we'll need torches too. It'll be getting dark soon.'

Connie walked away and back up the hill, calling her sister's name again. Pip must have been trying to protect Mandy. What other reason could there be? She remembered how he had taken off like a rocket almost as soon as they'd got out of the car. When she and Roger heard the delighted screams of the children, Pip must have heard something quite different. One of those screams had been a real scream. She thought about the relationship he had with Mandy. They really loved each other and the dog must have realised Mandy was in danger. So what had stopped him in his tracks? The dog couldn't have been knocked down by a car. The lane was too narrow and the ground too soft for vehicles. What about some sort of farm vehicle? There was a field almost ready for harvesting above them, but surely a farmer would have stopped to check if he'd hit an animal. There was only one other answer. Pip was deliberately attacked. Connie frowned as she tried to imagine what sort of an animal it could have been. Pip was fearless and there was no doubt that he would risk his very life for someone he loved, but what sort of animal knocks out teeth? A man with a stick, perhaps . . .

As Roger joined her, she said nothing. She couldn't bear to voice the things she feared the most, that Stan Saul had attacked her dog and done something awful to her sister. She had to find Mandy at all costs.

When the parents met the coach, Jane explained that although everyone else had come home safely, Mandy was missing. Gwen ran all the way home and Clifford shut the nurseries, got the car out and they came straight up the hill. Once they arrived, the locals on the hill were involved but there was little time for formal introductions. They all wanted to get on with the job of finding Mandy.

Connie and Roger took her mother and Clifford back to the place where they'd found Pip. 'I'm sure he was trying to get to her,' said Connie. 'You know how devoted he is to her. She has to be around here somewhere but I've called and called and there's no answer.'

Clifford took charge and they started a much more methodical search but after half an hour they had still drawn a blank. As the group came together again, they could hear more voices. Clifford made his way back to the path and found a whole crowd of people walking towards them. Mrs Bawden their next-door neighbour, the Frenchie, Isaac Light, Rev Jackson and Jane, Mr Stevens and Mr Luxton and a whole lot more friends and neighbours.

Connie felt a tear come to her eye. 'How did you all get here?' she gasped.

'We persuaded the coach driver to bring us back,' said Rev Jackson. 'Now where do we start?'

Roger explained where they had already looked and the area not yet fully covered. As soon as Connie noticed Eugène, her heart leapt. His eye met hers and she mouthed a silent 'thank you'. Before long the wood was ringing with people calling for Mandy. They walked beside ditches and lifted bramble patches. They prodded layers of leaf mould with long sticks and stared into rabbit holes and badger sets. Just when it all seemed utterly hopeless Connie heard Isaac shouting, 'Over here, over here.'

Everyone ran to the spot. Caught on a thick bramble they saw a red ribbon. Gwen reached out and grasped it as the tears sprang into her eyes. Now everyone was talking. Connie waved her arms to try and get some quiet but it took Roger's authoritative voice to get the silence they needed.

Connie nodded towards her mother and Gwen took a deep breath.

'Mandy,' she called. 'It's Mummy. Are you there, darling?'

Everyone held their breath then from somewhere deep below the earth, they heard a child's cry.

Twenty-Eight

They had no tools and she was obviously deep underground.

'How the hell did she get down there?' someone said.

'We should all move back,' said Roger, looking around. 'There's too many of us and this ground is very unstable.'

'I'll go down the hill and see if we can borrow some spades,' said Eugène and several of the men took off with him.

Connie and her mother felt a mixture of relief and panic. It was wonderful that they had located Mandy at last and that she was obviously alive, but how far had she fallen and how on earth were they going to get her out? Looking up, Connie could see that the tree canopy had once been shattered by something and Roger was right, the ground beneath their feet was very unstable.

The area was now largely neglected although during the war it had been the site of one of the many RAF wireless and Radio Location stations. It was within sight of another station on Highdown, a couple of miles away, as the crow flies, and they had helped the British forces keep a tab on enemy aircraft flying to and fro on air raids on London as part of the Ground Control Interception. Although there were plenty of bomb craters, High Salvington's greatest claim to fame was being the crash site of an enemy Heinkel 111 in August 1940. Back then, a crowd almost as large as the one on the hill now had gathered to see it.

The spades arrived and Roger began to organise a working party. Somebody had had the foresight to bring a wheelbarrow, which would make it easier to transport the dug soil away from the site. Tackling it from above increased the risk that the earth on top of her would simply collapse. They couldn't see her but they could hear her muffled cries. Clearly she was able to breathe without too much problem. It appeared that she had slipped down at an angle and gone under the damaged roots of a tree which leaned downhill at a crazy angle.

'I believe she's wedged in there by her shoulders,' said Roger. 'I have no idea how deep the hole is and I don't want to risk her falling even further.'

It was decided that they should dig alongside the opening rather than above it. That way they hoped to be able to persuade Mandy to crawl her way out without too much soil falling on top of her.

Eugène slipped unnoticed beside Connie. 'We will get her out,' he promised. As she turned to look at him, she was filled with a longing to feel his strong arms around her. He looked better. The dark rings had gone from under his eyes and his complexion seemed a lot healthier than when she last saw him. 'Did you go to see Kez?' she whispered.

He nodded. 'I did. Thank you, Connie. You are a true friend.'

Roger moved closer and interrupted them. 'Let's start getting the earth away from here,' he told the Frenchie. 'You can wheel it up over the ridge.'

'No problem,' smiled Eugène, taking off his jacket. Connie almost reached out to touch him but changed her move into a folding of her arms.

'I'll try and find another strong looking fellow to help you and you can do shifts,' said Roger glancing first at the Frenchie and then at Connie.

'That'll be me,' said Isaac, taking his shirt off as well.

Connie choked up. Roger gave her a quick side hug. 'You'd better brace yourself, darling. This is going to be a long, hard job.' And she saw Eugène look away.

The hill quickly became a hive of activity. Women living nearby had turned up with flasks of tea and later on, some sandwiches. Every now and then, Roger called for them to stop working so that Gwen could have the opportunity to call out to Mandy and reassure her that they were doing everything possible to help her. What they didn't tell her was that because of the unstable ground, this was getting more difficult by the minute. It wasn't just the moving hillock they had to contend with, they also had problems with the thick brambles and undergrowth which had to be cleared away before they could even get a spade into the earth.

As the evening wore on, the word had got around and a tidy crowd of would-be helpers gathered in the lane and PC Noble turned up on his bicycle. Connie was glad that they still had double summer time. 1945 was supposed to be the last time it was used but in view of the terrible food shortages in the country, the government had decreed to reinstate it in 1947 giving more hours of daylight to enable farmers to keep up the good work. The clocks would go back one hour on 10 August and then the final hour would be on 12 November.

Later on, someone put a blanket on Connie's shoulders and as she pulled it around her, she realised for the first time how terribly cold she was. She had no cardigan and her arms were bare. Eugène and Isaac who had stripped down to their vests, glistened with sweat and the dirt on their bodies made them look like a couple of miners. As the gloom turned towards dusk, the first of the oil lanterns was lit and a hurricane lamp hissed nearby. The first group of men were beginning to get tired, so a shift pattern was adopted and slowly but surely they were making progress. They shored up the sides as they went and once they were actually tunnelling, they had to shore up the overhang too.

Roger was a careful overseer, checking everything thoroughly as they went. 'No slacking,' he told Eugène who had stopped to wind a handkerchief around his blistered hands.

'Roger!' Connie exclaimed. 'He's doing his best.'

'It's important to keep up the momentum,' said Roger, unrepentant. 'We can't afford passengers.'

Eugène was about to react but Isaac tugged on his arm and the two men carried on.

Everything was going so well until someone's spade hit something metal.

'What the hell was that?'

Rev Jackson looked around wildly. 'Didn't they have guns up here during the war?'

'No, you've got that one wrong yer reverent,' said a voice. 'I've lived up here all my life and there's never been a gun up here.'

The man who hit the metal was running his hand along whatever it was he'd hit. 'There's definitely something down here and it's quite big.'

Roger scrambled down the bank. He traced his hand alongside the other man's and even in the gathering gloom they all saw his face pale. 'Have you ever been bombed up here?'

'What for?' someone cried. 'There's nothing up here.'

'What about the RAF Wireless and Radio Location during the war?' someone else remarked. 'Could be that somebody was aiming for that, I suppose.'

'Wireless and Radio Location?' Rev Jackson queried.

'Part of our air defences, sir,' said Roger. 'The German Luftwaffe were intercepted by our aircraft thanks to the boys working on Ground Controlled Interception.'

'Really?' said Rev Jackson. 'I never realised.'

Roger nodded sagely. 'We're all indebted to a lot of people we don't know about, sir.'

'Tell you what,' another man said, 'the Germans sometimes dropped the odd leftover bomb before they reached the Channel.'

'So did our boys,' a woman called out. 'If they were heading for Tangmere or Ford, they couldn't afford to land with an unexploded bomb still on board.'

'Then I'm afraid we have to stop what we are doing,' said Roger. He jerked his head towards PC Noble. 'Could you tell everyone to get well away, please?' The policeman saluted and scrabbled up the bank. 'And ask your sergeant to call my HQ and dispatch a unit.'

PC Noble seemed slightly confused.

'What's up?' said Clifford, sliding down the bank to join him. 'Why have you stopped digging?'

'I'm sorry, sir, but we can't carry on,' said Roger. 'That feels like a UXB to me.'

'A bomb!' someone cried. There was a collective gasp and several people moved away. PC Noble flew up the bank, mounted his bicycle and rode as fast as he could towards the houses further down the lane.

'How can you be so sure?' Clifford said desperately.

'Roger is a bomb disposal officer,' said Connie. 'He was the man who defused that bomb in Worthing High Street a few months ago.'

Clifford seemed to wither in size. Gwen burst into tears as Eugène took it upon himself to clear the rest of the people from the scene. Some left reluctantly, but most of them were only too keen to go back down the hill.

'You can't leave her there,' cried Gwen.

Connie's face was stricken. 'Can't we pull her out first?'

'I'm sorry, darling, but we cannot risk it,' said Roger. 'We've been really lucky so far not to set it off. It has to be checked and made safe before we can go on.'

Connie stared at him in horror. 'But she's underneath.'

'I know,' said Roger, 'and I will get her out. It's just going to take time.'

'I want to speak to her,' said Gwen. 'Let me talk to my daughter.'

Roger hesitated for a second and then said, 'Okay. But try not to let her panic. Tell her we're all going to have a rest. Tell her

306

it's night-time. Don't tell her what's really happened. Try to make everything sound as normal as possible.'

Gwen's eyes filled with tears and she looked helplessly at Connie and everyone knew what she must be thinking. How could she possibly sound normal when every part of her body was screaming in panic for her child?

'I'll do it, Mum.'

'Connie.' The sound of Eugène's voice made her hesitate. She turned and her eyes met his. Eugène glanced back at Roger watching them then turned to Connie. 'Be careful,' he said quietly.

Her chin quivered slightly as she nodded in thanks and then Roger reached out his hand to help her down. As she took it, Connie stepped on the boards the men had laid down for the wheelbarrow. Her foot slipped slightly and she felt Eugène's strong arm make a grab for her from behind to hold her steady.

'I've got her, thank you,' said Roger coldly as he reached to help Connie.

Connie couldn't look back but somehow it was Eugène's grip that gave her the strength she needed. Taking a deep breath, she knelt and then lay on the ground in front of the hole. It was damp and smelled earthy. 'Mandy . . .'

'Let me out,' Mandy sobbed. Her voice sounded far away but Connie could see a small gap tapering away in the distance. This must have been where she went into the hole, pulling the earth in behind her but luckily still giving her enough access to air. If it had closed right around her entirely she would have been buried alive. 'I will be good. Please, Connie.'

It took every ounce of strength Connie had not to break down. 'Mandy . . . darling, listen to me. It's hard to get down to where you are. We are going to have to get some special things to help us.'

'But I want to come out now.'

'I know you do, darling. But everybody is going to have a little rest first and then we'll get you out. Promise.'

Silence.

Connie chewed her lip anxiously. 'Can you hear me, darling?'

'I'm thirsty.'

Connie looked helplessly at Roger. 'That's okay. We can give her something,' he whispered.

'All right,' Connie shouted down the hole. 'I'll see what I can do. We'll have you out soon, Mandy, I promise. Do you think you can be a good girl for just a little bit longer?'

She waited for what seemed like an eternity and then Mandy said, 'Do I have to touch Mr Charles?'

For a second, Connie's eyes widened and her blood ran cold. Aware that every eye was upon her she fought with herself not to start shaking. Her heart was already pounding with rage. So she had been right after all. This had something to do with that damned man. Dear God. What was she going to do? Her mother and Clifford were already demented with worry. If she said something now it would only add to their misery. She swallowed hard. 'You don't have to do anything you don't want to, darling.'

There was another pause then Mandy sighed, 'All wight.'

Out in the lane, the coach driver had already decided it was time to go. 'If there's a bomb down there, I can't risk my motor being blown to kingdom come,' he told Rev Jackson. 'You either get your people back on the coach or you all stay here at your own risk.'

Although he himself wanted to stay, it seemed prudent to Rev Jackson to get everyone else home. 'I know you all want to help,' he told everyone, 'but the best way is by giving the authorities plenty of space to do what they have to do.'

It was his diplomatic way of assuaging any guilt they might feel at leaving Connie and her family to it.

Jane and Arnold sought Connie out first. 'We'll come back in the morning,' she promised Connie. She and Arnold were full of apologies. 'Please don't feel bad,' said Connie, giving Jane a hug. 'You've both been real pals. Thanks, and take your dad with you. He looks completely done in.'

'The vet says he's doing all he can for Pip,' said Arnold. Connie sucked in her lips, unable to speak. 'I think he might make it,' Arnold went on. 'He's a plucky little dog.'

The driver started the engine and a reluctant Rev Jackson began to close the door. 'We'll pray for you,' he said helplessly.

The School of Military Engineering began in Ripon in Yorkshire in 1940. Once the seriousness of the country's position was fully realised, the military formed a specialist Bomb Disposal School. They began with a basic unit which consisted of one officer, and fifteen other ranks which were divided into two subsections, one for the removal of a bomb and the other for its sterilisation. Roger came into the system in 1943 when the total Bomb Disposal force numbered some 10,000 men, who were stationed in every theatre of war and in the three services. His unit was based in Horsham which was only a twenty-mile drive away. Without even the basic equipment, there was little Roger could do except wait. He did his best to appear calm and in control but in truth he did have some serious concerns. He could only hope that the strike of the spade hadn't been enough to restart any dormant timing device. The bomb itself was badly damaged and most likely exceedingly dangerous. Not only that, but it was only held in place by tree roots and highly unstable earth works.

Connie was being very brave. She was a plucky girl and the way she was behaving only made him admire her all the more. He wasn't so sure about that other chap sniffing around. He had made short work of emptying the wheelbarrows at the top of the incline, but he seemed to be hanging around Connie a bit too much. Who was he? She'd never mentioned going out with anyone else and Eva had never mentioned it either. He was beginning to regret leaving it so long before declaring his hand. Connie was definitely the girl for him.

Roger managed to rig up a rubber tube and after he'd pushed it down the little gap, Connie came back onto the boards to explain to the child what was happening. When Roger had spoken to her, Mandy had become agitated, but Connie's voice calmed her.

'Can you see a rubber tube coming down, darling?' Connie lay on the boards looking down. 'If you put it in your mouth, we're going to put some water down for you.'

Once they'd made sure Mandy was able to reach the other end, Roger dripped a little water down the tube for her to drink. At least, he reasoned to himself, her arms must be relatively free, and she wasn't too tightly wedged in. The one thing he had to make sure of was that she didn't flap about too much and cause the earth to slip or the bomb to shift. The longer she was there, the greater the danger that the whole thing would go up. He was very concerned about Mandy and the way he felt about Connie made the thought that she might be hurt unbearable.

Mr and Mrs Craig had been taken in by some people further down the hill. The houses nearest the UXB had been cleared by PC Noble and his sergeant who had turned up soon after he'd been informed about what was going on. Plenty of people further down the hill were only too willing to open their doors to give the onlookers shelter. It wasn't until later that the first sign of trouble came when a large formidable woman climbed out of a taxi and demanded to see whoever was in charge. She was followed by a smaller woman who looked rather overdressed for the occasion. It was Ga and Aunt Aggie.

PC Noble came to see what was happening as Ga boomed and shouted, hardly giving any of them the chance to speak. 'Someone told me Mandy had fallen down a hole. So why aren't you getting her out? Don't just stand there, young man, take me to her. She was supposed to be in the care of that drippy girl from the vicarage, but she's come back home without her. Where is the child? And where's Constance?'

Connie and Roger, thinking the commotion might be the arrival of the bomb disposal unit, came down the hill to see what was going on.

'There you are,' Ga shouted as soon as she saw her. 'Where's Mandy?'

'Ga, this is Roger,' Connie began. 'He's been helping us with the rescue and . . .'

'So why isn't he still down there getting her out?'

'We have to wait . . .' Roger began.

'Wait? Whatever for?' she fumed. 'You get back there right this minute, young man.'

Roger seemed taken aback being spoken to like that. 'Madam, I have no equipment,' he said. 'As soon as my unit comes from Horsham . . .'

'Horsham?' Ga gasped angrily. 'But that's miles away.'

'Olive, dear,' said Aggie. 'Keep calm.'

'Keep calm?' roared Ga. 'That's what they told us all through the bloody war. Keep calm and carry on. Well, this isn't bloody Hitler we're talking about. This is a member of my family.'

'The bomb disposal squad will be here at any minute,' said Roger stiffly.

'Bomb disposal . . .' Ga choked. 'Constance, what is he talking about?'

Connie took her great aunt's arm.

'Let go of me, Constance,' Ga snapped. 'I don't need holding up.'

'Mandy has fallen underneath an unexploded bomb,' said Connie, struggling to be civil. 'Roger is a bomb disposal officer.' There was a stunned silence. 'It has to be defused.'

'Then tell him to get on with it.'

'And he will, Ga,' said Connie. 'As soon as the team get here.'

Roger marvelled at her patience. Clearly the aunt was used to saying 'jump' and everybody saying 'how high'. She was a monster. He turned to look for the unit and spotted his mother and sister

311

walking up the hill. He waved but didn't wait. Before they came, he decided to check one more time that everything was still as it was at the site.

The five women met in the lane.

'What's she doing here?' Ga demanded when she saw Eva's mother and addressing Eva she said, 'Been cavorting half-naked in any more fountains lately?'

'Olive, dear . . .' Aunt Aggie began again.

'Oh, shut up, Aggie,' Ga retorted.

'Ga,' Connie scolded. 'Please.'

Eva pretended she hadn't heard and gave Connie a hug. Theirs was a mutual sense of shared concern. Ga harrumphed and moved away from them.

'Hello Olive, Aggie,' said Cissy. 'How are you both?'

'Don't you speak to me,' said Aggie stiffly.

'Can't we let bygones be bygones?' said Cissy. 'Especially under the circumstances . . .'

Ga wrinkled her nose. 'Did you hear something just then, Aggie? I thought I heard a sheep farting.'

'For God's sake!' Connie snapped. 'Can't you let up for just a minute?'

Cissy turned to Connie. 'This must be so awful for you, dear. How is she?'

'I don't know,' said Connie. Her head was pounding and she had a raging thirst. 'Asleep, I hope. She's had a dreadful experience.'

'Someone told us they'd stopped digging,' said Mrs Maxwell. 'Is that because it's getting dark?'

Connie shook her head. 'It's because there's an unexploded bomb there.'

Vi Maxwell took in her breath. 'Then Roger . . .'

Connie nodded. 'He's been wonderful but we have to wait for the team to come from Horsham.'

'But Roger said he didn't want to do it anymore,' said Vi

helplessly. 'He said he didn't feel safe because he had other things on his mind.'

Connie put her hand over her mouth lest she made a sound. 'You know why, don't you, Ma?' said Eva. 'It's because he's fallen in love. Roger loves Connie.'

'Eva,' Connie cautioned. She had just noticed the red glow of a cigarette in the gloom. A group of men, including Eugène and Isaac were leaning against the wall of the shop across the road. 'Don't.'

Ga had removed herself to the other side of the lane but she was listening to every word they were saying and quickly rounded on Connie. 'Constance, what is she talking about? Who is that man?'

'*That man*,' said Vi, her voice steeped in sarcasm, 'is my son.'

Ga looked as if she was about to have an apoplectic fit. 'Your son!' She glared at Connie. 'And here you are hanging around him like a lovesick cow? A Maxwell?'

Connie gritted her teeth. How she hated Ga. It took every ounce of strength Connie had not to lash out at her. She glanced helplessly towards Eva but she had already turned away.

Just then a front door opened and Gwen and Clifford having heard the raised voices came out of the house. 'What's happening? Any more news?'

Connie went to her mother and gave her a hug. She looked totally distraught. Her eyes were puffy and red from crying and her face was pale. 'Nothing yet, Mum, but the team should be here at any minute.'

'What are you doing here, Ga?' said Clifford.

'Surely you didn't expect me to stay at home and do nothing?' she snapped.

'Well, there's nothing you can do here,' Clifford said pointedly, 'so go back home and take Aggie with you.'

'It's a good job I *am* here,' said Ga. 'Did you know about Connie and that man?'

Clifford stared at her with a blank expression.

'She's in love with him,' Ga shrieked. 'Well, I tell you now, I'm not having a Maxwell as a member of my family. I'm going to put a stop to this once and for all.'

'For God's sake,' bellowed Clifford.

'Go home, Ga.' Connie spoke in such an authoritative voice everyone looked at her in shocked surprise. 'And this is neither the time nor place to fuel your stupid dog-eared family feud.'

'Dog-eared . . .' Ga spluttered. 'I'll have you know . . .'

'We don't want to hear it,' said Connie, covering her ears. 'All we care about is getting Mandy out of that hole alive and I don't care who does it. They can call Hermann Göring and the whole bloody German army for all I care. If they can get Mandy out, I'll cheer them all the way.'

'Well,' Ga harrumphed. 'I'll go to sea.'

'I wish you bloody well would,' muttered Clifford.

Connie turned towards Eva. 'I'm supposed to be on duty tomorrow,' she said. 'Can you get a message to Ward Sister?'

'It's my day off,' said Eva. 'I'll do the shift for you.'

Connie put her arms around her friend. 'Thanks, Eva,' she choked. 'You're a real pal.'

'Why don't you all come back inside?' called the homeowner. 'You'll catch your death out here.'

'I'm not going anywhere with a Maxwell,' said Ga.

'Suit yourself,' said Clifford, herding everyone inside and waiting until last. Ga glared at him and he closed the door.

The taxi driver was talking to some of the other residents as Ga marched back down the lane. 'Take us back to Belvedere Nurseries,' she demanded as Aggie hurried after her.

He gave her an old-fashioned look but said nothing. Ga didn't care. She was furious. How dare Constance speak to her like that? Who did she think she was? And as for that cocky Maxwell girl . . .

'Everything all right with the little girl then, missus?' said the taxi driver as they sped down the hill.

314

Ga didn't even hear him. She was still seething. Connie was getting far too big for her boots. What she needed was taking down a peg or two.

The driver pulled up outside the darkened house. He didn't get out to open the door for her so she had to do it herself. She baulked at the idea of shelling out 10/6 for the fare as well. 'It was only five minutes up the road,' she snapped.

'Twenty,' said the driver, his face expressionless. 'It was a round trip and there was two of you.'

She slapped the money in his hand. 'Don't go looking for a tip,' she said, 'and I shan't be using this taxi service again.' She stamped to the door and fumbled for her keys.

The driver checked the money, exactly right. 'I wouldn't take you anyway, you miserable old bat,' he mumbled.

Aggie went inside first and Ga turned to glare at the taxi driver one more time. As soon as she was sure he was looking at her, she stuck her nose firmly into the air. The taxi driver pushed the taxi into gear and stuck up two fingers.

Twenty-Nine

The team arrived about fifteen minutes later. Roger briefed them and they set about working out a plan of action. Major Owen was in charge and he invited suggestions.

'Can we carry on digging underneath, sir?' said Lance Corporal Parker. 'One of us could crawl in and work on it from underneath.'

'Too dangerous with the child still in there,' said Roger. 'If the earth started moving she's just as likely to panic or distract you at a crucial moment.'

'First, we need to fix a stethoscope on it to check there's no timer,' said Major Owen.

'It's doubtful that the timing mechanism is still intact,' Roger said, looking at his watch. Usually there was a half hour or an hour's delay before detonation. They had passed both.

'That's what Lofty Greenways thought in Hastings,' said Private Taylor grimly.

They stopped talking for a couple of seconds as they remembered Private Greenways, blown to bits when a chance tap on the casing of a bomb restarted the timing device leaving him with no time to get clear.

'All right, so we'd better strap a magnet to the bugger to prevent any clock starting up again,' said Major Owen. 'Then what? Cut a hole in the casing?'

'And use the steam steriliser you mean?' said Roger.

Major Owen nodded.

'I'll get on to it right away, sir,' said Roger, standing up.

'Not you, Captain Maxwell,' said the Major.

'This has been my case from the start, sir,' Roger protested. 'I should like to see it through.'

'Not possible, I'm afraid,' said the Major. 'You're too emotionally involved. You've just said the child is your girlfriend's baby sister.' He shook his head. 'Absolutely not.'

'She's not actually my girlfriend,' Roger lied, desperate not to be sent away. 'Just a friend.'

'Nevertheless,' said the Major. 'No.'

Roger had no alternative. He was outranked.

They set up arc lights run from a generator and got to work. Roger stood above them in the lane, the recommended two hundred yards distance between the UXB and the team, wishing that he could be hands on. The sappers had laid down a sandbag barrier. It was small comfort because Roger fretted knowing that Mandy didn't have that sort of protection. However, they were a well-oiled machine and beautiful to watch. The idea was to dissolve the explosive filling with steam until it was rendered harmless. He could only hope and pray that they managed to get it all away before the detonator activated.

As the first light of dawn trickled over the horizon, they heard the child crying. At least she's alive, he thought, but as Mandy's wails grew louder and more desperate, he began to worry again. It sounded as if she was starting to panic. The obvious thing to do was to get the child's mother or Connie but he knew the Major would never allow them that close to the hole until the bomb was safe. It was a mammoth task to stop himself from dashing down there to comfort her, and he could only imagine how devastated the family would be if they could hear her.

A man stood up further down Honeysuckle Lane. Eugène Étienne yawned sleepily. Isaac was still snoring gently as he sat up. PC Noble had tried to move them on but they had been reluctant to go, so they had bedded down against the wall. Connie meant too much to both of them to leave. Isaac had come to realise for the first time what she had done for him and his family and he didn't want to let her down. Eugène had his own reasons for being there. He had known as soon as they'd laid together on that horsehair sofa that he would never feel about another woman the way he felt for Connie. As they made love, his passion for her only grew stronger. He didn't just love her, he adored her. He had wanted to tell her that morning but then she had pre-empted him by telling him she'd made a terrible mistake. He couldn't have her, he knew that now. She was with Roger. It cut him to ribbons to see them together but if Roger made her happy that was all that mattered. He got up and came sleepily towards him.

'She's crying,' he said unnecessarily.

'I hear that,' said Roger tetchily.

'Do you want me to get Connie?'

Roger shook his head. 'I can't allow her any closer.'

'We could sing to her,' said Eugène.

'Sing?' Then all at once Roger half remembered a conversation he'd had with Connie once when she'd talked of her little sister. She'd told him of Mandy's favourite song. Dear God, what was it?

The Major must have thought he had gone completely mad when Eugène stood in front of the sandbags and burst into song. '*You are my sunshine, my only sunshine . . .*' As his rich baritone voice filled the misty dawn air, Roger joined in. The men working around the bomb heard her quiet down and finally understood what they were doing. After a while, Major Owen gave them the thumbs up and Roger clambered down to him.

'False alarm,' said the Major. 'Bloody thing was filled with this.' He lifted his hand and poured a pale substance from one hand to the other.

318

'So we can get her out now?'

The Major nodded. 'The only danger now is falling earth.' Eugène climbed back up the bank and called Isaac. He came back down the plank walkway with the wheelbarrow.

The back door was unlocked. Roger opened it quietly and looked around. Clifford and Gwen were locked in each other's arms asleep on the sofa. Someone had covered them with a blanket. Connie sat at the kitchen table, her head on her arms. As he opened the door, she felt the cold air on her legs and sat up. She looked terrible. Her hair was wild and she had dark circles under her eyes. He longed to take her in his arms and tell her it was going to be all right, but it wasn't over yet. He put his finger to his mouth and motioned her forward. Connie crept outside quietly and they didn't speak until they were on the lane.

'The bomb wasn't dangerous after all,' he told her.

Connie frowned. 'I don't understand.'

'It was filled with sawdust,' said Roger and as he saw her jaw drop he added, 'Probably sabotaged by the forced labour who made them.'

Connie flung her arms around his neck and squeezed him until he could hardly breathe. 'So we can get her out now?'

Coming back from the hole with a full wheelbarrow, Eugène saw them together. He closed his eyes in agony and leaned his head back. It was hard watching the girl he loved with someone else. Connie and Roger were running back to the site hand in hand.

After all the waiting, it didn't take long. The soldiers had supported the weight of the bomb with shoring and they'd made short work of the remaining soil. As soon as it was safe, Connie lay on the boards and reached out her hand. She moved her arm around the opening, calling Mandy's name softly and then she felt a fluttering on her fingertips.

'I can feel her!' she cried. 'Mandy, we're coming. Oh, I can't quite reach.'

'Here, miss, let me,' said Private Taylor. He was a tall man and quite thin. His arms were definitely longer than hers so Connie moved away. Taylor reached down the hole. They heard Mandy whimper and then Taylor pulled.

She came out smoothly although the earth was falling all around her. When she saw Taylor, she looked absolutely terrified until Connie scooped her into her arms and hugged her tight. The child felt very cold and of course she was filthy dirty. She smelled of urine and her dress was wet. Roger handed Connie a tin mug of lukewarm tea and when she put it to her lips, Mandy drank greedily. The men, their faces wreathed in smiles, applauded.

'Mr Charles . . .' said Mandy, burying herself under Connie's armpit.

'You don't have to see him,' Connie whispered, the old rage rising up inside once more. There was a shout from the bank and the next minute Gwen and Clifford were scrambling down.

'I'll get the car,' said Roger as Connie put Mandy into her mother's arms. 'We should get her checked out in hospital.'

They squeezed into Roger's car, Clifford in the front and Gwen on the back seat with Mandy straddled across her lap. Roger pulled Connie towards him and kissed her. 'I'll be as quick as I can,' he said earnestly.

As they sped away Connie looked around. Eugène and Isaac came across to stand beside her. A clod of damp earth fell from the front of Connie's dress. She was crying now . . . tears of relief, joy and exhaustion. Eugène reached out his arms and she leaned gratefully onto his chest. He didn't say anything. He just let her cry and held her tenderly. When she was done, he gave her his handkerchief. 'Not very clean, I'm afraid.'

Connie didn't care. 'Eugène, I know you're tired, but would you and Isaac do one more thing for me?'

'Of course.'

'You heard what happened to my dog? Take me to see Pip.'

It was still very early but there were lights on in the vet's house. He had his surgery in two rooms purpose built onto the side of the house. When she got out of Isaac's old motor, Connie was conscious for the first time how dirty she was. She tried to smooth down her crumpled dress and run her fingers through her messy hair. She was embarrassed to be out and about looking so awful but the need to see Pip overruled everything else.

Mrs Fielding opened the door to the three of them in her dressing gown.

'I'm sorry to . . .' Connie began.

'Come in,' said Mrs Fielding stepping aside. She was holding a cup of tea. 'My husband was hoping that you would come soon. He's been up all night. Go straight through.'

Mrs Fielding followed them through the surgery door and put the tea down on the desk where Mr Fielding was sitting. He had his back to them. 'Your tea is there, dear,' said Mrs Fielding, 'and Connie has come.'

When he turned, he was hollow-eyed and unshaven. He stifled a yawn. 'Ah, Connie,' said Mr Fielding smacking his lips. 'You'll be pleased to hear he's still with us.'

After taking a gulp of his tea, Mr Fielding led them into the other room. Pip lay on a couple of blankets. He looked much the same as he had done when they'd found him, except that there was now a large blood-stained bandage around his middle. His eyes were closed. Mr Fielding knelt and began dripping water from a dropper onto his mouth and the dog moved his tongue.

'I don't know how he's managed to keep going this long,' he said. 'These injuries would have taken a much younger dog hours ago.'

'Any idea how he got them?' Eugène asked.

'My guess is that he was hit several times with something

heavy,' said Mr Fielding. 'A piece of wood perhaps and he's been viciously kicked as well.'

'So it was no accident then?' said Isaac.

'Absolutely not,' said the vet. 'There's a definite imprint of the boot on his side. I heard what happened to your little sister, Connie, so I took a photograph just in case this had anything to do with her being in that hole.'

Connie knelt beside Pip and stroked his head. His tail flickered slightly and he opened his eyes.

'Can you save him?' Eugène asked. 'If it's a question of money . . .'

Mr Fielding shook his head. 'There's nothing more I can do, but he's got this far . . .'

Connie and Pip locked eyes. She could feel her throat getting tighter and it was hard to hold back the tears. 'Oh, Pip,' she said softly. 'You're such a brave little dog. I love you so much. I'm so sorry.' She kissed the dog's muzzle. 'We got her out,' she said. 'Mandy is safe now.'

Again the tail flickered and Pip gazed up at her, adoration in his eyes. Connie could hardly see as her tears fell freely, but as she cradled his head in her hands and kissed him she saw something pass across his eyes. What was it? Fear? No, Pip was fearless. Sadness? No, it wasn't that either. Pip was at peace with himself. The look stayed for a second and then he slowly closed his eyes for the last time. As his head relaxed in her hands, Connie realised what she'd just seen. It was the last tender goodbye.

Thirty

Connie didn't feel a bit like it after the trauma of the previous day and losing her precious dog, but by 2 p.m. that day she was back on duty. There was no chance of taking the rest of the day off. Home Sister had made that very clear when Connie came back to the hospital.

'But Nurse O'Hara was happy to do my shift,' she protested.

'Nurse O'Hara will be sent off duty,' said Sister Abbott.

Connie had managed to get a little sleep before returning to the ward but not much. She had too much to think about. What was she going to do about Stan? She had no proof but it was obvious that if Mandy was talking about 'Mr Charles' he was still up to his dirty tricks. She should have told the police there and then but somehow what with the worry about the bomb and Ga making such a terrible scene, she couldn't bring herself to add to her mother's troubles. Her mind went round and round what might have happened before Mandy fell down that hole. Pip must have been trying to protect Mandy. Dear Lord, had he managed to prevent Stan from touching her? The man had to be stopped once and for all.

Another problem was Roger. What was she going to do about him? She didn't love him but he was a good and kind man. If she couldn't have Eugène, maybe she should settle for Roger. Connie tried to imagine what it would be like being married to him. It would be fun having Eva for a sister-in-law. It would also upset Ga and the thought of that made her smile. She could get her own back for the way in which Ga had in effect sent her mother and Clifford away, but then she'd come back to how unfair it would be to use Roger like that. He had gone back to Horsham, promising to telephone the call box outside the hospital as soon as Connie came off duty. Eugène had taken Pip's body in the back of Isaac's car and Clifford would bury him somewhere on the property.

Connie lined up with the rest of the staff for Sister's hand inspection and thankfully passed the test. It had taken a great deal of scrubbing to get her nails clean after yesterday and thanks to the local press, the word had got around. Everyone wanted to know how her sister was. 'She's at home now,' said Connie. 'My mother is exhausted but she's looking after her.'

As they sat down for the afternoon report, the telephone rang.

'Matron wants to see you in her office,' said Sister, putting the receiver back on its rest.

Connie smiled to herself. Obviously Matron had heard about Mandy and wanted to hear about it first-hand. 'Shall I go as soon as I've heard the report, Sister?'

'No,' said Sister. 'Matron was most insistent. You have to go immediately.'

Ten minutes later, Connie walked into Matron's office but far from the welcoming and gentle enquiry she was expecting, Matron wore a thunderous expression. Connie could feel herself panicking. She'd done something wrong again, but what? As she stood to attention by the desk, Connie knew she was about to get a telling off, but she hadn't a clue why.

Matron had a sheet of pale cream writing paper in her hand and Connie caught a glimpse of a lion's head watermark. It was good quality paper. As Connie trembled, she began reading aloud.

'Dear Matron,

I witnessed two of your nurses skylarking with a dead body in the lift. I saw one of them, Nurse Dixon, hit the other nurse on the bottom with the dead man's hand and then they both laughed . . .'

Connie's jaw had dropped and Matron glanced up at her with a cold stare. It took Connie a second or two to realise that whoever had written what was in Matron's hand had seen Eva and her with Mr Steppings' body. But that was ages ago. Why tell Matron now . . . after all this time?

Connie frowned. 'That's not true, Matron,' she began. 'It wasn't like that.'

Matron ignored her and began reading again. *'I do not wish to cast aspersions,'* she went on, *'but I think this sort of behaviour brings the hospital into disrepute.'*

Connie could feel herself trembling. Who was doing this, and why?

Matron looked up again. 'I tend to agree with that, nurse. And this is not the first complaint I have had about you.' She indicated two other sheets of identical paper contained within a buff-coloured folder on her desk. 'Since I had those letters,' she went on, 'I have kept a close eye on you and there have been quite a few times when I have found your nursing care sadly lacking.'

'Matron,' Connie said. 'I can explain.'

Matron held up a hand to stop her. 'I'm afraid I have no other alternative but to ask you to leave.'

Connie stared at her in horror. 'But it's not true!'

Matron put all three pieces of paper together in the folder and closed it. 'Were you and another nurse in the lift with a body?'

'Yes, but . . .'

'Did the arm of the dead man hit the other nurse's bottom?'

'Well, yes it did, but . . .'

'No buts, nurse,' said Matron coldly. 'This hospital stands for decency and respect for both the living and the dead. I will not allow you or anyone else to sully its reputation. You will surrender your uniform and give your house keys to Home Sister with immediate effect. I expect you to be off the premises within the hour. That will be all.'

'But Matron,' Connie began again.

'That will be all, Miss Dixon,' said Matron standing up and opening her door.

Connie turned miserably to go.

'By the way,' said Matron. 'Who was the other nurse with you in that lift?'

Biting back her tears, Connie drew herself up. 'I'm afraid I don't remember,' she said.

For the first time that day, Connie was in luck. There was no one about as she walked into Belvedere Nurseries through the back way. She had decided on the bus coming back home that she wouldn't tell her mother she'd been sacked. Not yet, anyway. After all the trauma of yesterday, she wanted her mother to enjoy a bit of calm for a while. Connie hid her extra bags of luggage in the woodshed and carried only her small case into the house.

'Connie!' cried Gwen. 'What are you doing here?'

'I've been given a few days off,' said Connie, avoiding her mother's eye as she put the case down. She knew Gwen had a knack of knowing when she was lying.

'How lovely,' Gwen said taking her into her arms. 'Oh, it's so good to have you at home and Mandy safe and well.'

'Are you all right, Mum?'

Gwen pushed back at arm's length and smiled fondly. 'I'm fine.'

'You look tired.'

'That's only to be expected, dear. Like you, I didn't get a lot of sleep last night.'

They hugged each other again.

'Mandy is upstairs,' said Gwen. 'She's awake now. She's been sleeping and sleeping but I suppose that's no bad thing.'

'Can I see her?'

'Of course, darling,' said Gwen. 'She was asking for a glass of milk a minute ago. You can take it up to her, if you like.'

Connie took off her coat and hung it by the door.

'Those wretched birds have been at the milk again,' said her mother as she poured a glass.

Connie smiled. The milkman left the milk by the back door and if her mother didn't take them in straight away, the birds would peck through the cardboard milk bottle top and drink the cream at the top. It was a marvel to Connie that they did it. Which bird was the first to discover the delights of cream and how long did it take him to work out how to get at it? The ingenuity and craft they deployed to get something they wanted was amazing and she couldn't help admiring such determined thieves.

'By the way,' said her mother as Connie put one foot on the stair, 'who is Mr Charles?'

Connie froze, glad that she already had her hand on the banister or she may have stumbled. 'Mr Charles?' she said with a smile that she worried was a little too bright.

'Mandy keeps saying she doesn't want to meet him,' said her mother barely noticing the effect the sound of that name was having on her other daughter. 'I just wondered if you knew what she was talking about.'

Connie pulled the corners of her mouth down and shook her head.

'Ah well,' said Gwen turning back to the kitchen. 'Perhaps it's some storybook character she's been reading about at school.'

Connie walked up the stairs anxiously. All her own problems paled into insignificance now. This was too much of a coincidence . . . seeing Stan Saul and the mention of Mr Charles again.

Clearly something had traumatised Mandy in the woods. Connie may have deliberately blotted out the memory of the day it happened to her but she could never forget the revulsion she'd felt when she saw 'Mr Charles' for the first time.

As she walked slowly up the stairs, Connie remembered how her head was banging like a drum and her mouth felt dry. 'I need to go back to Kenneth,' she'd said, and that's when she'd realised that her words were all slurry. She had been confused and couldn't understand why she felt so strange. Of course now, with an adult head on her shoulders, she realised that he had made her drunk. And yet when she and Kenneth had talked about it, they'd realised that neither of them had had enough to be drunk. Stan must have put something into the cider. Either that or it was exceptionally strong.

Stan had pushed her into her bedroom and she stumbled backwards onto the bed. Full of trust, Connie had closed her eyes and relaxed. Her head had been spinning and she was desperate for some sleep but when she opened her eyes a second later, Stan had slipped off his braces and was unbuttoning his trousers. He was staring at her with a strange look in his eye and she didn't like it. She remembered how much her stomach was churning and she knew she was going to be sick. As his trousers fell to the floor, she'd gasped. 'What's that?'

'Meet Mr Charles.'

That's when the fear kicked in. She'd tried to get up but he pushed her back down and yanked at her dress. 'You're going to love him.'

As young as she was, it was at that moment that Connie knew everything was out of control. She didn't know what he was going to do but it was too scary and she was helpless to stop him. 'No. No,' she'd begged. 'Don't.' Even now, after all these years, thinking about it made her feel queasy. She gripped the banister a little more tightly and waited for the moment to pass.

As she and Stan began a tug of war with her knickers, she'd become aware of voices downstairs. Her befuddled mind couldn't make sense of it and her arms had little strength to resist him. Stan was much bigger than she was and he had a power which was overwhelming. He'd lifted her roughly further up onto the bed and pulled at her knickers again. They were coming off and she couldn't do anything about it. She began to cry. 'Please . . . don't.'

The voices downstairs were getting louder but Stan didn't seem to hear. He was in a hurry. He was fully aroused and needed satisfaction. What little gentle coercion he had used before had turned into an ugly rough-handling. He pinned her to the bed with one hand around her throat and finally tore her knickers off. 'Come on, you little tease. Don't fight me. It's nice. You'll like it.'

Back in the present day, Connie swayed at the top of the stairs. She closed her eyes again and the memory, as vivid as if it were only yesterday, came flooding back. He'd prised her legs apart using his free hand and his knee and then mounted the bed. At the very same moment the door had swung open and her great aunt had come into the room. Ga gave Stan's bare buttock a resounding slap and he leapt away.

'Get out of here, you dirty little swine,' Ga had bellowed, 'and if you ever come into this house again, I'll have your guts for garters.'

Connie braced herself against the banister. She hadn't thought in depth about that day for years but if Mandy was talking about Mr Charles, she had to find out if a similar thing had happened to her. Connie felt the familiar rage and indignation building inside her. That man had ruined her family and blighted her own life. Until Eugène, she had been unable to let any man get really close to her. Now that she was being honest with herself for the first time, that was the real reason she and Emmett hadn't made a go of it. She'd always pushed Emmett away because she'd hated the thought of seeing his Mr Charles. Perhaps that was why she'd hesitated for so long about Roger.

It was because of what Stan did that Kenneth had been sent away. Connie took a deep breath. She must not allow him to do it again. Stan or Graham as he now called himself, was obviously popular with Rev Jackson and the other people in the church but they were such trusting souls and Stan could charm the birds off the trees. She couldn't let it go this time. Somehow or other, she had to find out what really happened on High Salvington. Connie took another deep breath. Stay calm, she told herself. Don't frighten the child and take one step at a time. Then she slowly opened Mandy's bedroom door.

'Eva, Eva, open the door.'

Betty's banging was very persistent. Eva was dog tired and she had had a long day on the ward. In the end, after being sent off duty she'd been called back and she'd done the whole of Connie's shift, finishing at 9 p.m. After spending a worrying time on High Salvington, Eva had managed to keep going all day but as soon as she'd come off duty, she'd downed a cup of tea and lay on the bed. Even though Betty's knocking was urgent, Eva had been so dead asleep it was hard to make her body respond. She had been sleeping on her back and was aware of a dry crusted dribble down the side of her face. Her head was thick and frankly she felt awful.

'Eva,' Betty insisted. 'This is important.'

Eva dragged herself upright and shuffled to the door. Betty burst into the room and as soon as she saw the sight of her, Eva was alarmed. 'Good Lord,' she said pulling herself together, 'whatever's happened?'

'It's Connie,' said Betty. 'Eva, you'll never believe this but she's been sacked.'

Betty was right. Eva didn't believe it. 'Sacked? No. You've got it wrong.'

330

'She's left us a note,' said Betty waving a piece of paper in the air. 'All her things are gone.'

Eva snatched the note. '*Dear Betty and Eva,*' she read, '*I have just come from Matron's office and I've been asked to leave. There's very little time to explain because I have to be gone within the hour and Home Sister is waiting outside the door. Someone reported seeing us in the lift with Mr Steppings. Don't worry, I haven't said anything. Destroy this when you've read it. Thanks for being such good pals. I shall miss you. Love Connie.*'

'Do you think Home Sister saw this?' Eva asked anxiously.

Betty shook her head. 'She put it in my jewellery box. I only found it when I went to get my pearls. I thought she'd gone home for a couple of days . . . you know, after all that happened to her little sister. When I found the note, I looked through her drawers and everything has been cleaned out.'

Eva opened her wash bag and wiped her face with the damp flannel. She still felt a bit peculiar but her brain was slowly coming back into gear.

Betty still seemed confused. 'What does she mean about Mr Steppings?'

Eva told her about the night she and Connie became friends. 'His hand fell off the trolley and bopped me on the bottom,' she said. 'Connie made a joke about it being his last chance to touch a pretty girl, that's all.'

'But if all this happened while you were alone in the lift, who could have seen you?'

That was puzzling Eva as well. They had been alone in the lift when the incident took place. By the time they'd reached the ground floor, the pair of them had been careful to look as dignified as possible. Of course they had repeated the story to umpteen people since then. They'd meant no harm. It was part of the black humour of the hospital. No offence was intended and the nurses were always discreet in front of the patients, but joking about incidents like that between themselves helped to lighten some very dark moments.

There was a soft knock on the door and Eva opened it. Several other girls stood outside. 'We heard you talking,' said one, 'and we guessed it must be about Connie. Isn't it awful?'

'I was with her on the ward today,' said another. 'None of us can believe this has happened.'

'Come on in,' said Eva. They squeezed into the small room, some sitting on the bed and the others on the floor. Everyone was upset and a few of them were crying. The big question was, what on earth could they do about it? What Matron said was as unalterable as the law of the Medes and Persians. With odds like that stacked against them, what hope did they have of getting their friend reinstated?

Thirty-One

His mother stared at the washing basket. Stan's trousers were covered in mud and his shirt was very dirty. She didn't want to think about it, but she was beginning to feel uncomfortable. When he'd come home on Monday night, he'd told her he'd been playing hide and seek with the children on High Salvington but it was odd that his things were so messy. She wouldn't have bothered about it if it weren't for the fact that almost as soon as he'd come through the door, he'd taken himself straight up to his room. She knew better than to follow him or disturb him once he had shut the door but she remembered the pattern from when he was a little boy. He usually shut himself away when he'd been up to mischief and he couldn't face her. He didn't come out again but she could hear him listening to the radio. She'd called up the stairs at supper time but when he didn't appear, she'd left some cold meat and salad on a tray outside the door.

Later, when she'd come up to bed, he'd eaten everything and left the tray outside on the landing but that unsettled feeling in the pit of her stomach was getting stronger. She'd spent a restless night but by the time she'd got up this morning he'd already left for work.

It was Ethel Durrent from next door who made the connection with Mandy. 'They say they were up half the night looking for her,' she said, her eyes bright with excitement. 'Wasn't your Stan there too?'

His mother put her fist into a ball, hardly daring to listen. Why hadn't Stan mentioned this when he came home last night? 'And was she all right?'

'Oh, yes,' said Ethel, 'but she was under a bomb.'

Mrs Saul relaxed. So nothing else. Thank God for that. The missing child was nothing to do with Stan.

'Did you hear what I said, dear?' Ethel was obviously waiting for some kind of reaction. 'She was down a hole with a dirty great bomb on the top of her.'

Mrs Saul shook her head and looked suitably alarmed. 'Poor kid. How awful. So what happened?'

Ethel Durrent gave her a blow by blow account but in truth, she wasn't really listening. What sort of a mother was she when her first thought was an accusation against her own son? Rev Jackson trusted Stan. All that rubbish about using his second name. He needn't have bothered. Rev Jackson said he was a wonderful pianist and he was so grateful when Stan, or Graham as he now wanted to be called, had volunteered to go with Jane Jackson on that outing. There weren't many men who were willing to help out. Most blokes thought it was unmanly to be running around with a bunch of Sunday school kids, but then, Stan wasn't like most men. He bought her cut flowers and he'd mowed the lawn for her. He was a good boy, was Stan.

But when she'd emptied the washing basket and seen the trousers and the shirt, something didn't sit right. The old worry was back again. Supposing . . . Had Stan . . . What if . . .? His mother shook the bad thoughts away. Jane Jackson would have kept a close eye on those children and Stan would have been in plain sight of everyone. She'd managed to convince herself it was her imagination, until she went through his pockets and found a bright red hair ribbon.

It wasn't until that evening that Connie finally sat down with her mother and Clifford to talk about Mandy. Ga was out. It couldn't have worked out better for Connie. They were alone in the house. This wasn't going to be easy, but it had to be done.

Clifford sat with his newspaper and Gwen sat concentrating on her knitting, a complicated Fair Isle patterned waistcoat in 3 ply wool for her husband.

'I need to talk to you about something that happened a long time ago,' she told Gwen.

At the end of her row, Gwen looked up uncertainly. Clifford folded his newspaper and stood up. 'I think I'll just go outside and check on the greenhouse,' he began.

'If you don't mind, Clifford,' said Connie, 'I'd prefer you to stay.'

He lowered himself back down into his chair.

'This is hard to talk about,' Connie began, 'but it is important that you both know what happened.'

'You're scaring me,' said Gwen, putting her knitting on the arm of her chair.

'I don't mean to, Mum,' said Connie, 'but please try not to interrupt while I do it. Okay?'

'Okay.'

So she told them. She told them about that meeting with Stan Saul on Long Furlong twelve years ago. She told them how she and Kenneth had brought him home to the house in Patching. She told them about the cider he'd given them and how Kenneth had fallen asleep with his head on the table. Then she told them how she had ended up upstairs with Stan and how he'd got undressed. Clifford stared at the floor in shocked surprise and Gwen at first put her hand to her throat and then reached for Clifford's hand when Connie described her fear and panic as Mr Charles was revealed.

'Oh, God,' Gwen whispered faintly. 'So you think . . .? And Mr Charles . . .? Oh no, no . . .' Connie nodded and her mother began to cry softly.

Clifford looked helplessly from one to the other. 'Am I missing something here?'

'It's Mandy,' said Gwen. 'She keeps saying she doesn't want to see Mr Charles.'

It took a second or two for the penny to drop then Clifford leapt to his feet, his face white with fury. 'Tell me who this bastard is,' he demanded. 'Where is he? I'll bloody tear him limb from limb.'

Connie put her hand on Clifford's arm. 'Clifford, I know you're upset . . .'

'Upset!' he bellowed.

'Shh,' said Connie, looking anxiously up at the ceiling. 'Whatever you do, don't let Mandy hear you.'

He forced himself to lower his voice but he was still white hot with anger. 'Then tell me where he is,' he spat.

'Clifford, the man needs to be behind bars,' said Connie. 'If you go after him, you'll be the one in prison.'

'Tell me or I swear I shall see Ga and make her tell me.'

'No!' cried Connie and Gwen in unison.

'For God's sake, don't do that,' said Connie. 'You'll do more harm than good. It took every ounce of courage for Mandy to tell me and if you tell Ga, she'll go up there like a bull in a china shop.'

'But you can't expect me to do nothing,' he cried helplessly.

'Yes,' said Gwen. 'No,' said Connie at the same time.

Shocked, Connie stared at her mother.

'I don't want my child being interrogated by the police,' said Gwen. 'That's what it'll mean, won't it?'

Clifford put his hands to his head and ran his fingers through his hair.

'We'll be gone soon,' Gwen said, taking hold of his arm. 'A few more weeks and we'll be on our way to Australia. Don't you see? It'll blow over. It's going to be all right.'

'Mum,' said Connie, 'I understand how you feel but believe me, this won't blow over. Mandy will need help. Right now she thinks it's her fault. She thinks she fell down the hole because she wouldn't do what he wanted.'

Clifford moaned in pain and turned around in a tight circle.

'And if Stan did the same to me all those years ago,' Connie continued, 'it stands to reason that he's been doing it to other little girls in between. He has got to be stopped.'

Gwen looked at Connie as if seeing her for the first time. 'I didn't know,' she apologised. 'Oh Connie, why didn't you say something at the time? Why didn't you tell me?'

'Because Ga told me not to,' said Connie. Her mother's expression hardened. 'Actually, I think for once in her life she did it for good reasons. To protect me, just like you want to protect Mandy, but it has to end here. How many other little girls has that monster frightened out of their wits in between? We can't let it go on.'

'She's right,' said Clifford.

'No,' Gwen insisted. 'I won't have you going to the police. And anyway,' she said rounding on Connie, 'just because he did it to you, doesn't mean he actually touched Mandy, does it?'

Connie put her hand over her mouth. Her mother obviously had no idea how much that hurt. She sounded so indifferent to what had happened to her. Yes, she was an adult now but that day Stan had robbed her of something. From the moment he had exposed himself to her, she had lost her childhood innocence. Connie knew her mother was frantic with worry over Mandy but she could have done with a little more understanding and a hug.

'Did Mandy tell you he touched her?' said Clifford. He was quieter now, but just as angry.

'I don't think he did,' said Connie.

'How can you be sure?' Clifford asked.

'I think when he showed her Mr Charles,' said Connie, 'that was the moment Pip went for him.'

'Pip,' said Gwen. 'Oh yes, I'd forgotten about him.'

'The vet said that Pip had been hit with something, a piece of wood or a log,' said Connie. 'Someone viciously beat him and left him for dead.'

Gwen took in her breath. 'And you think Mandy saw all that too?'

Connie nodded.

'But why didn't she take the opportunity to run away?' Clifford cried.

'She was too frightened,' said Connie. 'My guess is that after she saw what had happened to Pip, that's when she ran away.'

Clifford put his head in his hands. 'And then she fell down the hole.'

'But Stan went back with the others to look for her,' said Gwen. 'Why didn't he tell everybody where she was?' She saw Clifford and Connie share a glance and at last Gwen understood. Stan didn't want Mandy to be found. He'd left her down the hole to die.

'I know we should go to the police,' said Gwen choking back a small sob, 'but I keep thinking how awful it would be for her. She's only a little girl. How can we put her through all that as well?'

Neither of them had an answer to that. They heard the back door open and close again and Ga walked in. She seemed surprised when they turned towards her. 'What's the matter with you lot?'

'You'd better tell her, Gwennie,' said Clifford. 'I don't think I've the stomach for it. I'm off to the pub.'

'You won't say anything, will you?' Gwen said frantically.

'Of course not,' he snapped. 'What do you take me for?' He reached for his cap on the back of the door. 'But it isn't right, Gwennie.'

'What isn't right?' said Ga as he slammed the door.

'This is all down to you,' Gwen snarled at Ga. 'You and your

338

bloody interfering. If you had left well alone, none of this would have happened.'

'Mum, that's not fair,' said Connie. 'Ga was trying to do the best thing for me, just the same as you're doing for Mandy.'

'Will one of you tell me what's going on?' Ga demanded.

'Stan Saul was with Mandy on High Salvington,' said Connie.

Ga lowered herself into her chair as Connie began to explain.

'No,' she said when Connie had finished. 'That can't be right. His mother told me he was a changed man.'

'What are you saying?' said Connie faintly.

Ga looked up sharply. 'He never actually touched you, did he?'

Connie laughed sardonically. 'You know as well as I do that he came this close,' she said, holding her thumb and forefinger together.

'You were drunk,' said Ga defensively.

'I was thirteen years old!' Connie retorted. Connie was aware that her mother had begun to cry again. 'And actually, I wasn't drunk. He'd put something in my drink, Ga. And he did the same to Kenneth's. I'd hardly had more than a mouthful when I felt funny and couldn't stand up properly. Kenneth flaked out altogether.'

Ga stared at Connie in disbelief. 'But he said . . .'

'He said, he said,' said Connie angrily. 'That's the trouble, isn't it? You never once bothered to ask Kenneth and me what happened, did you? You assumed . . . and just because Stan was older than the both of us you took his word for it.'

There was a thick silence as the two of them digested what Connie was saying.

'He promised me it would never happen again,' said Ga. Her voice was a lot smaller now. 'What was I supposed to do? Stan is all his mother has got. She dotes on that boy. It would have broken her heart if I'd gone to the police.'

'But I was your family,' cried Connie passionately as she crossed both hands over her chest.

Gwen was still furious but Connie felt strangely moved with compassion. She'd never seen Ga quite like this before. 'Don't you see?' she said sitting down next to her. 'By not going to the police all that time ago, you separated this family and put count-less other little girls in danger.'

Ga looked up at her. Her face was white. 'He said it was all your fault. He said you'd egged him on and teased him. He said you were up for it.'

'You're not listening, Ga,' Gwen snapped. 'They all say that. Men who want to be with little girls. The man is sick . . . evil . . . He'll say anything to justify what he's done.'

'But he got married,' Ga protested loudly.

'And she killed herself,' said Connie. 'Didn't you ever wonder about that, Ga? I certainly did, especially when you told us that his wife had been a widow with a little girl of her own.'

The full horror of what Connie had implied shocked them all. The sound of the clock on the mantelpiece seemed to grow louder by the second.

'So what do I do now?' said Ga eventually.

'I don't want Mandy to have to talk to the police,' said Gwen helplessly. 'One day they might treat a child with kindness and care but I know that right now they'll try and get her to say she's made it all up. They'll shout at her and frighten her and I can't have that.'

Connie put her head in her hands. They were back to square one. Her mother began to cry again.

'It's all right, Mum,' said Connie, rubbing her mother's arm gently.

'And I'm sorry about you,' said Gwen brokenly. 'I wish you could have told me. I should have been there for you, darling.'

Ga fished out a handkerchief from her apron pocket and moved away from them to blow her nose.

'Anyway,' said Gwen. 'We'll be out of the country soon. We can make a fresh start.'

Ga spun around. 'Out of the country? What are you talking about?'

Gwen sniffed loudly and drew herself up. 'Clifford and I are going to Australia. There's a new scheme for migrant workers and we're taking Mandy.'

Ga's jaw dropped. 'But why?'

'Don't give me that, Ga,' said Gwen, her voice loaded with sarcasm. 'You know perfectly well why. We want a life of our own. Clifford wants to be the master of his own destiny, not a slave to your beck and call.'

'But all this is for you . . .' cried Ga. She waved her hands expansively.

'You've trotted that one out for years,' said Gwen, angrily stuffing her knitting back into the knitting bag, 'and yet every suggestion Clifford makes, you won't allow. He's stifled here and I can't bear to see him so unhappy anymore.'

With head high, she marched out of the room and went upstairs.

'I don't believe this,' whispered Ga. 'What on earth is happening to this family?'

'I think you'll find it's discovered its backbone at last,' said Connie.

Connie was up early but Ga was already sitting at her writing bureau. She was in her dressing gown and her plaited hair hung over her shoulder. Connie, who was already washed and dressed, put a cup of tea on the drop-down lid. She was still annoyed with Ga but she had made up her mind to try and be civil. Ga moved her arm quickly to cover the page and stopped writing. All at once Connie realised that the paper she was using was exactly the same pale cream paper that Matron was holding in her office. Anger exploded in her chest.

'It was you, wasn't it?' she snarled.

'What?'

'You wrote to Matron and got me the sack, didn't you?'

341

'What are you talking . . .?' Ga began.

Connie snatched the page and held it up. 'Don't bother to deny it. I saw the letter. It was written on paper just like this.'

'I have never written to your Matron,' Ga bellowed indignantly. 'I have no idea what you are talking about.'

But Connie was on a roll now. 'How many others have you written, Ga? What about those horrible letters to Sally Burndell?'

'Sally Burndell,' Ga blustered, 'was a silly airheaded girl who was cheeky to the customers.'

'And you tried to destroy her for that!' Connie shrieked.

There was a small sound and Gwen stood by the doorway. 'What's going on now?'

'It was Ga who wrote those poison pen letters to Sally,' Connie accused. 'And she's the one who got me the sa . . .' Connie only just stopped herself in time. 'And while we're on the subject . . .' she began again. She ran from the room, up to her bedroom and back again. Throwing a piece of paper on the bureau in front of Ga she added breathlessly, 'Perhaps you'd like to explain that.'

They were looking at a childish picture of a house. It had a red roof and smoke coming from the crooked chimney. On one side was a mummy, a daddy and a little girl. The little girl was holding the hand of another adult, a woman, wearing what looked like a frilly cap. On the other side of the house was a much older woman.

'What's wrong with that?' Ga said defensively.

'Mandy said you stopped her from taking a piece of paper from your bureau,' said Connie. 'She wanted to make Mum a birthday card.'

'She took it without my permission,' said Ga indignantly. 'Theft is theft no matter what the reason for taking it.'

'Mandy also told me you dropped this when you were burning something in the range,' said Connie. 'If stealing a piece of paper is theft, what would you call this, Ga?'

Connie turned the paper over and Ga paled. It was now obvious that Mandy had drawn on the back of an envelope. The envelope was addressed to Mrs G. Craig and in the top left-hand corner it said Royal Victoria Hospital, East Grinstead.

Thirty-Two

Rev Jackson was speechless. His face had paled and he fiddled with his cassock. Connie didn't bother telling him about Ga and what she'd been up to. She was only interested in telling him about Stan and by the time she had finished what she had to say, Connie was trembling.

They were sitting in his office in his own home. They were alone, apart from Mrs Jackson who had been cleaning in the hallway when Connie arrived. She had brought them a pot of tea.

'This is certainly a sorry tale,' said Rev Jackson when Connie had finished, 'but I hesitate to act upon this information. It was all a very long time ago and perhaps your memory has eroded what actually happened.' Connie must have shown her disappointment because he added quickly, 'I really don't doubt that you believe you have spoken truthfully, my dear, but Graham, I mean Stan, is bound to deny it and all I am left with is your word against his.'

He gave her an apologetic stare. He was right of course, and Connie couldn't go against her mother's wishes. She had only told Rev Jackson about her own experience. She hadn't mentioned a word about Mandy.

'I just felt the need to warn you, that's all,' said Connie, getting to her feet. They walked out into the hallway. 'I don't think it would be such a good idea to let him have contact with the children . . . especially unsupervised.'

'We are always very careful about looking after the children in our care,' said Rev Jackson. 'Changing the subject, how is your sister? What happened to her on High Salvington was most unfortunate. Tell your mother I shall call around this afternoon.'

Connie shook his hand and walked away. Without Mandy's testimony she wasn't going to get anywhere, was she? She could understand her mother's reluctance, but it was frustrating. She still felt physically sick every time she thought about Stan and yet she had been one of the lucky ones. If Ga hadn't have come back at that very moment, God alone knew what would have happened. From what she could gather, Mandy had been just as fortunate, but how many other children hadn't? If only there was some way she could stop that monster in his tracks.

Connie trembled as she stood outside of the house. She had waited by the gate for some time, trying to pluck up courage to knock on the door. The house itself was the most attractive in the road. The garden was neat and tidy with roses around the door and delphiniums, goldenrod and lupins waving in the borders. She had never been here before and she didn't want to be here now. She had chosen her time very carefully. It was time for the Golden Hour Meeting and Stan would be at his place on the piano. On Wednesday afternoons, Rev Jackson held a service for the pensioners of his congregation, followed by a cup of tea, which was why he was dressed in his minister's robes when she'd seen him in his office.

Connie was banking on the fact that Stan's mother would still be at home. She never went to church so it was now or never. She took one last deep breath and walked up the path.

Mrs Saul looked a little surprised when she opened the door and saw Connie.

Connie didn't wait for an invitation to come in, she simply

barged past. 'I'm sorry, Auntie Aggie, but this is important. I need to talk to you.'

Roger looked at Gwen anxiously. 'I've come to see Connie.'

Gwen smiled. 'You'd better come in. You're not the first and I'm in the middle of baking bread.' She indicated her floury hands.

Roger followed her into the neat kitchen. Connie's great aunt was sitting hunched up by the kitchen range. She glanced up as Roger came in but far from the torrent of abuse she usually dished out when she saw a Maxwell, she nodded curtly and lowered her eyes.

Roger looked around at the other assembled people and was dismayed to see that one of them was the French Canadian and the other, the chap who'd been with him on the hill. They apparently brought gifts for Mandy and Roger was immediately annoyed with himself that he hadn't thought of doing something like that too. He couldn't help admiring the beautifully hand-crafted doll's cradle and a little chair. It must have cost a packet. They weren't the only people in the room. There was someone else, a girl with flame-coloured hair and an interesting weather-beaten face.

'This is Kezia,' said Gwen. 'She's an old friend of Connie's. Kez popped in on the off chance of seeing her as well.'

Roger and Kezia exchanged a nod of greeting.

'And you know Eugène and Isaac of course.'

Roger nodded politely and looked away.

'We're here to say goodbye,' said Kez by way of explanation. 'The Frenchie is moving to Slinden with us and I came to thank Connie for looking after my brother.'

'I hope you don't mind,' Gwen said, holding up her floury hands again, 'but I must put this in a warm place to rise.'

'No, no,' said Roger. 'You carry on. That's fine.'

'I owe you an apology Captain Maxwell,' said Ga.

346

Roger lifted his hand to stop her. 'You were distraught. It really doesn't matter.'

'Oh but it does,' said Ga. Her tone was contrite and her voice small. 'I've done a lot of thinking since last I saw you and I'm ashamed of my behaviour. I have come to see that I may have confused my loyalties.'

'Please . . .' Roger protested, then turning to Gwen he said, 'Is Connie here?'

Mrs Craig and Kez shook their heads.

'She said she was going to see Reverend Jackson,' said Ga dully. 'If I had known Stan was going to turn out like that, I would never have gone along with what Aggie said.'

Roger frowned. 'I'm sorry?'

'There's no need to go into all that, Ga.' Gwen glared at her aunt and then added, 'We've all had a bit of a shock what with one thing and another.'

'Oh, so you know about Connie?' Roger asked. 'I must say, not to put too fine a point on it that I was appalled by what Matron had done.'

He looked around at their puzzled expressions and started to feel uncomfortable. He cleared his throat and lowered himself onto one of the kitchen chairs. 'Look, I don't know how much she has told you,' he began, 'although knowing Connie probably nothing at all because she wouldn't want to upset you.'

Gwen's face paled. 'Is something wrong? This sounds serious, Captain Maxwell.'

'Roger, please,' said Roger. 'Haven't you all wondered why Connie is at home and not in the hospital?' He glared at Eugène and noted with some satisfaction the anxious look on his face. The man didn't know. Roger resisted the smug smile playing at the corners of his mouth.

The three women looked at each other. 'It's her day off,' said Ga.

'I'm afraid not,' said Roger. 'It seems that someone made an

347

allegation about Connie behaving inappropriately. They accused her of being disrespectful towards a patient.'

Gwen clutched at her chest leaving floury marks all over her apron. 'What?'

'I don't believe it,' said Kezia stoutly.

'Apparently Matron had an anonymous letter,' Roger went on. 'Connie has been sacked.'

'I don't believe it,' Kezia said again. Ga moaned.

'Sacked?' said Eugène. He and Isaac exchanged a worried glance.

'But she never said a word about it,' Gwen gasped.

'Yes, she did,' said Ga. 'I remember it now. She told me but it didn't really register. It was when we were fighting over that envelope. Don't you remember? She was about to say that I'd got her the sack from the hospital.'

Roger raised an eyebrow. 'Don't look at me like that,' Ga challenged. 'I had nothing to do with it.'

Nobody spoke.

'Like I said,' Roger went on, 'in view of the terrible day you all had on Monday, she probably didn't want to upset you. All her friends, including my sister feel it's grossly unfair and for that matter, completely untrue.'

'An anonymous letter, you say?' said Ga.

'But who could have done such a thing?' cried Kez.

'Who indeed,' said Roger.

'I saw the way she looked after my father,' Kez went on. 'She's a wonderful nurse.'

Ga was staring into the hearth.

'Can nothing be done?' asked Eugène.

Roger pulled a face. 'Apparently Matron is adamant.'

'What's she supposed to have done . . . exactly?'

Roger repeated the story about Mr Steppings.

'I remember her telling us about that,' said Gwen. 'It was an accident. No harm was intended.'

'I'm sure of it,' said Roger, 'but the fact remains, Connie has lost the opportunity to do the thing she wanted most, to be a nurse.'

They heard the sound of a bed creaking upstairs and everyone's eye turned towards the ceiling.

'Mandy,' said Gwen, looking directly at Roger. She glanced down at her dough. 'I must get this out of the way before she comes down.' She was pushing the dough into tins and covering them with a clean tea towel.

'Forgive me,' said Roger. 'I forgot to ask. How is she?'

'She was up quite early this morning so she's having a rest now,' said Gwen. 'I want to thank you for everything you did to help us.'

Roger shook his head. 'It was nothing. What happened to the dog?'

'He died,' said Eugène. 'Clifford and I buried him in the orchard.'

'I'm sorry,' said Roger. 'Connie was fond of that dog.'

'Pip is dead!' Kez cried in alarm. 'When he wasn't here, I simply thought he was out for a walk.'

'Someone attacked him,' said Gwen.

'Whatever for?' cried Kez.

'It's a long story,' said Gwen, 'but we think Pip tried to help Mandy and her attacker lashed out.'

'I didn't realise,' said Kez.

'Have you managed to trace the man?' Roger asked.

Gwen and Ga exchanged looks and then Ga blew her nose again.

The floor above their heads creaked again. 'Ga, why don't you go up and sit with Mandy?' said Gwen. She had put the dough to rise next to the range and was busy clearing the table to do the washing up. 'It would be good for her to see a familiar face when she wakes up.'

The older woman rose to her feet and left the room.

'I don't know how much Connie has told you,' Gwen said to Roger.

Kez stood up. 'I'd better be going.'

'I'd rather you stayed, Kez,' said Gwen. 'You too, Eugène. Along with Eva, you are the most important people in her life and Connie is going to need all the help she can get if she's to get through this.'

Aggie Saul sat white-faced at her kitchen table. She had listened to everything Connie had told her without once interrupting. It was far worse than she'd ever dreamed. Her mind drifted back to when Stan was a boy. He was such a lovely looking child and it wasn't until he was about twelve that she realised he was a little different. That's when she'd caught him with little Estelle from next door.

He'd persuaded the child to take off her knickers and do a wee by the back door. While she performed, he was watching her and touching himself. Aggie had scolded him of course. At the time she'd put it down to natural curiosity but in her heart of hearts she'd known it wasn't right. Estelle was only six, for goodness sake. Stan's father had wanted to give him a thrashing when Aggie had told him what had happened. Aggie had tried to stop him of course but Leslie had been too enraged to listen. Having called her boy every name under the sun he'd reached for his belt but Aggie made sure he never laid a finger on her son and from that moment, she'd raised her little lad on her own.

She'd known about Olive catching him with Connie but she didn't feel that counted because they both blamed Kenneth. Olive had found some money on the table and said Stan had paid Kenneth to go with his sister. Well, what red-blooded young lad wouldn't make the most of an opportunity like that, and Stan had been most apologetic.

She took a deep breath. How dare Connie come here and accuse her Stan of wrongdoing all those years ago? Why didn't she say something at the time? Connie was going on about Mandy now. Agatha frowned. There was no proof that Stan was anywhere near the child. He'd been with Jane Jackson all the time. With a sister like Connie, it was far more likely that the girl had made the whole thing up.

They heard the back door slam and Stan's voice called, 'Mother, I'm home.'

Connie's face paled. He was back a lot sooner than she had expected. She rose to her feet as he walked in the door. Her heart began to pound. She shouldn't have done this on her own. She should have waited for Roger or asked Clifford to come with her, or even gone to the police.

Stan stared at both of them. 'Connie, what an unexpected surprise,' he smiled affably.

He took out his cigarette case and Aggie's mothering instincts kicked in. Her eyes narrowed as she walked to her son's side. 'Connie's been saying bad things about you, son,' she said. 'She's been telling me that you like little girls. She says you had something to do with Mandy going missing on the Sunday school outing. Tell me it's not true, son. Tell me it's not true.'

Stan shot her a wounded look. 'Of course it's not true, Mother,' he simpered. 'How could you believe I'd do anything like that? Why, it's disgusting.' He glanced at Connie and said in a much sharper tone, 'Whatever she's said, she's a liar.'

A wave of revulsion and nausea flooded over Connie. 'You're sick, Stan,' she said. 'You need help.'

'It was you who went to see Reverend Jackson, wasn't it?' said Stan.

Connie was relieved. Perhaps it was going to be all right after all. Rev Jackson must have spoken to Stan straight away. 'He's a good man,' she said, softening her voice. 'I'm sure when you both have a chat, he'll make sure you get all the help you need.'

Stan smirked. 'Reverend Jackson and I have already had a long chat.'

'That's good,' she sighed.

'I told him not to believe a word of it,' said Stan in a superior tone. He took out his cigarette case and tapped a cigarette on the lid. 'He was very embarrassed having to bring it up but after I explained everything, he reckoned it would all blow over soon. All I've got to do is sit tight.'

Connie's jaw dropped.

'He could see it was untrue, Mother,' Stan continued. 'As a matter of fact, he said that his daughter was most impressed by the way I helped out with those kids on the outing.'

Connie's eyes filled.

'He said he would do all in his power to . . . what was it? Ah yes, "to purge this village of gossip and innuendo",' said Stan confidently. 'In fact, I think he was going into his study to prepare his sermon on Sunday.' Stan waved his hand as if creating a headline. 'No gossiper shall inherit the kingdom of God.'

Connie couldn't believe what she was hearing. When she'd left Rev Jackson he was confident that what she had told him was true and yet somehow this silver-tongued monster had turned the tables yet again.

'You know me, Mother,' Stan continued. 'Would I really do all those terrible things like she said?'

Aggie looked up at him with trusting eyes. 'I never believed it for a moment, son, but what are we going to do?'

Connie suddenly felt very vulnerable. She took a step towards the door but Stan was right there barring the way. 'Don't be a fool, Stan,' she began. 'I've already told my family where I am.'

'Let me see,' said Stan, stroking his chin and play-acting a part. 'Yes, Connie was here. She stayed for a cup of tea and then we both saw her leave, didn't we, Mother?'

As he lunged towards Connie, she pulled the chair over between them. She backed away but there was nowhere to go. Stan and Aunt Aggie were both blocking the only way out of the room. Connie did her best to fight them off but within minutes they had pulled her from the kitchen into the hallway. Stan grabbed her painfully by the arm and Aunt Aggie opened another door. Stan shoved her in front of it and then Connie was slipping and falling down the cellar steps.

Thirty-Three

Rev Jackson was slightly surprised to see Eugène and Kezia at his front door. Eugène he had long admired. The man had done such a lot for the community during that long horrible winter and it seemed grossly unfair that he should be struggling with his business now. Rev Jackson was never one to listen to gossip but he had heard that the engagement with Miss Hampton was off. She had apparently fallen for an Earl and preferred to be known as a Countess rather than plain wife. Rev Jackson was aware of the gypsy woman because he'd had words with her grandmother about telling fortunes on the doorstep. He couldn't think why they should both want to see him. As they followed him to his study, it crossed his mind that perhaps they wanted to marry. They seemed a rather unlikely pair but the war had changed so many things.

As they left Connie's home, Eugène, Isaac and Kez had agreed that they couldn't sit around twiddling their thumbs the same as everyone else. Ga had said Connie had gone to see the minister, so Eugène had suggested they start from there. He and Kez went to the door, while Isaac waited in the motor. He had no time for Rev Jackson. After all, it was his testimony that helped to put him behind bars.

Eugène got straight to the point.

'Connie?' said Rev Jackson. 'Yes, as a matter of fact, she came to see me this morning but I haven't seen her since.'

'Did she talk to you about Stan Saul?'

Rev Jackson put up his hand in a stop signal. 'I'm afraid I am not at liberty to discuss a confidence.'

'Sir, we have reason to believe he's a child molester,' said Eugène firmly.

'Oh, I think not,' said Rev Jackson smiling benevolently. 'Connie was a little confused, that's all. After the events of yesterday that's hardly surprising . . .'

'Connie wasn't making it up, Reverend,' said Kez. 'I know she's telling the truth 'cos he done it to me an' all.'

It was dark in the cellar. The only light came from a dirty window near the ceiling. Connie sat miserably on the stair and cried. Her leg hurt like hell from where she'd fallen and she'd done something to her finger. She'd been an absolute idiot. No one knew where she was and there was no telling what Stan and his mother would do next. Even though no one believed her, it was in Stan's best interest to shut her up somehow. The cottage was isolated so there was no point in shouting for help. No one would hear her anyway. There were other cottages in the road but Aggie's place stood apart from them. Gradually, as her eyes became used to the dimness, she looked around for some sort of weapon. She was no match for the two of them, especially with a bad leg, but, by God, she'd go down fighting. The one person she found hard to cope with was Auntie Aggie. Surely the woman could see what her son was like and yet she'd closed her eyes to what he was doing again and again.

Connie looked around. She found a rolled umbrella with a long spike in a corner. It looked as if someone had hammered it a bit and she couldn't open it up but it might come in handy. There was a steel ruler on a table by the wall. She practised a couple of jabbing movements with it. She would have to be really close to someone to make a difference but in a desperate situation, it was better than nothing. She put them both near the bottom of the stairs.

The light was fading. Soon it would be completely dark and Connie knew that's when she would be in the greatest danger. She rubbed her cold arms. She wished she'd kept her cardigan on now but it was still upstairs in the sitting room. She looked up at the cellar door. Was there some way she could barricade herself in? He wouldn't be expecting that. She hobbled back to the stairs to look at the lock. The stairs were quite rickety, but the door at the top was stout. It was opened by a latch and a keyhole but the key wasn't on the other side of the door. Her only hope of stopping them from getting in and buy a little time was to block the latch.

Back downstairs, she scoured the cellar for something to use as a wedge. The whole place was surprisingly clean. Rows of kilner jars with preserved fruit and pickles lined the shelves. The floor was nicely swept and there was a table and chair in the corner. She tried the drawer in the table and cried out in surprise. Inside she'd found a fountain pen and some paper, a pretty beige with a watermark, neatly laid out. She held it up to the fading light and saw the same lion's head watermark that she'd noticed in Matron's office. Whoever wrote the damning letter that got her the sack had used this very paper. Connie sat down on the chair to think. In her own mind, she had accused Ga. Ga had some of this paper in her desk. Mandy had got into trouble for trying to take a sheet because Ga always said it was for her and her alone. Yet Auntie Aggie had some too. Could it be that it was Auntie Aggie who had written to Matron? But how would she have known what happened in the lift? Then Connie remembered telling the family about it. Had Aunt Aggie been there too? Even if she wasn't, she and Ga told each other everything so it was perfectly possible that Ga had told her the story about Mr Steppings. Connie's heartbeat quickened.

There was a letter opener and a small hard-backed book at the back of the drawer. The book seemed to be a list of names, all beautifully written in the same copperplate handwriting. But before she examined anything else, Connie climbed the stairs again and forced the letter opener through the latch. It was rudimentary, but it would give her a little more time, if nothing else. Then she went back downstairs to have another look at what was in the drawer.

Eva had been busy collecting signatures. It seemed that the whole hospital was shocked by Connie's sacking. She'd obviously made a huge impression on people and everyone wanted to help. Eva was on duty at two.

At twelve thirty, Eva had gone back to the nurses' home to change. A man accosted her outside the door. He had already stopped three other girls but they had rebuffed him.

'Brendan Beardsley, *Worthing Gazette*,' he said. 'Have you any comment to make on the new National Health Service which comes into being next year? I'm sure our readers would be very interested to know the feelings of an ordinary nurse.'

Eva smiled. All at once, she realised she had stumbled on a way to get Connie's plight noticed. If she could get the reporter interested, it would be a whole heap more powerful than a few signatures. She slipped her arm through his and led him back out to the road.

'Yesterday your newspaper ran a story about the little girl lost on High Salvington,' she began. 'Would you be interested to hear what happened to the heroic nurse who helped to rescue her?'

PC Noble had a problem with believing their story. He may have dismissed it altogether if had just been the gypsy, but Rev Jackson was a respected member of the community and when Captain Maxwell turned up to talk to him about the same matter, PC Noble realised that he would have to tread carefully. He didn't hesitate to tell them that he'd had his eye on Saul ever since he'd turned up in the area and decided to change his name. 'I thought to myself, what man with nothing to hide,' said the policeman, 'changes his name?'

357

'Quite so,' said Roger, although changing your Christian name didn't seem to be such a big deal to him.

'But after a few enquiries,' PC Noble went on, 'I discovered that Saul's wife had committed suicide.'

'She didn't kill herself,' said Kez. 'He pushed her. I saw him.'

The policeman gave her a sceptical look. 'I should be careful, young lady, making accusations like that.'

'The point is,' said Captain Maxwell, 'we want the authority of the law present when we go to the house. We feel that this man should be questioned about the little girl.'

Half an hour later, PC Noble parked his police bicycle in the hedge, took off his bicycle clips and straightened his tunic. The others were already waiting in the lane. They had driven to the house in Isaac's car and Captain Maxwell's car.

'I think it would be best if you leave me to handle this, sir,' he said, leaning into Captain Maxwell's window. 'By coming to me, you've made it a police matter.' To Eugène and the others he called out, 'Wait here.'

Roger nodded his agreement reluctantly. In his opinion, Noble was as gullible as the rest of them when it came to Saul. He was annoyed that Eugène had got to the police house before he had. They might have been friends of Connie's but he thought them all a bit shifty.

Eugène had never felt more anxious. Had Connie come here? He worried that she had got herself into deep water. Kez squeezed his arm encouragingly. 'She'll be all right,' she said. 'Connie is as tough as old boots.'

Roger was proved right almost immediately. PC Noble came back almost straight away. 'Mrs Saul tells me Miss Dixon was here but she left about two hours ago,' he said.

'You did go in?' said Roger.

'I have no reason not to believe her, sir,' said the policeman. 'I can't just go barging into people's homes with no good reason.'

'But what if she is in there?'

'I'd need a warrant, sir, and there's no reason to suppose that even if she is in there that she's come to any harm.'

'Did you ask to see Saul?' Eugène asked.

'He wasn't there.' Noble turned his bicycle round and touched his helmet. 'I'll be keeping an eye out, sir, don't you worry. Now if I was you, I'd go home. She's probably there waiting for you.'

Roger hit the steering wheel in frustration.

'She's still in there,' said Kez.

'You heard the man,' said Roger. 'She left. She probably wandered off somewhere to think.'

'You're not going to leave it at that, are you?' cried Kez. She climbed down from the motor. 'We have to make sure.'

Roger wound down the window. 'Let's go back to the nurseries and make sure she hasn't gone home first.' He started up the car.

'I'm going in there,' said Kezia, producing a few tired looking sprigs from her skirt pocket. 'I'll make out I'm selling lucky heather.'

'No,' said Roger firmly. 'I think my idea is better.'

'Fine,' said Kez. She turned towards Eugène and her brother. 'If I'm not back in an hour, come looking for me.'

'Don't be such an idiot,' cried Roger. 'You can't go barging in there.'

'Watch me,' said Kez.

Roger watched her walk up the lane, turn onto the path and knock on the door. Mrs Saul, he presumed it was her, opened it and Kezia offered her the heather. The older woman shook her head but Kezia kept talking. A couple of seconds later, Kezia went inside. Eugène and Isaac used the opportunity to creep around the side of the house. Roger stared at the front door anxiously. What now? Kezia was gone for ages and by the time the door opened again, he was beginning to think he would have to drive back to the police station and get Noble again.

'What on earth were you doing?' he gasped as Kezia returned to his car and climbed in.

'Telling her fortune,' Kezia grinned. She opened her palm and showed him the ten bob note Aggie had given her.

'For God's sake . . .' Roger began crossly.

'You don't think I believe in all that stuff, do you?' she said. 'I told her a load of rubbish and then Stan come in and turfed me out.'

'So he was there!' cried Roger. 'Did he recognise you?'

'Why should he?' said Kez bitterly. 'How many of them remember the kids they ruin? I was only eight when he got me.'

'I'm sorry, Kez,' said Roger genuinely. 'That copper is a bloody idiot. He said he wasn't there.'

They were quiet for a second or two, and then the door of the car opened and Eugène slid in the back seat. 'What the hell . . .' Roger began.

'Are you all right, girl?' Eugène's voice was quiet but full of concern.

She shrugged. 'If I'd had a knife, I'd have stuck it in his black heart.'

Eugène gripped her shoulder. 'If Connie is in there,' he said, 'she's most likely in the attic. Isaac's gone to take a look.'

'She's in there all right,' said Kez. 'I saw her cardigan on the arm of the chair.' She grinned. 'I didn't say a dicky-bird and it's obvious they haven't even noticed it's still there.'

'But you haven't seen her for months,' Roger protested. 'How do you know it was hers?'

'In case you haven't noticed,' said Kezia good-naturedly, 'we girls don't have a lot of clothes these days. Believe me, it was hers.'

'Well spotted then,' said Roger grudgingly. He turned towards Eugène. 'You obviously know the woman. Why don't you go in and demand Connie back?'

'There's no love lost between me and Aggie Saul,' said Eugène with a shrug. 'She was very upset when I refused to let her have extra coal during the big freeze.'

360

'So what do we do now?' said Kez.

'My guess is he'll get her out of there tonight,' said Eugène.

'Do you think he'll kill her?'

Eugène nodded. 'Yes but he'll do it somewhere else. He'll want it to look like suicide or something, especially now that he knows the police have been around.'

'But she'll kick up a fuss,' said Kez. 'How will . . .?' She stopped in her tracks as if remembering and added, 'He'll give her something to drink. That's what he did to me.'

'You mean he'll drug her and then carry her out?' said Eugène.

'Don't you think that's all a bit far-fetched?' said Roger.

'I can't risk hanging about,' said Eugène opening the car door again.

'*You* can't risk hanging about?' Roger snapped. 'I care about her too you know.'

Eugène hesitated. 'Then help me find her!'

It was getting more difficult to see in the light. The sun was going down and the amber dusk was giving way to evening. Connie thought she heard a strange rustling sound and hid. Stan was coming back. After a minute or two of hiding under the stairs, she realised it wasn't Stan. Perhaps it was an animal creeping about in the undergrowth outside. She wasn't sure if the noise came from outside the door at the top of the stairs or the little window but when she came out of hiding, she called softly at the window a couple of times but it was quiet as the grave. It must have been a cat, she told herself. She'd spent some time looking at the book in the drawer and quickly realised that it contained a list of names. They didn't mean anything until she came across two names she recognised, Sally Burndell and then her own. Her heart sank as she realised that these must be the people who had been the victims of the poison pen letters. On closer inspection she'd come across Mrs Ranger. Connie lowered herself onto the chair. Mrs Ranger had jumped off the end of Worthing pier at high tide. No one knew the reason why. She'd always seemed such a contented woman. There was no note either. It was a mystery. Could it be that . . . no, no, it didn't bear thinking about. It would have been easy to give way to tears at that moment but instead, Connie pulled herself together. She still needed to find something, anything which would help her fight Stan when he came back. He would come back, she was absolutely sure of that and she had to keep hold of this book. It was evidence.

She looked at the preserves. She could throw a few of them at him, but she had a rotten aim. She looked around again. There was a low table under the stairs. She noticed a draught as she walked there and wondered if there was an opening somewhere. The air circulated nicely just here. The walls seemed solid although there was an air brick higher up the wall.

She lifted the cloth on the low table and discovered it wasn't a table but a blanket box of some sort. Perhaps she could hide the book in there. Aunt Aggie mightn't miss it straight away and with a bit of luck, Connie could get it to the police before she knew it was missing.

It wasn't locked. Connie threw it open and jumped back, grabbing at her throat and stifling a scream of horror. The shock was immense. Even in the failing light she could see what it was straight away. A dull musty smell filled the air as Connie trembled uncontrollably. She was looking at the mummified remains of a man.

Thirty-Four

Kez was the only one who kept her cool. It was obvious that both Eugène and Roger were in love with Connie. 'Pack it in you two,' she snapped. 'This is neither the time nor the place.' The two men settled into an uneasy truce.

Isaac came back a few minutes later. 'I've found a way to the roof and there is an attic all right.'

'Is she there?' Roger asked anxiously.

Isaac shrugged. 'I'll need something to open the window,' he said.

Roger was feeling very uncomfortable. Breaking and entering wasn't his style.

Connie heard the key turn in the lock and Stan tried to push the door open but the letter opener did its work. She heard him curse her through the wood. Connie looked around wildly. Where was the best place to be? If she was to get up the stairs without him seeing her, she had to be close enough to make a dash for it and yet hidden enough so that he wouldn't spot her straight away.

He came back a few minutes later and took the wood axe to the door. Connie's heart was in her mouth. This was it. This was the moment when she started to fight for her life. It didn't take long to break the latch and the door flew open. Stan swung a torch around the cellar.

'I'm coming to get you,' he called as if he was playing a child's game. Connie shuddered as he began walking down the stairs. 'Ready or not, I'm coming.'

She waited until he had entered the cellar and was walking towards the desk then scrambling on all fours she came out from under the stairs, stood up and made her dash. She was halfway there when Stan roared in anger. Panic constricted Connie's throat. The man of her childhood nightmares was right behind her and her legs couldn't move fast enough.

Connie's heart was thumping wildly and she could hardly breathe for the panic that seized her at that moment, but somehow she managed to reach the stairs and began the race for the top. Terror was making her whimper now. Her eyes were wide with fear, her head hurt and she had developed a discernible tic on her cheek. Her only thought was getting through the door, a mere eight steps away, and out of the house. She could almost feel Stan's breath, cold on her neck but that was imagination because all at once something stopped her in her tracks and she couldn't move her foot anymore. Connie looked down and realised Stan had reached through the open stair and grabbed her ankle.

Connie snatched at the rails and clung on for dear life as Stan's fingers dug deep into her flesh. Then he shook her ankle like a dog. It was becoming impossible to stay on the stairs. She could feel her body titling towards the floor again and the rickety frame wobbled alarmingly. As the pair of them wrestled to gain mastery over her leg, Connie found her voice again and screamed. Stan uttered not a sound.

Try as she may, Connie couldn't get away from him and she knew if she let go of the handrail there was every possibility she would be pulled off balance and catapulted over the side and onto the flagstone floor beneath. If the fall didn't kill her the madman holding her heel most certainly would. Whatever happened, she couldn't let Stan grab her other leg either.

Connie lay on the stair face down and tried to press Stan's

fingers against the wood. Her assailant had his mouth open and he had bared his teeth. The fear of being bitten gave Connie renewed strength. Her fingers found the umbrella and she poked it through the stairs, managing to jab him in the neck. It only took a second, but Stan let go of her foot and grabbed the umbrella.

Connie didn't wait. She gathered herself together and made another dash for the top. Three rungs from the door she felt Stan's weight on the bottom of the staircase. He was right behind her.

Connie burst into the kitchen and grabbed the cellar door. Splintered and broken as it was, she had to get it shut before Stan came into the room. She almost made it . . . almost . . . A black leather glove had grabbed the edge of the door and Connie couldn't get it shut. She had all her weight against it but Stan was too strong for her. She could feel her foot slipping on the linoleum so she turned her body until she had her back to the door. That's when Auntie Aggie laid into her with a broom.

'You wicked, wicked girl. You hurt my boy with your wicked lies.'

'No, no . . .'

'You're evil, Connie Dixon. Evil.'

It was hard for Connie to fight her off but somehow she managed to keep herself on the other side of the door and away from Stan.

'Connie . . .'

Connie held her breath as she thought she heard someone in the distance calling her name. Auntie Aggie stopped hitting her and turned around.

'Connie, are you there?'

It was Roger. Thank God. Thank God . . . Roger . . .

'Roger,' she screamed at the top of her voice. 'Oh Roger, help me. I'm in the kitchen, help me . . .'

'We're coming, Connie, we're coming.' That was Kez and she heard them banging on the front door. A wave of relief flooded over her but from behind the door, Stan found new strength.

He had become Samson. Connie slid a little further forward. Whatever she did she couldn't let Stan win now. If he got into the kitchen, Connie knew she'd be dead long before Roger and Kez managed to get to her.

'Mum,' Stan shouted. 'Stop her. Stop her.'

But Aunt Aggie had dropped into a chair at the kitchen table and was sobbing.

Far away down the hall, Connie could hear thumping and banging and the sound of splintering wood. It was becoming harder to stay upright. If Connie's feet went any further forward, she would land on her bottom, and yet if she relaxed her grip so that she could reposition herself, Stan would come in. Connie could hear Stan's laboured breathing right behind her ear.

'Roger!' She was almost hysterical now but then she heard a noise coming from upstairs.

'Connie!' It was Eugène. Connie almost lost it then. She was sobbing and her panicking heart was pounding so hard in her chest she thought she would die anyway.

'Help me . . . I can't,' she choked, 'I can't . . .'

Someone was thundering down the stairs. For a split second, Stan stopped pushing and Connie snatched at a heavy saucepan right by her hand on the shelf. She missed and the lid clattered to the floor.

'Mum!' cried Stan.

Out of the corner of her eye, Connie saw Aunt Aggie jump to her feet and with a primeval scream, swing the broom one more time. Behind the door Stan used all his strength to push it open and Connie's feet began sliding at an alarming rate across the floor. At the last second, Connie ducked and the emerging broom hit Stan full in the face. There was a sickening crunch and Stan roared. At the same time, Connie was jolted onto her bottom as the remains of the cellar door slammed shut again. Eugène and Isaac burst into the kitchen just as on the other side of the door, Stan let out one last frantic cry as he overbalanced

366

and then they heard a series of loud cracks as the stairs came away from the wall. The pounding at the front door stopped and Connie heard more footsteps coming towards them. Roger and Kez stumbled into the kitchen but by then Connie was already in Eugène's arms.

'Oh God, what have I done?' Aggie dropped the broom and ran to the cellar door. She opened it and Roger only just grabbed her in time to stop her falling headlong on top of her son. 'Stan,' she shrieked. 'Stan. Can you hear me, son?'

But Stan didn't answer.

Epilogue

Connie leaned back in the passenger seat of the car and smoothed her bump. It was the summer of 1951 and she was expecting her first baby. Hot and swamped under the yards of material in her maternity dress, the novelty of being pregnant was beginning to wear off. She was excited about being a mother and couldn't wait to meet the first of her husband's promised fourteen kids. The nursery had been decorated, the cot was in place and the pram would arrive as soon as the baby was born. Any sooner and everybody deemed it bad luck.

Eva climbed into the driver's seat. She and Connie had just had tea with Sally Burndell and her husband Terry. Their friend stood in the doorway of their sweet and tobacconist shop to wave goodbye.

'She's bigger than you,' Eva remarked out of the corner of her mouth.

'She's only got a couple of weeks to go,' Connie reminded her.

'Well, all I can say,' Eva smiled, 'is that it's a good job you're not driving, Connie Étienne. I don't think you'd get your arms up to the steering wheel.'

Connie waved to Sally and then stuck her tongue out at Eva.

They were on their way to the church at Patching with the hope that this trip would clear up the rift between their two families once and for all.

The past few years had been momentous to say the least. Aunt Aggie and Stan were put on trial for concealing the body of Leslie Saul, their husband and father, and for Connie's false imprisonment. At first Connie and the family were upset that the pair were not tried for Leslie Saul's murder, but the pathologist couldn't find an actual cause of death. The body had obviously been in the cellar for some time and the dry cold and free movement of air meant that rather than decompose, Leslie had been preserved in a mummified state. Stan had broken his back in the fall from the stairs and would be confined to his bed for the rest of his life. At least Connie, Kez and Gwen had the satisfaction of knowing he no longer posed a threat to children and Mandy had been spared a police interrogation. Over time, Connie and Kez compared notes and found a great deal of help and consolation in talking to each other about their experiences.

'I was dead lucky to find a man like Simeon,' said Kez. 'I told him what happened and he still wanted to marry me. Any other gypsy girl in my position would have been mullered.'

Largely through Eva's efforts, and a campaign in the local paper, Connie had been vindicated. Of course, Matron never apologised for believing the letters she'd received nor for judging Connie so harshly but it was enough that Connie was allowed to continue her nursing. Several other people came forward as victims of Aggie's poison pen but because she was already in prison on a much greater charge, no case was brought against her. Connie and Eva had passed their exams at the end of 1949 under the umbrella of the new National Health Service but Connie didn't stay long at her post. She had married in the summer of 1950. Eva had to wait another year until her fiancé would be a fully qualified doctor and then they could marry, but at last her wedding plans were underway.

Connie continued to visit Kez and the family and it was during a meal with them that Peninnah began her family discourse again. Connie had heard it many times before but this time something resonated with her. 'Little Mac took the tattooed lady's mare,' Pen recited, 'and Abe gave Little Mac a piece of bread and a quart of ale but there was none for 'e, so he died . . .'

'Can you say that again?' said Connie. Pen went back a further couple of generations and returned to the same sentence. Connie could hardly breathe. Didn't Cissy Maxwell once tell her something about a Little Mac in her family? How did the same name belong in both stories? Or was it only one story? As far as she knew, Cissy and the gypsies weren't related and yet this incident had apparently had a big influence on them both. But who was the tattooed lady? And more to the point, who was Little Mac? She and Eva had gone back to Cissy who had filled in some of the blanks. She had explained to them that Little Mac was Tobias Maxwell who had lived in the last century. A small, vain and greedy man, he had been ostracised by his community but even though they'd probed her with questions, Cissy didn't know why. Cissy had dug out some old photographs and Connie and Eva were surprised to see that in quite a few of them, both of their families were together. They found pictures of the Maxwells and the Dixons on picnics, on an outing somewhere in a large farm cart together and as part of a country dancing troupe.

'They were all friends back then,' said Eva. 'So what happened?'

Cissy shrugged. 'I was only a little girl,' she said, 'but I think it was something to do with Tobias and money.'

'Do you know any more?' Connie wanted to know.

Cissy shook her head. 'Abraham Dixon was a stonemason. It could have been something to do with that.'

Intrigued, Connie and Eva agreed to spend an afternoon in Patching looking for any trace of her ancestor. His cottage was still standing but his workshop was long gone. The lady who lived there had never even heard of Abraham.

'You should find Ernie Sinclair,' she said. 'He's lived in this village for nigh on sixty years. He usually sits on the bench outside the pub.'

'You mean Mr Sinclair the road sweeper?' asked Connie. She remembered him from her childhood when he'd walked through the streets with a wheelbarrow, a long-handled brush and a spade. The streets of Patching were spotless.

Eventually they came across him and were pleased to find he remembered Connie and her family.

'I remember you when you were knee high to a grasshopper,' he smiled. His gums glistened in the sunshine. 'And now you're having one of your own?'

Connie told him about being a nurse and about her marriage to the most wonderful man in the world.

'I'm glad,' said Mr Sinclair. 'Your father would have been very proud of you. He was a good man, Jim Dixon.'

'We wanted to ask you about our families,' said Connie.

Ernie Sinclair remembered the story well. So well that as he told them, he could hardly contain his amusement. 'Abe agreed to carve old Mrs Maxwell's headstone,' he said.

'That would be Tobias Maxwell's mother?'

The old man nodded.

'So was it a case of taking the money but not doing the work?' asked Connie.

'Oh no,' chuckled the old man. 'He done the work all right. It still be up the church yard. Caused a right stink I tell ye. I remembers my granfer telling me, nobody spoke to him after that.'

The two women found their way to the church and spent the afternoon walking around looking at the inscriptions on the headstones. Some of them were almost impossible to read but as far as they could see, Maude Maxwell's stone wasn't there. Just as they were about to leave, they came across the grave-digger. 'The old Maxwell stone? It's up by the yew tree,' he said. 'They turned it round so no one could see.'

Connie's heart skipped a beat. 'Then it's still there,' she gasped.

The graveyard was in pristine condition apart from one

overgrown area where the yew tree crowded out the sunlight and created a dank atmosphere. The ground was uneven and Eva was afraid Connie might trip. There was one stone leaning against the flint stone wall and a few broken bits of headstone scattered among the brambles. The broken stones were pieces of headstones which had been erected in the path of the prevailing wind and had eventually come off.

'It's got to be that one,' said Eva, pointing to the large stone against the wall.

'Let's hope so,' said Connie, 'or this has all been in vain.'

It was only with great difficulty that they managed to move the heavy stone. Eva wanted to wait until they could find some strong men to lend a hand bearing in mind Connie's condition but she was far too impatient. They had to pull away the grass and get rid of some brambles but at last they uncovered the inscription which had caused Little Mac to be ostracised by the whole village and the two families to stop speaking to each other.

Eva began to laugh first, but Connie seemed puzzled. One line had obviously been defaced and the last line looked like an afterthought.

'That "gl" was once an "s" wasn't it?' said Eva pointing to the inscription. 'Sadly has been changed into gladly.'

'So it has,' said Connie beginning to chuckle.

'I suppose it's a bit tame by today's standards,' said Eva, 'but back in Victorian times it must have been quite shocking.'

'So this was the start of it,' said Connie. 'By the time Arthur married your Gran, the families had been at loggerheads for more than twenty years.'

'It's got to end,' said Eva. 'It's not our fight.'

'We should get everyone to come here for a picnic,' said Connie, suppressing a grin.

'I can't see your great aunt agreeing to that,' said Eva.

'Well, she's going to have to,' said Connie. 'Perhaps if she sees this, she'll realise how ridiculous it is to hold grudges.'

They both giggled. 'When shall we do it?' said Eva.

'How about Bank Holiday Monday?' said Connie.

Unusually for a Bank Holiday, the weather was perfect. Mandy burst back through the open door, with all the exuberance of an over-excited eleven-year-old. 'Hurry up, Mummy. They're all going to go without you!'

'Nobody's going without your mother, Mandy.' Connie was relieved to hear Clifford's calming voice coming into the room behind her. He walked towards Gwen and beamed, 'Come on now, my lovely. Take my arm and we'll be off.'

Connie couldn't have been happier. Just a few years ago she had dreaded that her family would be twelve thousand miles away and that she might never see them again. If the incident with Aggie and Stan had a positive side, it was that it had brought the family closer together. Once Ga realised how devious Stan had been and how manipulative Aggie was and the terrible things she had done, she was utterly repentant. It took Gwen a while to forgive Ga but things were a lot better now. Aggie's name was linked to the thefts as well. She'd obviously done it because she was so miffed that Eugène and Isaac hadn't given her logs during the winter of 1947 and had done her best to blacken his name. Having seen Reuben's caravan, one gypsy home was much the same as every other and so she had planted the watch. A search of the cellar revealed Mrs Wright's pearl brooch.

Ga was still awkward around Cissy Maxwell but with Roger and Eva being such an integral part of family occasions, her tongue was gradually becoming more civil. The thought of poor Leslie's body hidden all those years in the trunk in Aggie's cellar was almost too much for Ga.

'I said such awful things about him,' she lamented. 'May God forgive me.'

As for Roger, he'd been upset that things didn't work out for

Connie and him but not for long. He may have been disappointed, but Roger wasn't the sort of man to hold grudges.

Ga and Kenneth had had a tearful reunion and she had helped him and his new wife to set up a small business and find a flat of their own. Clifford was a changed man too. Ever since Ga signed the nurseries over to him and moved out, he'd had the place buzzing. There was a proper shop now and a small café where Gwen served teas. A new start in Australia was forgotten. They had all they wanted in Worthing.

Outside in the yard, already baked in August sunshine, friends and family waited patiently. Roger had collected Cissy and Vi from Durrington. He looked a lot more relaxed now that he'd come out of bomb disposal. He was working as a military advisor for the government now. He blew Connie a kiss as she emerged through the door. Kenneth and Pearl were behind Roger in their Ford Prefect, with their two children, Dick and Johnny in the back seat. It was unusual for Kenneth to leave his cabinet making business but he had given himself and the three disabled servicemen who worked with him the day off. Ga sat in the back of Clifford's car and Gwen sat next to her husband.

Connie made her way to a battered Humber and gazed into the face of her beloved husband. There hadn't been a day since he'd held her in his arms in Aggie's kitchen that Connie hadn't thanked God for Eugène Étienne. Things had finally looked up for him when the boggy wasteland he'd bought along the seafront fell under the watchful eye of three developers. Eugène held on until the price had almost doubled. He used the cash to buy a cottage and had it done up before selling it on. Having done it more than once, by the time Connie finished her training, he had enough money to buy a house with an outhouse which he converted into a studio. With the Festival of Britain sweeping the country, Eugène's paintings were selling like hot cakes.

'Ready sweetheart?' he said softly.

'Ready,' she grinned.

The picnic was wonderful and later, when the children were all tuckered out, Connie and Eva explained why they had brought them all back to Patching.

'We've found the reason why our two families fell out all those years ago,' Connie explained. 'When I heard Peninnah telling the story of the tattooed lady, I realised that must have been Aunt Gertrude.'

Gwen took in her breath. 'Not the same Aunt Gertrude who ran off with the chap from the fairground?'

'Only she didn't join the fairground,' Connie nodded. 'She became the wife of a gypsy. Aunt Gertrude was Pen's grandmother.'

'So our family and Kez's family are related?' cried Ga incredulously.

''Fraid so,' Connie grinned. 'And it gets better.'

She told them how Abraham Dixon had made the edifice for a Maxwell tomb. She pointed out the masterpiece, complete with crowns, trumpets, exotic plants and the inscription, which was magnificent but it seems that Abraham wasn't paid. And when he wasn't paid for another tombstone, that of the man's widow, Tobias Maxwell's mother, he was very upset.

'When Pen tells her oracle,' Connie went on, 'she says Abe, that's Abraham Dixon gave Little Mac, that was Tobias Maxwell, a piece of bread and a quart of ale but there was none for him and so he died . . .'

Gwen frowned. 'So, what does that mean?'

'On the day they struck the deal,' Eva explained, 'the two men shared a meal.'

'But Abraham Dixon wasn't paid,' Connie continued, 'and shortly after he'd completed the work he died.'

'But that's so sad!' cried Vi Maxwell. 'I feel terrible now.'

'I think he may have known his time was coming,' said Connie, 'because he had time to exact his revenge.'

They took the family into the churchyard and showed them

Abraham Dixon's handiwork. It took a few minutes to sink in and then everyone was laughing.

> *'In loving memory of Margaret Maude Maxwell.*
> *b. June 21 1813 d. Jan 31 1883.*
> *Gladly missed by her son.*
> *What is life without you?*
> *Peace, perfect peace.*

Connie watched them laughing, all the people she loved most in the world, together and happy. Best of all, Ga and Cissy stood together, arm in arm.

Read on for two exclusive
short stories from Pam

A Girl Called Emilie

The letter had come as a bit of a shock.

Of course he knew he had been there. It was the place where they'd stayed in that amazing old manor house. He'd been with a crowd of mates on a so-called cultural exchange to Poitou-Charentes in France, organised by the local council. The idea was to foster relations with the people of the area as part of the twinning of their two regions.

Jason worked in the Parks department and his older brother, Tom, worked in the electoral registration department.

'There's a whole crowd of us going, Jase,' Tom had said. 'You should come too. It'll be a laugh.'

'What, boring civic dinners and a load of OAP coach trips?' Jason had laughed. 'I don't think so.'

'One civic dinner,' said Tom holding up a single finger, 'followed by a trip to the local brewery, a prize-winning vineyard, and a newly opened flying school . . . Oh, and the area is famous for its cognac.'

Jason could feel himself being reeled in. 'But would they really want someone from the Parks department,' he began.

'Just give me the word and I'll wangle it somehow.'

Yeah, that's about right, Jason thought. You could wangle just about anything.

He'd gone, and of course, Tom was right. It had been a blast. He'd loved every minute of it; the scenery, the hospitality and the locals. After his painful break-up with Tanya, it had been exactly what he'd needed. It was even better when he'd got back. Tanya had contacted him and they'd made it up. They were back together again now, and once they'd saved enough for a deposit on a house, they'd get married.

Tom was getting married tomorrow. This was his stag night. Why did the letter have to come today of all days? Jason didn't want to spoil anything but he had to know. He turned it over in his hands and looked at the name on the back of the envelope . . . Emilie Grosjean, followed by the address. He had a hard job remembering her. Yet if what she was saying was true, he must have been there. How could he have forgotten doing a thing like that? And more importantly, how was he going to explain this to Tanya?

Bringing it up in the pub probably wasn't the best idea, but Tom might know something. Jason glanced at his watch. The others would be here soon but there was still time to quiz his brother.

Tom came back from the bar with two brimming pints. 'Get that down your neck,' he said, spilling one glass as he downed his own. 'My last night of freedom and I intend to get plastered.'

'Do you remember when we went to Niort last year?' said Jason, wading in.

'Was that the place with the Roman dungeons?'

Jason nodded.

'I remember you getting trolleyed.'

Jason cringed. He didn't recall how he got there but they'd found him the next morning, fast asleep and curled up on the lap of a big statue in the town's square.

Tom roared at his discomfort. 'Wish we'd had the camera.'

Thank God you didn't, thought Jason. If Tanya had seen . . . he frowned. Was that why he couldn't remember being with Emilie? Was it because he was too drunk?

Tom leaned towards him. 'Why do you ask? What's up?'

'I've had this letter,' he began. 'From a girl called Emilie.'

Tom sat back in his chair and took a long swig from his glass. 'Emilie. Emilie who?'

'Emilie Grosjean. Do you remember her?'

'I might do,' said Tom.

Tom was stalling and that's when it struck Jason. He'd never been with Emilie had he? It was Tom. Tom must have spent the night with her. And afterwards, when she said, 'Comment vous appelez-vous?' Tom, suddenly remembering his fiancé back home, had said his name was Jason.

Jason's eyes narrowed. 'Tom, this is important. Did you go with her?'

His brother shrugged again. 'Dunno, might have done. Can't remember.'

'Come on Tom,' Jason insisted. 'It was only nine months ago.'

Even though the light in the pub was dull, he could see his brother had gone very pale.

'Why do you want to know?'

'Like I told you, I've had this letter,' said Jason. 'And…'

Tom leaned forward again. 'Listen Jase,' he interrupted, 'this is my stag night. I'm getting married tomorrow. Whatever she says it's nothing to do with me, OK? It was only a bit of fun. Don't mess up the rest of my life, please.'

The door burst open and the rest of the lads came in. There was a lot of shouting and plenty of distraction as they hustled their way to the back of the pub where Jason and Tom were sitting, and from then on, the drinks flowed like water.

Tom was almost legless when they handcuffed him, just in his boxer shorts, to the lamp post outside the police station. As the rest of the lads made their way noisily down the high street, Jason came back.

Tom rattled his chains. 'Don't leave me here, Jase,' he slurred helplessly. 'They'll come out and arrest me. If I spend the night in the cells, they'll take me to court in the morning.'

'Answer my question then,' said Jason.

'What question?'

'Did you tell Emilie your name was Jason?'

'You're a hard man, Jase,' said Tom, his teeth chattering with the cold. 'Yeah, all right. I was with her. Proper little goer she was and all.'

'You had a good time with her then?'

'Oh yeah.'

'So,' said Jason, the relief sweeping over him. 'You've had your fun and left me with the consequences.'

'Just forget her, Jase,' said Tom.

'I can't do that, Tom,' said Jason unlocking the handcuffs. He threw his coat over his brother's shivering body. 'You see, *you* gave her such a good time, she entered *my* name in the town lottery. I've just won a fortnight's holiday in a chateau in the Poitou-Charentes.'

The Wedding Suit

Dee couldn't pinpoint the exact moment when she decided to take the suit back. It could have been when she saw the creases in the back of the jacket after Mark had sat down for a ten second photograph. Or maybe it was when she hung it up and saw the state of the trousers. Each leg looked like a dance band concertina. How could she let her one and only son get married looking like that?

Mark was back on duty and not at home until three days before the wedding so there was no chance to discuss the matter with him and she could hardly ask Sally what she thought about it. If it was considered bad luck for the groom to see the bride's dress before the big day, surely the same thing applied in the opposite direction? She searched for the label. Lion Stores, the most expensive shop on the High Street. Dee folded the suit carefully and took it back to the shop.

'I'm afraid,' said the assistant, a rather overly made-up woman of uncertain age, 'that I cannot change the suit. You've no receipt. How do I know the suit is ours?'

'The label,' Dee pointed out. 'Your store is unique isn't it? At least you claim you are when you advertise.'

Reluctantly the assistant called the Manageress.

'Madam,' said the Manageress, a snooty woman who held her head back and peered at the offending garment as if it had a very bad smell, 'there is nothing wrong with the suit. It's the material.'

Slightly confused, Dee frowned. 'But surely that's the same thing?'

But the Manageress was implacable. 'We never have complaints. There is nothing wrong with the suit,' she repeated.

'A suit is made of material,' Dee pointed out. 'Without material there would be no suit and this material is very creased.'

But the Manageress refused to budge. Dee could feel herself getting quite cross. How dare they look down their noses at her? She gritted her teeth and stood her ground.

'Give me the name and address of your head office,' she said, raising her voice for the first time.

The Manageress was reluctant, but it was obvious she didn't want a scene. A scrap of paper was pushed into her hand and Dee was escorted to the door.

Back home, Dee composed a letter. She explained the problem very carefully. It took her the best part of the afternoon to work out what to say and she used three quarters of the Basildon Bond she kept for best.

'If the suit creases this much,' she wrote politely, 'what will it look like when he poses for the wedding photographs?'

Dee enclosed a self-addressed envelope with the letter to ensure a speedy reply. All she had to do now was wait for the cheque.

A week later, Dee recognised her own handwriting on the envelope as it fell on to the mat. She sat at her kitchen table with her coffee to savour the moment.

'Dear Madam,' the letter said. 'We regret you are dissatisfied with our merchandise. However, as Mrs Gambol, the Manageress, pointed out, Lion Stores' suits are second to none. The cut and style are immaculate and the colour is the very latest fashion. We suggest to avoid further creasing, your son should wait until the last minute to put on his suit.'

Dee almost choked on her digestive biscuit. Then she reached for her notepad once again.

The local paper made her simple request a generous headline.

'Crumpled suit good enough for local hero?' certainly captured everybody's attention and sold a lot of newspapers.

The Manageress was given the opportunity to put her side of the story in the next issue. She repeated her first edict and posed outside the front door of Lion Stores. The photograph was a little unflattering, especially with her arms folded over her ample bosom, and everyone agreed that the unfortunate smudge under her nose made her look like somebody else entirely.

It was after that, that the national press began to show interest and 'there's nothing wrong with the suit, it's the material' became the new buzzwords.

Dee was alarmed when she was asked to give a TV interview, but she was quite excited to be sitting on the sofa with Sophie on the Beeb and then with Lorraine over on the other side.

'Surely they can't expect,' she asked innocently, 'my son to arrive at the church in his boxer shorts and shirt and then to put his suit on in the car park?'

The TV presenters agreed that it was ridiculous to ask any man to do that. Lorraine seemed positively appalled, and when she held up a picture of the tearful bride holding a photograph of her fiancé, the whole nation was stirred into action.

Clothwise Fabrics were none too pleased when their shares suddenly plummeted on the stock market. A furious Board of Directors met to consider legal action against Lion Stores, and when the local MP bumped into the Lion Stores MD at their golf club, the intransigence of the managerial department was suddenly reversed.

When he came back home on leave, Mark was stunned to find he had a five star wedding all lined up for him. Everything, the cake, the reception, the cars, the photographs, had all been generously donated by those who wanted to make sure that 'one of our boys' had a day to remember. Everyone agreed that his designer suit, personally paid for by the owners of Lion Stores, Clothwise Fabrics and the local MP, was superb. Bride and groom were happy to be photographed, videoed and filmed for all the glossies . . . for a small fee of course.

The world cruise honeymoon was a terrific surprise and the Brigadier (who went to the same golf club), made sure the groom had enough leave to enjoy every minute.

Satisfied at last, Dee kissed her new daughter-in-law and son goodbye as the honeymoon car waited to take them to the airport. One hundred yards down the road it stopped and reversed back.

'Mum,' said Mark, 'do us one more favour will you? Could you take the suit back to the shop for me? I got it from "Seconds for Hire" on the high street.'

'A vivid and authentic tale about life after the war'
ANNE BENNETT

There's Always
Tomorrow

For better, for worse 'til death us do part...

Pam Weaver

Can a wife ever really know her husband?

Dottie's husband Reg has never been the same since returning home from WWII. The man she fell in love with all those years ago has become selfish and cruel.

Out of the blue, Reg receives a letter informing him that he is the father of a child born out of a dalliance during the war. Now the sole care of the young orphan, Patsy, has fallen to him. Dottie is struggling with the idea of bringing up another woman's child, especially as she and Reg are further away than ever from having one of their own.

However, when eight-year-old Patsy arrives, it becomes clear that Reg has been very economical with the truth. But can Dottie get to the heart of things before Reg takes a step too far and shatters their lives forever.

A gripping family drama for fans of Kitty Neale and Maureen Lee.

A V O N

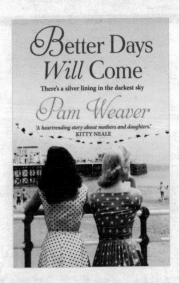

The war may be over but the hard times have only just begun for the Roberts family.

Worthing, 1947. Pregnant Bonnie leaves on a train bound for London, excited to meet boyfriend George. But he never turns up. Somehow she must look after herself and her baby, too ashamed to go home again.

Her mother Grace is devastated by Bonnie's disappearance and struggles to provide for herself and her other daughter Rita. But when Grace accepts the offer of help from her boss Norris Finley, she has no idea how much he'll want in return . . .

Rita thinks that marriage to Italian Emilio is her ticket to a better life. But he is hiding a long-kept secret. As each woman faces her own battle, can the bond of family love bring them back together in time?

Full of family drama, this is the perfect read for fans of Maureen Lee and Katie Flynn.

AVON

Follow Avon on

Twitter@AvonBooksUK

and

Facebook@AvonBooksUK

For news, giveaways and

exclusive author extras

A V O N